Night Sirens

Review

I loved the suspense, mystery, and drama in *Night Sirens*, and I am amazed by Stefan Vučak's attention to detail and creativity. I enjoyed getting to know the characters. Frank is a confident man who wants to live a seemingly ordinary life, and Nadala is a strong female character who knows what she wants and fights for what is right. I loved how I learned about the history and biology of the feeders at the same time as Nadala, who is new to this underground world. Frank and Nadala have great chemistry and natural interactions. Their first encounter was perfectly placed in the storyline. Vučak introduced readers to the motivations and lives of the characters before they interacted. The shady organizations, governments, and taskforces in *Night Sirens* are all unique and realistic. If you need to read a suspense novel with a great storyline and interesting characters, this is the book for you.

Readers' Favorite

Books by Stefan Vučak

General Fiction:
Cry of Eagles
All the Evils
Towers of Darkness
Strike for Honor
Proportional Response
Legitimate Power
Autumn Leaves
F/X-26
28th Amendment
Night Sirens
Broken Rose

Science Fiction:
Fulfillment
Lifeliners
All My Sunsets

Shadow Gods Saga:
In the Shadow of Death
Against the Gods of Shadow
A Whisper from Shadow
Shadow Masters
Immortal in Shadow
With Shadow and Thunder
Through the Valley of Shadow
Guardians of Shadow

Non-Fiction:
Writing Tips for Authors

Contact at:
www.stefanvucak.com

Night Sirens

By

Stefan Vučak

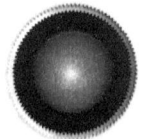

Copyright: Stefan Vučak ©2022
ISBN-13: 9780645116373

Dedication

To Mirko ... when reaching for the stars

Acknowledgments

To Kelly Smith for additional proofreading and insightful suggestions.

Partners in Crime Book Services
https://partnersincrimebooks.wixsite.com/authorservices

Cover art by Laura Shinn.
http://laurashinn.yolasite.com

Chapter One

Frank Hram waited for the brown-tinted glass panels to slide aside, then stepped onto a crowded sidewalk. A wave of traffic noise along the always busy Collins Street made him wince with distaste. Funny, the endless footfalls of people were almost silent. He would ponder the mystery one day over a snifter of cognac, but not here, not now.

A lingering scent of acrid car exhausts produced a passing scowl…a problem seemingly without any solution, wanting to breathe crisp air laced with the scent of oily eucalyptus. This weekend perhaps, he'll drive into the Dandenong hills and indulge himself in nature to replenish what the city had drained from him.

Along the boulevard's median strip, golden elm branches swayed to the whisper of a light breeze. The leaves rustled in protest as a hot northerly gust suddenly raced up the canyon-like street, the effect created by towering buildings on both sides. They witnessed it all before, including the smog. He took it all in and exhaled softly.

Tempted to walk back to his empty air-conditioned apartment, devoid of warmth or somebody waiting for him, he turned left and merged with the flow of pedestrians pushing past him on their way toward the Southern Cross railway hub to catch a train to some suburb and faraway home. Others like him jostled up the street in search of a convenient bar to tank up before finishing the day. Endless rivers of people, and streets were arteries that channeled the never-ending streams. Blank faces, tired faces, animated faces, an anonymous tide ebbing out of the city. To-morrow morning the flood would carry in those same faces. A treadmill stuck on fast with no off button.

Frank could have waited for the evening peak hour to subside before venturing out without having his senses battered. Unac-countably restless, not wanting to spend the evening alone, he gave into the urge to mingle. Weekend afternoons were best to be out, the central business district almost deserted, until evening when a minor surge of excitement seekers ventured out looking to forget reality for a while in a restaurant, theater, cinema, or some other place of earthy entertainment. Right now, he only saw suffering weariness of office slaves who faced a dull trip home by train or car along clogged highways, and they did it twice a day. Mentally exhausted by the time they came to work, and to-tally wrung out when they got home, some still had energy to go out someplace for distracting amusement. He shook his head, not understanding any of it.

A two-bedroom apartment in the same building as his busi-ness had lots of practical advantages, but silence, greenery, and a backyard were not one of them. It still beat the hell out of facing a twice-daily commuter crush, and made up for everything else. When he wanted silence, greenery, fresh air, he took a drive out of the city somewhere to connect with a saner world.

At the Queen Street intersection, a tram clattered through as he waited for the walk sign to turn green. Swept along by the throng, he made his way toward Bourke Street, past the corner Cbus Tower, and stopped in front of the Emporium Hotel, one of his favorite watering stops. After a relaxing drink, a dinner en-gagement at the fashionable uptown Ishizuka restaurant would cap a fine day. He loved the cuisine, subdued lighting, and wait-resses tip-toeing around in traditional kimonos, smiling and bow-ing politely. Every décor detail and soft Japanese background music designed to promote an ambiance of tranquility for sophis-ticated patrons. Frank saw few young people there, the setting far removed from preferred Western-style gregarious establishments. For him, such places lacked cultural refinement, he decided phlegmatically. He always sought restaurants with character where he could immerse himself into their subtle atmosphere. As for discos, the image of gyrating, arm-waving couples thinking they were having fun made him shudder. Old-fashioned stylized mating rituals. A symphony to pluck at his emotions and make his mind soar, a tumbler of something in hand, made living worth enduring.

The Emporium dining room specialized in Mediterranean dishes, and he always enjoyed superb meals there. A little pricy, but as with Japanese diners, that little extra separated living from mere existence. Besides, someone once said indulgence filled the soul, or perhaps he made up the thing as a reflection of his own self. He strode into the lobby, glanced at the still mostly deserted restaurant with its brown paneled walls, square tables covered with genuine lace cloth, cut glass chandeliers, and turned left toward the noisy Blink's Bar, many of its small round tables already occupied. Apart from an odd snack, no meals served here, the tables did not have to be large. Like any bar, the place smelled of spilled beer and sharp spirits. It never ran short of lunchtime customers having a quick one before returning to the office grind. In the evening, after work suit types perhaps wanted a badly needed alcohol fix to close off what might have been a stressful day, or maybe dreading tomorrow. Then again, a drink might fortify them for what waited at home.

Frank did not give a toss why somebody came here. He liked to sit quietly, sip his mix, and watch people. They were funny, silly, solemn, depressed, and lots had all those attributes in one package. The problem with some, he decided, they took themselves too damn seriously. They lacked a sense of humor to laugh at themselves and everything around them. That's how he beat the game. The world still kept turning whether he worried or not.

He pushed through standing groups and strode toward an

empty stool beside the bar. Soft music filled the background, the kind of stuff popular in the seventies and eighties. The drinks were not watered and the bartenders would talk to him if they had a spare minute. Cheaper than a session with a mind twister and delivered about the same level of service.

Maybe the slow pace and the square atmosphere attracted young up-and-coming executives. According to Walt, some came to enjoy the dated sounds, liked the mood, and became regulars, proud to have discovered a really cool place.

He sat down and Walt nodded to him from the other end of the bar. The portly bartender, laugh lines crinkling his eyes, bald head slick under the lights, a cleaning rag always in hand, ambled over. He could be fifty or sixty, unchanged in the eight years Frank knew him. The man must have seen and heard just about everything in his time, and laughed at it all. Somewhere in his checkered past, he also learned how to beat the game.

"How's life, big guy?"

"If I wanted decent booze, I wouldn't be here," Frank told him amiably.

Walt shrugged. "There's a pub down the street if you don't like what I serve. The usual?"

"Make it a double." Frank cast a quick glance at the mixed clientele. Easy to be picked up here by either sex, knowing from personal experience, but he wasn't hunting this evening, and would not need to for a while yet. He simply wanted a drink with bodies around him.

"Hard day at the office?" Walt asked as he squirted a dash of ginger ale into a tumbler of bourbon, no ice. Casual chitchat came free with the drinks.

"It's money coming in," Frank said indifferently and dragged a bowl of mixed nuts toward him. "You know, figuring out how to invest a few spare bucks isn't all that difficult. All it takes is some research and a bit of common sense." He popped two roasted cashews into his mouth and chewed.

"I hear 'ya." Walt slid a cork coaster across the bar and placed the tumbler on it. "The thing is, buddy, if sense was really common, you wouldn't be enjoying your fancy Collins Street pad."

Frank picked up the tumbler and took a sip. "I guess." He cocked an eyebrow at the bartender. "Are *you* looking to invest some spare cash?"

"Hah! If I had any spare cash, I'd be sunning my butt somewhere in Queensland. Too steamy this time of year, though," Walt reflected. "Still alone? No good living alone. Take me. Married for twenty-four years and the fire hasn't gone out. We've had our ups and downs like everybody, and Marica even left me once. Came back after a week at her mother's. We talked it over and sealed the reunion with a romp in bed." He chuckled at the memory and absently wiped the bar top. "That's the trouble with kids these days. No patience. They have an argument and bam! The next day, they're divorced."

"Yeah, so I heard," Frank agreed.

"Hey! How about some service here?" a bulky individual demanded from the other side of the bar.

Walt shrugged. "Catch you later or I'll get beer thrown in my face."

Frank smiled after the retreating figure. Pushing thirty-eight, he often wondered what it would be like to have a warm bundle beside him in bed to love, share secrets in midnight pillow talk, go places together, have kids, and be normal like everybody else, whatever the hell that meant. He missed his chance to have it all with Rainey. Memories bubbled to the surface and he spent a few moments raking over the more pleasant ones. After a couple of sips, they faded into yesterday's scrapbook. That's where he ought to be, in a scrapbook. Then again, Walt might be right. Time to let go and move on. Owen told him as much more than once. Happily married, his business partner dispensed marital advice like a gumball machine.

He took another sip, letting the bar's ambiance wash over

him, soaking it all in.

Someone gave a heavy grunt beside him and Frank turned. Perhaps in his mid-thirties, dressed in a dark gray suit, yellow tie pulled down, clear blue eyes regarded him with amused cynicism. Streaks of white at the temples added a touch of formality and dignity to an otherwise rugged face and powerful figure women liked. Frank gave a mental shrug. Some guys had it all, knew it, and made many self-conceited bastards. He wondered if this guy fit the mold, prepared to be surprised.

A young waiter brought a fat glass of red wine and placed it before Frank's new acquaintance. The man took a pull, nodded in appreciation, and lifted the glass in a salute.

"Not bad actually. How's your stuff?"

"Drinkable," Frank said with a grin. "Coming here is a diversion from the unforgiving madness outside."

"Wow, heavy stuff for this time of day," his friend growled and turned slightly to check out females cruising to be picked up.

"You're wasting your time, my boy," Frank told him with a shake of his head. "All the good ones are already taken. These are strictly one-nighters."

"Can't shoot a guy for looking. They haven't passed a law against that yet, but give them time." The deep laugh lit the man's eyes with open humor. "Name's Dan," he said and stuck out a meaty paw.

"Frank."

No pretense there and he began to warm to him.

Dan's hand cool and dry, both maneuvered for a knuckle crusher. Childish, but what the hell. Frank left all the serious bits he wanted in the office. Time to chill out as the kids said. He had an advantage in height and reach, but did not underestimate Dan's powerful grip. From a confident smirk, Dan's expression changed to a surprised grimace of pain. Frank let him go before the encounter became too uncomfortable.

"Damn!" Dan grunted and massaged his fingers. "It's been a

while since I came off second best."

"I'll be around whenever you want a reminder," Frank told him with a smile.

They clicked glasses and Dan suddenly sat up. "Man! Check out that chassis!"

Frank followed his gaze and almost missed her standing at the bar entrance.

Early twenties, not tall, she carried herself with power and maturity, something he liked to see in a woman. Black hair spilled down her back and hung above a slim waist. Oval eyes, highlighted by blue eyeshadow, drew attention to a delicate face, small upturned nose, and full lips brushed with gloss. He could not tell if she wore any other makeup. Dressed in a loose beige blouse with a generous cleavage, the clinging brown knee-length skirt showed shapely legs. Black stiletto heels, open at the toes, fixed at the ankles by thin straps, gave an impression of extra height. For a second, he swore silence drowned all conversation as every male eye in the room clicked to focus on her. Her confident posture and an almost visible glow gave her away. An energy feeder, he wondered what prey she would catch tonight. She hunted openly, wanting men to see her ready for some close entertainment.

It takes maturity, training, and a lifetime of experience to recognize a feeder, provided one chose to be recognized. There were little mannerisms a feeder can adopt to prevent recognition, and Frank used them all. This woman flaunted her desire.

He turned and shrugged. "Not bad," he said offhandedly.

"Not bad?" Dan shook his head and gave him a pitying sigh. "You happen to leave your eyeballs at home or something? Step aside. This is man's work, sonny." Without taking his eyes off the woman, he placed his wineglass on the bar and stood up.

Amused, Frank watched him walk to her, beating another suitor vying for her attention. Dan leaned toward her and said something. She gave him an appraising look as though measuring a side of beef, nodded, and smiled. Dan wound her arm around his, winked at Frank, and they strode out. He expected Dan to have a very interesting night.

Frank lifted his tumbler and sipped, figuring it was none of his business how the woman hunted, and she would not take too much from Dan. Ordinary men provided what she needed to survive, and women provided what men like Frank needed. Simple as that. He could link with a man, but that wasn't his stuff. Life went on, and nobody could figure out why it had to be like that. Philosophers, priests, and mystics tried over the millennia, and some thought they had it. He never read anything yet that explained it to his satisfaction. Best to stick with his Zen *shikantaza* and forget trying to understand it all. Let the all be his total self without conceptualization, grasping, goal seeking, unencumbered by traditional *bodhisattva* rituals.

He finished the drink and dismissed Dan from his mind. Right now, he had a culinary appointment to keep. He stood, threw bills on the bar, waved to Walt, and headed for the lobby, looking forward to dining on some superb Japanese cuisine.

* * *

Fingers locked behind his head, Frank gazed absently at the far wall of his bedroom. Dawn broke and he heard muffled sounds of cars moving outside. Nice and snug, his thoughts wandered, not dwelling on anything in particular. A jumble of random associations he used as an excuse not to get out of bed. To get up meant shattering his contented mood and face a harsh, indifferent world. *Only a few moments more*, he told himself and closed his eyes.

A car horn blared as a driver vented frustration at some offending miscreant. His fantasy dissolved and he became fully awake. He pursed his lips, threw back the light blanket, and padded into the bathroom. A shower and a shave perked him up and he dressed quickly, not fussing over his appearance, but as managing director of Urbi Investments, he needed to project a professional front for the company's existing and prospective clients.

With the percolator going, filling the kitchen and living room with an enticing aroma, he prepared breakfast of homemade muesli, the ingredients bought at Victoria Market—the packaged supermarket stuff mostly sugar bombs—cut up a red capsicum, then added blueberries and tomato slices to the mix. Sadly, most vegetables these days lacked any smell and were almost tasteless. Lately, the apples and pears he'd been eating started an argument with his stomach. Probably all the chemicals in them to force growth or keep them from rotting on shelves. On his weekend trips out of town, he always picked up fruit and veggies from local farmers that had old-fashioned substance and flavor.

A second fix of coffee, warm mug held between his hands, he glanced at the electronic wall clock screen: 8:05 AM, Wednesday, December 6, 2023. The rest of the week would be all downhill toward another Saturday. As he watched the thing, the number changed to 8:06. Coffee finished, he washed up, brushed his teeth, slipped on a dark maroon tie, and pulled on a black cashmere jacket to finish off. A last glance at the mirror showed a hard face, granite gray eyes below a full crop of almost charcoal hair brushed straight back. At 179cm, he still looked good; no eye bags or drooping jowls, his body kept trim with regular exercise at the downstairs gym. He nodded and headed for the door. With the monitored alarm system enabled, he strode quickly toward a bank of three elevators. The Oaks on Collins apartments, located in the Collins Street Tower office complex, made getting to work almost a pleasurable experience. As with everything, some days were better than others.

As an added security measure, a wireless camera installed in the ceiling aircon grille kept five days of takes in cloud storage. Personal safety and security were priority life items for every Keeper who contemplated ongoing survival, which Frank did.

One hint of his true nature to anybody and the exterminators would come sniffing. His parents may have suspected during his turbulent teenage years when the urge to feed first manifested itself, but they never broached the subject. Perhaps better for all concerned.

In December 2010, the debilitating effects of the Global Financial Crisis starting to fade, he bought his two-bedroom pad and persuaded Owen Emerson, a longtime friend, to start a financial consulting business. If they wanted to make serious money in life, slaving for somebody else on a salary would not do it, regardless how high the salary, he told Owen. Frank had two other buddies; the four of them attended the same high school. After graduating, each pursued a different course of study and career, and over time drifted apart. Except for Owen. They all got together once or twice a year without the wives in tow to yarn over old times and pontificate on the new, but the close connection they enjoyed before faded as the years marched. Flotsam on the river of time, that's what they were. Like time cared where it took people riding it.

Many investors, large and small, badly burned during the GFC, were ready for someone honest to tell them what to do with their money. The industry had a deserved 'buyer beware' dictum and people were wary. An office opposite the Rialto Tower added a veneer of prestige and reassurance to nervous clients not sure two young looking entrepreneurs could handle their millions. It took five years of long hours and many missed weekends to build up a solid reputation and goodwill in the cutthroat financial market before things picked up and real returns started to come in.

Although only twenty-seven at the time, Frank brought into the business KPMG work experience and investment knowhow gained at Lodge & Porters, one of the most respectable trading houses in Melbourne, a bachelor's degree in commerce, and a master's in finance. A year older, Owen held an accounting and law degree, which gave Urbi the required spread of practical professionalism and academic snobbery clients appreciated. Everybody liked to see framed diplomas on an office wall. They handled a portfolio of $716 million, distributed in shares, various managed funds, and cryptocurrency. So far, Urbi's clients did well sticking with the relative newcomers, because he and Owen treated them with scrupulous honesty, prepared to steer them somewhere else for a better deal. Many came back when that better deal turned out not to be so good.

The elevator door opened on the 14th floor and he faced a long frosted glass panel, his business name set in black-bordered gold script. The single clear entrance panel slid away when he pressed a glowing green pad, and he walked into the tastefully furnished reception area.

Catherine Rossen looked up from her curved, grained wood workstation flanked by two tall potted plants decorated with tinsel and colored glass balls in anticipation of Christmas, and smiled. Behind her, a floor-to-ceiling window revealed a jagged city skyline. The modern, clean décor always went down well with clients, in contrast to some firms who still thought the 1900s dark paneling look spelled stability and respectability.

"Morning, Frank," she said cheerfully and held out several message slips.

With them since he and Owen opened the firm in mid-2011, of average height, short auburn hair highlighted bright brown eyes and small mouth, Cathy served as receptionist, office manager, and general gofer. Whatever needed doing, she took care of it. Not a partner, but Frank made sure her salary and benefits kept her with them. She did not need the money really, moderately wealthy after following Frank's investment advice. As she pointed out over coffee more than once, work kept her mind busy. Better than staring at a TV all day and slowly going batty. Happily married, two teenage boys a handful at home, she added cheerfulness and a sunny disposition to some dull days. Like any business, Urbi had them.

"Anything I need to know?" he asked as he grabbed the slips.

"You have a Miss Tammy Rezing at nine. The rest are call-me-back things. One is from an old client, Gregory Forster. He wants to see you soonest."

"Is Owen in?"

"Not yet."

He shoved the message slips into his jacket pocket and headed for the small kitchen/lounge. A mug of strong black coffee in hand, one sugar, he walked into his office and powered up the networked tower computer sitting on a large black-grained gray executive desk. Apart from a ceiling-high wall unit stuffed with books, magazines, odd trinkets, two seascapes on one wall, Frank liked his office bare and functional. A window behind him took up the entire wall and provided all the natural light the room needed.

He quickly scanned several financial websites for latest market developments, stock movements, and general heads-up items. The vibes from everyone were strong that the Federal Reserve Bank would lift interest rates before Christmas. Otherwise, the local and international trade, monetary and fiscal climate, looked fairly stable, already having factored in a possible rate hike designed to keep inflation in check. Coal futures were down again as the world slowly weaned itself off this energy source, but gas had rallied.

The Greens Party wanted to kill all coal and gas usage in the name of reducing global carbon emissions, but reliable, cheap renewable supplies were still years off in their ability to provide base load power for houses and industry. This cold fact did not stop them beating the drums of change. At the last federal election, Elena Griffin, the new Labor Party Prime Minister, refused to adopt the Green's radical and economically damaging policy, and promoted investment in gas exploration and delivery infrastructure. She insisted all companies must reserve at least 20% of all supplies for the country's internal consumption rather than seek best deals through international sales. No more nonsense pegging the domestic market to the international spot price. The big exploration companies grumbled and threatened to pull out, and Griffin told them to go ahead and leave. In reality, reserving a percentage of production for domestic consumption meant a miniscule drop in annual earnings. Not worth incurring the government's wrath and public ridicule for being heartless profit gougers, which everybody knew they were.

Homework done, he checked the message slips, shot off several email replies, and slotted Forster for three PM into the appointment system.

The phone rang and he picked up.

"Miss Rezing is here," Cathy announced, and Frank glanced at the clock weather station on his desk, startled to find it showed almost nine.

"Show her in." He hastily dragged on his jacket and straightened loose papers. *Perception rules everything*, he told himself.

He recalled Rezing's file and two previous meetings when she approached Urbi for investment advice. Twenty-nine, a geologist at BHP, single, around 162cm, raven hair tied in a severe bun, which made a startling contrast with her pale features. Frank remembered a long, somber face, large green eyes with penetrating directness, and a sharp delivery when she spoke. Slim, fashionably dressed, he would not have minded dating her. A passing fancy.

A knock and Cathy opened the door, ushering in his guest. He stood and offered his hand.

"A pleasure to see you again, Miss Rezing." He squeezed her small hand, smelling fresh perfume.

"Thank you for seeing me, Mr. Hram," she replied coolly and sat in the visitor chair without waiting for an invitation. She clearly expected deference and made sure she got it. Legs crossed, she tugged down her navy blue skirt over tanned legs.

13

"Can I get you a coffee or something?"

"I'm fine."

"In that case, what can I do for you?"

She bit her lower right lip and frowned. "I'm in a bit of a bind. As you know, apart from my shares portfolio you helped set up, I own thirty Bitcoins my father bought for me in 2012 as a flyer. Since then, I accumulated an additional twenty before the 2021 peak. With the current price hovering around $89,300, I want to sell some to finance purchase of a central city apartment to better suit my work requirements and lifestyle. The alternative is to offload some of my shares for the purchase. I would appreciate your input what to do."

"Both are sound options, but have you considered taking out a fixed rate home loan for the apartment? The current bank rate is around 6.5% for a 20-year loan. If you pay off some of it over twelve months, you'll be making money on the deal."

She arched her eyebrows. "I'm surprised to hear you say that. The fortnightly repayments would be an impossible drain on my operating liquidity."

"Your income and dividend yields will service the loan comfortably." He smiled and leaned over the table to concentrate on her face. "In twelve months, you can sell a few Bitcoins to unload the loan balance."

"But if I sell now, I can purchase the apartment without any outstanding liability."

"That's true, but you'll be doing it by sacrificing future Bitcoin appreciation, which is far more than 6.5%, even if you're not getting any dividends from it now."

"I don't understand."

"When Bitcoin first came on the market in 2009, it had a fixed issue of twenty-one million virtual coins. Some 19.2 million are already in circulation. Roughly every four years, Bitcoin miners go through a block reward subsidy halving. Right now, miners are rewarded with 6.25 Bitcoins for every transaction block they create, which releases more Bitcoins for people to buy and sell. In May next year, that reward will drop to 3.125 per transaction block. As the available supply of Bitcoins shrinks, miners will have less incentive to create transaction blocks. This means you can expect to see a sharp increase in Bitcoin price. By March next year, the market is predicting a value of $120,000 per Bitcoin. If you take out a bank loan to finance your apartment purchase, you'll be able to repay it by selling far fewer Bitcoins than if you sold now, and you'll be preserving your investment."

"Mmm, I think I understand. A tantalizing tactic, but what if Bitcoin value doesn't go that high? I'll be stuck with an expensive loan."

Frank shrugged. "You'll still be in a better position, as a price increase is an absolute certainty. All investment is based on perception, not mathematical formulae. If every cryptocurrency suddenly bottomed out, they'll be in a mix of other investment instruments, and the world economy would face another GFC. All of us would have survival on our mind, and repaying a bank the least of your problems. It's not a scenario we're facing, though."

She allowed herself a small smile. "So, you're recommending I hold onto my investment portfolio and borrow, the loan serviced by asset appreciation."

"That's right. All economic indicators point to an expanding domestic and international future, with no political threat indicators in the medium timeframe to cause a downturn. If you have some cash capacity, consider investing in Ethereum crypto. Right now, it's cheap, but growth over the last eighteen months suggests it might overtake Bitcoin as a favorite investment."

"Why not invest in shares? Are you saying I should dump them in favor of crypto?"

"Not at all. Diversification is a good thing. I am merely pointing out a possible opportunity that's likely to become very competitive next year."

Rezing flashed him a broad smile, rose, and held out her hand.

"Thank you, Mr. Hram. Your advice has always been reliable."

"Whatever decision you make, Urbi Investments will execute your transactions." They shook hands and he escorted her out.

He checked his email Inbox and went over what he said to Rezing. Perhaps he should follow his own advice and extend his holding in Ethereum. He could easily afford to put in another $20,000. Perhaps the firm could also apply some surplus to increase its portfolio. He'll have a chat with Owen.

Frank stood before the tall plate window and gazed absently at a profusion of towers clawing for the sky, reflecting how Bitcoin got him started.

In January 2015, he bought eighty coins when they were at $304 and basically forgot about it. A very risky venture, crypto still an unknown investment quantity then. In April 2021, the price unexpectedly soared above $79,000, and he offloaded everything, which netted him over $6.3 million. The windfall allowed him to retire all personal and most company debt, and he used the balance of the initial six million to service his capital gains tax liability. The government always made sure it got its cut from any enterprise.

By July, the price dropped to roughly $43,500 and he bought 100 Bitcoins. At his urging, Owen, Cathy, and some clients, came out of that rollercoaster trading cycle financially secure, as did Urbi itself.

His parents also did well following his advice, retired, and bought a property at Airlie Beach in Queensland, gateway to the Whitsundays, and now enjoyed luxury living and first class travel.

As an only child, he recalled a rocky relationship with his father. A rather stern personality, which, according to his mother, he passed to his son. A senior Commonwealth Bank manager in their retail division, no dummy when it came to technology and the evolving world of personal computers in the early 1980s, mobile phones in late 1990s, email communication, and the Internet, Attard Hram drove Frank hard to get a university education. This invariably generated a rebellious response. Never wild, Frank's late teens were years of experimentation and impulsive decisions all teenagers indulged in. His mom, a partner at the time in the downtown Central City Realty, a practical, down to earth woman, tempered his rashness and resentment of his father's stifling authority with quiet talks and wise guidance.

Frank weathered the discipline of high school and found himself in a free world of Melbourne University where he enrolled in a Bachelor of Commerce degree. He liked all sciences and read widely, but never considered an academic or engineering career. The higher mathematics turned him off.

He enjoyed university life and became active in the Student Union for a while, until it started to encroach too much into his study time. Undergrads could attend lectures and tutorials or not. Nobody drove them to do anything. The Uni got its fee and did not care how the students spent their time. He barely scraped through the first year, and many of his classmates fell by the wayside. This left him with a sober realization that the safe, comfortable existence he enjoyed living with his parents did not prepare him for the tough and indifferent world he found himself in now. Predictably, he blamed his dad for letting him down. One evening, Hram senior walked into his room and gave Frank a brutal choice. Get a degree and secure a future for himself or become a menial worker. The world owed nothing to anyone. Opportunities lay everywhere, but he must reach out and grasp them. He would never realize them from a factory floor.

The somber talk gave Frank a lot to think about, resenting his old man's blunt dressing down in the process.

He got his degree and immediately joined KPMG in their Management Consulting division. The four years he spent there gave him a solid grounding in the impersonal cut and thrust of corporate finance that knew no quarter. A lot more mature, he came to appreciate what his parents had done for him, and the relationship with his dad improved immeasurably. These days when they met, they talked as equals, and Frank valued the words of praise and approval from his father.

As he gazed out the window, life unfolded from his memories and he found himself uncharacteristically despondent.

A thriving company, fancy apartment, nice car, financial security, he should be riding high. Instead, when he opened the door to that fancy apartment, no one stood there to share his successes, and his nights were lonely. Did that explain why he liked going to Blink's and other bars, because he wanted surrogate companionship? There used to be someone four years ago.

Rainey…

Engaged to be married, his life turned dark when a week before the wedding, a speeding truck driver ran a red light, hit her car, and drove it against a concrete light pole. The rescue crew had to cut through the mangled wreckage to get at her torn body. Six years, that's what the driver got, but it did not bring Frank any satisfaction, or filled the emptiness he still felt inside.

Endless days, months, and years providing personal and corporate financial advice, growing richer in the process, maintaining his cover as a Covenant Keeper, was that all life held for him? More than once, he reflected that professional achievement meant little if no one shared it with him. He figured a mind twister would find him a very messed up client. Sometimes even Zen contemplation did not help lift his mood.

Still morose, he walked back to his desk and got the computer working. Time for some paid work, and screw all psychiatrists. Whom did they consult when they needed straightening out?

He secured two new clients before lunch. Both middle-aged, successful executives looking for options. They typified the kind of people he saw. With a bit of due diligence, they could have managed their investments themselves. Most could not be bothered, did not have the time to research, or were overawed by the stock market mystique. Urbi Investments made a lot of its money from such people. Corporate clients were usually more savvy and required careful handling.

At noon, Frank walked out onto Collins Street and paused to soak in the streaming traffic, hurrying pedestrians, and the city's pervasively noisy atmosphere. A deep blue sky reflected warm sunshine and cast sharp shadows. Not bothering with a tie or jacket, he ambled toward the Southern Cross railway station, the street festooned with Christmas decorations. At the food court, he snagged a salad roll, a cup of freshly squeezed orange juice, and perused a small bookstore. Not finding anything of interest in the limited collection—for a serious bookworm like himself, Dymocks had it all—he made his way toward Bourke Street a block up. His latest brain prodder, *Ethics*, edited by James P. Sterba, made for thoughtful reflection. Some articles induced instant slumber. By the time he completed the circuit back to the Collins Street Tower, he felt prepared to tackle more clients.

He and Owen Emerson jointly handled any firm with an annual turnover of more than $10 million. Each contributed specific expertise to every discussion. As Frank admitted more than once, he did not know everything, something Owen did not let him forget.

At one, Cathy showed a severely dressed lawyer into the meeting room, and the three of them shared small talk over coffee. The rake thin individual represented a company based in the city's western suburbs that made various stainless steel containers for milk processors, beer fermenters, chemicals suppliers, and custom storage tanks. The company's profits had increased substantially and the owners did not want surplus funds languishing in a bank interest account paying a miserly quarter percent.

"What is your medium term expansion strategy, Mr. Lewis?" Owen asked.

The lawyer pushed up his rimless glasses that slid down a sharp nose and cleared his throat.

"We're building a new plant in Sydney. The property is already acquired and the architects are waiting for the local council to approve the drawings. We're hoping to get it next week before the process gets bogged down because of Christmas and New Year holidays."

"How are you financing the new plant?" Frank put in.

"From general revenue."

Frank exchanged a quick glance with Owen, the response typical from small companies not versed in corporate financing.

"Mr. Lewis, have your owners considered borrowing the required capital instead of drawing down your earnings?"

"We have, but they're averse to leverage the business, and in the process, burden it with subordinated debt or substantial loan repayments."

"Which are tax deductible," Owen pointed out.

"But still payable up front."

"Effectively, a loan costs you nothing, and your earnings profile shows you could service it comfortably or you wouldn't be here."

Lewis gave a strained smile. "That's what I told them. However, the firm is family owned and they have a strong policy of financial prudence."

"Mr. Lewis, we can advise your owners how to invest surplus funds at minimal risk," Frank told him, "but we can do much more for you that will increase your returns without damaging the firm's financial discipline. Do the owners have a background in management accounting?"

"Small-time business experience only before they started manufacturing."

"We can help them change their mindset," Owen told him. "Running two plants requires a broader outlook and professional management if they want to be successful."

"We'll provide you a list of investment options, including cryptocurrency, and your owners can make an informed decision how to proceed," Frank added quickly. "However, if you restructured your financial profile for the new plant, your owners will be in a greatly improved fiscal position. We'll email you some material for your consideration. I suggest you bring in your principal owners and we'll explain the reasoning behind our recommendations." He stood and held out his hand. "It's been a pleasure, Mr. Lewis. Don't hesitate to call us if you need more information."

He saw his guest to the elevator and returned to the meeting room. Owen refilled his mug and gave a wry smile.

"You hurried him on purpose without giving him time to consider what we said."

Frank grinned. "Lewis knows I'm right. He only wanted my confirmation of his position. The owners are using a flawed, outdated operating model, and I wanted to reinforce that impression. Take my word for it. They'll be here next week asking how to restructure the company."

"With a slice of their earnings landing in our pocket."

"Of course. We value add whenever we can."

Owen shook his head and laughed. "You're a thief, Frank."

"That's the business we're in."

His next two clients were simple status update sessions, a review of their portfolio holdings and possible changes in the mix within a growth marketplace. Both left happy, and Frank made himself ready to meet Gregory Forster.

The fifty-eight-year-old import/export entrepreneur had $14 million in personal and company savings invested with Urbi. He was also a feeder. The Covenant network regularly channeled such clients to Urbi, Owen and Cathy thinking they were random referrals. Some of those clients suspected Frank to be a feeder himself, or even a Keeper, but he never allowed himself to admit anything. A client might be a friend today, but could turn into a bitterest enemy tomorrow. Exposure would be a personal disaster and ruin for Urbi. With the US-based Project Purple, cooperation from the Australian Federal Police Taskforce Crimson, Interpol, and most governments around the world hunting feeders and working to unmask the Covenant, he did whatever it took to protect his identity as a Keeper. Sometimes a damn hard thing to do when he needed to feed.

Promptly at three, Cathy introduced the short, overweight Forster. They shook hands warmly and Frank offered the man a tumbler of Willett Distillery bourbon. Forster took an appreciative sip and settled himself in the visitor chair.

"Still serving cheap booze, I see."

"Can't afford anything else, Greg. Business is tough these days."

"You don't know what tough is, you con artist."

"With all your millions, I can see how you suffer."

"Screw yourself."

Frank smiled, not taking offense. They indulged in such banter all the time. "How's Christy? The cruise to the Bahamas still on in January?"

Forster sagged and suddenly looked seventy. He took a long pull of whiskey and placed the tumbler on the desk with a loud click.

"She's fine, but I may have to postpone the cruise."

Immediately concerned, Frank leaned forward. "Something happened to the company?"

"I need you to liquidate five million and have the funds in my bank account by three PM tomorrow."

"Christ! What's going on?"

"Can you do it?"

"Not a problem, but—"

Forster raised his hand. "No questions, okay?"

"Listen, Greg. We've known each other for eight years now, and I consider you a friend. If you have troubles, perhaps I can help. Nobody asks for five mil on 24-hour notice. Talk."

Forster gave him a hard look. "Under the rose? If this got out…"

Frank lifted his hand, palm out.

"It's Melany. Always a little wild and prone to an occasional excess. With wealthy parents behind her, she overindulges sometimes. Two weeks ago, she met some smooth-talking sleazebag at a St. Kilda bar and allowed her sexual appetite to get the better of her. After three days, she dumped him. She tends to do that with men she meets. The thing is, this character suddenly developed aches and pains and became extremely lethargic for several days. You know how these things work. He recovered, but his family are now on my case and want retribution."

Frank felt his mouth go dry. Greg's daughter could be a possible feeder.

"Who are they?"

"The guy is a son of someone in the Pomperi Family clan."

"Pomperi? You're kidding."

"That's what he told her during one of their pillow talk sessions. Of all the jerks to get involved with, she picks a mobster! They practically own the Maritime Union."

"I heard."

"Nothing moves on our docks without them knowing about it. They're major smugglers with links to local and overseas crime syndicates. The federal police regularly raid their offices and arrest the small fry, but they can't make anything stick on the Pomperi. They're always several layers behind the front men."

"And they're blackmailing you, threatening to expose your daughter as a feeder, right?"

"An energy vampire," Forster growled. "Gods!"

Frank hated the term, coined by popular cultist literature, but they were not far off the mark. No one could explain, not even the Covenant, why some people needed to draw energy from a sexual partner or from a crowd to sustain themselves, but they do. Frank fed at least once every five weeks to maintain his vitality. If he abstained, the urge became relentless as he turned steadily weaker. The problem, and why the world hunted feeders, if one took too much, the partner could suddenly die of apparent old age as though life was sucked out of them. Which in a way, it had been. Greg's daughter apparently came perilously close to killing her lover, and one of the most powerful criminal families in Australia was now after her.

"Does Melany know she's a feeder?"

"She suspects, and I talked to her about it, but she doesn't want to know," Forster replied miserably. "I think she secretly hates me for it. I'm so totally screwed."

"About the Pomperi Family—"

"They want the five million by five PM tomorrow. Given the business they're in, I fear this will only be a down payment. They'll keep sucking until I have nothing left, then probably expose my daughter and kill her. Once this comes out, I'll be ruined, unless they kill me as well. Might be better that way."

Frank took out a small pad and wrote quickly. "Here's a number for Ardor Helpline—"

Forster snorted. "I've seen their ads. Sounds like a pimp outfit."

"It's not. Get Melany to call them. They'll help her. I mean it, Greg."

A worldwide front set up by the Covenant, the Helpline steered youngsters and some not so young who exhibited unusual sexual urges to respectable psychology/psychiatry clinics. They confirmed if a person was an actual feeder and instructed them how to manage their condition without exposing themselves. If they were not, the clinics provided normal counseling. With taskforces everywhere hunting feeders, the Covenant could not say how long this program would last before exposure destroyed everything.

Forster tilted his head. "How come you know about all this stuff, Frank? Are you a feeder? I always suspected you might be one."

"I read up on it and I'm simply helping a friend. Don't worry about the Pomperi. I'll take care of your problem."

"How will you take care of it? Do you realize the muscle they wield? Cross them and you'll end up in a pine box."

"I know people who know people who handle such things." Frank stood and held out his hand. "Make sure Melany calls that number."

Forster slowly rose. "If whatever you have in mind fails, she's dead. I'd rather pay up than see something happen to her."

"Trust me," Frank told him with more confidence than he felt, and walked his friend out. Many things never turned out as planned. This one needed to work perfectly. "Give my regards to Christy."

At his desk, he picked up the cellphone, set encryption mode, added a ten digit PIN, and tapped in a number ingrained into his brain. He had no idea how encryption worked, and didn't care as long as it worked. When he became a Keeper, the taciturn man who gave him the phone said all calls Frank made in encryption mode were totally untraceable. He also told him not to use it for personal or professional calls.

"Manuel de la Kass," an electronically altered voice answered after three rings. "Identify."

"Frank Hram."

After several seconds… "Okay, you're you," the Melbourne Master's executive assistant declared amiably. "How's the investment racket going?"

"We're raking it in."

Manuel gave a booming laugh. "I don't doubt it. What can I do for you, amigo?" The third-generation Australian loved to flaunt his Spanish ancestry.

Frank summarized Forster's problem without embellishment.

"The Pomperi Family, eh? Your friend has a problem, all right, and Melany definitely sounds like a feeder. You gave him the Helpline number?"

"He has it."

"Well, if the girl doesn't call in the next few days, we'll chase her down. We can't let her run around loose. As for Forster, we'll make a persuasive statement to the Pomperi to drop the blackmail or they'll come in for some bad karma."

"Thanks, Manuel. He's really beating himself up over the whole thing."

"No doubt. Leave it with me. By the way, when are you doing Lenny?"

"This weekend. Probably Saturday night." He would still have most of the day for a trip into the countryside.

"Take care."

"All the time." Frank chuckled and hung up, relieved the Covenant would handle the Pomperi. He had no idea what Manuel had in mind, but he did not underestimate the Covenant's resources or reach.

Lenny the Finger…He looked forward to offing the pimp and Taskforce Crimson informer. The little weasel only thought of himself and pointedly ignored the harm his carnal activities caused all feeders. The Covenant warned him to curb his excesses, and Lenny told them to shove it, certain the underworld mob behind him would keep him safe. He killed two women within six weeks, leaving them desiccated and old, and the Covenant decided he had to go. Frank drew the short straw with the other five Melbourne Keepers for the job.

Despite counseling, some feeders still turned rogue and killed. Some did it without ever becoming aware of the Covenant or understanding why intimacy suddenly made their partner die of old age. Others, men and women, took a life because they enjoyed inflicting ultimate pain and suffering. Rehabilitation helped many manage their excesses. Those who persisted were cut out like cancerous cells before the disease spread, and Keepers did the cutting. The Covenant could not really refer such cases to the police, although on occasions they did share information anonymously with local taskforces to take care of business.

Nine years ago when he trained to become a Keeper, he questioned the binary live/kill doctrine applied by the Covenant. In centuries past when death stood at every corner with no shortage of customers from numerous diseases and constant wars, a feeder could satisfy his or her need in utter secret. With Europe under the Inquisition's horrible excesses well into the 18th century where individuals were seized, tortured, and often burned at the stake on someone's mere say-so, feeders were rightly wary of exposure. To protect itself and normal feeders, the Covenant issued an unbending edict: a rogue must be eliminated without mercy, lest the whole society rose up in a program of even more extreme extermination.

It might already be too late for all of them. With rapidly advancing technology, it was only a matter of time before Project Purple researchers developed the capability to recognize feeders, which might set off a worldwide purge. If existence of feeders became public prematurely, there could be riots, vigilantes, protest marches, and political overreaction. Project Purple and the Covenant operated programs of population conditioning to the existence of feeders, but he feared premature disclosure.

What if everything did become public today? Across Australia, less than two people a week died of sudden old age. On average, twenty-five lost their lives in road accidents. Nobody marched in protest or rioted, desensitized to the carnage despite police warnings and graphic advertising. Why should people riot over old age deaths? Riots and protests did not happen spontaneously. It took planning, organization, and communication to create rampaging mobs. Incidences of sudden old age deaths had not reached the necessary flashpoint.

The flashpoint might be reached if he added the word 'vampires' into the equation. Something dark lurked in man's psyche that would awaken at the image of energy vampires walking the streets. Countless books and films had firmly embedded visions of blood-sucking evil things who damned every soul they touched. Although rampant fiction, many actually believed such creatures existed, fostered by religious dogma.

Authorities were pouring billions into research to ascertain the cause of sudden old age deaths without reference to feeders as the cause. From what he knew, special research centers and large pharmaceutical companies pursued two lines of inquiry: a virus vector and genetic variance. Most leaned toward the letter, as decades of study failed to find any virus. Understandably, people were getting impatient, as incidences of sudden old age deaths steadily increased. As the world's population grew, so did the deaths in direct correlation, more noticeable in poorer countries with high birth rates. As usual, irresponsible media sensationalized the situation with wild innuendo that fueled public unease and unrest.

* * *

Frank liked Fridays. Mornings attracted mostly corporate clients. Mom-and-pop and small corner store investors usually came early in the week. A pattern beyond unravelling, ripe for some sociology student's paper. Afternoons tended to be easy as people decided to leave the city early and avoid the exodus crush, which, of course, created the crush as everybody else came up with the same bright idea. From the 14th floor, his senses were spared the sight of jammed cars and horn blasts from frustrated drivers wondering if they would ever get out of the mad city.

What made this morning special and added a spring to his step were news clips on all channels as he prepared breakfast. Reporters talked learnedly about organized crime as they stood in front of the luxurious Pomperi Family's suburban Toorak mansion, with police in the background keeping back the overly curious. Panning cameras showed the entire front brick fence wall painted with blood, according to the forensics people still taking samples.

Greg Forster called him yesterday afternoon, very nervous at what might happen to his daughter if he did not pay up. Frank told him to take a drink and sit tight. About to close for the day, he received an encrypted text saying his friend no longer had a problem. A text to the Pomperi, according to Manuel, far less pleasant. The Italian crime syndicate understood symbolism and what a blood wall feud represented.

This morning, Greg rang, gushing his profuse thanks and relief. An anonymous text he got basically said he could forget the five mil payment, and his daughter would not be touched. He showed his gratitude in a substantive way by depositing $50,000 into the Urbi account. Frank knew better than to knock it back. It would only insult his friend if he tried. He accepted, glad to see the matter settled satisfactorily.

The rest of his day progressed less dramatically.

By four o'clock, he finished updating his billable hours and expenses sheet, and allowed the computer to crunch the numbers. When they started the practice, Owen insisted that every hour and spent dollar must be accounted for. Not only to provide a legal basis for client billing and tax deductions, but time records generated valuable engagement profiles of busy and slack weekly, monthly, and seasonal patterns where promotional advertising could be employed to attract more clients. This required getting an accounting package able to do all those things in addition to churning out normal general ledger reports, profit and loss statements, balance sheets, and other paperwork necessary to run the company. Frank did not argue the need for such a system, although the drudgery to keep it fed with data sometimes became an irritant.

Tonight, a reservation at Rialto's Vue de Monde, nothing would keep him from that gastronomic rendezvous, not even administrative chores. He made the reservation some six weeks ago—not a place where someone could simply ring for a table. He pictured himself in the quiet atmosphere, all the décor done in black, tall windows gave a stunning view of Melbourne under lights. But first, he'd have a quick one at Blink's.

Around five, he powered down the computer, slipped on his jacket, and walked to Owen's office. He knocked and opened the door. His friend looked up and nodded, busy straightening a pile of papers.

"If it's a client, I'm not here."

His partner lived in a fancy three-bedroom apartment in a St. Kilda Road condominium not far from the formidable Shrine of Remembrance memorial. Frank urged him to buy a pad in the Collins Street Tower, but Owen liked open spaces and parkland that ran from the Yarra River to the Shrine where he could take a peaceful jog. Exercising in a gym simply wasn't the same thing, he declared flatly more than once. No argument from Frank there. The condo an easy tram ride to Collins Street, Owen did not get stressed out having to commute into the city. Having money came in handy sometimes. Karen and his teenager Merva also liked some open space. Owen could argue with anyone about many things, but not with Karen when his wife set her mind about something, and the Emersons never moved into the CBD.

"I wanted to tell you I'm off," Frank said. "Give my regards to Karen."

"I'll do that." Owen peered at him. "Why don't you come over on Sunday for lunch? You haven't visited in a while. We'll have a few drinks and talk crap. Merva is having a sleepover at a friend's place and we'll have the apartment to ourselves."

"Sounds good." Frank genuinely appreciated the invitation. Karen would try to get him married to one of her friends, but he did not mind the matchmaking routine.

"Great! I know a nice woman who'd love to see you."

"Not you too!" Frank moaned, and Owen laughed.

"Time to plow a new field, my boy. See you around eleven? We'll sit on the balcony, puff on a cigar, and drink fine wine."

"You talked me into it." Frank waved a hand at him and walked out.

In his apartment, he took a quick shower and dressed casually in dark blue jeans, gray runners, and a black microfiber T-shirt with collar. He would put on something more formal for his dinner. One last thing to do…

He picked up the multi-purpose remote that controlled the TV and surround sound system. A double click on the blue Pip Input key, the small LCD screen lit up as the nonlinear junction detector activated. It took him almost three minutes to check every room for planted eavesdropping devices and cameras. Satisfied, he nodded and headed for the door.

Almost six, he pushed through the flowing pedestrian mob and strode into the Emporium. He never took a table, preferring a bar stool where he could observe fellow connoisseurs. That way, he could also chat with Walt or one of the other bartenders.

He paused at the entrance and winced. A weaving ocean of heads and bodies filled Blink's. He stood a better chance winning a lottery than finding an empty stool. No chatting today. Determined to have his bourbon mix in company, reluctant to try another bar probably equally crowded, he moved in. He found an empty standing spot at the end of the bar and tried to catch a bartender's eye.

An older man, fading hair streaked white, a blue shirt and black pants propped up what still looked like a powerful body. A bartender walked over and Frank ordered his drink. Not an extrovert, he often wondered why he frequented Blink's and other bars, putting aside earlier philosophical ponderings. An unconscious study of human group behavior, or silently laughing at man's antics? Perhaps a session with a mind twister would give him an answer. It might also tell him something about himself he did not want to know. What if it stopped him visiting his watering holes? He never saw a shrink and never got that answer. Anyway, the bars he frequented also provided him with ready females he could feed on.

He leaned against the bar for emotional support and plucked

a handful of nuts from a handy bowl, filtering out animated background chatter and music. The old geezer beside him nodded and
grinned.

"Pops," Frank said pleasantly, hoping the guy wasn't after a
free drink. The man did not look like a bum, but he hated hang-
ers-on.

"How you doing, my boy?" the geezer growled, an amused
smile tugging his mouth.

Frank stared hard at the blue eyes and did a double take as the
face resolved into startled recognition.

"Dan? What the hell happened to you? You look…" He
trailed off. He knew what happened to his acquaintance and the
realization made him furious.

"I know. I look like shit and I feel like I'm pushing eighty. I
had to see you one last time, and Walt said you're here on most
Fridays."

Frank's drink arrived and he emptied half of it in two gulps.

"I'm dying," Dan added wearily.

"Dying? From what?" Frank did not have to ask. He already
knew, but could not very well say so.

"Would you believe love?"

"Come on. I'm serious."

"So am I." Dan's eyes sparkled with some of his old inner
vitality. "It was her."

"Don't be ridiculous. You must have caught something,"
Frank retorted to maintain the charade.

"I did, and it's killing me."

"How can you die from making love?"

"Beats me."

Frank stared at him. "Did you see a doctor?"

"Yesterday, my GP took one look at me and wanted to rush
me to a hospital. I walked out on him. He knew something, but
wouldn't tell me. Bastard. I'm simply another case of someone

suddenly dying of old age you read in the papers or see on evening news. She did it to me, I tell you.

"Remember Tuesday and how we met? Something about her made her different from any other woman I ever knew. She made herself that way for me. For every man in the bar. I could tell. Never mind I was cheating on my wife, I wanted her. She took me to a room at the Grand Hyatt, of all places, and we spent the whole night making delirious love. When I got tired, night service brought us snacks."

A wishful smile lit his face and some of the years fell away, and Frank saw the man he first met. The moment passed and Dan turned into someone simply old and weary, lost in yesterdays and what might have been.

"When I picked her up, or maybe she did the picking. It doesn't matter. We both knew where it would lead. She captivated or bewitched me. I don't know. Her magnetism drew me to her and I couldn't pull away. Not that I wanted to," Dan added with a wan smile and took a quick sip of wine.

"You were right. She wasn't beautiful in the classic sense, but when she looked at me with those large, dark eyes, I knew I was the only man in the world for her. That's a powerful aphrodisiac, my boy. Something in the back of my mind told me to run, but I couldn't. My hormones were doing my thinking for me."

Helped by the woman's bioelectromagnetic link, Frank thought.

"Our fling only lasted a night, but in that night, I lived a lifetime. When I woke the next day, I felt fine, and she had already left. Yesterday, I walked around as though somebody had beaten me up. I looked in the mirror, saw a stranger, and I knew. She took it all. And you know something, Frank? I didn't care. I really didn't. Who knows? Perhaps she left that for me as some kind of compensation. My wife came into the bathroom, went hysterical, and immediately drove me to our GP. Poetic justice for cheating on her, eh?"

"How do you know it was the woman?" Frank demanded.

"You know she did it. I can see it in your eyes, so don't bull-shit me. All women take something from a man when you love. Ask my wife. The life-sucking nag drained me for years. Despite everything, I still love her. Isn't that a crock? This one just took a bit more than most. All I know, as we made love, she grew stronger, more radiant, more compelling, and I felt weaker. The thing is, I couldn't stop myself. All that corny guff about feeders and energy vampires? I believe it all."

Frank nodded, knowing what Dan meant. Every copulation entailed an exchange of energy between partners that can lead to deep bonding, understanding, and wellbeing. Most people are not aware of the phenomena, accepting it as something one feels when in love. When one-sided, the affected partner can over time become physically and emotionally weak, age prematurely and, carried to the extreme, die. That's what happened to Dan.

Now, he would have to hunt her down.

Never close to a rogue feeder victim before, seeing his degen-erating friend made what he did as a Keeper far more personal. It also gave him an intimate insight into the quality of suffering the victims and those around them endured.

Dan grabbed his arm with surprising strength. "If you see her, don't wait. Run like hell. I'd hate for you to end up like me." He tossed back the last of the wine. "I'm glad I had a chance to see you, Frank. I have a feeling it's for keeps."

"What are you going to do?"

Dan shrugged. "My GP wants to send me to the Victorian Institute of Forensic Medicine at Southbank for some tests. It won't do anything to cure me. From what they say on TV, once you get this thing, it's terminal, but what the hell. They can carve up my body if they want. Perhaps they'll find something to help some other poor bastard."

"Are you going to tell them about your date?"

"You crazy? They'll think I'm a dingbat. I'll just tell them we had a good time. Let them figure it out for themselves, if they don't already know. There might be something to this being a government conspiracy."

According to the Covenant, governments everywhere already knew.

Established in 1947 by President Truman, Project Purple had now run for seventy-six years. During that time, authorities learned a lot about feeders, Keepers, and the Covenant from apprehended subjects without penetrating the organization itself...yet. The Project operated a worldwide deception campaign to explain incidents of sudden old age deaths as a virus or genetic mutation, with hints that feeders were responsible. A deception now wearing very thin among the general public. The authorities dared not reveal the truth that among them lived feeders. Should the truth become known, and many Western countries feared that Russia or China might leak it in order to sow discord among their enemies, governments would be overthrown as the populace rose up to exterminate the vampires among them.

What a tangled web we weave...

Dan grunted and pried himself off the stool. "I guess I'm through talking. I should go home, pack a bag, and get my wife to take me to Southbank." His mouth twitched as he stuck out a hand. "Look after yourself, buddy. If things had turned out differently, I have a feeling we could have been pals."

Frank grasped the hand and grinned when Dan tried for the knuckle crusher. His friend suddenly let go, turned, and hurried out. Frank stared a long time at a knot of bodies where Dan disappeared.

Walt ambled over. "Who was the old pop? He asked about you last night, but didn't seem that old then."

"Just a nice guy I chatted with once," Frank told him softly. "Tell me something. Do you remember the woman who came on Tuesday? She wore a beige blouse and a brown knee-length skirt."

"The one with long black hair?"

"That's her."

Walt bit his lip. "Lots of women come here to cruise, and I remember you picked up one or two. Mmm, I think I know which one you're talking about. She's a regular. Usually comes in on a Tuesday or Saturday, but not all the time. Why? You want to pick her up? Take it from me, my boy, she's bad news. Has that look."

"What look?"

"The hooks. She'll drive them into you and you're gone." Walt glanced at Frank's tumbler. "Want a refill?"

"No thanks. I have a dinner appointment. I appreciate the info about the woman."

"Any time. See 'ya around."

Frank nodded, wondering why he never saw the woman before if she came here often.

Outside, a cool breeze picked up, too uncomfortable for only a T-shirt. Surrounded by hurrying, indifferent pedestrians, traffic, and assorted city noises, his thoughts raced, thinking how to take care of another rogue feeder. As per standard SOP when a rogue demanded termination, he'd call Manuel and see if the Covenant had something on her. Without a photo, he could only give his contact a description, which might not be sufficient to identify her. Dan wasn't anything to him, but he could not allow the woman to hunt indiscriminately. He would pop in next Tuesday and see if his target showed up.

He turned right and stopped at the Bourke Street intersection to cross. Time he did himself up, hoping what happened to Dan would not spoil his dinner.

* * *

The antique tram clattered to a stop opposite the St. Kilda railway station and the door panel snapped open. Frank got up off the hard plastic seat and followed others out without using his Myki card to check off, not wanting an electronic record he'd been on the tram. Several passengers sprinted across the road toward the adjoining Woolworths supermarket to the blare of horns and screeching tires. A few seconds later, the walk sign turned green and he crossed to the other side of the brightly lit Fitzroy Street. The idiots running to Woolies saved themselves a few seconds, but they could have been injured or worse. However, those few seconds appeared to represent a moral victory against the system, and Frank hoped they enjoyed them.

The old refurbished tram clanked its bell and he watched thirty tons of sudden green death, as Melbournians affectionately called the old clunkers, clatter toward the beachfront. The City Council kept a number of them in operation as tourist attractions, together with WW II wooden City Circle relics on which passengers could ride free to tour downtown attractions on a hop-on hop-off deal.

Misty drizzle fell from a dark sky and blurred outlines where it touched. In the west across the Bay, thick cloud cover gave way to a faint orange sheen that colored the water with copper. It faded even as he watched and night claimed its domain. A large cargo ship, its superstructure a blaze of lights, crawled toward the Heads and the open Bass Strait deeps on the other side.

The gloomy evening somewhat different from the bright, sunny morning. Chores taken care of, he took his Subaru Impreza to the leafy, quiet, Bacchus Marsh nestled in the rich agricultural Parwan Valley west of Melbourne. Instead of taking the direct Western Freeway, he went along Calder Freeway and took a back road from Gisborne. He had not visited Bacchus Marsh in a while, and intended to pick up a supply of fresh fruit and vegetables. Along the way, he stopped when the valley fell away before him to admire the view and took some snapshots with his phone camera.

Morning should have made him keen to hit the road and leave the city with its problems behind. Instead, the breakfast news curdled his coffee somewhat. More sudden old age deaths across Europe and the United States cast a shadow on his tomorrows. The National Rally Party, a single issue far-right anti-energy vampire quasi-vigilante group, planned to hold protest marches in Melbourne and Sydney next Saturday, the presenter said, demanding that Prime Minister Griffin take steps to eradicate what they saw as a growing menace threatening to destroy the country.

Beijing saber rattled with renewed threats to reclaim Taiwan by force as legitimate Chinese territory. During the week, J-15 and J-20 fighter aircraft made several incursions into Taiwan's Air Defense Identification Zone, and were intercepted by Taiwanese F-35s. Both sides snarled at each other and peace returned. China's Belt and Road Initiative stalled as several African and Pacific nations canceled existing projects or rejected new proposals, prompted by economic and defense measures from Australia and the United States, wary of Beijing's encroachment into the Pacific, which they considered theirs. Elements of the US Coast Guard, supported by warships from the 7th Fleet, clashed with several Chinese Armed Maritime Militia fishing trawlers violating Pacific Islands Exclusive Economic Zones, the small nations lacking capability to drive off the trawlers pillaging their fishing grounds. Nothing new, Frank mused.

All the gloomy news made him depressed and he switched off. He finished breakfast, wondering why the world had to be so screwed up. Once he hit Calder Freeway, his outlook on life improved and he began to enjoy the warm sunshine coming from a deep blue sky.

There is a thing in the world he called the Self, comprised of every living thing. Not a God or some supreme creator—he did not believe in such stuff—but nonetheless something that watched over everything. When they philosophized, Owen often kidded him about this apparent contradiction.

When he meditated, Frank sometimes felt a connection and became one with the thing, aware of everything and nothing. The

Self existed and continued even when things inside it died, knowing new life would replenish it. Connected, he thought he understood the purpose of it all and his place in the encompassing vastness. When he opened his eyes, reality would rudely crash into his senses and the feeling of oneness faded, leaving him just another insignificant mote to the indifferent Self. Did it mean anything? Frank did not know. What he did know, it helped him cope.

Bacchus Marsh itself remained unchanged, maintaining its rustic, country feel that welcomed visitors. Away from the town center, residential lots spread up the surrounding low hills like a growing infestation. After a simple, tasty pub lunch, accompanied by a tall glass of cold beer, he drove down the Avenue of Honor—towering memorial trees on either side of the road representing fallen war heroes—and made three stops at local farms to stock up. Satisfied that life still had some compensations, he hit the Western Freeway to take him into the city.

The relaxing, diverting drive prepared him mentally for what he must do later.

Back in the real world, he surveyed the brightly lit Fitzroy Street decorated down its entire length with tinsel and glowing balls hanging from overhead wires. Every establishment festooned with some decorations behind a plate glass window to celebrate the coming of Christmas.

Boutiques, restaurants, ice cream parlors, and souvenir shops lined the entire side of the street all the way to the beach. Although warm, around 24C, the drizzle and cool air coming off the Bay made walking in casual summer gear somewhat uncomfortable for the streams of pedestrians ambling in both directions wearing all kinds of attire. Mostly young couples and singles looking for action at one of the numerous bars, restaurants, and discos.

The tourists were easy to spot. Many held smartphones or tablets taking snapshots or movie clips. The smooth sandy beach at the upper end of the street always a popular destination for a leisurely dip. A discerning stroller could find almost anything here, from sea shells and strip joints to establishments of more earthy pleasure. St. Kilda held a deserved reputation as the city's premier red light district. The downtown Arts Center complex provided attractions for those with more refined tastes. Frank visited both.

Almost nine o'clock, he inhaled a mixture of pleasant smells coming from various eateries. He walked casually past a couple gawking at trinkets in a jewelry store, stopped briefly to study a menu stuck to the front glass panel of Peppe's Italiana, then paused outside the Kitten Club.

Wearing a yellow cardigan, black pants, gaudy alligator shoes, Lenny the Finger strode up and down the front of his joint urging passersby to come in and enjoy the delights waiting inside. Evenings along the street were busy year round, especially during the summer months, but Fridays and weekends drew the big crowds. That's what Frank relied on. Another unremarkable face in a sea of anonymous faces.

Last weekend, sporting a limp, thin mustache, ragged jacket and pants—several people even offered him coins—he walked around the railways station, the Woolies store, and the street, checking for surveillance cameras. Some of the stores probably had them, but he could not see any mounted facing the street. Satisfied his presence would not be recorded, he considered a number of alternatives how to off Lenny. In the end, he decided to keep it simple. Keeping things simple meant fewer things that could go wrong, and Murphy never slept. The beauty of his plan, it allowed him the luxury of waiting for the optimal opportunity to strike.

A group of five laughing youngsters jostled each other as they approached the Kitten Club, making a nuisance of themselves for other pedestrians trying to walk past them. Frank reached into his lightweight gray windcheater, grasped the Ruger .22 automatic with a fitted suppressor, and pushed through the group.

Lenny beamed a huge smile and tugged one of the boys toward the club's entrance. The others talked it over, snickered, and began to shove each other inside. Frank stopped behind Lenny, smelled cheap aftershave, lifted the automatic, and fired two rounds through the windcheater into his upper body level with the heart. The rogue pimp pitched forward, almost dragging down two boys. Frank slid the automatic into the inside pocket and kept walking, not concerned about the small hole the bullets made in the fabric. It took almost two seconds before a shrill female voice screamed. Making like any curious pedestrian, he stopped and turned to check out the commotion. A small group gathered before the club to stare at Lenny's body sprawled on the sidewalk, laughter gone from the five boys. Frank kept walking up Fitzroy Street toward a lit intersection and tram stop for those wanting a return trip to the city, happy with his work.

The cops would figure Lenny to be another victim of underworld crime, write a report, file it, and close the case. Given the pimp's checkered past and several short-term prison tours, nobody would look too closely at circumstances surrounding his death. Tomorrow, the Deputy Police Commissioner for Public Safety and Security would stand before TV cameras, solemnly report another gangland killing, and promise that those responsible would be apprehended. The police will not tolerate violence in any form, he would declare ponderously. Anybody with dashcam footage, please hand it in to help with the investigation. Stirring stuff. Fitzroy Street would get free publicity and draw more visitors.

Frank nodded as he waited at the tram stop. Light rain continued to fall. He had heard it all before.

He could not say positively the shots killed Lenny, but his training and practice at a deserted patch of forest near Woodend—he could hardly practice at a shooting club—a little satellite town west of Melbourne, made him fairly confident. A

.22 round might be small, but its unusually high velocity made it lethal at close range. It would rip through any tissue in its path, and the heart represented very soft tissue. Lenny probably hit the sidewalk dead before realizing what happened.

Frank rode the tram all the way down St. Kilda Road, up the CBD's Swanston Street, and got off at the RMIT University. Not many attractions this far uptown, the street had only an occasional lone pedestrian. Thankfully, the drizzle had stopped, but a fresh breeze made walking unpleasant.

He walked toward Victoria Market and dumped the Ruger and his windcheater into a drop box. Somebody from the Covenant would pick up the items, dispose of the jacket and clean the Ruger, ready to be used by some other Keeper or disposed. He now needed to thoroughly wash his clothing and scrub himself to remove any gunpowder residue that might have stuck to him. Always take care of the small things, his trainer drummed into him, and he would live to enjoy a long life. The chances that cops would come after him for Lenny's murder were vanishingly small, but he could not afford to be complacent, mindful of that long life.

He hurried down Queen Street, his black cashmere cardigan barely keeping him warm. He smiled as he walked past Blink's Bar, the inside packed with reveling customers. Tempted to go inside, Frank kept walking. He would have his drink after taking care of the chores.

At Oaks, he pulled out a clean tissue and used it to press the elevator pad. When the door opened, he did the same thing to touch the button for the sixth floor. He pressed the keycard against the door sensor to his apartment and it gave a solid click. A new tissue wrapped around the handle made sure he did not contaminate it. He would wipe the card later. Inside, he deactivated the alarm system, walked quickly into the bathroom, and thoroughly cleaned his hands. He stripped down and threw all his clothing into the washer, then wiped down the floor tiles. His precautions extravagant and probably unnecessary, he believed being thorough at what he did.

A long, hot shower perked him up and he hurriedly pulled on jeans and a warm shirt. In the lounge, a tumbler of bourbon in hand, Vivaldi's *Four Seasons* filling the room, he allowed himself to relax. As termination jobs go, this one went smoothly. How many over the last nine years? He stopped counting after eleven.

The rogue woman feeder, on the other hand, required some thinking as he gnawed on the feedback from Manuel. Likely name: Kaneel Mercer, and she killed four times as far as they knew. The Covenant warned her twice to curb her indulgences, clearly without effect. If Frank wanted to eliminate her, Manuel would provide whatever equipment he needed.

Frank could put a bullet into her and end it. Neat and simple, but he wanted to make her suffer for what she did to Dan and other victims. Training told him not to get personally involved with his work, but he felt this woman deserved it. He decided to repay her in her own coin.

"Poetic justice, Dan," he murmured and lifted the tumbler in a silent salute.

Tomorrow, lunch with the Emersons to scrub Lenny's memory.

Frank placed both feet on the glass-topped coffee table, leaned back against the soft recliner, closed his eyes, and allowed the music to create random images in his mind.

Chapter Two

Tuesday evenings were easy at Blink's Bar, and Frank always managed to get a stool. The after work crowd still to arrive in force, he could hear snippets of subdued conversation and actually listen to the background music. Neil Diamond sang *I am…I said*, sounding particularly poignant. For some reason the tune struck a responsive chord. Frank also had this emptiness inside and could even say why. Not caught between two shores, though, unless he considered them metaphorical…stranded between feeders and ordinary humans. There were not many palms in Melbourne, and the rents sure as hell weren't low.

He leaned against the bar and turned his body enough to see everybody and watch pedestrians and the crawling traffic outside. Like eavesdropping secretly on the world. The world eavesdropped on him. So, all even.

Where were all those people going? What did they do in this sprawling city? He often wondered at the point of it all. Work, pay bills, procreate blindly to make more people who would do the same thing over and over, then die, leaving only dust behind. No point to it at all. Damn, he did not want to get moody. He contemplated handing out death and needed to remain sharp or he could easily end up like Dan.

Around one PM, he received a call from Manuel de la Kass that brightened his day. Melany Forster called the Ardor Helpline and they referred her to a clinic run by Covenant psychologists. After some tests, they confirmed she was a feeder and explained the grim facts of life to her. All good, according to Manuel, which relieved Frank of a minor concern. A nice guy, Greg did not need his daughter's condition or the Pomperi Family hanging over him. Life dished out lots of other shitty things to worry about.

Neil Diamond finished his lament, which left Frank deep in thought and somewhat nostalgic, wishing for a place with palms where rents *were* low. Outside, golden elm branches swayed, lashed by a strong wind. Around 18C, decidedly not summer weather. Melbourne can have four seasons in one day, so they said. On some days, he could believe it. Today, it only had one…misery. Without a heavy jacket, he'd be courting a cold. If it were not for some unfinished stuff with Kaneel, he would not have bothered going out.

He took a sip of bourbon and held the tumbler in his hand, drawing comfort from the warm glass as background bar sounds washed over him, the customers sounding particularly cheerful.

Last night on the ABC seven o'clock news, among the usual serving of car smashes, a gangland murder, Prime Minister Elena Griffin jetting off to Paris for a NATO meeting, branch stacking by the Victorian state Labor Party—good for a chuckle, as both major parties did it and indignantly denied the practice—the report finished with a clip of a sudden old age death victim: Daniel Poole, father of two with a surviving wife. Two hundred and thirty-nine cases this year so far Australia-wide. Compared to some 4,300 around the world, the Aussie statistics were insignificant. Medical authorities were no closer to understanding why people simply died like that, the presenter commented solemnly. A genuine mystery that stymied the world for a hundred years of fruitless research. Longer if newspaper articles dating back to the 18th century were to be believed.

Frank shrugged. No mystery to him.

A Sunday morning news item on the demise of a small-time underworld figure, Lenny the Finger, outside his St. Kilda brothel made him smile. The police did not seem overly heartbroken and would go through the motions to apprehend the killer. Nobody gave a toss if one less crim soiled the city. Let them kill each other off, people would say. He shared that sentiment.

He saw his target walk in and pause to survey the men inside the bar. A tight, ankle-long black dress revealed a pleasantly full figure. A white pearl necklace accentuated a long neck. Matching earrings adorned small, nicely shaped ears. Part of her long raven hair fell down her back. The rest covered the curve of her left breast. She did not carry a handbag, but clutched a small black purse.

Her large eyes pinned him and she slowly walked toward the bar. A smoldering look of desire radiated from her as she sat on the stool beside him. She fed off Dan last week and should not need to feed again, but Frank could not afford to be careless. He felt her magnetic attraction even as he admired her clear skin, delicate features, and a mouth made to be kissed. She could have picked any man, but when she looked at him, he projected his own magnetism and desire to draw her to him.

A bartender sauntered over and waited.

"A glass of house chardonnay," she said huskily in soft contralto that invoked a surge of passion from him. An enchanting woman regardless of her predatory tendencies.

She turned her head slightly, touched the corner of her mouth with the tip of her tongue, and smiled, revealing even teeth, not recognizing him as a kindred spirit. He would need that illusion to protect himself.

"You look as though I remind you of someone."

"You do remind me of someone," he told her easily. He would be forever damned if she did not remind him of Rainey, if only superficially. Or perhaps he wanted the image in his mind to shield him from the task ahead. How messed up can he be, still clinging to a memory?

"It must have been a powerful reminder. I can see the pain in your eyes, and I'm not after pain. Perhaps I should go."

"No! It's only a memory of a thing long ago."

With another smile that did not touch her eyes, she placed a delicate hand on his forearm.

"I can make you forget her," she whispered and her eyes seemed to expand. "There will only be us…forever. You have a quality about you I like. Do you want to leave? And I don't want your money."

He knew what she wanted, but she would not get it tonight.

The bartender brought the chardonnay, but neither looked at him.

"What's your name? Mine is Kaneel."

"Frank."

Without touching the wine, she stood up and waited. He threw some bills on the bar top, took her hand, and headed for the lobby. Outside, the keen wind made him wince, but Kaneel did not seem to feel any discomfort.

He steered her toward the Bourke Street intersection and they walked across when the lights turned green. She stopped and arched puzzled eyebrows.

"The taxi rank is back there."

"My apartment is a lot closer than what you may have in mind," he told her firmly.

She gave him an amused smile. "An apartment? You must be rich."

"You don't want my money, remember?"

Her clear laugh reminded him of water tumbling over rocks.

In the Oaks lobby, he pressed the elevator triangle and waited. The light above the center one snapped on to an accompanying *ting*. When the two door panels slid back on the sixth floor, he turned right and led her down a brightly lit corridor, their footsteps muffled by the hard ocher carpet. In front of apartment 62, he opened the door and automatically stood to one side to let her in.

All the lights were on and she paused to survey the living room fitted with a large LED TV and surround sound system, racks of CDs, DVDs, and Blu-rays, a couch and two cloth recliner chairs that flanked a coffee table on which rested an opaque glass chess set, a filled bookshelf, and bar cabinet. She pursed her lips and nodded.

"Nice, Frank. Somewhat austere, but it suits you. What do you do that enables you to afford a place like this?"

He switched off the alarm and turned to look at her. "Financial consulting. I can help you invest any spare cash you might have," he added with a grin.

Unmoved, she dropped her purse on the coffee table and walked toward the spare bedroom door.

"This way," he said softly and opened the door to the master suite facing Collins Street.

She slipped past him and looked quickly around the elegantly appointed room with its queen bed, vanity night stand, a hung round wall mirror above it, doors to a walk-in robe and *en suite*. Her back to him, he placed his hands on her smooth shoulders and felt her stiffen as his fingers slid down the curves of her body. She turned, melted against him, and lifted her face.

Her lips soft and cool against his, he kissed her with unreserved hunger. Just because he intended to kill her did not mean he could not have some fun first. After all, that's what she might be planning for him.

Fire raced down his back when their tongues touched. He stared into cold, unblinking pools of her dark eyes and wondered if things could have been different were she not a rogue. The zipper hardly made a sound as he dragged it down her back. Breathing rapidly, a slight flush colored her cheeks as her breasts strained against him. She pulled back, pushed down his jacket, and her delicate fingers began to work on the buttons of his shirt. He jerked it off and her cool hands slid across his broad chest.

"You're strong, Frank. I like mature men who know what they want."

His head whirled with longing, keeping one part of himself

reserved and remote.

He tugged at her dress and it slid past the swell of her breasts to make an untidy pile at her feet, leaving her clad in wispy black panties. Her warm flesh pressed against him, hair cascading down her back, her slim arms wound around his neck.

"You're mine," she whispered into his ear, pinched it with her teeth, and his body responded.

He picked her up, a slim doll in his powerful arms, and laid her on the bed even as part of him welled with black thoughts. She had it coming to her.

His body primed, he dragged off the rest of his clothing and lay beside her. Kaneel immediately rolled on top of him and clamped her mouth against his, her tongue probing. Before he could wrap his arms around her, she sat up, gave him a smoldering smile, and took him in.

As waves of pleasure coursed through him, he felt her connect with his bioelectromagnetic field and begin to slowly draw. He felt the drain and set up a block, allowing only a trickle for her to feed on, enough not to alarm or arouse suspicion. Perhaps she only wanted a little, but he would give her more than she bargained for. He lifted his arms and massaged her full breasts, which made her groan and toss back her head in ecstasy.

She did not let him rest, demanding he use various positions. When both became exhausted, they raided the kitchen for nibbles, talked inconsequential things, and resumed business without any emotion on his part. He merely satisfied a physiological need. Emotions only got in the way, although he made appropriate noises for Kaneel's benefit. Despite her unsavory sexual tendencies, she was nevertheless a compelling, desirable woman. Judging by an almost perceptible glow of satisfaction surrounding her, she thought she conquered him.

Somewhere in the small hours, he sensed she'd had enough. *Time to finish this*, he told himself, before she did it to him and triggered massive cell apoptosis, although he did not know if

Kaneel intended to kill.

He knelt, held her spread arms firmly against the bed, positioned himself, and thrust into her, thoughts grim. His link with her field strong, he sucked relentlessly until he reached the irreversible threshold and kept going. Eyes screwed shut, moaning with pleasure, she suddenly stiffened and her eyes flew open in panic. She began to struggle, but his powerful arms held her down.

"No!" she screamed and arched her body in an effort to throw him off. "No! Get off me!"

He kept thrusting into her until he climaxed. Satiated, he leaned over her and brushed her lips with his.

"For Dan, darling," he grated, rolled off the bed, dragged on his boxers, and stared down at her.

"You bastard! You unspeakable piece of shit!" She sat up and clutched the sheet across her breasts.

"You only had to take a little, but that wasn't enough for you."

"I gave him an eternity of love! It's more than his wife ever gave him."

"You took too much and turned your lust into sport. You took everything without giving your prey a chance to recover, and the trail of bodies you left behind threatens to expose us all. You were warned."

"The Covenant? Who are they to set themselves as my judge and executioner? You're a feeder like me, needing what people out there must give us."

"That's right, I am, but I don't abuse them!"

"They're food, nothing else."

"So are you."

"I didn't kill every time!"

"But you did kill, Kaneel. That's the difference. You could have had your fun without going over the edge."

Her eyes filled and her lips quivered. The fight suddenly left her. She buried her face between her hands and sobbed quietly.

After a moment, she looked at him.

"Please! I don't want to die."

Frank believed her. Too late for second thoughts, though. Too late from the moment she took her first victim. They did not want to die either, but that did not stop her.

"You didn't have to kill!" he grated, in a way regretting having done this. The shitty parts of life.

Tears glistened on her stricken face. "You don't know what it feels like, Frank. The power, the thrill of having total control over someone. To push them over the edge when they think they're in control." She sniffed and wiped her eyes.

"That's the thing, Kaneel. I do know, because I've been there myself, but I didn't take more than they could give."

"How…how much time do I have?"

"Four…five days. You just fed, so it might take a little longer. Then again, I hit you pretty hard."

She threw back the sheet, eyes flashing hate. "You heel!" she hissed.

"You did it to yourself."

"I'll go to the cops, the newspapers, and tell them everything!"

Any feeling of sympathy for her vanished and he clenched his jaw. He walked to the coffee table, picked up her purse, and rifled through it.

"What are you doing?" Naked, she ran after him and tried to snatch it.

He pushed her back, pulled out a driver's license and memorized the address.

In his first year at Melbourne Uni, his psychology professor took him to one side and taught him techniques to read faster and retain almost everything. Not quite an eidetic memory, but the skill helped him wade through all the material he needed for his studies. It also came in handy with his business.

He held up the license. "See this? I know who you are now and where you live. You talk and I'll come after you. Not only you, but your family and close friends. Yours won't be the only funeral."

"Worth it to see you destroyed!"

"Fine. Then talk." He knew she would not, but if she did…

Without saying anything, she snatched the card from his hand, shoved it into the purse, and stomped toward the bedroom. Dressed, she walked to the door, paused, and gave him a look of utter loathing, eyes flashing fire. If she had a weapon, she would have killed him. The door banged after her, echoing in the sudden silence.

Alone, he sighed and padded into the bathroom. After a long, hot shower, he fixed himself a shot of bourbon and tossed it back to wash out her taste, then slipped back into bed. Tomorrow, he'd get Oaks services to launder the sheets to remove any trace of her presence.

Fingers locked behind his head, he stared at the dark ceiling and inhaled the lingering scent she left behind.

She didn't have to do it to them!

Last time he did this, he underestimated the woman's powerful field and allowed her to slip through his defenses, blocking her in time before she became dominant. Two days later, his hair showed streaks of white, his joints ached, and he looked fifteen years older. He took a few days off work and recovered quickly, determined never again allow himself to be seduced.

The gauzy curtains hung limp, a shield for the smart glass window to ensure silence from a city that never really slept.

He pictured himself sitting on coarse sand beneath a dark sky. A cold wind tugged at his hair, but he did not feel it, or smell the iodine in the air. Thundering rollers reared up and smashed themselves against rocks, shooting up white spray as the ground trembled. The surf gurgled and hissed as it raced up the beach and swirled around his legs. The water receded, leaving behind glistening sand. Overhead, circling gulls screeched in protest. Golden rays suddenly slanted down as the clouds broke and turned the churning sea blue. One of them splashed him with color and he luxuriated in its warmth. After a while, the vision faded.

He turned over and pulled the sheet under his chin. Sometime later, darkness descended.

* * *

Nadala Robinson twitched the pink carnations around the single central white bloom into place, nodded, and slid the cut glass vase to the corner of her desk. It would do. A tall potted green thing blocked the workstation in front of her to provide a semblance of privacy. Somebody must water them, as she saw droplets on the drooping leaves when she got in.

She glanced out the full wall window at the Docklands sprawl bathed in sunshine. The weatherman said the city could look forward to a pleasant Wednesday with light southerly breezes and a top of 24C. Possible showers in late afternoon. December can have gorgeous hot days, but can also be patchy.

Her second full day at work…Funny how quickly a person's life can change.

On Friday morning, prepared to tackle a formidable stack of case files sitting on her desk, the office devoid of natural lighting, an email popped in her Inbox and her eyebrows climbed when she read the sender's name: Deputy Commissioner Neville Trusk, Australian Federal Police. It said she'd been selected for a transfer to Taskforce Crimson. If interested, present herself for an interview with Inspector Kurt Porter at three PM on Monday at the Spencer Street Police Center. She heard the usual office grapevine stuff, but nobody really knew what this mysterious taskforce did. Tired of general detective work chasing down petty criminals and road violators, eager for a change of pace and a push up the career curve, she sent back an affirmative reply. It could not hurt to have a chat with Porter and find out more about this taskforce.

Excited and a little nervous, she showed up on Monday and asked security to announce her. Prada Vishnu, the formidable detective senior sergeant who escorted her to the eleventh floor after asking to see her police ID card, turned out to be easygoing and friendly. The Inspector, she said with an engaging smile, looked stern and forbidding, but a real human type underneath, provided everybody did their job. At her workstation, she shoved a hard plastic chair not much softer than concrete toward Nadala and did things with her computer.

Robinson allowed her eyes to roam around the half floor occupied by Taskforce Crimson. Festooned with tinsel, bright glass balls, and cotton wool, lush potted plants scattered around eight workstations broke up the bare, sterile feel. Glittering loops hung from the ceiling to add additional Christmas cheer. Seeing them, Nadala reminded herself to decorate her apartment and not leave it until the last minute—again. High time also to buy presents for everybody. In line with established tradition, her mom called last Thursday, saying the Christmas day lunch would be at their place. She loved the spread of foods and desserts Mom lavished on everybody, bemoaning the weight gain she would have to work off later. Valerie would go nuts tearing wrapping off presents, insisting Granddad light sparklers on the Christmas tree, and indulge in assorted torte. Twice a year, Nadala's sister Angela allowed her irrepressible little bundle of trouble to run wild, the other time being Easter. Well, three times if she counted birthday.

Apart from Prada, only one other desk had an occupant, a cute looking man peering at a screen. Sitting rigid on the edge of the chair, she wondered if accepting this transfer had been such a good idea. It definitely looked like an opportunity on Friday. She must have been totally tired of her job to fall for a sight unseen. Not even a job description! A simple yes or no if she wanted the position. Well, she could still say no after she saw Porter.

Prada's phone rang and she picked up. After a clipped, 'Yes, sir', she stood and glanced at Nadala.

"Come with me," she said and strode briskly toward the only office on the floor.

Prada knocked and opened the ceiling-high wood-veneered door after hearing a muffled 'Come'. Robinson hastily patted down her conservatively cut dark blue business jacket, hoping her ash-blonde hair had not gone awry—she should have visited the ladies room to check everything—and walked into the almost bare office devoid of traditional steel filing cabinets, which she found odd. She knew modern offices were meant to be paperless, but this never worked out in practice. People liked handling paper documents, simple as that. Her professional life to date required going through endless reams of papers and files. A rather small bookshelf stood tucked against the left wall, filled with what looked like law manuals and assorted magazines.

"Thanks, Prada...Sit down, Detective," Porter said pleasantly enough without getting up or offering to shake hands, which annoyed her a little. Could he be one of those macho martinet types?

Before coming, she studied his publicly available personnel file and photo, and heard the usual office gossip stuff, but his powerful personality intimidated her a little. Thirty-seven, 180cm, black hair, trim, second generation Australian from English parents. Someone told her he lived in Sunbury, a rapidly growing satellite city west of Melbourne, and commuted to work by train. With the Southern Cross station an easy five-minute walk from the Police Center, despite available underground parking, Porter wisely spared himself the twice-daily traffic crush.

She lived in Carlton and used her little red Suzuki Swift to commute to the Collingwood police station. She spent her first two years on the force in Altona, which she believed took five years off her life, the place utterly dull. Followed by two years at the modern Broadmeadows complex before posted to Collingwood. Somewhat of a letdown, but promotion to detective sergeant made up for it, and she ran a team. Plus, as a detective, she no longer wore a uniform—most of the time. All good things on the career ladder.

Porter earned a bachelor's in Criminal Justice—she had one too—and a master's in Criminology. After three years as a general duties patrolman, he joined the Criminal Investigation Unit as a leading senior constable detective. In 2014, promoted to senior sergeant, and in 2018, to inspector. Office rumor said he was tapped for superintendent next year. She figured some guardian angel must have steered him through the office politics traps, as he did not look like an ass crawler to her.

"Welcome to Taskforce Crimson, Detective," Porter told her in an even voice devoid of emotion. "You signed a nondisclosure confidentiality agreement sent to you on Friday. As you've gathered, while here, you'll be operating under an extremely tight security regimen. We have no secrecy classification. The mere existence of one is an invitation for someone to find out what lies under it. Our existence is not secret, but what we actually do definitely is, covered by the Crimes Act 1914. Everybody knows we deal with organized international crime and its impact on Australian commerce, and we promote that image. You accepted this assignment without a background brief, a test of sorts." Porter leaned forward and fixed his amber eyes on her. "From this moment on, you will not refer to or discuss any aspect of your activities with anyone. Not your family, boyfriend, confessor, or God. That clear?"

She swallowed and blinked. "Yes, sir."

"If you cannot operate under these constraints, you can return to your current duties without fear or prejudice. Well?"

Digesting the impact of his words, she took a deep breath. "I want to be part of your team, Inspector."

"In that case, you can look forward to some interesting work. Not always exciting or dashing, but definitely interesting. Prada will give you a 24/7 access keycard, a new cellphone, and show you your workstation and all computer logon protocols." He sat back and gave a small smile that transformed his rugged face into something almost handsome.

"You're no doubt wondering what you've gotten yourself into. Without supporting information, a natural and expected reaction. You've heard of sudden old age death cases?"

"I've seen clips on TV and social media," she said guardedly, not certain how they could be in any way construed as criminal. "I remember an ABC *Four Corners* program about it a year ago."

"A lot of people around the world are spending their time trying to find out how some die an accelerated death. Most believe the condition is caused by a virus. Although not true, it's something we don't publicly refute. Several decades of research points to genetic variations as a causal factor, and largely promulgated for public benefit. Have you heard of feeders?"

Nadala stared. "Energy vampires?" Taskforce Crimson is chasing an occult fantasy? *Jeez!*

Porter scowled. "Although in essence accurate, it's an exaggeration used by cheap tabloids, cultists, and most social media platforms. You're not to use it, and you should know why."

"I know why." The word 'vampire' immediately conjured horrible images in people's minds, a bias almost impossible to erase, even though a fantasy.

"I thought you might. Feeders can link with a person's bioelectromagnetic field to draw energy by their mere presence or through physical intimacy. In extreme cases, they can trigger onset of sudden old age death. Most people don't even know this field exists or the subtle effect it has when subconsciously or consciously used to influence those around them. Extrovert personalities seem most adept at this.

"Our job, and the job of similar taskforces around the world, is to capture as many rogue feeders as we can lay our hands on to enable researchers uncover genetic markers that drives their need to feed and why some victims die. We don't work alone, of course. ASIO and intelligence services around the world provide valuable support."

Nadala scowled. "You're talking about arbitrary detention of a citizen, and that's against the law."

"It may appear so at first glance. Prada will show you background files that will explain everything. Study them. Next time I talk to you, I expect you to be a subject matter expert and put you to work. That's all, Detective."

Somewhat nonplussed, Nadala slowly rose and walked out. She closed the door with a soft click and strode quickly to Vishnu's desk, tempted to head straight for the elevators, not sure she wanted any part of this nutty taskforce. The Indian woman looked up and smiled pleasantly.

"Joining or leaving?"

"Joining…I think," Nadala told her uncertainly, and the woman laughed.

"Outstanding! You'll regret every minute of it."

Prada stood and steered her toward a window workstation. "This one is yours. When you're not in the field playing old-fashioned detective, you'll be spending a lot of your time here researching." She dug into her trim navy blue jacket and held out two cards. "You must click the access card against the sensor to get in or out. Don't lose it or building security will jump all over you. The other is your new ID. You're now a federal police officer. You'll find it handy when talking to people."

Nadala took the proffered cards and smiled. "The Inspector must have been confident I'd take the job to have these ready."

"He's a great judge of character. Never misses. I'll text you how to log on. There'll be an email in your Inbox that'll tell you about directories where to find stuff and open your own case files. First, you need to do some homework. I suggest you get yourself a large mug of coffee or tea. You'll need it. Probably more than one. The stuff you'll be covering is intense. Straight out of *The Twilight Zone*."

Prada reached into her pocket and held out a Motorola smartphone and a card. "Military grade encrypted cell, courtesy of ASIO. Have it on 24/7. To use it, plug in the SIM from your current phone. The card has your six digit PIN and instructions how to use the encryption mode. Memorize the PIN and destroy the card. By the way, you also have a basement parking spot on the fourth level—D64."

Nadala raised both eyebrows. "Wow. That'll be handy."

"Believe me, it will. Okay, let's get you started." She sat down, logged on, and brought up a directory. "Have fun, darling." With a flutter of fingers, she sauntered back to her desk.

Still uncertain if she made the right choice joining the team, Nadala retrieved the SIM from her phone, slipped it into the new cell, and shoved both into her bag. A quick rub of her palms, she clicked on the displayed folder, opened the first file, and began to read.

Chasing energy vampires? For goodness sake.

She initially sampled all the material to gain an overall mental picture, and felt the small hairs on the back of her neck rise, unable to believe any of this could actually be true.

The legends and early history of the so-called energy vampires quickly dispelled her skepticism as mere recent occult phenomena. Events in the 20th century and the two world wars made her bite her lip. The exponential growth of knowledge and technology gave governments everywhere tools to initiate scientifically based research programs into feeders and sudden old age deaths.

Finished, she snagged another mug of tea, opened the first file again, and began to read slowly, summarizing and ordering the material in her head. Porter told her the next time they talked, he expected her to be a subject matter expert. She took that literally and did not intend to disappoint him. The Inspector did not look like a man who liked disappointments.

Her knowledge of vampires in general came from the popularized legend of Dracula, occult literature, and Hollywood films. She actually saw the *Twilight* movies and liked them. If she dumped the sensationalist lore, she readily understood what feeders really were. Like Porter said, they drew energy from a person to sustain themselves. Existence of the bioelectromagnetic field acknowledged only recently by mainstream medical and scientific communities. Nobody knew why they fed, hence all the international research programs to find out. The process left the victim drained physically and emotionally sluggish, and depressed. Nadala easily related to that.

Her former husband washout, a law professor at Swinburne University where she studied for her degree, six years her senior, left her absolutely exhausted after some sex episodes, unable to resist him in any way as though he somehow depleted her will. Desperately in love, they married a year after she graduated.

Ordinarily gregarious, a genuine people person, he liked to party. His students adored him and his cutting dry sense of humor. Too late, she found Leo to be a two-timing son of a bitch. Having a loving wife at home clearly not enough for him, she filed for divorce. Thankfully, no children, although she wanted some. Could he have been a vampire? Since then, she tried sex with a woman, found it unsatisfying, and used other methods to relieve her needs. She dated, sometimes an intimate encounter, but most men were immature boys after only one thing. The sober ones she knew were already taken, to her regret.

Sidetracked by a memory bump, she continued to read.

A lot of cultural nonsense circulated among pyramid power and crystal healing followers who provided guidelines how to recognize and protect oneself from narcissist vampires, dominators, and plain evil individuals who thrived on inflicting pain, and sometimes death, on those they met.

Things became interesting when she delved into ancient writings. Many old Mesopotamian cultures had stories of blood-drinking demons. The Persians and Babylonians were one of the first civilizations who formerly incorporated such tales into their mythology, which flowed into old Hebrew writing. The Greeks and Romans were firm believers in gods, mostly female—*men wrote history,* Nadala reminded herself—who preyed on babies and mothers, drinking blood and eating their flesh to sustain themselves.

Early and medieval European writings were replete with vampire legends able to reanimate the dead, who in turn became vampires. Victims turned sickly, withered, and died after a sexual encounter. Stories of energy-sucking monsters abounded on every continent, and could not be dismissed as mere mythical lore.

Then came the rise of the Covenant.

The Roman and Spanish Inquisitions decimated upward of 300,000 victims accused of heresy, demonic possession, or practicing witchcraft—again, mainly women—often based on innuendo, jealousy, or plain revenge for some misdeed. The religious purges ensnared many energy vampires in the same net. Taskforce Crimson called them feeders, a more accurate description of these people. The poor individuals often did not know why they had exaggerated sexual needs, or why a partner suddenly aged and sometimes died after an episode of intense sex. The survivors would denounce their partner, male or female, accusing them of demonic possession. After a mock trial, the Church handed the luckless individuals to civilian authority, where they were tortured to obtain a confession, then executed, often at a fiery stake. No evidence ever emerged of genuine blood-sucking creatures. Knowing this did not stop the Church from its program of wanton persecution.

To protect themselves, a group of elderly male and female feeders gathered in Paris and, in 1637, created the Keepers of the Covenant. In succeeding centuries, they inserted themselves into positions of religious and secular power, set up programs to identify fellow feeders, educate them how to control their sexual appetite, and stay socially invisible. The Covenant also established the Keepers—men and women—trained assassins who eliminated rogue feeders to control incidences of sudden old age deaths, still relatively low even today.

As she read, Nadala found one thing puzzling. Why didn't the Covenant resort to outright blackmail of legislators and intelligence operatives to deflect attention? Then answered her own question. To do so would reveal it as a criminal organization and openly hunted as such. Perhaps they did some underhanded things, but no evidence existed to substantiate the suspicion. Anonymity demonstrated its neutrality and simple desire to protect feeders from discrimination. As far as they were concerned, the bad guys were Project Purple taskforces. The Covenant may not be wrong, she decided. The bottom line? Nobody knew what influence it exerted on economies and political systems, but authorities knew it did. Hence, the intense interest by governments everywhere to dismantle it. She understood it then. It rubbed everybody the wrong way that a world-powerful organization existed politicians could not control.

The Great War saw a spike of sudden deaths in militaries of both sides as men did each other in absence of available females. During the Great Depression, governments were too busy keeping people fed and employed to worry about odd sudden old age deaths.

The problem reared its head again in WW II. America in particular believed a virus to be the causal factor, genetics at the time still poorly understood. In 1947, President Truman created Project Purple and tasked the Johns Hopkins University in Washington, DC, to study those deaths. In July 1968, President Lyndon Johnson transferred the project to the Centers for Disease Control and Prevention facility in Atlanta, Georgia. At the same time, he urged the UN World Health Organization to establish a guiding body to coordinate worldwide research. Lack of subsequent funding saw the initiative die, and the United States decided to take control.

Because of the Cold War, little data trickled from the Soviet Union and its satellites, and nothing from the Chinese Communist Party. Hardly anything came from Africa, South America, Asia, and Pacific countries, including Australia.

As affluence increased, an improved standard of living saw population levels explode, incidences of sudden old age deaths also increased. In August 1971, President Richard Nixon gathered the most influential Western leaders to codify Project Purple as the governing authority to oversee investigation of and research into those deaths. Coordinated by the CDC, nine special research units were set up around the world, which included Johns Hopkins, Babraham Institute at the University of Cambridge, Bayer Group, Pfizer, the Royal Melbourne Hospital in Australia, Institut Pasteur, and facilities in Moscow, Beijing, and at the time, Bombay.

The Washington meeting turned into a watershed of international cooperation that drew resources from police and intelligence services of participating countries. The Soviet Union and China were not invited, even though reports indicated both faced the same problem. Predictably, the two authoritarian regimes accused the United States and the West of conducting biological warfare.

In February 1972, Nixon held a historical meeting with Chairman Mao Zedong. In May the same year, he saw General Secretary Leonid Brezhnev in Moscow. The visits served to mollify the two prickly leaders, and Nixon agreed to a mutual sharing of information from Project Purple to address what was perceived as an existential worldwide threat. For TV, photo-snapping reporters, and the world at large, the goodwill visits were designed to improve bilateral relations and promote trade. Newspaper editorials and TV commentators extolled Nixon's diplomatic skills, unaware how close civilization avoided chaos had Russia or

China revealed everything.

In 1982, Malcolm Fraser, the Australian Prime Minister, established Taskforce Crimson, run by the Federal Police, subordinate to Project Purple.

Nadala took a break to refill her mug, surprised to find her black Rado wristwatch show 5:26 PM. Determined to finish the brief, she went back to her workstation, giving Prada a nod of acknowledgment along the way. She decided this job would not do much for detectives with families.

The Covenant...

Apart from historical generalities, Project Purple knew very little about the secretive organization and its dealings that managed to elude penetration for centuries, the information obtained in the only way possible—captured city Masters and a rare Master Keeper, the people who actually ran the Covenant, often carried out under a questionable cloak of legality. Authoritarian and Muslim regimes discarded all pretense at legality. Project Purple authorities discouraged such practices, but took data from taskforces in those countries anyway, done in the name of a higher cause. A slippery slope history repeatedly showed led to social disintegration. Since the coordinated worldwide effort in 1996, nobody ever managed to apprehend a Master Keeper, Nadala noted with interest and a degree of amusement. Although clearly not amusing at all to Project Purple and the politicians.

Western countries could not maintain a veneer of moral indignation, as they themselves employed quasi-legal methodology in their investigations, supported by intelligence organs and plain old detective work. She feared that Taskforce Crimson also operated under a thin veneer of legality, something she found difficult to reconcile as a police officer.

According to the brief, ordinary feeders did not know the Covenant existed at all, but if threatened with exposure, they could contact the Ardor Helpline for counseling. She had seen some of their sophisticated, tastefully done ads on TV and social media. It seemed every country around the world had an Ardor variation to suit local customs and laws, having to be particularly discreet in conservative Muslim regimes. The Helpline had to have some serious backers to support a network of international call centers, but the brief did not provide any details. Raids on their clinics yielded nothing, as patient records were kept on inaccessible networked servers protected by two factor authentication protocols. Barging into a clinic without a warrant, guns drawn, demanding access to records, generated too much negative public backlash and embarrassment for authorities to be a sustainable tactic.

Subtler attempts were made to penetrate Ardor clinics by inserting Project Purple psychologists and psychiatrists, all without success. The clinics were legitimate businesses with patient records to prove it. When a taskforce did manage to place one of their own, they handled ordinary patients—if patients who needed a psychologist could be classified as ordinary. It quickly became apparent why infiltration attempts failed. A new patient went through an initial screening process handled by one of the clinic's established residents before treatment by someone else. According to planted psychologists and psychiatrists, if the screening process identified a feeder, they never saw them. They suspected some clinic residents were probably feeders themselves, but nobody could verify them as such, and no scientific test exists to prove them as one.

Taskforces gave a captured rogue feeder or Keeper a simple choice. Become an informer snitching on their own kind, or undergo immediate medical/scientific testing, sometimes to destruction. When a feeder, male or female, outlived their usefulness, they were handed to researchers, a fate Nadala did not want to delve on. As wanton killers, their life was effectively forfeit. Them or us, the rationale went. That higher cause can hide a multitude of sins, Nadala decided.

Over time, the Covenant found Paris politically untenable

and, in 1842, Project Purple suspected it relocated its operating headquarters to Zurich, Switzerland. A neutral country, it avoided much unpleasantness that subsequently afflicted Europe. The secretive banking laws also made it easier to manage their finances. Conjecture, as nobody actually knew where the Covenant set up its headquarters.

What they did know, the organization maintained a simple hierarchy, its genesis founded under a Middle Ages mentality. A Grand Master presided over a world Council, which consisted of Master Keepers from member countries. A Master Keeper in each country headed a separate Council of Masters who administered activities in major cities. When it became necessary to resolve policy issues, Master Keepers from the most powerful European countries met as a body, initially in Paris. This worked well for two centuries, as they considered the rest of the world uncivilized, the belief promoted by Judeo-Christian cultural snobbery.

After WW II, the political and economic center of gravity shifted to the United States. City Masters and the American Master Keeper, speaking on behalf of Japan, Australia, South America, and other minor Asian countries, demanded greater autonomy to formulate policy more relevant to their regions. The Grand Master and European Master Keepers resented what they perceived as erosion of their authority, and sent an assassin in a failed attempt to remove the American Master Keeper. In response, the Americans arranged to leave a disarmed bomb on the Grand Master's desk, the message clear: We can kill you anytime we want. The US Council declared its breakaway and set up their own Grand Master, probably based in New York, although unverified. Short of an all-out internal power brawl that would destroy everybody, the European Grand Master reluctantly accepted the new order of things and relinquished authority over half the globe.

According to sources, in 1950, every Master Keeper and city

Master the world over signed a new Covenant in a spirit of mutual preservation of feeders everywhere. With Project Purple actively hunting them, they could not afford to be locked into a medieval European mindset, as everybody's security became a paramount consideration. In late 1980s, the advent of personal computers, emails, the growth of the Internet, proliferation of cellular telecommunication early in the 21st century, maintaining social anonymity became singularly difficult.

Initially, the founding members financed the Covenant's operational needs. However, as its tentacles reached further into Society, royal courts, and businesses, the organizational support structure expanded, which required the setting up of formal funding and investment mechanisms. How those mechanisms operated and who provided donations were items of keen interest to taskforces everywhere. These days, shell companies, offshore tax havens, and electronic banking made it easy to syphon funds into seemingly innocent accounts, which made life for taskforce auditors more difficult, especially since the Covenant appeared to operate scrupulously within established legal frameworks. What Project Purple wanted to unravel were the Covenant's tentacles of economic and political power and how they used it.

In 1984, Project Purple achieved a breakthrough. President Ronald Reagan received a letter from the American Grand Master offering cooperation to design and implement programs to publicly reveal existence of feeders in a way that avoided global unrest and economic upheaval. Governments around the world must stop treating feeders as social enemies and recognize them under law. The Covenant would actively work with Project Purple and its taskforces to apprehend rogues, and support research institutions in an effort to identify biological mechanisms that trigger sudden old age death in an endeavor to find genetic blockers.

President Reagan appeared willing to negotiate, provided the

Covenant divulged details of every feeder in their records...worldwide. The Covenant would also be required to reveal details of its internal operations and disclose the identity of every Master and Master Keeper. In addition, Keepers must immediately cease and desist assassinating rogue feeders. Maintaining civil order was the responsibility of duly appointed police forces.

The Grand Master agreed to disband the Keepers, but predictably, refused to provide lists of known feeders, saying handing over personal records would expose feeders to violation of common rights and increase illegal incarcerations already happening everywhere. As for revealing its internal operations or individual identities, no country had jurisdiction over the Covenant's lawful business dealings.

Reagan declined to negotiate and the overture failed. Nadala shook her head. Instead of working for the common public good, politics, power maneuvering, and the desire by governments to control everything seemed to derail most well-intentioned initiatives. Since then, an uneasy coexistence remained in place. Despite fundamental disagreements, Project Purple and the Covenant maintained channels of communication with taskforce branches, and sometimes passed them information on rogue feeders, which set her thinking.

Did Porter have a link to the Covenant?

Starting in the 1990s, Western governments began to release information tidbits about feeders in an attempt to discredit unproductive feedback the energy vampires tag generated in the public psyche through media outlets, scientific papers, and documentary films, something she noted with approval. Project Purple polling showed the program had a measurable positive impact. However, nobody expected full disclosure to happen anytime soon, people's veneer of civilized behavior still uncomfortably thin.

Attached appendices provided a lot of supporting material,

including details of past taskforce operations. At the wrong end of 6:25 in the evening, she skimmed the material, promising herself a detailed look tomorrow, but one ops caught her eye. In 1996, Project Purple initiated an extremely dangerous global campaign to capture as many Keepers and Masters as possible in an attempt to infiltrate the Covenant. The operation worked and netted 164 Keepers and eighteen Masters captured or killed at a cost of thirty-nine operatives shot or eliminated in some other way. One week into the operation, the Covenant must have gotten insider information about the campaign and that ended it. Similar campaigns were launched over subsequent years without any results. It became obvious to everybody that Project Purple and its taskforces were penetrated, which created a new set of headaches. This made her scratch her head why the 1996 effort succeeded. Something the report neglected to explain.

Eyes burning, Nadala gave a long sigh and called it a day. She shut down the computer and walked slowly toward the exit, her mind buzzing with a history few people knew existed. Prada's workstation stood dark and empty.

A hell of a day, she told herself as she touched her keycard against the sensor. She looked forward to a long, hot bath where she could forget everything…until tomorrow.

As she stepped out into the noisy, smelly Spencer Street full of afternoon rush pedestrians making their way toward the Southern Cross station, she dug out her new cellphone. She simply had to tell Angy all about the new job. Not the details, of course, but her sister must be gnawing her fingernails waiting for the latest update.

Always close, Nadala the traditional big sister who guided her younger sibling through the turbulent teenage years and protected her from prowling wolves. A respected investigative journalist for *The Age* newspaper, Angela now had a husband and a precocious four-year-old bundle of trouble who wound her aunty around her little finger with giggling ease. Nadala did not mind, loving Valerie as though she were her own.

She and Angy enjoyed a terrific childhood growing up in a modest Clifton Hill weatherboard house close to shops, entertainment, schools, and churches. Nadala winced at the memory. Catholics, her parents dragged the kids to Mass every Sunday, an hour of torture for her. When she turned fourteen, her dad saw religious indoctrination did not work for her and allowed her to skip Sunday services, much to Mom's displeasure and Angela's annoyance, until she also turned fourteen. Their parents loved them, scolded and punished them, taught them how to handle boys, and life in general. Both tall and beautiful, Angela's flowing honey hair a hit with dates, neither lacked suitors for weekend outings. Mom curbed their wilder tendencies with sober talks and soothing encouragement. Nadala appreciated that support and those words of wisdom when she entered Swinburne University and came face to face with hordes of prowling boys eager to devour young flesh.

She scrolled down the Contacts list and pressed Angela's icon. After three rings, her sister answered.

"You beast! I've been simply dying to hear from you. How did it go?"

"Wait till you get a load of this, Angy!" Nadala gushed.

She sat back and smiled at the memories. To think all that happened on Monday, and she did have the hot bath.

More homework to do, she took a sip of tea and began to read a case file, forty-four to go.

* * *

Detective Inspector Kurt Porter sighed in frustration, wishing they would abolish Wednesdays and go straight to Thursday. He pushed back the computer keyboard and leaned back against his comfortable ergonomic cloth chair. He longed to take out his pipe and puff on the mild blend of rum-flavored tobacco. Regrettably, he could only do that at home in the backyard as Estella would give him hell if he smoked inside. At work, nobody would burst into tears if his habit killed him, least of all the city's rogues, but the powers that be frowned on passive smoking that could contaminate others and open a door to possible duty of care breaches. Soon, he would need to wear a spacesuit to walk anywhere because somebody would be inhaling his exhales if he did not. Trust the tree huggers to think of that one.

Damn them all.

He turned and gazed absently at the sprawl of condominium high-rises that had sprung around the harbor. The Westgate Bridge spanning the Yarra River loomed in the background. He could just make out the flowing traffic going both ways. Gnats on the back of a dormant monster. The view came free with the job. One advantage of having a spacious, if somewhat sterile office befitting his lordly rank.

At thirty-seven, his career so far on the planned track, time to make the next step on the promotion ladder. In August 2020, Chief Superintendent Marlow himself called him into his office and announced Porter's immediate transfer to Taskforce Crimson, where he would head a small team of investigators. The Superintendent did not say what they would be investigating. Porter despised Marlow, considering him a political weasel who cloaked himself in glory on the back of successes by his subordinates. The creep had a nasty habit of inserting himself into an operation likely to close a major case, his name prominent on the report the Crime Command deputy commissioner would read. When an operation pancaked—some things simply did not work out—Marlow made sure his teflon image wasn't spattered with acrimony. A posting to the secretive Taskforce Crimson meant no more scraping and bowing to Marlow. At home that evening, he celebrated his release from purgatory, much to Estella's amusement. Later, both celebrated in a different way.

Estella…An anchor that held him firmly to reality. With a master's in chemistry, teaching at RMIT University, he readily acknowledged her superior intelligence. Her urging to get a master's in Criminology from Melbourne Uni undoubtedly helped his rise up the promotion ladder. A chance meeting on a tram one lunchtime sealed the relationship, both sensing they met the right one. Every marriage went through rough waters, but they weathered minor storms, and along the way had two fine boys to fulfill their life.

After three years running a team of eight detectives, Porter wondered if the posting was a sidewise move by the Chief Superintendent to rid himself of a bright subordinate who could one day become a professional threat. The secrecy that surrounded his work and the Taskforce in general started to wear him down. At night, entwined in bed with Estella, he could not tell her what he did with his days. Chasing bad guys, he would whisper. True in a way, but not the kind of bad guys she saw in cheap TV flicks. As a woman filled with unquenchable curiosity, she resented his reticence, but thankfully did not ride him about it.

When Deputy Commissioner Trusk first told him what Crimson did, Porter goggled in disbelief. He figured that this time, Marlow shafted him properly. He sobered quickly after Trusk said he personally picked him for the post. That spruced up Porter's ego somewhat, but when he learned Crimson represented only one small piece in a worldwide mosaic run by the US-based Project Purple, his enthusiasm turned into dismayed incredulity. After seventy-six years, they were no closer to uncovering the Keepers of the Covenant cabal and the protective umbrella it held over all feeders. What the hell were they doing?

He quickly came to understand what they did. On one side of the coin, not much suitable for public release. Behind the scenes, quite a lot. After an intense two days of background indoctrination at Canberra headquarters, he appreciated the need for a security blanket over all Project Purple activities tighter than what he used to protect his bank account password. Accidental or deliberate public disclosure meant possible world chaos that made nuclear war an irritating distraction. In an all-out war, everybody died. End of problem. A world politically, economically, and socially ripped apart by knowledge of feeders walking loose everywhere represented years of unrest, with a likely nuclear exchange to boot at the end of it.

He watched cars crawl across the Westgate Bridge.

If Project Purple and some of the best researchers in the world could not crack how feeders caused old age deaths, or integrate them peacefully into the social fabric, the contribution his seven geniuses would make scant impression. Eight with Robinson on deck after one of his men had the disgusting bad luck to fall off a ladder and break his hip. He liked Nadala Robinson and hoped the twenty-eight-year-old leggy, 172cm tall sergeant would work out. Her record suggested she possessed the tenacity and a wide-ranging mind backed by intelligence necessary in this job. When he walked in this morning at eight, he found her staring at a computer screen. Five of his other investigators were also staring at screens.

What he kept telling himself, feeders were not responsible for being born like that, but Project Purple did not care to dissect the human side of the equation. They wanted a pill to turn feeders into normal people, if such creatures actually existed, Porter decided. Decades of worldwide research failed to develop such a pill, and he figured time might be running out for everybody before the whole thing blew up in their faces. A more aggressive approach might be required.

As he came to learn from briefly studying the subject, the human genome, especially the noncoding parts that early in the mapping program some halfwit termed junk, turned out to be a giant switchboard that controlled everything the body did. Unfortunately, nobody had a manufacturer's manual to tell them what those switches did, or what happens if one is flipped on or off; not for most of them anyway. This contributed to mounting frustration by Project Purple's political masters who wanted answers how to handle rising public disquiet about sudden old age deaths and what caused them. If a pill could be invented to cure some cancers, why can't someone invent one to prevent old age death? Increasingly acerbic murmurings of government conspiracy worldwide gave severe nausea to politicians who knew what Project Purple did. At least they could take a pill for nausea, Porter mused sardonically.

He should not worry about such weighty things, happy to leave them to the white-haired Neville Trusk and his higher-ups. Right now, a frustrating little problem nagged him, and he knew just the person to dump it on. The anticipation made him grin.

Get more live rogue feeders, Trusk told him in a clipped voice, and get them quickly. The federal twitch neglected to mention how Porter should go about doing that, as Keepers often eliminated them. Taskforce Crimson kept an office in every Australian capital city, New Zealand, and the Pacific Island states, who received the same directive. Tempted to tell Trusk that rogue feeders did not carry a glowing sign on their back advertising who they were, he refrained, mindful of keeping his job. Anyway, why the hell didn't Trusk simply ask city Masters to leave terminations to the Taskforce! A festering point of contention for everybody.

Dissecting victims of sudden old age death and running a zillion tests on those about to die went only so far to fill blank pages of knowledge. What researchers everywhere badly wanted were real live feeders to study how they promoted death in someone and pinpoint the causal genetic trigger. More likely several triggers were involved. Getting feeders presented an almost insurmountable problem not only for him, but taskforces everywhere. Unless identified by a rogue like Lenny the Finger, nobody could point to a person on a street as a feeder.

Since the collapse of Pauline Hanson's One Nation Party last year on charges of electoral fraud, the radical far-right movement rebranded itself as the National Rally Party. The exterior coat may have changed, but its policies had not. Affiliated with neo-Nazi groups in the United States and Europe, they became vocal exponents of energy vampire eradication programs and government conspiracies to hide existence of feeders from the public. People at large tended to ignore what they considered fanciful claims, but the tide started to turn as more credible evidence emerged from Russian and Chinese sources. Project Purple did not care whether disclosure resulted from internal leaks or were deliberate destabilization ploys by those regimes. They served to fuel public unease and growing demands for a cure of sudden old age death. Hence Deputy Commissioner Trusk's increasingly desperate demands for more experimental feeders.

However difficult the task, that's why Porter got the big bucks at the end of every month. He glanced at the flat computer screen…Lenny the Finger, his immediate object of frustration.

Apart from a multifunction phone station and computer, nobody kept paper records or files. If something needed filing, store it in the computer, the directive coming from on high. Any scribbled worthwhile notes should be transcribed into a computer work file, then shredded. Not a scrap of paper must leave anyone's office or workstation. One warning, followed by career oblivion for a repeat transgression, with probable posthypnotic conditioning to stop the individual from blabbing, accompanied by threats of dire consequences for the immediate family.

As far as Porter knew, no one talked, and he suspected a security breach saw the demise of his immediate predecessor. Then again, something like that would not be the subject of casual gossip in the kitchenette. Given the tens of thousands of people involved in Project Purple everywhere, somebody *must* have talked, which attested to the effectiveness of its sanitization procedures, and made him suspect the Russian and Chinese leaks were deliberate. Trusk as much said so. *Bastards.*

Porter glanced at the computer time display; almost 10 AM.

He reached for the phone and pressed one of eight preset number buttons.

"Yes, sir?" a pleasant low register soprano voice answered after two rings.

"My office, now."

"Yes, sir."

If he must do penance for sins yet to be committed, he saw no reason why he should not share the misery.

A knock on the door and he looked up. "Come!"

Robinson strode in, closed the door, and stood at attention.

"For Chrissake, Detective! Relax. This isn't a parade review. Grab a chair."

A faint smile tugged the corner of her mouth. She pulled up a chair, sat down, and crossed her legs.

He peered at her. "Are you a subject matter expert yet?"

"Almost there, sir. There's a lot to cover."

"It's Kurt, not Inspector or sir. You're on the team to work, not salute. That clear?"

"Yes, s…Kurt."

"Don't get worked up about digesting all the material in one gulp. It took me a while to come up to speed as well. As long as you have the important stuff down pat, you'll be able to do your job. Once you're happy with the basics, dig into our case files to get the down to earth flavor how we do things here."

"I'm already on it."

"Good. One piece of advice. This is not an us versus them deal. The feeders out there are people with rights, and we treat them as such, most of the time. They're definitely not the enemy. They could be turned into one by special interest groups—religious, political, and commercial—without appropriate social conditioning. Unfortunately for everybody, we may not have enough time for social conditioning to take root before things go into meltdown."

"I gathered that from the background material."

"No doubt. You may have taken it in intellectually, but you must also feel it in your gut. If you hold any ingrained prejudices or personal bias, scrub them from your psyche."

"Understood."

"What I'm telling you, Detective, to do your job, you'll violate existing criminal law. The situation we're facing, there is no specific law to tell us how to handle feeders. There cannot be any law if we don't admit feeders exist."

Robinson looked at him without wavering. "You're talking about arrest and illegal detention of a citizen without foundation or warrant. If feeders are people with rights, Kurt, how can we ignore those rights?"

Porter pursed his lips and nodded, pleased she stood up to him. "Law is merely a restraining yardstick that enables us to co-exist peacefully. It's not a behavioral template, and that's why societies have police to limit individual excesses. Remember your history. In times of trouble, minorities are the first to lose their rights. Life isn't fair, kind, or nasty. It just is. It dealt feeders the hot end of the brick, and that's tough. Our job and the job of taskforces the world over is not to make it any tougher for them than it already is…or us. Your part is a small component in a social jigsaw puzzle where feeders and ordinary people must fit to form a complete picture. That clear?"

"Clear enough."

"Project Purple doesn't have an issue with feeders as such. Our problem are rogues who exaggerate their need to a point where they kill by inducing sudden old age death. That's what frightens everybody, and why the Covenant exists. Some time ago, steps were taken to gradually condition the public to the existence of feeders and the relationship with sudden old age deaths. Until somebody decides to disclose everything, we operate in a legal no man's zone.

"Time for you to do some paid work. Do homework and moralizing in your spare time, but feel free to come and talk to me. Right! On Saturday night, someone put two .22 rounds into Lenny the Finger's back in front of his St. Kilda strip joint cum brothel. Dead before he hit the ground and nobody saw a thing. Despite light rain, Fitzroy Street had a full attendance of tourists and locals looking for entertainment. Homicide notified us immediately when they checked his file and found he worked for us. We did get some dashcam footage, but it's of limited value." Porter waited for her to ask the obvious question, but she sat there passively and waited. Clearly curious, she did not jump to conclusions. He liked that.

"Why he worked for us? Our Lenny was a rogue feeder. We told him he'll live as long as he kept locating other feeders who might have walked through his establishment, or heard something on the local underworld grapevine. The thing is, in the last six weeks, two of his girls succumbed to sudden old age death. Forensics couldn't pin anything on Lenny and he walked, but I suspect he sampled some of his merchandise and allowed things to get out of hand. Of course, that's not something I could tell the public prosecutor. The reason I think Lenny is dead, the Melbourne Master knew of his transgressions and decided to terminate him since we were not prepared to do so. Supposition on my part only as they declined to tell us anything. Given his underworld connections, anybody else could have offed him. Don't feel too sorry for old Lenny. The little pimp deserved everything he got.

"Once we were told the morgue had the body, we sent it to our section in the Victorian Institute of Forensic Medicine at Southbank. They're always hungry for new research subjects. From the brief you read, you know what Project Purple and research institutions the world over are after."

"They want to find genetic markers that make feeders different and come up with a cure for sudden old age death," Robinson told him calmly.

"That's right. You also know, and if you don't, bone up, our understanding of the human genome is still very limited. We need to find out which genes are switched on or off that makes a person a feeder, the effect manifesting itself after onset of puberty, which is earlier in girls than boys. Makes me wonder sometimes," Porter mumbled. "The need to feed drops sharply after fifty in men, and completely at onset of menopause in women.

"A lot of supercomputer power is invested in this. Some researchers think the DRD4 gene responsible for alcohol and gambling addiction also influences an individual's sex drive. If it were that simple, we'd have our cure and be out of a job. The thing is, experimental evidence suggests a number of hormones produced by the pituitary gland also influences sexual behavior. A curious observation about that gland. Researchers found that in feeders, it's some fifteen percent larger. Normally the size of a pea, fifteen percent is a huge increase in functionality. What that functionality does is a black box. However, the hypothalamus pretty much controls everything to do with the sex drive, among other things, but it's a complicated organ poorly understood, and nobody really knows how it works in feeders.

"The cleft stick everybody is sitting on, DNA and gene activity persists in a narrow time window after onset of death, two hours at most. By the time the boffins get a sudden old age death victim or a feeder's body, all useful gene activity has decayed. You see what I'm getting at, Nadala. We need warm body feeders to experiment on."

"Forensics ran tests on Lenny?"

"They did, and he contributed a small datum to our knowledge database. We need measurable evidence what happens when a feeder couples with a victim and triggers the onset of sudden old age." Porter lifted a hand. "You don't have to tell me the moral, ethical, and legal minefield such experimentation entails. Subject for another discussion. With Lenny, I decided he was too useful in an intelligence gathering capacity to waste him in a lab. His usefulness almost ended, we intended to send him to the Southbank forensics facility next week. Unfortunately for us, I think the Covenant beat us to it."

"I'll have to study up on genetics, but do we know what happens to a person who suddenly dies after coitus with a feeder?"

"Not only coitus. Your brief told you people can age prematurely through prolonged contact with a predatory feeder. Neither party may be aware why one partner is always physically and emotionally drained, and over time starts to exhibit symptoms of premature aging. When the parties are separated, the victim usually recovers fully.

"But to answer your question, what we do know so far, if not the how, a feeder somehow causes the body's epigenetic clock mechanisms to advance dramatically. Seconds become hours and the victim declines almost visibly. It takes four to five days of degeneration before onset of death, and the effect is irreversible. The process also truncates the cell's telomere sequences, which stops cell division and triggers apoptosis. The link between telomere function and the epigenetic clock is still largely a mystery, which doesn't make life fun for researchers around the world.

"You're no doubt wondering what all this has to do with Lenny. Somebody shot him. End of story. Except it isn't. Not to me. I want you to find out who shot him. If a Covenant Keeper did it, he committed murder regardless of any extenuating circumstances. The fate of the world isn't resting on your shoulders, Nadala. Taskforces everywhere want to lay their hands on live feeders. However, *should* you snag one, you'll get a red star in your report book."

She chuckled, revealing her human side. "I'm sure that will make up for all the angst in between…Kurt."

"We'll see. However, Lenny isn't your only target. On Friday evening, Daniel Poole presented himself at Southbank. He claims to have had sex with a woman he picked up on Tuesday the eighth at Blink's Bar, part of the Emporium Hotel on Queen Street. Three days gone, he didn't last long. Died on Monday."

"And you want me to find the woman?"

"That's right."

Robinson frowned. "I don't see any connection with the Lenny case."

"No apparent connection, Detective, and there might not be one. I get the wild ideas and it's up to you to connect the dots. If there aren't any, create them." He waved a dismissive hand. "I know. Easy for me to say when it's you doing the hard yards. Employ some lateral thinking. I know you can do this or you wouldn't be on the team."

She blinked, not swayed in the least by his attempted ego boost. Definitely a hardcase.

"If I find the woman—"

"*When* you find her! The dots, Nadala. Remember, all the federal resources of this taskforce are at your disposal. Use them. Everything on this is in the database. Case file KZ-9362-B11. That's all."

"Yes, sir."

Porter watched her walk out and grinned, figuring she'd kick some serious ass. If not, he'll be the one getting kicked by Trusk.

* * *

Hands clasped behind his back, Aiden Conrad, Grand Master of half the world, and the United States Master Keeper, stood before the plate window and watched large flakes drift down from a silent, gunmetal sky to cover Midtown Manhattan under a ghostly white blanket. From his nineteenth floor TD Bank Building penthouse-like office—a choice location for the Covenant's Hale & Associates, Importers, front—cars crawling along 8th Avenue were plaything toys, and the hurrying pedestrians anxious to get out of the bitter December weather two rivers of black ants. Ants that had to be kept happy and productive, consuming goods and services produced by enterprises around the globe, many indirectly controlled by the Covenant. The crushing weight of responsibility drained its chief executives in a way a feeder might, and described the Covenant perfectly: a feeder that kept sucking until only a dry husk remained.

Usually focused and not easily sidetracked, he allowed himself a momentary lapse of concentration and watched the snow fall. As he stared at the unbroken white expanse, it amused him to think the people below considered themselves masters of everything they saw and touched. An understandable reaction, although thoroughly misguided. They built monuments, towering skyscrapers, freeways, machines that levelled mountains, sought to reach the stars, and played with the genetic stuff of life. Despite their seemingly omnipotent power, those little ants nevertheless scurried for shelter when the sun burned, storms roared, or blizzards raged.

The little ants did not control the sky, and the sky controlled everything.

Likewise, mighty corporations shaped the world's economic sphere, bending the political process in the service of profits and growth. In the same way the Covenant, run by country Master Keepers, bent the most influential companies to mold the globe's social fabric and protect feeders. That power came with handsome side benefits. Control of the World Bank, the International Monetary Fund, and national treasuries gave it influence exercised only by dictators. The Covenant's levers were effective, but blunt instruments, whose application sometimes created undesirable social consequences.

He had one particular example in mind—the environmental movement. Promoted to preserve the planet's ecosystems and resources, despite the Covenant's best efforts, the radical socialist left had turned it into a force bent on destruction of corporate globalization. Planted operatives provided indisputable evidence of Russian and Chinese manipulation. Why wage a shooting war, always messy, when the West can be turned in on itself.

A few timely terminal accidents in the greens leadership might restore a degree of objective rationality. He would raise the issue at the next Council meeting, certain to obtain support for affirmative action from a number of Asian and South American Master Keepers, tired seeing their country's economic agendas disrupted by wild-eyed, chanting protesters. Time also to rein in some of the Russian oligarchs as a reminder where their prosperity came from. Sudden demise of one or two Chinese Communist Party Standing Committee luminaries would provide the same heads-up, the East-West political bickering bad for business.

Although a vital arm of its global activities, business did not rule the Covenant. Its charter demanded that it curb corporate open *laissez-faire* tendencies. That in turn allowed the organization to inject the human factor into the calculus, without which mutually beneficial coexistence with workers and consumers would not be possible. Dazzled by their materialistic successes, some Master Keepers on corporate boards had strayed and began to adopt the sterile mindset they were set up to restrain. To a degree, the Covenant itself had strayed, allowing itself to morph into a quasi-world government to keep the ants out there happy.

Conrad had to give the seventeenth century founders credit. They were practical realists, not a bunch of psalm-singing idealists. Bankers, politicians, industrialists, even highly placed clergy. They understood the workings of governments and economies, adhering fervently to Machiavelli's writings on the use of underhanded manipulation, fraud, treachery, elimination of opponents, and application of fear to achieve an objective and control subjects. Necessary tools used to protect their identity as feeders as they quietly inserted themselves into those organs. For almost three hundred years, the global geopolitical fabric readily lent itself to such massaging. The twentieth century however, saw the rise of corporate multilateralism and consolidation of geo-economic power in an increasingly hard corporate model some elements within the Covenant seemed reluctant to break.

He did not blame individual Master Keepers. They simply sought to maximize returns for their own country and thereby increase personal influence within the Council. He blamed past Grand Masters for allowing control to slip from their hands, interested at exploiting the political and economic landscape as a goal in itself, the wellbeing of feeders everywhere becoming an irritating impediment to growth under a threat of public exposure.

In his opinion, the Covenant should no longer babysit the world's feeders, not entirely. He intended that governments everywhere take on that long overdue responsibility. The game they all played for three centuries had become outmoded.

A month ago, he submitted a proposal to Sybille Konigen, his European counterpart, to redress the imbalance, and risked everything if she balked, perhaps even his life at the hands of a Keeper assassin. One whole month without a word, he had grown weary waiting for her to get into gear. Can't the woman see the obvious and get off the pot? But no, she had to consult with her Council. How much consulting does she need? If she continued to vacillate, he would go it alone!

Far from a homogeneous, unified global entity, the Covenant suffered from internal power struggles, petty jealousies, misguided ambitions, and possible betrayal that risked its very existence. He thought everybody would be above such foolishness by now. The situation not helped by Project Purple's rapidly growing reach and power. A thorn he wanted to pluck out and stomp on. Although totally penetrated, it still had powerful claws that could rip through the Covenant's vitals if it lowered its guard once. They should have stomped on it in 1947 when the thing germinated. An opportunity squandered because of internal Covenant power byplays. Subsequent Grand Masters had openings to neutralize Project Purple, but were instead happy to enjoy the trappings of their power, steeped in the seventeenth century mindset. Well, he lived in the twenty-first. High time to shake the tree of history and allow rotten tradition to fall off. He had no patience for it. If Konigen refused to be a player, he would send a Keeper to drill her head, and any Master Keeper anywhere who failed to fall into line. What use power if he could not use it.

His mind made up, he strode to his desk, sat down, and picked up the cellphone. Encryption mode enabled, he input the ten digit PIN and typed in a familiar number.

After several seconds of electronic silence, her rich contralto voice finally came through.

They met twice, once in Zurich and once in his office under the guise of corporate executives. Her ready smile lit her large blue eyes and accentuated short hazel hair streaked white, always bemused him. An easy outgoing personality, cold steel lay beneath that friendly persona, which he tasted more than once. Years back, still new into his position as Grand Master, thinking himself all-powerful, he tried to play the alpha male gambit with her and got chewed up. Even now, the memory of those experiences made him squirm. If only he could find a lever to bend her will. Instead, she maneuvered him with deceptive ease.

Not this time, my dear! You're dealing with a different man.

"Aiden, a pleasure as always. How's your morning?" she answered with a touch of German accent.

"It's bleak and it's snowing. And your afternoon?"

"Getting dark, and it's only four o'clock. I hate winter. The only compensation I get sitting in my office, the floodlights make the Jet d'Eau fountain a piece of sculptured magic."

Conrad nodded as he recalled the amazing Lake Geneva feature spouting up to 450 feet into the air. They hardly made such things these days. Everything sterile steel, smart glass, and concrete. Sterile like the unfeeling corporations.

"I remember. Fancy a holiday in Hawaii?"

Konigen laughed gaily. "At sixty-one, my boy, I wouldn't do justice to a bikini. Although the idea of soaking some rays on a golden beach sounds good. Your son, still in the Air Force?"

"A lieutenant-colonel now. I keep urging him to resign and do something useful with his life, but he's stubborn and refuses to listen."

"Not at all like his father, right?"

He sensed her amusement and smiled. "Well, I never listened to my old man either. What about your family? I understand you're a grandmother again."

"A second grandson! Holding the little cherub in my arms, it made me feel young."

"Yeah, that's how I felt with my granddaughter. I sometimes wonder where the years have gone."

"How's business?"

"Hale & Associates are doing well, thank you, but I think my personal assistant thinks we're a money laundering front for the Mob."

Konigen laughed. "Funny, I get the same reaction from my secretary. Talking about passing years, you didn't call about Hawaii or my family."

"No, I didn't, Sybille. Remember the old days when we were city Masters? Our only worry was letting a rogue feeder slip through the net."

"I started as a Keeper, you know. Those were fun days. Now, a Keeper must undergo training that rivals a military or intelligence community hitman. Even so, conventional termination has become increasingly risky, as has inducing sudden old age death in a rogue. Forensics is a sophisticated science these days."

"Hence my proposal. We should move immediately and I need your decision."

"It's a dangerous plan, Aiden."

"Meaning, your Council doesn't approve."

"I exercised my prerogative to reject the proposal with a recommendation to conduct a review."

Conrad pursed his mouth in anger. "When did the Council sit?"

"A week ago."

"Damn it, Sybille! And you didn't tell me? I specifically asked to be on the video link to present my case."

"I presented your submission to every European and African Master Keeper without alteration."

"Presented with your personal slant. Reading a dry paper is not a substitute for a face to face delivery and you know it!"

"As Grand Master, I made the call."

"Playing partisan politics as always," Conrad grated. "With Project Purple and its taskforces hanging over us, I thought we had moved past such nonsense. This is far too important to be playing power politics."

"It is, and you're being needlessly provocative. Just because my Council demurred on your proposal, doesn't mean it's without merit, and I resent your insinuation that we're playing power politics. The Covenant faces a crisis of identity that needs to be resolved, I agree with you there, but your plan lacks an implementation strategy."

"It's supposed to be a discussion paper, for Chrissake!"

"That's why I recommended a review."

"For your information, I do have an implementation strategy."

"Then you should have attached it."

"I wanted your initial reaction."

"And you have it."

Conrad gave a suffering sigh. "I don't want a fight. I want to move this thing along. What do you find objectionable?"

"Your intention to go public. Have you forgotten your history? Our founders created the Covenant to protect themselves and other feeders from discovery and persecution. You want to throw that away and direct focus on our business and political activities."

"I haven't forgotten anything. The whole point of going public is to force governments to recognize feeders in law. Right now, we're virtually *persona non grata*, and Project Purple task-forces are treating us as such. It's an intolerable state of affairs, I tell you."

"I agree."

"I believe our public conditioning programs have reached a tipping point that would, if properly controlled, avoid mass hysteria and social discord."

"By no means a certainty."

"We'll never have hundred percent acceptance. Some level of public disquiet is expected, but should be containable. The quid pro quo? President Everett must disband Project Purple and its taskforces, or at least curb their lawlessness, and the EU Executive must do the same thing."

"Even if Everett agrees, that's no guarantee that governments around the world will do it. They're focused on a need to capture feeders for experimentation in a drive to find a cure for sudden old age death and infiltrate and destroy the Covenant."

"Going public will pull their teeth," Conrad countered. "To sweeten the deal, we disband the Keepers. That's been a sticking point with every administration since Truman created Project Purple. They want responsibility for hunting rogues, they can have it."

"Why should he deal? He has no incentive to do anything. Project Purple gives him everything he wants now. Admittedly, he's getting it by operating outside the legal framework."

"That's why we need to curb or kill it. Everett will cooperate if we promise him a second term and a majority in both houses."

"The corollary being, if he doesn't, we decimate the Republican Party and the Christian nationalist movement that controls it," Konigen added. "Not only in the United States, but everywhere."

"They effectively stand above the law, having bought state and federal legislators. It promotes government autocracy and they like it that way. We must break that mold and restore social stability."

"Let's say Everett makes a public announcement to shut down Project Purple. He'll simply order the FBI, Interpol, and every intelligence agency to continue the program to penetrate us."

"I wouldn't expect anything else. The point of the disclosure is to clip Project Purple's authority. The FBI and the intelligence community operate within a framework of law. A crucial difference."

Konigen gave a sour chuckle. "Somebody should tell them that."

"At least there is *some* oversight. The thing I want to see done is recognition of feeders under law."

"We need that badly, I agree. What about the Ardor Helpline?"

"We keep it operating, of course. It's far too valuable to abolish. To remove the veil of secrecy we currently have in place, we can suggest that governments incorporate the service within their health system. Doable once feeders are legally recognized. A demand we make non-negotiable."

"You know what Everett will want in return, don't you? Something he wanted ever since he came to office."

"Ardor Helpline's records of known feeders. I know. That's one thing we cannot let him or anyone else have under any circumstances. Once feeders are recognized under law, those records will fall under doctor-patient confidentiality."

"Project Purple tried to hack our databases a number of times to get those records. Even if feeders are recognized, Project Purple won't stop its penetration attempts."

"We'll just have to make sure they never succeed," Conrad temporized. "I don't want to be put into a position to force our argument by relieving one or two Project Purple's executives of their existence."

"Not a wise course of action, Aiden." Konigen remained silent for several seconds. "Everett's a pragmatist. Something he learned well as a two-time New York governor. He may be willing to shut down Project Purple and the American taskforce, but he doesn't control taskforces the world over. Individual governments do. I doubt you and I will be able to shut them down."

"I want them brought under a legal umbrella, and we have levers to change their mind."

"That's my point of contention and frustration with your plan. Lack of detail!"

"Well, you're getting the detail now. As Grand Master, I expected you to maintain a holistic view instead of nitpicking. You disappoint me, Sybille."

Konigen laughed. "If I didn't know you better, I'd say you're peeved with me."

"I'm peeved at your never-ending procrastination. We need to act, not just talk."

"I sense your anger and the reason behind it, but I didn't make my decision to spite you. Young and vigorous, you're afflicted with the malady of impatience and intolerance, much like your country. Instead of pursuing an objective through consensus, you rely on intimidation."

"Sometimes, that's the only way to get things done," he replied stiffly.

"Not when so much is at stake."

Conrad gave a weary sigh. "Look, I'm sorry if I seem to be baiting you, Sybille, but after a month waiting for a response, I began to wonder if you were holidaying somewhere warm instead of doing your job."

"Like Hawaii? I should have given you a heads-up on what we were doing. My bad."

"Okay, let's move on. I want to go public before the start of the New Year."

"Why the rush?"

"You have all the important pieces in place to make a decision now. If we allow every Master Keeper to debate this, we won't move until next Christmas! It's never a right time to do something like this, Sybille. Congress isn't sitting and everybody is in a holiday mood. We have a perfect psychological moment to pressure Everett. Truman created Project Purple with an Executive Order. Everett can kill it with another Executive Order."

"Mmm, yes. If he baulks?"

"We go ahead anyway, and I'll carry out my threat. He'll deal."

"I can talk to my Council, but I'm not sure I can carry the EU Executive."

"Tackle individual heads of state. You have influence. Use it!"

"Let's say I get the go-ahead. You left out one vital variable in the equation. If the Covenant goes public, it might compromise our corporate and political operations."

"I didn't mention the point because it's a null value. Going public doesn't mean we expose our operating arm. We'll only play the feeder angle. We tell people the Covenant exists to protect feeders from persecution and takes care of rogues. They'll sympathize with that, and free the Covenant to pursue its primary objective—control the world's economic and political organs."

"What about our own intelligence network?"

"We leave it in place, of course. As you know, in addition to hunting rogues, they serve as an important data gathering mechanism for all our ventures."

"Okay, I'll bite. How do you propose we proceed?"

"I'll talk to President Everett. You handle the EU Executive. If they hesitate and want time to ruminate, I propose we implement the plan anyway by using a little misdirection to force their hand. Agreed?"

"I'll take it under advisement."

"Good enough," Conrad replied, realizing he could not risk pushing her too hard. As Grand Master, she had to win over her

Council. A prickly lot, all of them. Perhaps one or two obstructionists *should* be eliminated to bring others into line. "I'll send you the implementation plan."

"That would be useful," Konigen replied dryly. "A break in Hawaii afterward?"

He laughed. "I wish. When we trigger this, I fear there won't be much time left for Hawaii."

"That reminds me. I still have to do my Christmas shopping. Somehow, I always leave it until the last minute."

"Thankfully, I'm spared that chore. Trudy has those things well in hand."

"Give her my regards, will you?"

"I'll do that. Take care, Sybille."

"And you, Aiden. I have a feeling we'll be talking again very soon."

"I hope so."

* * *

Nadala sat back and her shoulders drooped in frustration. The case report from the St. Kilda police station gave her precious little to work with. Pictures of Lenny sprawled on the sidewalk, black sweater stained with blood; the victim looked almost peaceful. No more worldly worries. Approximate time of death: 9:04 PM. The officers on the scene interviewed everybody who hung around and took statements from the five youngsters about to enter the Kitten Club. Two of them thought they saw a man in a dark gray windbreaker push through them, but could not be sure. A passerby also said he saw a tall man, the descriptions too disjointed to be useful. Unfortunately, none of the stores in that part of Fitzroy Street were equipped with security cameras pointing toward the sidewalk. Why would they? She watched one piece of dashcam footage of a small crowd clustered in front of the Club, and a tall figure in a gray windbreaker walking toward the intersection, his back to the camera. One man among other passersby.

The local cops handed the case to the Criminal Investigation Unit as per SOP and washed their hands off it. The senior constable assigned to the case did not add anything useful to the file. According to his statement, they were checking Lenny's underworld associates to establish motive for a possible gangland murder. St. Kilda had a number of red light establishments, and major crime syndicates were always muscling on each other's territory to assert dominance. Lenny represented one case in a stack of cases on the constable's desk, and he did not expect a speedy arrest. When he saw a Taskforce Crimson flag against Lenny's computer file, he happily dumped the thing into their hands, he told Nadala, and welcome to it.

Thank you very much for nothing, Porter!

The Inspector told her to find the killer, but neglected to mention that he gave her a dead potato. No surprise there. Superiors unloaded tricky cases on subordinates all the time and expected speedy resolution, knowing such a thing to be often impossible. Police forces everywhere had shelves of unsolved case files gathering dust, and Lenny's might add to the pile.

No credible witness, no forensic evidence, no security camera footage, no…nothing. Except Porter's assertion, a reasonable one, she admitted, that a Covenant Keeper closed Lenny's insurance. Still only a supposition, of course. If done by a professional, she'd be better off consulting a psychic.

Apply lateral thinking, Porter said.

Okay, she'll do that. Blink's Bar an easy walk from the Police Center, she would start wheels turning on the Daniel Poole death, hoping the walk triggered a flash of inspiration on the Lenny murder. She connected her cell to the computer and uploaded several photos of Lenny and Poole as references.

Collins Street always a wind tunnel, Nadala winced as a cold southerly cut through her thin business jacket. Didn't somebody

say this was supposed to be summer? She merged with other pedestrians heading toward Queen Street and set a brisk pace to
keep warm, wishing for hot days. They could not come soon
enough for her.

She paused in front of the Emporium Hotel and approached
the thick glass doors. The panels slid aside. Subdued music and
conversation came from inside Blink's, accompanied by a perva-
sive smell of beer. She strode in and headed for the bar. A portly
bartender, cleaning rag in hand, ambled toward her.

"What can I get you, lady?"

She reached into her shoulder bag, pulled out the ID folder,
and flipped it open.

"I would like to see Walter Crnov."

"Federal cop, eh? You don't have to look any further. I'm
Walt. Am I in any trouble?"

She gave him a small smile. "I need all your security footage
from October until now. I understand you keep footage for three
months before it's recycled." Poole said he got picked up last
Tuesday, but she wanted to establish a movement pattern and see
if the mysterious lady pickup visited Blink's before.

"That's right. Anybody special you're looking for?"

She scrolled through her cell and held up Poole's picture. "He
died on Monday from sudden old age."

"Another one, eh? Tough shit for him." He scratched his
chin. "I think I remember the guy. He went out with this really
classy chick who had the look."

"The look?"

"Anchors. Gets them into you and you're gone." He gave a
boyish grin that lit his chubby face. "I ought to know. My wife's
like that, but I don't mind. Been happily married for twenty-four
years."

She stared at him. That was almost as long as she'd been alive.
What do people talk about for twenty-four years? Leo became
bored with her after only two, and they had lots of things to talk

about. She gave a small shake of her head, not understanding any of it. Men were basically egotistic, sexist, domineering bastards, and Porter fitted comfortably into that frame.

"When did he pick her up?"

"A week ago Tuesday."

Nadala nodded, matching what Poole said.

"What's that woman got to do with anything?" Walt asked.

"We think she might be a carrier."

"A carrier? As in virus?" He gave a hearty chuckle. "You guys still think sudden old age is caused by a virus?"

"Not my department," Nadala told him firmly. "I'm just running down people she may have met in the last few weeks. If she's a carrier, we need to find and isolate her."

He shrugged indifferently, then suddenly turned serious, cleaning rag forgotten. "Funny, last Friday, Frank asked about her."

"Frank?"

"One of my regulars," Walt explained, and started to rub the bar top. "A real classy guy. Money to burn, but for some reason likes coming here. Runs a business from the Collins Street Tower. Lives there as well. I guess men like him got to talk about ordinary things in life like the rest of us, not only finance, and I talk to him." He titled his head. "You also have that look."

"The anchors?"

He laughed. "The high-powered look. As a matter of fact, I saw them together last night."

An innocent encounter?

"Does Frank have a last name?"

"He never said and I never asked." Walt pocketed the rag and jerked his head toward the office. "Come with me and I'll get you the security footage."

Eager to go over the takes, Nadala took a cab back to the Police Center. The cold breeze had died down, but dark clouds were gathering overhead. The weather people might be right for once and it could actually rain. She always carried a little foldout umbrella in her bag, among other things, but it would do little to protect her in a downpour. Still, better than nothing, mindful of the motto to be prepared.

At her desk, she opened VLC Media Player—the thing could read almost anything—and plugged in Walt's 2TB drive. More than two months of data meant a lot of homework, but the bartender's information narrowed her immediate search. The nice thing about Blink's security system, it recorded in one hour blocks. Instead of starting from October 1, she opened the file for 6 PM on December 6 and began to watch the footage, keeping the volume down, Poole's photo open on her cell.

The single camera mounted behind the bar on top of the bottles rack gave a reasonable view of people coming in, patrons sitting at tables, and those at the bar. It also showed a fairly clear view of pedestrians walking outside. At 6:08, she spotted Poole pause at the entrance and walk toward the bar. After ordering, he picked an empty stool next to a nice looking man wearing a navy blue suit and dark orange tie. Nadala upped the volume. They had a brief exchange and swapped names. When it came to shake hands, both maneuvered for a knuckle crusher. She smiled at this juvenile behavior. Overgrown boys, she decided. They disengaged and clicked glasses.

Poole glanced at the entrance and sat up. A few moments later, he got up and strode quickly toward a striking young woman in a beige blouse and brown knee-length skirt. Nadala pressed Pause, took a screenshot, and watched Poole escort his newfound date out. Shortly afterward, the man Poole chatted with finished his drink and left.

Frank, the mysterious man who yesterday allegedly picked up the same woman.

She selected yesterday's file for 6 PM and pressed Play.

He showed up at 6:12, took a barstool and ordered a drink. What interested her, instead of looking down the bar as others were doing, he appeared to watch the tables, and possibly the entrance. Nothing unusual there. Staring at arrayed bottles of various drinks probably got boring.

Tall, strong without showing muscle bulges, thick charcoal hair brushed straight back, no white streaks at the temples, Nadala sensed a powerful personality that somehow did not fit a dull businessman. Then again, how should a businessman look? When he turned, his granite gray eyes seemed to look directly at her and she involuntarily pulled back. Clean shaven, his hard face bore character lines of someone who had seen and experienced things not usually found in an office. A visceral attraction tugged at her insides, and she fleetingly wondered what he'd be like as a date.

Concentrate, girl!

At 6:42 according to the date/time stamp, the woman appeared. This time in a tight ankle-long black cocktail dress. Nadala nodded with approval at the choice of attire. She saw Frank give her a concentrated look. Several other men were also giving the lady appreciative glances of interest. The woman walked to the bar and sat next to Frank. Nadala leaned closer to the screen, upped the volume, and listened to the conversation.

"I can make you forget her," the woman whispered.

Nadala winced at the cheap line. Nothing but a slut cruising for tricks.

"What's your name? Mine's Kaneel."

"Frank."

Eyes only for each other, both stood and walked out.

Lips compressed, Nadala felt a stab of disappointment. Frank did not strike her as somebody who would pick up casual trollops. Then again, a business suit revealed little about the man wearing it. Never judge a book by its cover, they said, which she found amusing, as she always picked up a book based on the impression the cover gave her. She never bought without reading the back blurb and several pages, though. Frank's book did not appear worth opening.

Walt did say he lived alone. She bit her lower lip, uncertain why that piece of trivia stuck in her mind.

She pressed Pause, rubbed her eyes, and sat back.

Last Tuesday, Daniel Poole went out with Kaneel and died. Yesterday, Frank picked her up and…

Both men dated her, and one of them is dead. Logic suggested Frank might be next if unlucky enough to fall prey to a rogue feeder. Her training emphasized that logical reasoning did not necessarily equate to correct reasoning. Perhaps, but Dan's deathbed statement strongly pointed to the possibility that Kaneel might be more than a strikingly attractive woman. Research into feeder behavior told her they went through numerous sexual encounters without being terminal, supported by testimony from rogue feeders themselves. They did not kill every time, or the incidences of sudden old age deaths worldwide would be in pandemic proportions. Simple self-preservation dictated prudence. Take a little from each victim and live to feed from somebody else…and undoubtedly more pleasurable.

Why then did rogue feeders kill at all? Unfortunately, the weight of research spanning more than seventy years did not help her. Rogue feeders themselves did not always know why a compulsion drove them to kill a partner, most of the time involuntarily. Some were plain mean and wanted to kill, like Kaneel. Human behavior, always a complex subject with no single neat definition. Hence the rise of psychologists, psychiatrists, and pharmaceuticals who saw pills as a solution for everything. If an ailment did not exist for a newly invented pill, create one. Serious university studies supported by clinical trials produced libraries of information without reaching a conclusive answer. The weight of evidence suggested that genetics controlled all human behavior— something Porter seemed to support—much to the vehement annoyance of behaviorists. Man has a thinking brain and will to overcome programmed urges, they argued. Nadala sometimes wondered.

She got up and slowly walked to the kitchenette for a refill, deep in thought.

Forget the humanistic claptrap, she admonished herself firmly, *and treat Poole's case as a simple murder investigation—yet to be proven.* Porter told her to do homework in free time.

The case files she read? This year, the Taskforce apprehended thirty-two alleged rogue feeders and one Keeper, but most involved running down mundane leads, old-fashioned footwork, and staring at a computer screen doing research that led nowhere. Taskforce Crimson and its sister taskforces around the world faced one insurmountable problem. In Western-style democracies at least, authorities could not simply haul in a suspect feeder for interrogation and medical testing. They were citizens with rights. Unless one broke the law by proved killing of a sexual partner, taskforces everywhere had some tough days, as Nadala began to appreciate. She preferred not to delve too long on unsavory methods used by Russia, China, and other authoritarian regimes to gather evidence and conduct research. A lot of useful information came from those countries, and Project Purple did not throw it back, even though it came tainted with blood.

When did expediency for the greater good override individual rights and freedoms? And who decides?

Nadala sipped her tea, not really wanting to go there, uncertain she could even make a personally satisfying determination. Still young, she lacked the breadth of knowledge gained from decades of life's experiences, which precluded her from making such a decision. Nevertheless, her conscience demanded she make one if she wanted to succeed in this job. Rely on philosophical and religious teachings? Obey orders from superiors and leave it at that? A solution she found deeply unsatisfying. Blind obedience all too often meant accepting evils committed by higher authority. She knew enough history to realize evil roamed freely when people turned away, not wanting to know.

"You seem to be in another dimension," a soft, Indian-accented voice said beside her, and Nadala looked up to see Prada smiling at her.

She gave an exaggerated wince. "It's a case Porter unloaded on me—two cases—and I'm starting to wonder if I'm being punished for something."

Prada chuckled and sat on the corner of her desk. "The Inspector likes to stretch his people's boundaries. Nothing personal."

"He's certainly stretching mine!"

"Don't get sidetracked and you'll be all right."

"When I walked in here on Monday, I saw this job as an exciting new adventure."

"Believe me, it is."

"My cases, though, made me realize I'm walking two roads, and they're not going in the same direction."

"An interesting way of putting it, and true. All of us faced the same dilemma you're confronting, and had to arrive at an emotional and moral settlement that allowed us to walk those roads. Some failed."

Nadala looked quizzically at her friend. "What happened to them?"

Prada shrugged. "Porter transferred them out."

"Just like that?"

"With conditional strings." She patted Nadala on the shoulder. "You're a detective. When you handle a case, be a detective. It helped me get over my hump. If you have a conflict of interest or a moral quandary, talk to the Inspector. He'll sort you out."

"I don't know. He sees the law as a roadblock for the Taskforce."

"He can be intense, but he's a cop first. Still, dealing with feeders often stretches boundaries."

"Have you stretched yours?"

"We all did, and so will you." Prada stood and smoothed

down her slacks. "When you get there, come and talk to me."

Nadala reached out and squeezed the woman's arm. "I might do that, but I'm not there yet. It's simply—"

"I know. Dealing with feeders for the first time churns up many things you took for granted."

"I keep seeing unimaginable chaos if this ever came out."

"Sooner or later it will, and lots of innocent people might die," Prada said soberly. "We can only hope we're not around to see such days. Then again, people might turn out to be more decent than we give them credit." She nodded and strode back toward her desk.

Nadala stared after the woman.

Philosophize at home, she admonished herself, *and concentrate on the job at hand.*

She wanted a change of pace in her life, and Taskforce Crimson certainly gave her that change. Instead of meeting the challenge, she questioned the legality and morality of her work. Was she subconsciously longing for the dull security of her old job because she did not want to confront the cruel reality of her new one?

Okay, if Kaneel is a rogue feeder, Frank might be in mortal danger if he consummated the encounter. Should she warn him? And tell him what? 'Excuse me, if you had sex with Kaneel, you'll be dead in a few days.' She vividly imagined his incredulous reaction, especially as she could not reveal to him existence of feeders. What then? Wait for him to die? Would he die, though? Rogue feeders themselves said they rarely took a life, and sometimes unintentionally in the heat of the moment. Frank's date with Kaneel may have simply been an enjoyable encounter for both.

She needed to find out more about Kaneel. With a photo in hand, she sent an email to VicRoads, responsible for issuing driver licenses. With a full name and address, she would be in a better position to unwrap Kaneel's life. After a moment, nibbling a fingernail, she sent another query with Frank's photo.

Nadala took sip of tea, then opened the file for Tuesday, October 10. Walt did say Kaneel tended to come on Tuesdays. If she picked up a man before she snared Poole, Nadala would ID them and see if any died of sudden old age. With evidence, she would pull the woman in and have a heart-to-heart.

She still had Lenny the Finger to deal with, she reminded herself. In all likelihood a much tougher case with no apparent leads. What did Porter say? Connect the dots. If there aren't any, create them. She did not think much of that advice.

A glance out the window showed rain coming down.

Great!

Chapter Three

A sweaty half hour workout at the downstairs gym, followed by a relaxing sauna, toned up the old muscles and made Frank more receptive to face the world. Relaxed, he switched on the 7:30 *France 24* news program and set about preparing breakfast. He preferred that channel or the *Deutsche Welle* broadcast for his news fix. His once favorite ABC *Breakfast* show fell out of favor when they revealed their hopeless left-wing bias. The commercial channels fed the public sensationalist mush devoid of serious journalistic content. This morning, he intended to eat high: fried slices of lean speck, onions and eggs on the side, chased down with freshly brewed coffee.

"...Global Times, *the English version of the Chinese Communist Party's propaganda sheet, the* People's Daily, *warned the United States to stop biological attacks on peaceful Chinese people causing a rise in sudden old age deaths throughout major population centers, or face serious consequences. The White House press secretary said China's claims were baseless. The entire world is suffering from this malady.*

"The People's Liberation Army Navy deployed two carrier groups into the East China Sea, reportedly heading toward Taiwan. The US 7th Fleet, supported by European Union and Quad warships, is loitering off the Pescadores archipelago in the Taiwan Strait to forestall any hostilities. The US Secretary of Defense said earlier today, America and its allies stand ready to defend Taiwan's sovereignty."

Frank filled his favorite mug and watched the summary with interest, eating temporarily forgotten. His interest spiked because mainstream and social media outlets were giving more airtime to sudden old age deaths and feeder stories. A leak from somewhere within the Covenant or one of the worldwide Project Purple task-forces, probably more than one? He spoke to Manuel about it only last week, but his contact did not say much. Frank knew why. In case of capture, he could not divulge information he did not have. Dark portents were gathering and he feared for tomorrow. Sooner or later, Project Purple would expose the Covenant. Unless properly conditioned, people on the street could turn into rampaging mobs in search of feeders, supported by professional agitator groups only interested in promoting social disorder without any policy platform of their own.

"Elena Griffin, the Australian Prime Minister, announced construction of three thorium power generators, which in six years would provide 36% of the country's base load needs. Historically opposed to anything nuclear, this represents a major policy shift for the Labor Party. The Greens vowed to block the initiative in the Senate, but with support from the Coalition Opposition, the government does not need the Greens to pass legislation."

About time Australia climbed out of the 19th century, Frank thought and took a long sip of coffee. The Greens…blinded by ideology, insensitive to the destructive effect their policies had on the country and people at large. Their objective, creation of a world government with them on top. Nothing but disguised communists hiding beneath an environmental umbrella.

"In an unprecedented move, US President Julian Everett imposed trade sanctions on Saudi Arabia, once a Middle East ally, for continued attacks on Yemen. As a major oil exporter in its own right, the United States foreign policy is no longer influenced by former dependence on Saudi oil. The Arab kingdom retaliated by cutting back oil exports to Europe and canceling an order for 120 F-35A Joint Strike Fighters in favor of Russian Su-57 fifth-generation Felons. Syria and Iran announced similar purchases, the move seen by Western think tanks as dangerous destabilization of an already fragile Middle East, the unrest fueled by an increasingly aggressive Israel seeking to bomb Iran's nuclear facilities.

"PBS, the American Corporation for Public Broadcasting, released a half hour documentary on research conducted by some of the most prestigious

universities around the world into sudden old age deaths. Professor Sigmund Bauer from Johns Hopkins University confirmed existence of a link between victims of old age death and genetic triggers present in some people, sometimes referred to as feeders by popular media. What is not understood, the Professor added, why an act of intimacy resulted in death. Some tabloids seized on the revelation to affirm existence of energy vampires walking among us."

Frank grabbed the remote and switched off, wishing for once, he could wake up to some cheerful news. A doomed hope, as people appeared to thrive on war, scandal, and death. The stark realization made him wonder a few times at the basic makeup of his fellow two-legged creatures seemingly determined to embrace doomsday. As long as he had his coffee, the rest of the world could screw itself. The conjured images made him smile as he strode into the kitchen to finish making breakfast.

Yesterday, he called Manuel de la Kass and asked for a complete profile on Kaneel Mercer and her family after explaining why he wanted the data. He did not know the resources behind the Melbourne Master's assistant, but they must be considerable because Manuel sent him a response within two hours. Set in encryption mode, Frank texted Kaneel a photo of her parents, together with their addresses, in case she thought he did not mean it when he told her he would target them if she talked.

Late in the afternoon, Manuel sent him another text. The Melbourne branch of Taskforce Crimson assigned Detective Sergeant Nadala Robinson to investigate the deaths of Lenny the Finger and Daniel Poole. He sent back a thanks, not overly concerned. The feds investigated everything related to old age deaths as a matter of procedure. Robinson would go over security footage from Blink's, connect him superficially with Dan and Kaneel, and run into a wall. No evidence existed to incriminate him, and Kaneel happened to be a random date he picked up. With Dan, a chance encounter at a bar.

The fling with Kaneel replenished his energy reserves, which meant he did not need to feed for a month or more. Long before then, he expected Detective Robinson to lose interest in him.

He nevertheless appreciated the heads-up, wondering who in the Taskforce provided the information. According to Manuel, infiltration of Project Purple hierarchy and its taskforces enabled the Covenant to sabotage penetration attempts into its organization. He could not say how long those measures would remain effective before the troubles started. The planted operatives provided something else: invaluable information on possible rogue feeders identified by taskforces.

Hram did not worry too much about it. He did, but nothing he could do except maintain his own anonymity.

Breakfast finished, he completed his bathroom chores, set the alarm, and walked out of the apartment.

Time to do some paid work.

Living as a feeder and Keeper might be personally inconvenient at times, but he had a company to run responsible for financial security of its clients. A responsibility he could not relinquish regardless of any countervailing circumstances.

* * *

Nadala dealt with dead end cases before and shrugged them off. Some could not be solved regardless of applied resources or the investigator's ingenuity. Contrary to popular opinion, the image promoted by TV shows, hardened criminals were not dumb, and CSI hero characters did not always get their perpetrator.

It looked like Lenny the Finger case would cause Porter a degree of disappointment. Only Thursday, the Inspector could not reasonably expect she already solved it. Lenny's voluminous case file of past murky deeds made for colorful reading, but nothing suggested he aggravated one of the mobs sufficiently enough to warrant assassination. He identified two feeders for the Taskforce who visited the Kitten Club. One a possible rogue, the other a husband cheating on his wife. Apparently, Lenny got a lot of business from such men. Porter could not haul them in for questioning or medical testing without some evidence. Things had not deteriorated sufficiently to warrant drastic violation of individual rights on mere criminal's word. The Taskforce could only watch the two. And when the situation did deteriorate? She preferred not to go there yet.

Lenny supposedly killed two of his Club escorts. The police could not prove he caused them to die of sudden old age, energy vampires still largely treated as fictional lore. However, Porter possessed sufficient evidence to bring him in and make him a snitch. At end of his use-by date, the Inspector said he intended to hand him over to the Southbank forensics facility, but Lenny had the bad manners to get himself shot first. Now, his body lay on some steel bench while green-garbed scientists slowly took him apart.

The initial autopsy yielded two .22 caliber bullets, both lodged in the heart, which suggested a professional hit or lucky shots. The rifling grooves meant nothing. Without the actual weapon, they were useless as evidence. Even with a gun in hand, it meant little unless covered with fingerprints, which she doubted a half-smart killer would be careless enough to leave behind.

Nadala recalled a Taskforce case she read of a rogue feeder murdered by two .22 rounds. Pen stuck between her teeth, she began a quick file scan, trying to remember some of the details. She stopped and grinned, castigating herself for being stupid. A single click brought up the cases home directory and she input 2023 and .22 in the search box. Two occurrences popped up and she clicked on the first. Not interested in the actual cases yet, she opened photos of the .22 rounds and printed close-ups of their rifling. She did the same thing with Lenny's bullets. Color prints held side by side, she nodded with satisfaction. The same weapon fired all rounds. So? *A datum of interest*, she told herself. Porter's dots.

She plucked the pen from her mouth and slipped the printouts into the shredder, then opened Lenny's file and added a cross-reference to the other files. Not prepared to write him off, not after only one day, she went over Lenny's activities as a brothel owner. It turned out, he canvassed Melbourne's YWCA and hostels to pick up girls with offers of easy money for a few days of enjoyable work. Many were foreign backpackers looking for casual jobs to support themselves, and turning tricks earned them far more than sweating on some farm picking fruit. His interview records showed he recruited several girls at The Village Melbourne on Franklin Street opposite the Queen Victoria Market. For backpackers, an ideal location close to everything.

She bit her lip. Lenny got girls at The Village? So what? Provided they were not underage, they could do whatever they damn pleased. All her hours of research brought her no closer to identifying his murderer. Like she really gave a toss who killed the disgusting pimp.

Porter's voice came to haunt her. Apprehending the killer may open a small peep into the Melbourne's Covenant chapter. *Well, bully for the Taskforce*, and immediately frowned. Lenny may have been a rogue feeder, but she agreed with Porter when he said the Covenant could not take the law into its own hands. Retribution rested with the courts.

If only it were so cut and dried. She got up to get a refill.

Back at her desk, she found an email in her Inbox from VicRoads. She glanced at her Rado, almost eleven. A nice sunny day, she intended to take a stroll up Spencer Street and grab lunch at the Southern Cross food court. She could eat at the downstairs cafeteria, and it served great food, but a brisk walk might get her mind off Lenny.

She opened the email and quickly scrolled through Kaneel Mercer and Frank Hram's basic details. Apart from address, date of birth, and type of car they drove, the records were bare. A license check gave her enough to start a more in-depth search.

She shot off an email to the Taxation Office requesting their returns. Nadala's federal police ID guaranteed a prompt response.

A change of screen, she logged into the Taskforce's Virtual Private Network and put in a search for Frank Hram, financial consultant. A list came up and she clicked on Urbi Investments at 480 Collins Street Tower, as Walt said. She wondered if the lobby mounted security cameras. If it did, what would it prove? *Connecting the dots*, she told herself.

A relatively young company registered in 2010, they opened for business on July 1, 2011, the beginning of a new tax year. The website looked crisp and professional without extraneous clutter. A brief About Us page gave summary resumes of the two partners, and a services list made it easy for prospective clients to see what Urbi did and why they should use the company to manage their investments. Thoroughly dry, the website said nothing intimate about Hram or Emerson, not that she expected to see a memoir.

She opened Facebook and hunted for Hram's personal page without luck, but did find one for Urbi Investments. Kaneel's page, on the other hand, a clutter of posts between Friends, some perhaps genuine. Without her tax records, Nadala had little to go on with. One thing she *could* check on were her movements. Walt told her Kaneel usually came to Blink's on Tuesday nights, and sometimes on a Saturday.

She already perused every Tuesday evening on the security drive. Kaneel picked up a date on October 17, and did not return until she met Poole on December 5. Her first date still alive and kicking, which left the weekends. If a genuine rogue feeder, Kaneel would be crazy to pick victims from a single bar and leave a clear trail. Nadala opened the security file for October 7 and started her search. Nothing on any Saturday to December 9. Scrolling through last Saturday's take, the time stamp showed 9:53 PM, she prepared to shut down. Although possible, Kaneel would hardly pick a date so late. About to press Stop, movement on the sidewalk made her blanch and sit up straight. She backtracked, watched the clip advance, pressed Pause, and stared at the frozen frame, recognizing him instantly. Frank Hram wore a dark cardigan, the street lighting too faint to make out clear color. Why walk past Blink's without stopping for a drink or chat? She pressed Play and saw him disappear toward Bourke Street. If he dined somewhere, she expected him to be better dressed. Anyway, there were no classy restaurants up Queen Street, and Frank did not strike her as the type who ate at a takeaway. Then again, everybody craved a taste of junk food occasionally.

Tantalizing as the clip might be, it left her with nothing but unsatisfied curiosity.

The prospect of canvasing a dozen or so pickup bars, demanding to see their security footage—if they had any—to trace Kaneel's movements, left her in a dejected mood. What did Porter say? She could look forward to some interesting work. Not always exciting or dashing, he added. She believed him.

Her Rado said 12:42. Time for that walk, fresh air, and sunshine.

She squinted at the bright assault outside and slipped on her shades. The streaming traffic noises hardly registered as she headed toward Southern Cross. Across the Bay, a low band of dark clouds appeared to drift toward the city. The weather people did not say to expect rain today, but they never actually opened a window to see what went on outside.

As she walked, mingling with office types and those in more casual gear, she flushed the cases out of her mind, more concerned what to get for lunch. Nothing heavy, probably an assorted salad. Not a diet follower or weight control fanatic, she watched her intake and jogged regularly in the Carlton Gardens.

About to cross Collins Street, she almost faltered when she saw him striding briskly toward her. Hram's dark gray suit, no tie, perfectly tailored with broad jacket lapels starting to come into fashion again. They were all the rage twenty years ago, followed by ultra-narrow lapels before things became more normal with something in between. She sensed latent power in his tall frame topping her by several centimeters despite her high heeled pumps. Not too high, as she did not fancy a broken ankle. He walked without looking at anything in particular, his gaze lost in some inner reality. Fit, rugged looking, Nadala felt an unaccountable tug of desire. He strode past her, swallowed by the throng. For a fleeting second, she considered following him, intrigued by his raw masculinity. The feeling passed and she continued her walk, the image of his face stamped into her mind.

The next half hour passed in a surreal dream. As she made her way back to the Police Center, she could not recall what she had for lunch. Nobody created such an impact on her before. Not even Leo at the height of their delirious union.

Mature, at the peak of his physical powers, successful, Hram monopolized her thinking for the rest of the day, something she found thrilling and disturbing, totally outside her parameters of normal behavior.

For goodness sake! I am not a swooning teenager.

Even emails from the Tax Office failed to divert her attention from him. Disgusted with herself and her juvenile behavior, she focused on the emails…Hram's first, of course.

A savvy entrepreneur, single, never married, with an apartment at Oaks on Collins. She needed to put meat on the skeleton and fill in the personal blanks in his profile. How did he spend his time when not doing financial consulting? Where did he go for fun and who did he see? Did he regularly pick up women, and Kaneel happened to be a casual one-night diversion? Did they spend the night together? For some reason, the image of them entwined in bed sent a stab of jealousy through her.

Kaneel Mercer's tax records revealed a single person who worked as a hairdresser at a St. Kilda Fitzroy Street salon, and had an apartment within easy walking distance. A brother working as a car mechanic, both parents lived in seaside Frankston. Unremarkable life, except Kaneel might be a rogue feeder.

Before rushing off to Oaks, she brought up the database of Australian sudden old age deaths and opened the Melbourne directory dates file. Forty-seven this year, including Lenny and Poole's. For a city of five million, almost insignificant. A spike of nine clustered around January 4 to 11. New Year party revelries pushed a little too far?

She should have used the database before. Porter told her the resources of his taskforce were at her disposal. Instead, she thought in terms of door-to-door footwork like an ordinary detective. *Of course* Taskforce Crimson kept detailed records of all sudden old age deaths!

Nevertheless, she did not look forward to wading through forty-five cases again—she knew about Mercer and Poole—most of them cold, and clicked the first in the list. Her eyebrows climbed when she saw Prada Vishnu's name as the investigating officer.

A neighbor found the victim, a woman of twenty-nine. An ANZ bank teller in the St. Albans branch, unattached, leading a quiet life. Except her death suggested not so quiet. According to the neighbors, she never brought anybody home. One claimed she might be a lesbian. The woman did not report her condition to a clinic or hospital, and apparently died alone. A rough way to go, Nadala decided. Clearly, a feeder got to her, but Prada could not establish any leads and closed the case.

The next two were men who apparently cheated on their wives and suffered the ultimate retribution.

She clicked on the fourth case, January 6, and pursed her lips. Prada again. Two bachelors who lived in Richmond shared a flat. One died, the other developed severe lethargy and joint pain, but recovered. The survivor reported picking up a date at Freddie

Wimpoles on January 2, a trendy bar in Fitzroy Street where anybody could meet anybody. He said the woman wore long black hair. The description and an identity composite sketch matched Kaneel's face. The two drove her to their place and enjoyed a night-long party. With no positive leads, Prada closed the file, which made Nadala frown. Why hadn't her friend dug deeper into both cases?

A quick gulp of tea, she opened Clearview AI, fed it Kaneel's picture, and told it to hunt through the entire case directory. Slowly, a pattern emerged. Where bars and clubs in greater Melbourne had surveillance systems, her search identified Kaneel fifteen times over five years. Excluding Poole's case, sufficient evidence existed to suggest she might have killed four times. Although circumstantial, in Nadala's opinion, adequate for the Taskforce to look more closely at her. In two cases, as investigating officer, Prada dropped them. She handled eight this year, closed four, apprehended three rogue feeders and a Keeper.

Nadala could understand why Prada dropped the first case against Kaneel—nothing there to push an investigation—but when the second one popped on her screen, it should have triggered a major in-depth look into the life and times of the long-haired predator. Instead, Prada closed it. Time for a chat with the senior sergeant?

Something puzzled her about those cases. If the Covenant took care of rogue feeders, why hadn't they taken care of Kaneel? It seemed completely out of character how the Covenant operated. Perhaps not. The most likely explanation, they probably did not know about her. Rogues did not advertise themselves, she reflected.

That left her with thirty-six cases to wade through, handled by six other Taskforce members. On impulse, she fed Clearview Hram's photo and told it to hunt, confining the search to 2023. She hardly lifted her finger off the Enter key when the system spat out four case file results. The first made her purse her lips.

An alleged rogue feeder killed on Saturday, April 15, by two .22 rounds. Case two, a feeder died from a single .380 round to the head on July 23. Bullet rifling suggested the gun was fitted with a suppressor, which made sense. No weapon recovered. Case three, a female feeder who suddenly died of old age on September 21. Case four—Kaneel Mercer. Taskforce detectives who handled the first three cases found nothing. Frank Hram simply happened to be at a bar where the victims enjoyed a drink. Coincidence? They never investigated him because nobody could connect him with the victims. The detectives never compared notes either, she saw. Each victim died on the same night Hram visited a bar they frequented. With Poole, Nadala had her connecting dots and did not like the conclusion.

First things first. She called the St. Kilda Police station, identified herself, and asked the constable on duty to pick up Kaneel Mercer and bring her to the Center for questioning. She gave him her cell number in case he needed to call.

Handbag on shoulder, she hurried toward the exit past Prada's empty desk.

At Oaks, the security officer said the lobby mounted a camera, and made a copy of the take from six PM Tuesday to eight AM Wednesday, hardly saying a word. In the main foyer, about to walk out, she hesitated, then read the office tower occupants directory. Still undecided, she slowly stepped toward the three elevators servicing the tower. On the fourteenth floor, she walked to the reception desk. The woman there looked up, brushed back a lock of wayward hair, and smiled warmly.

"Welcome to Urbi Investments. Can I help you?"

Nadala fished out her ID. "I would like to see Mr. Frank Hram if he's available."

"One moment." The woman spoke quickly into her phone and beamed. "Please wait in the meeting room. Second door on your right. Mr. Hram will see you shortly. Care for some coffee or tea?"

"No, thank you."

Nadala walked into the meeting room and paused in the doorway. A floor-to-ceiling window provided lots of natural light and gave a grand view of the city's expanse. The walls were lined with pale wood sheets, their matte finish pleased the eye. Cloth chairs surrounded a heavy modern conference table. Its polished dark finish mirrored the window vista. On her left, a large wall unit held odd memorabilia, books, what looked like law manuals, and two delicate glass bowls, their intricate colors flowing into each other. The opposite wall mounted a large LED TV, presumably used for videoconferencing. She stepped to the window and gazed at the little people crawling below.

The door opened behind her and she turned. Hram wore a dark blue tie with his suit, which made him appear distinguished. In some subtle way, he projected something akin to charisma that captured her attention and made her keenly aware of her femininity. She also felt annoyance that her hormones threatened to take over her brain.

"It's not every day I get a visit from the federal police," he said in a rich, vibrating voice that made her skin prickle, and extended a hand.

"Detective Sergeant Nadala Robinson," she replied in a neutral voice and took his dry hand, his clasp firm before he let go.

"You looked more mysterious with your shades, Miss Robinson," he said with a broad grin and pulled back a chair.

Startled, she tensed. "I don't believe we have met, Mr. Hram."

"Not officially. This afternoon…Spencer Street? You were heading toward the Southern Cross station."

She stared at him, then cleared her throat to collect her shattered senses. "You remember that?"

"You're not someone I could forget. Before you attribute me with superpowers, it's merely a memory technique I learned some years back. Make yourself comfortable and tell me what made you look me up." He cocked an eyebrow. "Want to make an investment?"

Her reserve broke and she laughed, which relieved her tension, finding him very approachable. "Not on my salary." Seated in what turned out to be a comfy chair, she folded her hands in her lap. "I believe you could be in some danger."

"Oh? One of our clients is after me?"

Her face lost all expression and her demeanor turned cold.

"On Tuesday evening, you picked up a date at Blink's Bar, Kaneel Mercer. We believe she might be a virus carrier that induces sudden old age death. If you notice any unusual symptoms, you must seek immediate medical help."

His intense gray eyes probed into her without blinking. Many people averted their gaze when talking, not this man. She found his directness disconcerting as though he peered into her soul, hating to think he could read her unladylike thoughts right then.

A faint smile tugged his mouth. "You had her under surveillance?"

"She apparently went out with Daniel Poole last Tuesday. You two chatted for a while, then you saw him again on Friday."

Hram shrugged. "A random encounter."

"Poole looked old on Friday, Mr. Hram. Blink's surveillance footage shows he told you about the woman and how she made him old. Yet you disregarded his warning and went out with her on Tuesday night."

"She interested me, and your concern is misplaced. As you can see, I look perfectly fine. We spent some time together in my apartment and she left around two AM. Oaks security will corroborate that. If she is an energy vampire—I read available literature and seen a couple of documentaries—she may have killed Poole. I can't say. Women can be dangerous, you know," he added with a grin.

"And so can men," she replied tartly and leaned forward a little. "How do *you* explain sudden old age deaths?"

"Genetic predisposition, but what triggers it is anybody's guess. Was there anything else?"

"Thank you for your time," she said coolly and stood, slightly miffed at the casual dismissal. "Here's my card. If you notice any adverse effects—"

"It will be too late."

She felt the pull of his eyes and could not look away. Long seconds passed before she gathered herself together and broke contact. His faint smile of understanding made her feel coltish and self-conscious. Suddenly, he straightened.

"How would you like to have dinner with me tonight?"

Startled by his directness, her emotions in disarray, she tried to find the words to brush him off, while something else inside her said to accept. She hadn't met a real man in a long time, and he definitely fit in the different mold.

"I'm afraid that's not possible."

"Why?"

"I'm a police officer—"

"But I'm not a suspect, or am I? I can tell you more about Poole and Kaneel."

"I have everything—"

"Blink's security footage, I know. What you need is the human element, Detective."

The absurdity of the situation overwhelmed her and she smiled. "I've been asked on dates by men who used some innovative pickup lines, but a first from someone I'm investigating." The word slipped out and she cursed silently for such carelessness.

Hram tilted his head with interest. "I'm a suspect?"

"A figure of speech."

His broad grin revealed even, white teeth. "If you want to investigate me, let's do it over dinner. Much more pleasant for both of us."

"You don't give up, do you?"

"And neither do you. So…"

She bit her lower lip. Part of her desperately wanted to get closer to this enigmatic man. Her professional side frowned at the idea. Sometimes professionalism had to stand in line. Anyway, what harm could come from having dinner with him?

"Well…"

"Great! Six-thirty suits you? I can pick you up at home."

She reached into her bag, pulled out a small notepad, wrote down her address, and tore off the page. He took the slip of paper, eyes fixed on her, his fingers lingering on hers longer than strictly necessary, which sent a tingle up her arm. She pulled away and stood.

Hram opened the door for her and escorted her to the elevators. "Goodbye, Detective." He turned abruptly and hurried toward his office.

In the elevator, she stood in front of two executive types, bemused by the encounter with Hram. Her feelings about him shaken, her emotions were not prepared for the intense physical impact he had on her. She recognized a hard, tough man who knew what he wanted and went for it. His directness when he asked her out supported that impression. Did she allow an emotional reaction to override her professionalism? He wasn't a suspect in anything, she reminded herself. Anyway, a dinner *would* give her a chance to know him better.

Nadala's job hat back on, her decision to meet him also saved her a lot of legwork and poring over dull security footage from numerous bars to pin down Kaneel's movements. Circumstantial evidence, although compelling, suggested the woman actively preyed on men. Once they hauled her in, she hoped to change perception into certainty. But how? No scientific test existed to prove an individual exhibited positive feeder tendencies. Although suggestive, an enlarged pituitary gland proved nothing. Unless she watched Kaneel couple with someone and wait for the victim to wither to nothing, there were no legal grounds to hold her. Couple…Some researcher somewhere must have thought of this and already looked into it. She pulled at her chin.

When she apprehended Kaneel, what then? She could send her to Southbank and wash her hands off her in clear dereliction of duty, and make a step closer to police state rule. Better to blow the lid on everything before condoning such a thing.

Hram…The man seemed unusually calm at the prospect of suffering sudden death, and she could not discern any symptoms. On the contrary. His energy almost palpable, she felt herself drawn to him, wanting to be in his arms. *I would not have minded*, she told herself with a small smile. Work wasn't everything, she decided.

The elevator stopped at the ground floor and she strode into the noisy street outside.

Her cell twittered and she dug it out of her bag. "Detective Robinson."

"Senior Constable Rowlan, Detective. No luck with Kaneel Mercer. She did not come to work yesterday or today, and she wasn't in her apartment. We checked. Nobody saw her since Tuesday afternoon."

Nadala bit her lip. 'Curiouser and curiouser', as Alice said.

"Put out an all-points search order, Constable. Check rail, bus, and airports in case she left town."

"Is she considered armed and dangerous?"

Dangerous perhaps, but not in the way he meant.

"She's merely a person of interest. Keep me informed."

"Will do."

Deep in thought, she crossed the street to the Rialto Tower taxi rank, not in the mood for a hike to the Police Center.

* * *

Frank sprawled against the chair, fingers locked behind his head, and gave a soft guffaw. His nemesis actually sought him out to warn him? Robinson could not come out and say feeders killed, hiding a publically unpalatable reality behind a virus smoke screen.

Why did the alluring woman really seek him out, and he did find her alluring. A sense of civic duty? Her lustrous ash-blonde hair cut short framed a classically beautiful face perfectly proportioned. He wanted to hold that face between his hands and stroke the soft skin. Small mouth, rose tinted full lips, nice nose, and green eyes large enough to wade in or sink into oblivion. He could not tell her age. Perhaps late twenties or early thirties.

He remembered her, all right, as they passed each other. Tall and willowy, her strides long and confident, he wanted to take off her shades and see those eyes. Well, he saw them and felt their pull. An attraction he did not want to resist. Importantly, he knew she liked him. Little involuntary mannerisms betrayed her, and he did not manipulate her bioelectromagnetic field to get that reaction. Realizing her emotions were taking control, her demeanor became cold and professional. A formidable lady indeed.

As much as they might like each other, a dangerous association for him to indulge…and perhaps for her. Right now, she saw him as one of Kaneel's victims, and he must maintain that cover. One hint of his true nature and she would come after him regardless of any personal feelings. Probably a very good detective or Taskforce Crimson would not have picked her. That's what made her dangerous.

A likely victim, not a suspect, she said. Not a suspect yet, he reminded himself. If she kept digging into Kaneel's death, as a good detective, despite his explanation, she would keep asking why he went out with the woman, disregarding Dan's warning. He let out a slow sigh. Once Robinson finds Kaneel's shriveled body, what then?

He made a mistake cornering Kaneel at Blink's. A clean shot on some busy street like he did Lenny, probably a wiser thing to do. Manuel delicately hinted as much, but no, he wanted to make her suffer for what she did to Dan.

The page written, he could not go back and erase it.

Tonight, another and more pleasurable page to write. He really should not get involved with Robinson, but he liked her and she liked him, or she would not have accepted the dinner date. Frank wanted to see more of her and build on the fleeting encounter in his office regardless of possible consequences. As a feeder and Keeper, it did not mean he could not have a life like any other normal person. Time he put Rainey into a memory drawer and moved on. Always a part of him, he needed more than a memory in his life, and Nadala Robinson might be someone who could fulfill it. The age difference? It did not matter. He wanted her.

He swiveled the chair and gazed out the window. Dark clouds were drifting in from the Bay. Let it rain and storm. Let lightning destroy everything. For sure as he lived, sooner or later, ordinary humans would wage unrestricted war on feeders, not realizing they were all feeders to a degree. Why didn't Project Purple hammer the public with that fact? The Covenant should also step up its own worldwide conditioning campaign. Under the circumstances, perhaps they were already doing as much as possible to shift the prevailing social climate. At any rate, nobody asked for his opinion.

Keepers around the world would not need to hunt if only the rogue elements among them controlled their urges. Sadly, men and women everywhere demonstrated a proclivity to satisfy individual desires at the expense of others, even if eventually those desires destroyed them. Not only individuals, corporations and governments were equally guilty. He only had to peruse overwhelming historical evidence for proof of this tendency. It did not say much for the quality of human kindness.

Bastards, all of them, he concluded.

Did it have to be, though? He liked to think man can rise above his base nature and reach for the stars.

You're a hopeless dreamer, Frank, something inside him said and laughed with derision.

Thoughts wandering, he reflected on the conversation with Manuel yesterday evening. His contact confirmed the seasonal rise in sudden old age deaths around the world. Once during the southern and northern spring, and at onset of winter. One celebrated the start of new life—feeders celebrated like everybody else—and winters demanded sharing creature comforts.

The trend exhibited itself everywhere, most noticeable in India and China, with women as principal victims. Both cultures revered male children as heirs and bearers of the family line. Women were merely a means toward that end, and girl babies often met an untimely death. Because of that practice, Indians—ordinary men and feeders—now found it difficult to find a bride and resorted to random attacks to satisfy their needs.

China operated under a similar social outlook, made worse by years of the Communist Party's one-child policy to stem population growth, relaxed in 2016. Girls who managed to survive family culling grew into young women who found they were in great demand by hordes of bachelors. They liked the new order and became fussy whom they chose. Without a job, car, apartment, a young man had little hope attracting a bride. Those who missed out sought women from neighboring countries. Childless labor doomed the rural poor.

Western, predominantly white, societies faced a more insidious problem. Declining birthrates saw an influx of immigrants from Africa, Middle East, and Asian countries, which began to change population demographics and created a gradual shift in power as ethnic background politicians assumed prominent social and parliamentary positions. The still white majority saw the old social norms change and did not like it, which in turn triggered rebellious responses from far-right extremists who reflected unvoiced disquiet of the silent majority.

Frank did not know what kept Manuel going through the evening, but he lubricated the conversation with several tumblers of neat bourbon.

Events were piling up on him and he decided on a Saturday trip into the countryside to put some perspective on everything. He thought of Daylesford. A while since he visited the touristy little town, the drive along the back roads among rolling farms to get there always soothing. The thought of luxuriating in mineral water baths appealed to him. He could pick up lunch at one of the quaint bistros on the main street, or have a takeaway and eat at the nearby Jubilee Lake. Afterward, he'd rent a canoe and drift on the placid water away from weekend campers and picnickers. His only danger lay in having a collision with another canoe piloted by reckless kids.

Not certain how thinking about Robinson got him philosophizing, he reached for the coffee mug, only to find it empty. Not wishing to expire from thirst, he got up to get himself a refill.

The phone rang and he grabbed the receiver.

"Your four-thirty appointment is here, Frank," Cathy announced cheerfully. "Owen is already in the meeting room with the clients."

Damn, he forgot all about Lewis, his conservative factory owners and their Sydney plant.

"Be right there!"

He switched mental gears, twitched the tie into place, and hurried out. No coffee! Cathy probably made sure they had a carafe in the meeting room. She thought of everything.

Owen spent several hours crunching numbers for Lewis, and Frank created a slick PowerPoint presentation. Laid out in four slides, the company owners liked the new business plan and committed to another meeting on Monday to discuss details. The session closed with handshakes and smiles all around.

Their clients dispatched, Owen gave him an inquisitive glance.

"Cathy tells me a pretty federal cop called on you. Anything I should know?"

"A hot date, that's all."

"Come on, Frank! You haven't cooked the books, have you?"

"On Tuesday night, I dated a likely feeder, and the lady wanted to check on my health."

"A feeder? Jesus, Frank! What the hell's the matter with you?"

"It wasn't anything, Owen. I didn't feel a thing, and she's probably not a feeder at all."

Owen sighed. "If you settled down—"

Frank lifted a hand. "Don't start, okay?"

Around 5:10, he shut down the computer, dragged on a jacket, and walked out with a nod to Cathy. In his apartment, he showered, shaved—although unnecessary—and fixed himself a shot of bourbon. Initially, he wanted to make a restaurant reservation close to Carlton where Nadala lived, and Lygon Street offered great choices, then changed his mind. For their first outing, he preferred something classier and booked Florentino at top of Bourke Street, a stone's throw from Parliament. A Thursday, he easily got a table. Almost time to go, he slipped into a superfine Merino wool black suit, pale blue silk shirt, carmine tie, and soft Gucci loafers. An up-market place, Florentino liked their guests more formal. He also wanted to make a favorable impression on the formidable detective.

At almost exactly 6:30 PM, the black Uber BMW 7 pulled up in front of a neat gray brick terrace. A red Suzuki Swift stood parked on the narrow street lined with tall elms. Still bright, the sun cast sharp shadows on the sleepy, comfortable lane. He strode down a narrow paved path toward the house, paused at the carved wooden black door, and tapped the round clacker.

Hurried footsteps came from inside and he gave a silent whistle when Nadala opened the door.

The short hair suited her delicate face, lips touched up with gloss, pale green eyeshadow highlighted large, sparkling eyes. She wore a clinging blue gown that went all the way to her pumps and showed off her height to best effect. A narrow choker with a single white pearl adorned a slim neck. She held a small crocodile skin purse to complete the accoutrements.

"Wow," he managed in an overwhelmed whisper.

She flashed him a warm smile and nodded. "Thank you, kind sir. You don't look half bad yourself." Her eyebrows climbed when she saw the BMW. "My, aren't we splurging tonight."

Frank hooked a thumb over his shoulder. "That? It's all I could get on the spur of the moment."

Nadala laughed gaily and closed the door. He stood beside her, conscious of her closeness and perfume, and offered his arm. After a brief hesitation, she wrapped hers around it.

"Gorgeous evening," she murmured as he opened the rear door for her.

The air warm without a breath of wind, the street silent, a far cry from where he lived.

"You like it here?" he asked as the BMW pulled away.

"It's quiet and restful, and the neighbors are great. My house isn't large, but comfortable enough for my needs. What about you?"

"An apartment in the middle of town has its advantages. When I want greenery and peace, I drive to the country. It helps to reset my perspectives."

Her eyes probed into his soul. "So, you're not a dull 24/7 businessman?"

He chuckled. "It can get dull sometimes, but I compensate."

"By taking out…" She stopped and her checks colored. "Sorry, I shouldn't—"

"It's okay. You can say whatever you want to me," he told her softly, and meant it. He wanted her to be open with him, and did not intend to hold anything back about himself. Well, almost anything. "Yes, I go out with women, only because I haven't found one yet I'd like to be with all the time."

She appeared to digest that revelation, and he longed to know what went on in her pretty head. He felt her, not only close physically, but something deeper, as though their bioelectromagnetic fields were linked. He had not felt such a connection in a very long time. Since Rainey, and savored the sensation. Tonight, he promised himself not to startle or drive her away by doing something dumb.

It took some ten minutes to drive to Florentino Grill. Most of the traffic headed out of the city, people keen to put the working day behind them. A tram rounded the corner and clattered down Bourke Street toward the Mall. Passersby strolled on both sides of the wide street looking for entertainment, a cinema, shops, or simply window shopping.

The driver stopped beside the restaurant and Frank escorted Nadala upstairs to the main dining room. He nodded to the elderly usher who stood inside the entrance.

"Georgio…"

"Mr. Hram. Nice to see you again, sir. This way, if you please." He showed them to a table at the back, seated Nadala in a tall leather upholstered chair, and walked off.

Still relatively early, only four other tables were occupied. Square wood murals ran shoulder-high around the narrow room, above which hung large paintings of Renaissance cities. At the bar, an attendant busily prepared a mixer.

She looked around with interest. "Somewhat rustic, but nice."

"They don't serve pizza," he observed, and she scowled.

"Then I've been had."

"I'll make it up to you. Care for an aperitif?"

"A cocktail?"

"Anything in particular?"

"They're all a mystery to me. All I know is a Bloody Mary, a Manhattan, and a Pina Colada."

"Allow me."

As if by magic, Georgio appeared and waited.

"For the lady, a Mike Romanoff. For me, a Johnnie Walker Blue."

The usher nodded. "Very good."

Nadala sat back and fiddled with the beige cloth napkin. "You've been here before?"

"Once or twice. By myself, with Owen—he's my partner—or a client. Not always for dinner." He grinned at her. "Before you ask, sometimes with a lady friend."

She rolled her eyes. "Are you going to give me a hard time over that all night?"

He laughed and moved his thumb and forefinger across his mouth. "Not a word. Seriously, Florentino is a great restaurant with excellent Italian cuisine, even if they don't serve pizza," he added.

"You apparently did well with your business." She tilted her head slightly. "Can you make me rich?"

"It wouldn't happen overnight, but you could make a start to ensure a comfortable life later on."

"That's my problem. I want the good things now, not when I'm pushing sixty."

"I tell you what. Make an appointment with Cathy and we'll talk."

Before she could respond, Georgio appeared with their drinks held on a stainless steel platter. He placed the conical cocktail glass before Nadala, served Frank, and silently withdrew.

"Not much into conversation," she observed.

"Georgio? He's a mind reader. Knows what the guests are thinking and anticipates."

"Well, I hope he doesn't know what I'm thinking!" she blurted, then colored. "I mean—"

"I'd also be in trouble," Frank told her. Her eyes grew round, then she rewarded him with a sunny smile. "When I first saw you this afternoon, I knew you were something special," he added.

"You have a forceful personality, Frank," she remarked after a moment, "but I learned to be careful."

"I left my wolf outfit in my apartment, if that's what's worrying you," he declared and lifted his tumbler.

She raised hers and they touched glasses. After a hesitant sip, she pursed her lips and nodded.

"Wow. I could easily get used to this kind of living, you know."

Tempted to tell her she could if she became his, he refrained. She could easily misinterpret his intentions, and she'd be right. He stared at her, traced the lines of her face with his eyes, and lingered on her full lips. He wanted her more than any other woman he'd met. He felt her connection and knew she also wanted him. A mere physical attraction or something deeper? He would take time to find out.

When Georgio appeared to take their order, she went for a dozen Kilpatrick oysters, and he settled on roast quail. For the main, Nadala chose ocean duck and gnocchi, while he picked a braised veal shin.

"Any wine, Miss?" Georgio queried in a subdued voice.

"A Riesling?"

"May I recommend Rockford? A delicate wine with a wonderful bouquet without being too dry."

She glanced at Frank, who nodded.

"For me, a Palozzo Chianti," he said.

"Very good."

Several more guests drifted in and the room filled with background conversation and odors of wonderful cooking, heavy on garlic.

Nadala took a sip of cocktail and her eyes probed him. "Frank, I don't want to spoil the evening, but—"

"Why I went out with Kaneel if I suspected she was a feeder? As I told you, I found her interesting. I wanted to find out what it might be like."

"She could have killed you!"

"Well, I'm here, and everything works. Is she a rogue?"

"You seem to know a lot about feeders," she countered.

"I studied up. They *are* one of the main topics of interest for everybody. Tell me. Why did you come to see me?"

"I was concerned about your safety."

Before he could reply, Georgio arrived with their entrées and wine. Business forgotten, he watched her relish the oysters. As he picked through his quail, he remembered her saying she considered him a suspect. A professional turn of phrase, she said. He doubted something like that would slip by her, but consider him a suspect?

He pushed his plate toward her, determined to forget everything and enjoy her company. "Care for some?"

"Well…" She sliced off a piece and gave him three of her oysters.

Finished, she dabbed her lips with a napkin. "That was so delicious."

"Not bad at all," he agreed and sipped his Chianti. "Did you always want to be a cop?"

She frowned. "Actually, I wanted to study at the Duntroon College and be an Army officer. Instead, I went to Swinburne University for a degree in law, but switched to criminal justice. Something I found far more interesting. There are enough lawyers already," she added whimsically. "Once I graduated, I applied for the police force rather than join a boring law firm. In two years, I'm looking at promotion to inspector."

"To get there means training?"

"Training, getting an Advanced Diploma of Police Investigation—nobody gets a commission without one—and passing a selection board."

"How did you become a federal officer?"

"Haven't been one for long, and it's only a temporary assignment. I'm on a taskforce looking at international crime syndicates."

Taskforce Crimson had an altogether different objective, though, he mused.

"Why the interest in feeders?"

"It's complicated."

He believed her.

Georgio showed up, cleared away the plates, and topped up their drinks.

"What about you?" she queried. "Always into finance?"

"Pretty much. I'm interested in all kinds of sciences, with cosmology on top of my list. When I finished high school, I wanted a degree in astrophysics, but my dad talked me out of it. He's a bank executive and a rather hard man. He said, 'Frank, you can gaze at the stars all you want, but you'll be eating thin sandwiches for the rest of your life. Study something that'll make you money and give you a comfortable life.' So I studied commerce." He gave her a lazy grin. "To be honest, I didn't like the tough math required for astrophysics."

"No mathematics in finance?"

"There is, and some of it complicated, but our software does most of it for me."

"You like it?"

"There are some down days, but it's satisfying to see people do well following my advice."

"You obviously followed your own advice."

"And swallowed my losses," he added with a smile. "Not everything works out as planned."

Georgio brought their main course, and both spent time satisfying the inner self.

A young usher walked out of the kitchen holding a candle-lit cake on a glass tray and brought it to an elderly couple near the front. He started to sing 'Happy Birthday', and everybody in the room joined in, then clapped enthusiastically as the woman blew out the candles.

"Nice of them to do this," Nadala observed.

"Florentino is a family business who believe in maintaining tradition," Frank replied and worked on his veal shin.

He enjoyed sparring with her. Once her reserve dropped, she relaxed and became more natural. Bright, a roaming mind, she nevertheless reflected an innocence only years of life's knocks would file away. She argued her position with passion and gave in graciously when he ground her down with overwhelming facts. He could not recall having such an uninhibited conversation with any of his casual pickups, the objective there purely sexual. With Nadala, he wanted more, and wondered if it were possible.

With the main course out of the way, he talked her into ordering dessert, a slice of tiramisu and an Amaretto, while he settled for a port. Both enjoyed an espresso with chocolate wafer sticks on the side.

She eyed the tiramisu, grinned, and dug in. A satisfied sigh made him smile.

"This is so wicked," she declared, "and you're an evil man for talking me into having it."

"An occasional indulgence is good for the soul," he told her seriously.

"It might be good for the soul, but it won't do anything for my waistline."

"Nothing wrong with your waistline."

"You're a blockhead, Frank Hram."

"That's me," he agreed and sipped his port.

Both finished, he regretted the end to a pleasant evening.

"I'm a working girl, and you have a business to run," she told him with arched eyebrows.

Frank asked Georgio to book an Uber and left him a hefty tip. Outside, night claimed the brightly lit city. Lots of people crowded the sidewalks, enjoying a pleasant summer atmosphere and twinkling Christmas decorations in store fronts.

Nadala did not say anything on the way to Carlton, seemingly preoccupied. When she caught him glancing at her, she averted her gaze. The connection he felt with her pulsed strong, and he longed to take her into his arms and simply hold her, not wanting anything else.

The Uber pulled up in front of her house and he opened the door for her.

"Thank you for a lovely evening," she murmured softly.

The streetlamp highlighted her silver face and he reached for her. She tensed when he kissed her, then her arms went around his neck and the kiss progressed into something passionate and serious. She pulled away and cleared her throat.

"I didn't plan that," she said shyly.

"I did. I'd like to see you again, Nadala. Saturday night? I'll leave out the wicked tiramisu."

She gave a tinkling laugh and shook her head. "You're mean."

"Saturday?"

"You move fast."

"I don't want to miss an opportunity to see you."

"Saturday is fine." She opened the front door and disappeared inside.

On the way downtown, the car whispering to him, he merged with the Self, feeling everything right with the world.

* * *

Thankful to see Friday roll around, Nadala cheerfully waved to Prada as she hurried to her workstation. Shoulder bag strap hooked over the chair, she powered up the computer and went to the kitchenette for a mug of tea. Government issue Lipton English Breakfast far too bitter for her taste, she brought her own loose leaf Earl Grey blend. Prada tried it and instantly became a convert. Nadala gave her a website where she could order, pleased to have won over another addict.

Mug in hand, the enticing aroma rising delicately to her nose, she could not get Hram out of her head. She swore the disturbing man haunted her. In a moment of weakness, she pictured his powerful arms pull her against him like he did last night, his steel gray eyes becoming large as he leaned toward her to clamp his hard mouth on her yielding lips. When he kissed her, she felt electricity race down her body, and his power made her feel secure and protected. When the kiss ended, she wanted more, but if she gave into her raging feelings, she knew it would end only one way, not ready to take that step yet.

In bed, restless, she tried to banish his image from her mind. Sleep eventually came. Dawn caught her wearing a contented smile as remnants of the last dream faded, but not the pleasant bits with the enigmatic Frank Hram. She stretched and gave a long sigh.

Annoyed at the flush of heat coming from her cheeks, she shook off the memory.

Saturday night, he said…

Two hasty slurps, back in the real world, she opened her email Inbox. A week into her new position, her Collingwood Station stuff still followed her. About to shoot off several terse replies, her cellphone jangled.

"Detective Sergeant Robinson."

"Constable Rowlan, Detective. Your person of interest, Kaneel Mercer? She's dead. Two joggers this morning found the body at the St. Kilda Beach. She apparently sat there for some time. Cause of death, sudden old age. We identified her from a driver's license she carried in a shoulder bag. Her parents were notified."

A grim chore, she reflected, having gone through such an episode herself. To stand helpless at the front door and tell someone a loved one is dead always left her feeling wretched. Nothing she said lessened the shock, denial, and heart-wrenching grief.

"No robbery or foul play indicated. Since this is your case, what do you want us to do with the body?"

"Send it to the Victorian Institute of Forensic Medicine at Southbank. I'll call them to expect it."

"Anything else, Detective?"

"Please email me a copy of the incident report."

"Will do," Rowlan acknowledged and hung up.

No foul play indicated…If she had a suspicious nature, the whole case reeked of foul play. Connect the dots, Porter said. Okay, she'll give him a whole raft of dots.

Kaneel picks up Daniel Poole and he winds up dead. Then she picks up Hram, and three days later, she is dead. Not just ordinary dead, but old dead.

Nadala already established to her satisfaction that Kaneel was a rogue feeder, although nobody could prove it in court. Not even the competent Senior Sergeant Prada Vishnu. Project Purple taskforces around the world had evidence that rogue feeders sometimes killed. However, no laws existed anywhere to tell the courts how to deal with such cases, and for a good reason. Legislating induced sudden old age death by a feeder meant public acknowledgment of their existence. Something authorities were not ready to do.

How then can anyone pin murder on a rogue feeder? Impossible, of course. Equally impossible to pin murder on a Covenant Keeper who killed a rogue feeder, unless the Keeper used something conventional. Like two .22 rounds found in Lenny the Finger's heart? Still only supposition a Keeper did it. Old Lenny had lots of unsavory friends who would love to see him wearing a funeral wreath. Her mouth twitched at the thought and sipped some tea.

She bundled everything into one mental bag and shook it, ready to do something radical.

Frank met Poole at Blink's and strikes up a casual conversation. Security footage showed they established a rapport. When Poole sees him again, already an aging man, Hram afterward asks Walter about Kaneel. On Tuesday, he goes out on a seemingly blind date, supposedly to find out what it might be like in bed with a feeder. She wanted to believe him, but her detective instincts told her Hram played her. When she connected all the dots, she reached a disturbing conclusion. What if Hram had an ulterior motive to seek out Kaneel? Such as exacting retribution for what she did to Poole in the most grisly manner possible. To do that...

Incredible as the idea seemed, Hram must be a feeder. Everything fitted. She recalled the almost palpable attraction she felt for him. A natural reaction because she genuinely liked the man, or did he prompt the feeling with subtle manipulation of her bioelectromagnetic field? Her research, although incomplete, proved that predator feeders could influence a victim's emotions and feelings to disguise the ultimate intent to feed or kill.

Did Hram do that to her? She did not want to believe it. Not of him, but what did she really know about him?

She pulled herself up and snorted. No. She allowed her imagination to lead her to an absurd assumption. He never manipulated her. Why would he? He picked up women. So what? She picked up men.

With her professional detective hat on, she worked through her suspicions and came up with what she considered a far more realistic scenario. Hram told her the truth. Clearly foolish to go out with Kaneel, but with the intent to kill her? That she happened to die three days later a coincidence? If Hram did not kill her, *somebody* did. Somebody powerful to induce death in three days—savage even by feeder standards, the norm usually four or five.

Two scenarios, two wobbly theories at best.

She sighed and carefully updated her case file notes with everything she knew, including the wild hypotheses, then lifted her workstation phone and pressed a glowing button.

"Nadala," the Inspector answered after one ring. "Talk."

"I need to see you about one of my cases."

"My office, now."

She found Porter's assertive attitude confronting and reassuring. Confronting because he unnerved her, and reassuring because he supported his people, Prada told her over small talk. He affected everybody like that. Build a shell around yourself, she advised, and stand up to him. Porter respected those who were confident, and loathed anyone who looked to ingratiate themselves.

Nadala strode quickly toward his office, knocked once, heard a 'Come', and walked in.

Porter looked up from his computer screen and waved at a visitor chair. "Which case is giving you heartburn?" he demanded gruffly as she seated herself.

"Daniel Poole. The woman he picked up—"

"Kaneel Mercer, and she's dead. I know."

Nadala took a second to digest that. *How in hell...*

"I think she was a rogue and killed Poole. What has me puzzled, Senior Sergeant—"

"Prada closed two Mercer cases. I wondered when you were going to notice that."

"She wrote lack of evidence in both files, but in my opinion, she should have instigated an in-depth investigation after the second case."

"A judgment call, Nadala. Talk to her about it. Now, what's bugging you?"

Porter appeared to like it plain and ungarnished. Okay...

"I believe it's possible Frank Hram murdered Mercer for what she did to Poole."

His black eyes bored into her. "You're saying he's a feeder or a Keeper?"

She did not flinch at his harsh voice. "There is nothing to suggest one way or another."

Dismayed at having said it, she realized she severed something important between Frank and her, and was not sure she could knit the strands together again. *She had a duty, damn it!* Saying it did not lessen the burden of her guilt.

"But you're suspicious. To prove it…"

"I need to put a 24/7 team on him and see how he spends his days."

Porter reached into the desk drawer, pulled out a post-it pad, and scribbled on it. He tore off the slip and held it out. "Call that number. They'll give you whatever resources you need. When asked for a code word, tell them 'crimson'. Once done, shred the note."

Nadala bit her lip. "I'm not sure I want to know—"

"You don't."

"Who do I see about getting a search warrant?"

"No magistrate will issue you a warrant for the kind of work we do, Detective. I thought you understood that by now. Do you?"

It went against all her training as a police officer, but she did understand…finally and brutally. Without legislated protection, feeders were effectively *persona non grata*—if they can be found. Taskforce Crimson could not operate following standard criminal investigation procedures. Most everything it did lay outside the accepted legal framework. A double-edged sword that gave taskforces freedom how to chase down feeders, but also constrained their activities within a social matrix that did not acknowledge feeder existence. Every victim and suspect must be treated as a normal person with rights. She could see why author-itarian regimes found such constraints limiting and ignored the rule of law. They also did it to their own citizens, so it wasn't a step too far. Hunting feeders probably did not cause them any conscience twinge.

"I do, but I don't like it."

"Until feeders are recognized under law, to do our job, we sometimes must walk in shadow. Where are you with the Lenny case?"

Disappointment…

"I've hit a wall, I'm afraid. No evidence, no reliable witnesses, no surveillance footage—"

He lifted a hand. "Spare me the litany. Keep at it."

Sensing dismissal, she stood and walked out. Porter might be a hard man, but he appeared to trust her without demanding an explanation, something she appreciated and gave her an ego boost.

At her desk, she picked up the phone and tapped in the number from the post-it note.

"Code word," a gruff voice answered after two rings.

"Crimson."

"What can I do for you?"

"I need a 24/7 surveillance team on a person of interest. I also need a camera installed in his office and apartment, including a trace on his cellphone."

"Duration?"

"Ten days should do it. I'll advise you of any change. If your men are spotted, or the equipment, it'll blow the whole thing."

"Give me the details and I'll get things moving. We'll keep you updated."

Finished, she added the number into a spreadsheet file where she kept her passwords, shredded the note, and sat back. It ap-peared Taskforce Crimson indeed commanded real pull. She reached for her mug, only to find the tea cold. With a weary ex-hale, she pushed herself up and ambled toward the kitchenette.

Tea at her side, she gnawed the end of her pen. Lenny the Finger…She really ought to knuckle down and do something about the little snitch. She logged into the computer—the thing disconnected itself if she did not use it for ten minutes—opened the Lenny file and began to sift through everything again.

Two witnesses alleged they saw a tall man in a gray wind-breaker push through pedestrians in front of the Kitten Club. Seconds later, Lenny lay on the sidewalk shot in the back. In the ensuing pandemonium, nobody remembered anything clearly. A tall man…There were thousands of tall men in Melbourne.

Pen clamped between her teeth, her thoughts drifted to only one tall man who captivated her interest. Why did Hram walk down blustery Queen Street last Saturday at 9:53 PM? With a mil-lion possible valid reasons, she pushed him out of her mind.

Connect the dots, Porter said. Hard to do if there weren't any damn dots. Then create them.

You know what you can do with your dots, Inspector.

She needed to clear her head and look at the case from a dif-ferent angle. First, she must send a spike to some of her Colling-wood Station colleagues.

The Uber ride to the Bourke Street Mall fought the usual war with other cars going the same way. At the entrance to the pe-destrian Mall, only trams allowed through, Nadala watched the crush of people jamming the sidewalks. Christmas only a week away, stores everywhere were doing brisk trade.

Thick tinsel streamers crisscrossed the Mall, hung from tram-line power poles, festooned with Santa cutouts, sleighs, wire stars, and bells. She could see two walking Santa characters up the Mall entertaining children. The sound of carols vied for attention above the noise of chatting, strolling, hurrying pedestrians, women trying to keep youngsters under control, and occasional clangs from a tram as it slithered through.

Behind tall plate glass windows, Myer displayed its usual nativity scenes: Santa riding a sleigh, reindeer wearing cheerful smiles, and snow-covered village views. Kids crowded in front of them, twittering excitedly. It all looked highly incongruous, having winter scenery when the city enjoyed 26C.

Nadala pushed her way through the crowd and sighed with relief when she entered the pleasantly air-conditioned Myer department store. She knew what to get her parents, her sister, and the bubbling Valerie. Before buying anything, she had to check out the goodies.

Her mom, a respected lawyer working for a firm at the Collins Street top end, might enjoy a new briefcase. Dad, on the other hand, a Virgin Air domestic pilot, might be tickled with a compass in case the aircraft instrumentation failed. He can always use it on one of his outback adventures with Mom, she mused. Then again, a compass might not be such a good idea if a passenger saw it. Angy would gush over a gold pen when interviewing someone important, although she regularly used a pocket recorder. As for Valerie, there were untold things for a four-year-old.

Mouth set, Nadala navigated among other shoppers and began to hunt.

Two hours later, a large shopping bag in hand—all presents wrapped by smiling attendants—she stopped at the food court for a late shrimp salad lunch. Chores finished, she snagged a cab to the Police Center rather than put up with a crowded tram.

Armed with a fresh mug of tea, she sauntered to Prada's desk, determined to finish an unpleasant piece of business. Her colleague looked up from her computer screen and smiled.

"I noticed you were out shopping."

Nadala dragged a visitor chair and sat down. "Out of the way for another year, until Easter. I tell you, by mid-January, everybody will be selling chocolate eggs and bunnies." She noted the red bindi dot between Prada's eyes. "Be glad you don't have to do this."

The Indian woman chuckled. "As a Hindu, we also observe festive customs. For the five-day Diwali, we're expected to share presents. This year, it fell last month. Parties, revelries, and I'm required to dress in traditional costumes. I'm not much into all that, but my husband's parents are devout followers and I make allowances for their benefit."

"My sister and I were raised as Catholics," Nadala put in, "but neither of us follow the Church. I think the Vatican is corrupt to the core, and it burns me up to see pedophile priests protected from civil prosecution. I'd string them up by their thumbs if I had it my way. My mom is a strong believer and my sister and I observe the two main calendar events for her benefit and for Valerie. That's my sister's daughter."

"It's pretty much the same with my two daughters, nieces, and nephews. Indians tend toward large families," Prada added with a small laugh.

Nadala took a sip of tea and studied the woman. To be a senior sergeant and a member of Porter's team, she must be competent and intelligent, which made her reluctant to broach what she felt needed clearing up. Prada noted the scrutiny and smiled faintly.

"You're a good interrogator, Nadala."

"Oh?"

"I don't mind the chat, but that's not why you're here."

"No, it isn't. I feel like a heel bringing this up—"

"I'll make it easy for you. It's Kaneel Mercer and my two cases. Don't look surprised. I know what you're working on. Kurt told me you have an issue with them."

Nadala stared at her, then grinned. "Porter doesn't let weeds grow under his feet, does he."

"Not where the Taskforce is concerned. He's on top of everything. In Kaneel's case, I made a judgment call, just as he told you. In hindsight, after the second case, I should have launched a more in-depth investigation into her activities, seeing how Commissioner Trusk is always screaming for more feeders to experiment on. I told myself if Kaneel became involved in another sudden old age death, I'd land on her, but she kept her activities below our horizon. When I learned about Daniel Poole, I went to see Porter to give me the case. You know what happened there."

"He unloaded the thing on me."

"It's meant to be a live fire exercise, Nadala. He does it to every new team member. You can have a sterling resume, but to him, the only thing of any consequence is performance. He wants to see how you perform. So does everybody else here." Prada cocked an eyebrow. "He speaks highly of you. Ordinarily, he only growls."

"Highly of me? Lenny the Finger is a dead end, and now, Kaneel a dead end, literally."

"You're investigating Hram."

Nadala frowned. "Are you snooping through my case files?"

"I'm the Inspector's 2IC. I oversee everybody's cases."

"Sorry, I didn't mean—"

"Forget it. I'd also feel annoyed. About Kaneel—"

"You told me what I wanted to know, Prada. Sometimes things don't work out the way we want them to. Any suggestions how I should handle Hram?"

"So far, you've ticked all the right boxes. Follow procedure and you'll be fine. One thing. You're an experienced detective. Follow your instincts."

Nadala stood and nodded. "Thanks for the heart-to-heart."

"My office is always open."

At her desk, Nadala logged back in and bit her lip. Follow her instincts, Prada said.

Something about Lenny the Finger's murder bothered her, but she could not quite pin down the itch. The dots...the dots...

The .22 rounds!

"Stupid!" she mumbled and gave a low growl of annoyance.

She brought up the cases directory and typed in '.22'. The first file held nothing of interest. The second file made her stare at the screen. A rogue killed on April 15 with two .22 rounds whose rifling marks matched those that killed Lenny. Clearview AI showed Frank Hram and the April 15 victim at the same bar.

Could he...She did not want to complete the thought that bubbled to the surface.

Chapter Four

Frank seethed with anger as he skipped across the TV channels, his plans for a carefree Saturday shot. Every breakfast show carried the same story. In United States—why in hell bad things always started there—Hacker Anonymous claimed they penetrated Project Purple's email server, copied hundreds of operational documents, and posted links on social media sites how to access the material. To see for himself, he opened a Facebook link and skimmed through some of the damning stuff. China and Russia, supposed enemies, did not leak this. Western corruption and vindictiveness against the system did. A sordid state of affairs, the image of a Hacker's leering mask vivid in his mind. He wanted to bash in that white plastic face!

As he read, a pattern emerged. If people were prepared to wade through all the information, they'd gain a basic understanding of Project Purple, its subordinate taskforces, research into sudden old age deaths, and critically, the Covenant as an entity, but no doomsday predictions of feeders running rampant sucking blood from victims. The Project revealed itself as a coordinating focus for governments everywhere to understand what caused sudden old age deaths and how to cure it. Although grave, the disclosure might not be totally disastrous. Without reading every document and email, he could not tell how far the damage extended.

If Hacker Anonymous intended to create popular panic, he reflected, their effort may have backfired. What the posted documents said, every person on the planet was to some degree a feeder, something many people could relate to. This cut the ground under the feet of extremist organizations such as the National Rally Party and similar far-right groups around the world. They no longer had a single segment within the population to focus their racist rants and action protests. He did not doubt they would invent spurious reasons to agitate and blame it on feeders.

To his surprise, the ABC *Breakfast* show provided a fairly balanced summary and editorial commentary on the social impact the disclosure might have. As always, *France 24* and *Deutsche Welle* programs were concise and factual without injection of unnecessary drama, the event dramatic enough in itself. The sensation-seeking commercial channels were predictably hopeless with wild claims that Australia and the world faced general unrest, even the fall of governments, suggesting that some federal politicians might be energy vampires. Unhelpful, although probably true, the announcement played directly into the Hacker Anonymous strategy to create public upheaval, something the National Rally Party already seized on. They demanded a Royal Commission into Canberra's involvement, promising direct action against the Prime Minister, those responsible within the Cabinet for this monumental cover-up, and a drive to rid humanity of feeders.

A small group stood on the steps of the Victorian parliament brandishing placards. A tough customer faced them, holding a bullhorn. Six uniformed cops stood well back and watched.

"What do we want?"

"Down with vampires!"

"When do we want it?"

"Now!"

How in hell did those protesters get organized so quickly? Disgusted, Frank switched off before he threw the coffee mug at the TV. His appetite gone, he put the breakfast remains into the fridge, refilled the mug, and sat in his favorite recliner, deep in thought. The tomorrow he dreaded had arrived, but would things be as calamitous as he and the Covenant feared? The agitators he'd seen looked prepared for the long haul.

The White House deserved credit for reacting quickly to dampen what threatened to turn into a major political scandal. For once, the Democrats chose not to play partisan politics and announced support for the Republican president. Most channels aired excerpts, and some in full, the Press Secretary's response refuting claims by Hacker Anonymous, saying they were wildly exaggerated, and everybody should go on with their lives as normal. The Administration directed the FBI to look into the matter, and those responsible for the security breach faced arrest. Frank chuckled, the image of that proverbial bolted horse coming to mind. She even inserted a humorous comment about an energy vampire descending on the culprits, inducing immediate death. Given the gravity of the situation, he felt the remark to be in extremely poor taste.

It mystified him how Hacker managed to crash the Project Purple email and database servers, supposedly totally secure. More likely an internal leak, something he felt far more plausible. Regardless how they did it, they pulled back the veil of secrecy that sheltered feeders for centuries. Having done it, what else could they do? They overplayed their hand and had no more chips to raise the bet. That left the National Rally Party and its sister organizations around the world to carry the persecution banner and encourage professional protesters to loot and destroy. From what he knew, researchers were still years away from identifying genetic markers that induced sudden old age death, let alone develop blockers.

His cell rang and he blinked at the flashing red encryption icon. He input the PIN to enable the call, not totally unexpected.

"It's Manuel, Frank. I suppose you watched the news?"

"And saw the protesters. The National Rally Party didn't waste any time."

"I'm sure there is more to follow."

"I don't doubt it. What's the reaction from the Covenant?"

"Still evaluating the possible public impact, amigo. No word yet from the US Grand Master. I figure he's having some high-powered talks with the President and Project Purple right now. There's a lot to take in and digest before the US Council can formulate a tactical response. In due course, something will trickle down to every Master Keeper and city branches. Melbourne isn't waiting for it to rain on us, though. The Master called for a ten AM meeting with all six Keepers. Can you make it?"

Frank pictured himself driving to Daylesford for some fun and relaxation, not aggravation. Life did not always cooperate, and today seemed to be one of those times. If the day did not end up totally ruined, he could still go somewhere in the afternoon before his dinner date with Nadala.

"Where?"

"There's a safe house at 322 Albert Street opposite the Fitzroy Gardens."

"I can make it."

"See you there," Manfred said brusquely and cut contact.

His friend did not have to tell him to be discreet how he traveled. A Collins Street tram went directly to Albert Street, stopping before the Eye and Ear Hospital. From there, a short walk to the safe house. What contribution he could make to the discussion, Frank did not know, but if the Master wanted him there, he would not disappoint her.

He never met the other five Keepers as a group. The few times he visited a Covenant safe house for briefings or training—always a different one—he saw one or two and exchanged brief pleasantries. Not a club, the Covenant discouraged intimacy between Keepers for a good reason. A captured Keeper represented a grave security risk should they know too much. They lost Bravo in March, which upset everybody. He did not even know where the Master had her offices. She had to work from somewhere for administrative purposes, if nothing else.

When they did meet, each used a codename. He used Foxtrot, which tickled his sense of humor, as one fellow Keeper called herself Tango. Around 170cm, straw-colored hair, trim, she hunted male and female rogues. On reflection, it made sense. Not every rogue walked the heterosexual street. Although not a lesbian, she confided with a mischievous grin that a girl can be a blast.

"I know," he told her with a straight face. "I do them all the time."

She laughed and slapped his wrist. "Dick."

The few times they met for training sessions, she repeatedly demonstrated she could handle herself. A formidable lady in every respect.

Gay, 'Charlie' hunted men. The rest were straight. He understood the need, but could never picture himself intimate with a man. The very idea made him wince with distaste. In all other respects, Charlie's outgoing personality made him approachable, and Frank enjoyed several lively discussions with the slightly chubby guy, always at a safe house.

With time on his hands, he cleaned and vacuumed the apartment, and fed the washing machine. A rogue that sucked everything from clothing it chewed up. When he returned from the meeting, he'd iron his business shirts, a chore he detested. Happy to occasionally iron a pair of pants, the prospect of tackling shirts made him look for excuses to get out of town. Building services could launder them for him, and sometimes did, but he did not like to throw away money on principle.

He took a tram to Parliament—the agitators still there, as were the police—and decided to walk the odd four hundred meters to the safe house. This time, he did not have to use the Myki charge card to tap on and off the tram, travel within the CBD free. From time to time, the City Council announced plans to abolish the perk to raise revenue, but State governments of both political persuasions always quashed the suggestion, mindful of public backlash come election time. The current Labor Party proposed to make Swanston and Elizabeth Streets pedestrian malls all the way to Flinders Street, something businesses decried. They protested creating the Bourke Street Mall when first proposed, saying it would ruin trade. Instead, when opened in 1983, the Mall drew crowds into the CBD. Some people needed their heads pounded before they got the point.

He paused in front of the old, gray brick terrace and pressed a large brass doorbell button. The thing clanged like an old telephone and he heard footsteps. Manuel de la Kass opened the heavy plain wooden door and beamed.

"Good to see you, Frank."

They shook hands, and the wiry man stepped back to let in his guest.

"I wish it were under different circumstances," Frank replied gravely, and followed his contact down a narrow, dark corridor.

"Yeah, me too. You're the last to arrive, but two couldn't make it, Oscar and Victor. The others are in the lounge."

"How's the Master?"

"Sierra? Worried, as you can imagine."

Manuel opened a white door to a comfortable nineteenth century drawing room fitted with pale chest-high paneling, ornate cornices, a yellow ceiling from which hung a glass chandelier mounted in a round plaster rose.

Frank nodded to Tango and Charlie, barely glancing at the always grim Echo. From his stern, chiseled features and crewcut, possibly a military officer or something, solid build, Frank never warmed to the man. Chemistry, he presumed.

Sierra, in her sixties, short and slim, turned from a small table set against the wall laid out with steel carafes of coffee and tea, a glass plate of pastries, and smiled at him. He longed to know what life dished out for her, something he knew would never happen. They did not discuss personal things. Brunette hair streaked white, probing black eyes that took in everything, small mouth made up with lipstick, completed a pinched face used to wielding authority. He figured her to be a corporate executive, but she could be a nice grandmother sitting at home knitting socks for all he knew.

Cup and saucer in hand, the Melbourne Master seated herself in a red-striped green lounge chair and waited for Frank to make himself comfortable.

"We all have things to do, so I'll make this short as possible," Sierra said in a pleasant, friendly voice. "Manuel will update Oscar and Victor later. Both send their apologies."

"The ladies busy doing their makeup," Echo declared sotto voce, which drew a disapproving glare from the Master.

"Enough! This is serious. The story broke in Washington at noon, six PM in Europe. Plenty of time for the two Grand Masters to converse and define a response strategy."

"And plenty of time for somebody to organize a protest," Charlie grumbled sourly.

Sierra nodded. "I've seen them."

"This is gonna get ugly," Tango added.

"The word from the Australian Master Keeper is to lay low," Sierra said. "All sanctions against rogue feeders are suspended. We'll pass what information we have on them to Taskforce Crimson and they can take appropriate action. Our priority is to keep all of you alive and safe."

Dressed in a conservative dark gray business jacket and pants, Tango leaned forward. "Innocent people might die if we stop pursuing rogues."

"Can't be helped. Project Purple wanted sole jurisdiction how to deal with them for some time, and now they got it. Although Hacker Anonymous compromised Project Purple and its taskforces, the disclosure might not be as grave as initially expected. Public conditioning has progressed to a point of general acceptance that feeders live among them, although commercial media and radical far-right groups are still pushing the unhelpful vampire theme. Their problem is lack of proof. They're unable to parade a single blood-sucking vampire in front of City Hall. Moreover, polling shows people have become somewhat jaded to alarmist propaganda."

"That hasn't stopped the protest!" Echo declared flatly. "I understand similar rallies are going on in Sydney and Canberra."

"All we can do is hope the authorities contain them. The world faces the realization that feeders exist, and some kill by inducing sudden old age death, close enough to brand them vampires, which I'm sure the National Rally Party and allied overseas organizations will exploit fully to foster unrest. Apart from waving placards, what form that unrest will take remains to be seen. What we dread is the emergence of self-appointed vigilante groups hunting feeders. A situation might develop where mere insinuation that someone is a feeder will result in personal attacks."

"Witch hunts," Charlie remarked gravely, sitting opposite Frank.

"I pray we never see such days," Sierra announced soberly. "I'm told the Grand Master spoke to President Julian Everett, urging him to place all police forces on high alert to curtail signs of vigilante activity. Prime Minister Elena Griffin had a similar conversation with our Master Keeper. Don't be surprised if she enacts Article 4 of the International Covenant on Civil and Political Rights by declaring rogue feeders a national threat."

Echo snorted. "An open invitation for extremists to agitate."

"You could be right. It's too soon to know how the world will react to the Hacker Anonymous revelation. People need time to read leaked documents and digest the information. The most valuable protection we all have is normalcy. Despite what we've seen on TV, everybody still needs to work, pay bills, buy groceries, and look after their family. Australians are naturally concerned, as is everybody else, at incidences of sudden old age deaths. However, they should be relieved it isn't caused by a virus or some genetic disorder they can catch. The fact that such deaths result from an overly enthusiastic sexual episode should, in a quirky way, be humorous. Understanding the cause is likely to make people guard themselves against wanton promiscuity."

"That won't do anything to rein in rogue feeders," Frank pointed out.

"Or religious organizations everywhere to clamp down on what they regard as something sinful, unless directed at making another baby," Tango added.

Sierra lifted a hand. "Let's not inject unnecessary alarmism here, okay?"

Echo stared hard at the Master. "Tango is right. We're in for years of political and religious ultraconservatism."

"The Covenant addressed this with Project Purple, and contingency plans are in place to avoid overreaction. Rogues are everybody's problem, not normal feeders, and they'll continue to be a problem until researchers develop blockers to suppress an exaggerated feeding impulse or reverse the onset of sudden aging. Now that they're officially exposed, we hope simple preservation will make rogues more circumspect with their activities. We all must feed to survive, but millennia of history has demonstrated that we can coexist peacefully with normal humans. That's the platform the Grand Master is asking President Everett to promote. Coexistence, not predator and prey mentality, as extremist groups and some religions will promulgate in an effort to stamp us out. An impossibility, as every person on the planet is a feeder. It's part of our genetic makeup." She paused and took a sip of tea.

"You told us to suspend all rogue assignments, but there's more. Isn't there?" Tango prompted.

"If there is, nobody told me. Right now, go home and do your Saturday chores."

The remark raised several chuckles.

"On Monday, resume your normal life and do whatever it is you do. Manuel will update you as events unfold. In meantime, when you must feed, keep it discreet," she added with a grin, which everybody shared.

Frank cleared his throat. "What about Taskforce Crimson, Sierra? I'm under investigation."

"I know about that one. I'll talk to Kurt Porter to drop all action against suspected Keepers who killed using non-conventional means. We can't do much about the rogues we shot, as he views those as murder."

"And he's right," Charlie pointed out.

Frank again wondered at the level of penetration into taskforces by Covenant operatives.

"Technically, but he can help everybody by not pursuing some cases. Hacker Anonymous may have blown the lid on the Covenant, but research institutions everywhere are still desperate to acquire live feeders for experimentation. The demand will remain until they come up with a blocker pill. Legally, Porter cannot do anything to you, Foxtrot—"

"If the Prime Minister enacts Article 4, they'll come after him," Echo interjected, daring somebody to refute him.

Sierra scowled at him. "The Master Keeper will take this up with Deputy Commissioner Trusk. We don't want to swap one vigilante group with an officially sanctioned one."

"Trusk might not have a choice," Tango added softly. "With the Hacker disclosure, governments everywhere will be under terrific pressure to find a cure for sudden old age death. They'll authorize taskforces to arrest suspected feeders using the greater good argument."

Clearly weary, Sierra sighed. "I hope they don't push it that far. However, the Covenant wields considerable political clout, and we'll use it to suppress government overreaction."

Frank exchanged looks with Tango. "You may have the party machinery in your pocket, but parliamentarians answer to people at the ballot box. Griffin will do the expedient thing, as will other governments."

Echo nodded vigorously. "He's right. Your promise to keep us safe might not amount to much."

"There is a way we can put heat on Griffin," Charlie announced promptly. "We can go public and expose the Southbank and its sister Sydney forensics facility if Porter arrests one of us."

Frank shook his head. "The public might be willing to look the other way in exchange for a pill to stop them dying suddenly, regardless how many feeders it takes. It's them or us."

"The Covenant would initiate a slew of legal actions against the government and police forces for unlawful detention, Article 4 notwithstanding," Sierra pointed out, and her mouth firmed. "If any federal member—state politicians don't really count—supports a bill designed to prosecute feeders, the Covenant will have their party disendorse them. Every politician's paramount driver in life is to keep their seat, no matter what. Griffin may be the Prime Minister, she can also be compromised."

"While the Covenant and Canberra play with each other, Foxtrot may not survive a stay at Southbank or some other facility somewhere," Echo added ponderously. Hating to admit it, Frank shared his sentiment.

Sierra lifted her hands. "We can hash this all day without getting anywhere. I don't make these decisions. All we can do is remain vigilant, watch the situation develop, and hope Project Purple and governments everywhere don't overreact."

"Instead of exposing Southbank directly as Charlie suggested, what if we launched a dissembling action against Porter's taskforce?" Frank asked quietly, and every face turned on him. "We find a perfectly innocent person and claim Porter had her—better a woman, it generates more sympathy—arrested and subjected to illegal medical testing."

"Porter would deny it," Tango shot back.

"Of course, but the action will cast a glaring public spotlight on what's going on there and make people think. What if one of them is arrested on mere suspicion and subjected to dissection? We make this as gory as possible. I doubt Taskforce Crimson and Griffin would enjoy such exposure."

Sierra frowned. "An ingenious idea, Foxtrot, but it's not something I can approve. However, I'll take it up with the Master Keeper and he can raise it with her as a counter threat."

"Despite the Covenant's back door influence, if the government legislates open season on feeders…" Tango murmured, and Sierra nodded.

"It would set an extremely bad legal precedent that might not stand up to a High Court challenge, but we're facing an unprecedented situation. We'll wait and see what the government will do. Go home. Resume your lives and hope sanity prevails. We cannot meet as a group again. Much too dangerous. If Porter is looking into your activities, don't give him an excuse to arrest you. If he does, contact Marrick, Ward, and Thatcher. Good luck to us all." She stood and briskly walked out, leaving a hint of citrus fragrance in the air. Manuel followed close behind.

Echo got up, fixed himself a cup of coffee, and grabbed a blueberry Danish. Two large bites almost demolished the pastry as he returned to his seat.

"It looks like we're all pretty much screwed," Charlie remarked affably.

"As Sierra said, there's nothing we can do individually except wait and see how events unfold," Frank countered. "As for grand strategy, the Covenant higher-ups will handle it."

Echo put down his cup. "Handle what? Clear away the protesters? Stop the vigilantes? Sierra hasn't told us everything. I've been in Navy counterintelligence long enough to smell a smoke screen."

"So what if she hasn't told us everything?" Charlie countered. "We operate on a need-to-know."

"This time, we have a need-to-know," Echo snapped. "All of you are missing a vital point here. We don't know how the Covenant operates and what are its long-term objectives. They're supposedly protecting ordinary feeders, but I am certain there's more to them than we were told. As Keepers, we're given the minimum information necessary to do our work, nothing else. They know everything about each one of us, but what do we know about them? We were given what's probably a heavily redacted history during our training. We only have their word that we're acting for humanity's good."

"Are you saying wiping rogues off the pavement isn't good for humanity?" Tango demanded. A faint flush colored her face.

"Don't get me wrong. I believe rogue feeders deserve to be castrated, but I'm suspicious when the only contact I have with the Covenant is Manuel's phone number, and don't give me any crap about security. What I'm getting at, this one-way knowledge pipe makes us vulnerable. The bottom line? They've cut us off from the herd, boys and girls. They don't need us anymore. We're on our own. I suggest you pack a bag and be ready to disappear. The next knock on your door could be from one of Porter's cops. I for one am not hanging around to find out."

"You're full of shit, Echo," Tango told him bluntly.

He laughed at her. "And you're naïve, my dear colleague. Shed that innocence and grow up. Did any of you ever wonder where Sierra gets her intelligence on rogue feeders? We get a call from Manuel to hit someone and we do it. How does he find out? The Covenant must run an extensive intelligence network we know nothing about. Sierra said that Southbank forensics researchers are always hungry for more test subjects. We're the price she might be prepared to pay to protect her network. That bag I spoke of? I packed mine before coming here. My Keeper days are over. You guys can stick your neck into Sierra's noose and wait for her to pull the rope. Hang around and be sacrificial lambs. I'm outta here." He stood and walked out without a backward glance.

"I never liked the pushy creep," Charlie declared wearily. "It burns me to admit it, he made a lot of sense. It's time we seriously considered our own survival."

Frank wagged a finger. "Call me naïve as well, but I'm with Tango. I can't believe the Covenant would shaft us. Sierra never deceived us. Granted, in the larger picture, we may be expendable, but not in the way Echo thinks. If I ran somewhere, I'd have a large 'I'm a feeder' label on my back, with every cop in the country after me."

Charlie pulled at his chin. "From what we were told, the Covenant infiltrated governments, the military, police forces, corporations, religious orders, and what not. That's a lot of power and influence—"

"And control," Tango murmured.

Charlie pointed a finger at her. "Right you are! Ask yourself this. Control of what? The world?"

"You're saying there's an underground world government nobody knows about that manipulates everything?" Frank demanded. "You're getting pretty melodramatic, aren't you?"

"Take it any way you like. Look at globalization over the last sixty years or so. You really think governments and corporations could set up such a complex network without some overall guiding hand? Who benefits? Certainly not the ordinary person on the street. Power is created to be used, and those in control will do anything to see it doesn't disappear."

"You're getting as bad as Echo," Tango shot back with a wry smile.

"I agree with him on one thing. We don't have a job anymore. You and I are now ordinary feeders, and the Covenant holds a sword to our necks. I say he had a point when he said to pack a bag. I for one might do just that. I don't want cops coming after me and be sacrificed for that nebulous greater good." The chair creaked as he heaved up his bulky frame. "Nice knowing you, guys. Ta ta." He fluttered his fingers at them and stomped out.

Frank watched him leave and turned to Tango. "After that bucket of cheery news, what are you going to do?"

"Echo may be able to pull up stumps and disappear, I can't. I have a life outside the Covenant. If somebody comes after me, I'll make them pay. What about you?"

"Same here. Look, I skipped breakfast and I don't want to rile my stomach with more talk of gloom and world domination. Do you want to go out for brunch somewhere? I know a great place in Chinatown." Ironing shirts be damned.

She broke into a sunny smile. "That's the most sensible thing I've heard all morning. While we're at it, you can tell me all about yourself so I can hand you over to Porter."

He laughed at the idea, got up, and opened the door for her. Nobody waved bye-bye to them as they left.

His day not totally ruined, he could still take an afternoon drive somewhere.

* * *

A piece of buttered toast topped with Mom's runny apricot jam partway to her mouth, Nadala gaped at the TV. Protesters already agitating in front of the Parliament? Hacker Anonymous dumped on the world without any inkling or warning. Simple spite in nobody's interest. Is that how they get their hots off, sowing discord?

Her cell gave a ping, announcing a text message. Her eyebrows climbed when she read it. Prada said Porter wanted everybody in the office by nine. Given the current events, the development not altogether unexpected. The planned outing with Angela to Luna Park, followed by some serious relaxation at the St. Kilda Beach soaking in the UVs while Valerie chased seagulls, now utterly shot. She should have switched off the damned cell and shoved the thing into a drawer.

Only 7:46, she finished breakfast, did the washing up, and headed for the bedroom to change. She then called Angela with the bad news. Her sister told her not to worry about it, which only made Nadala feel guiltier. Valerie so looked forward to their outing. They could come to her place in the afternoon to put up the Christmas tree, she offered.

To save herself the stress driving in, she had Uber take her to the Policer Center. An official trip, she'd claim it as an expense. Although Saturday, it made no difference to the road crush. For some people the only day they could take care of specific chores impossible to do during a working week. By afternoon, things should ease off. She preferred doing her shopping on a Sunday, and most stores were open. As the driver threaded her way along Flinders Street, Nadala hoped Porter would not ruin her day further with lots of tedious meetings. She enjoyed life as a police officer, and put in extra hours when required, but with Christmas one week off, even the crooks were taking a break. Hacker Anonymous could have held off their announcement until the new year and allowed everybody to enjoy the festive season without a blanket of troubles draped over them. She decided Hacker were not nice people.

The Uber driver dropped her off and immediately merged into Spencer Street traffic. She rode the elevator to the eleventh floor and headed directly for the kitchenette to fix herself a mug of tea. Two days ago, she caught Rosalyn helping herself to her Earl Grey, and Nadala chewed her head off. If Rosalyn wanted it, she could buy it or stick with the Lipton lawn clippings. The word must have gotten around, for nobody else messed with her tea. Her fellow detectives might be cops, but it did not mean they were above a little casual office pilfering, but not her tea!

Mug in hand, she joined everybody clustered around Prada. They parted ranks to let her in without a break in conversation.

"Nothing will happen, I tell you," Simone Washnik declared, her chestnut ponytail waving from side to side, both hands shoved into black jeans.

Nadala found the junior detective sergeant amenable; an expert in all forms of electronic banking tricks bad guys used to launder money. Her soft Slavic features belied her twenty-nine years. According to Prada, when Simone joined the team, two male colleagues started to hit on her, but she quickly put them in their place. Like Porter, she also liked it plain and took no crap off anybody. Not married, she lived with a partner somewhere in Deer Park.

"Christ, Simone! Where have you been all morning? Protesters are already on the street!" Randal Young shot back. On the short side, skeletal, clothes hung on the elderly detective senior constable as though from a coat hanger. An apparent stickler for detail, everybody said he approached each case as a personal affront. "On Monday, the National Rally Party will have hundreds agitating on parliament steps in every capital city. Tonight, the channels will be flooded with documentaries and talk shows about feeders, the Covenant, and Project Purple. Don't be surprised to see gangs everywhere painting white Fs on store windows."

Simone laughed. "Wearing brown shirts, no doubt. Jesus, Randal, you're off the planet."

"Wait and see," Young shot back.

Kurt Porter emerged from his office and the conversation died as he strode toward them. He stood at parade rest, hands clasped behind his back, and gave them a hard look.

"I regret the necessity to spoil your morning, but things happen we cannot always control. In case you're wondering why you're here, I take it you've watched the news. For us, the Hacker Anonymous announcement is both good and bad. Good because people on the street finally know what's really going on and we can speed up our operations. Bad because they don't know everything. Hacker haven't completely compromised Project Purple because they don't know everything either. How they pulled this off is under investigation by the FBI and every intelligence organization in the States. Our IT people assured Commissioner Trusk that such a penetration of our system isn't possible."

"It shouldn't have been possible to crack Project Purple either," Simone quipped, which earned her a glare from Porter.

Nadala did not need to have it explained. The Taskforce might be able to secure itself against external attack, but not from an internally planted Covenant agent.

"For those of you who haven't read the leaked emails and documents, do so," Porter went on. "At least some of them. Part of the bad thing about the Hacker revelation is that nobody knows more about the Covenant than we did yesterday. They penetrated us for decades, but our efforts to do the same to them amounted to nothing. They obviously have excellent internal security, and operatives planted inside Project Purple undoubtedly tipped them off on any infiltration attempt. They played this game for three centuries and are very good at it."

She cast a quick glance at her colleagues. Was one of them a feeder and a pipeline for the Covenant? Porter could not say it without damaging team integrity and morale, but his grim expression suggested he had no doubts. Then again, it might not be true. Judging by the long faces of concern around her, everybody understood the situation without having it spelled out. All of them must have speculated on the possibility already. It came with the job.

"About an hour ago," Porter continued, "I came off a lengthy teleconference with Deputy Commissioner Trusk and heads of all Australian taskforce branches, including New Zealand, on possible negative reaction to the Hacker disclosure. He conducted individual sessions with our Pacific Island colleagues and briefed Prime Minister Elena Griffin. I'll not be surprised if she gets a call from the Australian Master Keeper, or even the US Grand Master.

"Despite Senior Constable Young's dire warning, nobody expects riots, mass marches, or general unrest. Gatherings will be broken up and the organizers arrested. We cannot stop protests altogether, but we can confine them to small groups. It will take the public a few days to digest the leaked data and decide what effect if any it might have on them. The same cannot be said for the National Rally Party, or even the Greens. They will no doubt twist the Hacker leak to push the energy vampire theme to the fullest. Griffin will be on TV this evening with a statement designed to maintain general calm. If commercial channels deny these groups a pulpit to air their propaganda—the Prime Minister will talk to the networks—the government expects the public to remain calm. What we anticipate is demand for accelerated action to produce a pill that stops sudden old age death. Unless somebody comes up with one soon, public patience might deteriorate to a point of active unrest nobody will be able to control."

Porter looked at each of them in turn. "If you haven't already worked it out, I'll tell you. For researchers to develop such a pill, they badly need live feeders. You'd think after seventy-six years they'd have one, but genetics is complicated and you mess with it at your own risk.

"Each of you will continue to work your cases, but with one additional caveat. If you suspect the person or persons you're investigating is a feeder or Keeper, you're to arrest them and hand them over to the Southbank forensics facility. You, not the state police! Where sufficient evidence is obtained, the detainee will be subjected to a full regimen of testing. If you have informers on the street, squeeze them. Warned, your suspects might flee, so act quickly. That clear?"

Everybody exchanged concerned glances.

Porter lifted a hand. "I know what you're thinking. We're about to walk the dark side where law doesn't exist. Something as police officers we swore not to do. The updated Crimes Act 1914 gives us limited legal authority to detain suspects for twenty-four hours without charge. To overcome this limitation, the Prime Minister has activated Article 4 of the International Covenant on Civil and Political Rights, and we'll be able to hold them almost indefinitely. The news should be on all the media by now."

"That's a fig leaf, Kurt, and you know it," Randal Young retorted with a snort.

"It will do until the government enacts specific legislation. I'm told there's a bill in a drawer waiting for a trigger to pass it. Well, they've got their trigger. The PM has recalled Parliament for a special sitting and the government will table the legislation in the House on Monday. With Coalition support, it should sail through the Senate without debate. By Tuesday, we'll have more than Mr. Young's fig leaf."

"The High Court may deem such legislation unconstitutional," Simone observed.

"This is not a debate!" Porter snapped. "Our mandate to date covered arrest of rogue feeders and Covenant assassins. It's now expanded to include capture and detention of any and every feeder for reasons I outlined. If that's not clear to you, remember one thing. Police forces protect the public and apprehend criminals under enacted legislation. In a rapidly changing world, legislation doesn't always cover everything, and politicians are forced to play catchup. We face such a scenario now. Lawyers can argue how we do our job all they want. The ordinary person on the street won't give a crap. He wants the government to get that pill for him. Everybody on the globe wants it. Keep that in mind before you gallop off in moral indignation."

Nadala felt she needed to make a stand.

"The country will tread very dangerous ground, Kurt. Today, it's feeders. What about tomorrow? Do we arrest someone for driving twenty kilometers over the speed limit and experiment on him? The idea that I can apprehend somebody on personal suspicion in the name of greater public good is a violation of our oath as police officers. We'll be joining China, Russia, and other authoritarian regimes. Is that what the Prime Minister wants for Australia?"

Porter pursed his mouth and glared at her. He looked totally weary, and she suspected the teleconference he attended probably addressed those same concerns. Right then, she felt a little sorry for him. Can she in good conscience continue to execute her duties as a Taskforce officer?

"What the Prime Minister wants, Detective, is that damn pill! If you still have a problem, take solace in the fact that you're not the final arbiter to what happens when you detain a suspect. Checks and balances exist to prevent abuse of your authority…me. You don't arrest someone merely because he or she happened to piss you off for some reason, or we'd hold half the country in detention. You must have reasonable suspicion supported by a chain of activities conducted by a suspect.

"The entire world faces a potential social crisis if we don't handle this properly. You and everyone here is in a position to help ameliorate such a crisis. If you cannot work under the parameters I gave you, I'll accept your resignation, not only from the Taskforce, but as a police officer. You're either part of the solution or a problem. Right now, I have all the problems I can handle. That clear?"

Nadala felt the force of Porter's stare and wondered what went on in his mind. Did he walk a moral and ethical tightrope? To command, he must project confidence and authority, even when things may go against the grain. Canberra may enact legislation to protect Taskforce Crimson's activities, but the fig leaf Young mentioned still applied.

He turned abruptly and walked quickly toward his office.

Randal Young sighed. "Okay, boys and girls. Who's walking?"

Simone Washnik fisted him in the ribs. "I thought you'd be the first to head for the door."

He raised both eyebrows in mock surprise. "Me? You always misunderstood me, my dear. Porter is a hardass, but he's right when he said we have a job to do, and I want to be part of the solution. I've got a case to run, and the feeder I've got my eye on has an appointment at Southbank." He gave everybody a nasty grin. "What about the rest of you? Are you players?" He pushed past Nadala and headed for the kitchenette.

Simone shrugged. "I also have a case, but I'm not going to be on it today. If my suspect makes a run for it, so be it. Porter can shove it. It's Saturday, for Chrissake! Protests or no protests, I've got things to do at home. The world won't collapse if I'm not chasing feeders. I'll see you guys on Monday." She gave a perfunctory wave and walked toward the door.

Nadala recalled that Lenny the Finger identified two rogue feeders, but Porter did not bring them in due to lack of sufficient verifiable evidence. Under the new mandate, she'd take a fresh look at both. She made a decision.

"I'm sticking," she declared with resolve. "Project Purple and its taskforces are the only things that can maintain peace in the face of potential public upheaval. As a police officer, I swore to uphold that peace, and I intend to fulfill it. Right now, we'll be straying into territory where questionable law applies, but as Kurt said, we'll know more on Monday. Until then, I'll do my duty as necessary."

"And so will I," the seasoned Neil Ferris announced in a deep voice. The heavyset bald man looked like a banker, not a former Special Forces lieutenant. "Keep one thing in mind, everybody. When we joined up, Porter told us what this taskforce did without qualification or holding anything back. Nothing has changed except to work more quickly. He needs us to do our job, simple as that."

"My, you even talk like him," Prada chided, which raised several smiles.

"Shove it," Ferris growled at her.

Nadala gulped down the remains of her cold tea. "I'll moralize at home with a glass of Riesling. Right now, I have a case file to review."

She walked to her desk and logged on. On the bottom right corner of the screen, it said 10:21 AM. Definitely too late for a beach outing.

Hram!

She completely forgot about him and their dinner appointment, and the realization sent her into panic. Under Porter's new mandate, she should arrest Frank immediately. She had sufficient circumstantial evidence to do it. Sufficient to warrant arrest? Ordinarily, she would not even bother with such a flimsy case.

Why did that man make her heart flutter and her insides melt whenever she thought of him? He managed to snare her somehow and she could not pull away, or wanted to. After Leo, did she fear committing herself to someone else? Someone who might be a Keeper? It wasn't fair, she decided. Everybody would live happily ever after if it were not for rogue feeders.

How messed up could she be?

Be part of the solution, Porter told them. If researchers needed feeders, get them. What could be more straightforward? She studied feeder genetics as he suggested, but most of the highly technical material simply did not register. Nadala lacked the necessary background training to understand the difficulties researchers faced. Several trials on feeders to suppress disruption of a victim's epigenetic clock mechanism showed promise. Tampering with poorly understood genetic switches inherently dangerous as Porter said, old age victims and feeders often suffered gruesome death.

Some institutions pursued an intermediate line of research. Instead of suppressing the onset of sudden old age, they sought to slow it down. Better several months or even a few years of life than death within four or five days. Not a solution, but it would take pressure off research programs to develop something permanent. Understandably, governments found this politically unacceptable. How do they tell someone you have a few months to live, but you'll die anyway? It merely deferred the problem and placed terminal victims and families through months of emotional torture, with eventual death as the only release.

Nadala decided to visit the Southbank facility and have Professor Zimmer or somebody fill gaps in her knowledge. She planned to visit the facility during the week to see what they did, but events sabotaged her time.

She understood why people would turn on feeders as the cause of their misery and hunt them to extinction…if they could find them. Better to destroy every suspected feeder than let a vampire loose among them. An easy fix for all the social ills, and a swift slide into chaos.

She went to Porter to voice a hypothesis. On that basis, she arranged a black ops team to install surveillance equipment in Frank's office and apartment. Had they done it? Probably not. She only made the request yesterday. Call them off? And tell Porter what? Forget Mr. Hram because she became emotionally involved with a suspect? She could vividly picture his reaction to such a revelation. Goodbye police career.

In hindsight, she should not have told Porter anything without some verifiable evidence to back up her allegation. She linked dots in a pattern of behavior any detective would say were entirely random, and convinced herself Frank killed Mercer because she wanted to impress Porter. Could she condemn the man to possible horrid medical examination and testing based on a flight of overheated imagination?

Be a detective and go back to fundamentals, she told herself.

Motive, means, and opportunity. Primary markers any good investigator should establish before arresting a suspect. Did any of them apply to Frank?

Motive…Frank wanted to exact revenge for what Kaneel did to Poole, if he suspected her to be a rogue feeder. Then again, revenge might be too strong. They just met twice. Everything she read about the Covenant said they authorized terminal sanctions only after rehabilitation failed. Nothing suggested they attempted rehabilitation with Kaneel…to her knowledge. Perhaps Poole happened to be the trigger that warranted her death and Frank volunteered to be the executioner.

As for means, if Frank was a Keeper, he certainly had the means to kill Mercer during their one-night stand, which also gave her opportunity.

Logical, consistent, and useless! A wobbly stack of unsubstantiated suppositions. Follow your instincts, Prada said.

She believed Frank Hram represented a pivotal point in Mercer's death. If he did kill her by inducing sudden aging, he could never be prosecuted even if the government enacted legislation to enable the courts to act. Every prosecution must prove guilt beyond reasonable doubt based on tangible evidence, which she did not have. Why then did she subject him to surveillance?

She found herself in a vicious circle with no way out.

Should she confront him over their dinner date? He would probably laugh at her, and rightly so. End of a possible relationship, something she badly wanted to continue, which left her with an unpalatable option—arrest him and let the Southbank boffins work on him.

First, pick up Lenny's rogues. They were nothing to her, even though something to their wife, family, and friends. It made it easier for her to simply think of them as anonymous faces. Afterward, a talk with somebody at Southbank. *With Frank, wait for a surveillance report before doing anything*, she told herself.

Nadala opened Lenny's case file and scrolled through the report until she came to the names of two feeders he claimed he identified. She lifted the phone and punched in the number for the Criminal Investigation Unit duty desk.

"Sergeant Dansk," a crisp, businesslike voice answered roughly.

"Detective Sergeant Robinson, Taskforce Crimson."

"Ah, the people all over the news. I often wondered what really went on at the eleventh floor."

"Now you know."

"What can I do for you, Detective?"

"Please send a squad car to 26 Page Street, Middle Park, arrest Mr. Frederick Goldsmith, and transport him to the Southbank forensics lab."

"Is he a rogue feeder?"

"Only a person of interest, Sergeant."

"If you say so. Anything else?"

"I need a car to take me to St. Kilda."

"Front entrance, ten minutes."

"Thank you."

"Any time, Detective. The sooner we wrap up these vermin the better," Dansk growled and hung up.

She stared at the receiver. The news only hours old, it disturbed her that a social rift had already opened. If others shared Dansk's hard attitude, there might be serious trouble, glad that only the Taskforce can authorize an arrest, but would he and others like him obey the decree?

After a moment of reflection, she pressed a glowing direct line button.

"Victorian Institute of Forensic Medicine. Marjorie speaking. How can I help you?" a pleasant female voice answered.

"This is Detective Robinson—"

"Hi, Nadala! I don't have to ask why you're at your office. Most of our team are also in."

Nadala never met the effervescent receptionist, but they chatted a couple of times, and the woman's bubbling personality always gave her a lift.

"The reason I'm calling, sometime this morning a squad car will bring in Frederick Goldsmith. If he's in, please let Professor Zimmer know."

"He's in, but Dr. Bayer handles routine inductions."

"I'll be coming in with another potential feeder. By the way, Goldsmith may be a rogue."

"I sense things are likely to become busy around here," Marg said and chuckled good-naturedly. "Until then." She hung up and Nadala smiled, looking forward to meeting her in person.

She logged off, shouldered her bag, and strode out without looking at any of her colleagues. A squad car waited at the front. Seeing her, the uniformed constable in the passenger seat got out and opened the rear door. Not used to such courtesy, she nodded to him.

"Detective Robinson?"

"That's right." She got in and clipped on the seatbelt. "Fourteen Mitchell Street, St. Kilda, please."

Although busy, traffic flowed easily along Kings Way. As the car sped past the Albert Park Lake, she caught snatches of Port Phillip Bay on her right. A container ship crawled slowly toward the Heads that led to the open ocean. A warm, sunny day, she wanted to be on the beach, not chasing feeders. The two officers up front noted her solemn expression and remained silent. Not in a talkative mood, she kept her eyes on the passing scenery.

She made numerous arrests during her career, but a first for a feeder. Not exactly criminals, society decided they should be treated as such, and worse. It did not feel right, regardless of her duty. Duty…a shield that hid many wrongs. She pushed back her lurking misgivings and watched the scenery.

The squad car entered the bare Mitchell Street and stopped behind a blue Camry in front of a beige brick house, red tin roof, and two large evergreen bushes in a tiny front yard. The lots here did not usually have room for a garage, which left the street packed with cars on both sides.

"Come with me," Nadala told the two constables, strode to the red front door, and pressed the entrance button.

The bell tinkled and she heard a patter of small feet. The door opened and a little girl, perhaps five or six, long black hair tied into two ponytails, peered at her, round cherubic face set in a frown. Her pink shorts and white T-shirt smudged, she looked adorable.

"Daddy! Someone's at the door!"

"Tindel! I told you never to open the door by yourself!" a stern voice came from inside.

The little girl gave Nadala a conspiratorial smile. "Daddy always shouts at me when I do it."

A young man of average height in black trousers and collarless shirt appeared and suddenly froze when he saw the constables. He lost all color and tensed.

"Mr. Homer Woods?" Nadala asked more stiffly than she intended, her insides unexpectedly churning.

"Yes?"

"You're under arrest under Criminal Act 1914 on suspicion of being a feeder." She glanced at one of the constables and nodded. The cop pulled out a set of cuffs and strode briskly toward Woods.

Round-eyed, mouth open in surprise, Tindel suddenly screamed, wrapped her small arms around her dad's waist, and began to sob uncontrollably.

"Don't hurt my daddy! Don't hurt my daddy!"

Face tragic, Woods glanced at Nadala, and crouched before his daughter. He gently wiped her cheeks and smiled wanly.

"It's all right, grub. They're not going to hurt me."

"They're going to take you away, Daddy! I just know it," Tindel wailed and clutched her dad's neck.

Woods gathered her into his arms and held her tight. "Shh, it's all right."

The sight of the little girl sobbing brokenly, looking so much like Valerie, Nadala felt something squeeze her chest and her resolve crumbled. This man might be a feeder, but his little girl did not deserve to see her father dragged away in cuffs. Nobody deserved it, unless he wantonly killed, and she did not know if this man killed. He did not look like a killer, but then, how is a killer supposed to look? She turned to the constable with the cuffs and jerked her head at the squad car.

"Wait for me," she ordered curtly.

The two cops exchanged glances and walked off.

She squatted and stroked Tindel's head. "Look at me," she cooed softly.

The girl sniffed, eyes large and tragic, swimming in shining tears, and waited.

"I won't hurt your daddy. Promise. We need to talk a little, that's all."

"Is that a promise?"

"Cross my heart."

"And hope to die?"

"And hope to die."

Woods kissed his daughter's cheek and patted her shoulder. "Go inside, okay?"

"They won't take you?"

"I promised," Nadala told her and stood up.

Uncertain, Tindel let go of her father's neck and slowly walked into the house, glancing back every few steps, fearing betrayal. Woods rose and swallowed hard.

"Thanks for making this easier on her."

Nadala stood and searched his face, wondering what he did in his life. Lenny's file did not say anything about the two feeders he snitched on. "Are you alone?"

"My wife's out shopping. Before you say anything, Detective, I know why you're here. I always knew that sooner or later somebody would come knocking. After watching the news, I realized my time had come, but I didn't expect it this quickly."

"Did you frequent the Kitten Club on Fitzroy Street?"

Woods' face contorted with anger. "So, that bastard Lenny the Finger ratted on me. I heard somebody shot him. Well, it couldn't have happened to a nicer guy. To answer your question, I did go to the Club from time to time. I also picked up women in bars, but I never killed. Never!"

"Does your wife know?"

Woods nodded. "It's not something I could hide, or wanted to. She tries to satisfy me, and most of the time it works, but every four or five months, I must feed more strongly. That's why I pick up women and escorts, and she knows. It's merely fulfilling a biological urge, Detective, although I don't know why. I love my wife desperately and never cheated on her. Although what I must do can be interpreted as cheating. It's complicated," he said and gave a long sigh. "What now?"

Before her stood an ordinary man and she saw a side of feeder's life she never considered before. An individual who struggled with a compulsion to draw energy from someone to survive while trying to have a normal existence, one eye over his shoulder waiting for the cops. How did Woods bear the never-ending pressure and remain sane and functioning? Did he deserve what Zimmer's people would do to him? Rogue feeders must be exterminated, but should the same net snag an innocent like Woods?

Nadala bit her lip and crossed the line between duty, self-respect, and social decency. She had to live with herself.

"I won't arrest you, Mr. Woods. Go to your little girl," she whispered hoarsely.

He gaped at her. "You're letting me go? Why?"

She gave him a long look. "Let's say I want to see a little justice done and leave it at that."

"What about tomorrow and the day after?"

"Nobody will come after you. My report will say it's a case of mistaken identity, but if you ever kill, I'll come after you, and I'll shoot you."

His eyes expressed more gratitude than mere words could say. "Thank you, Detective," he managed to whisper. "You gave me back my life, and there is nothing I can give you in return."

Nadala smiled fleetingly. "Your girl already gave it to me. Goodbye, Mr. Woods." She turned and hurried toward the squad car.

"Tindel! Come and say bye to the nice lady," she heard Woods call out, paused, and looked back.

The little girl ran out, hesitated, and slowly walked toward her, worrying the bottom of her T-shirt.

"Take care of your daddy," Nadala told her warmly.

Tindel beamed and suddenly hugged her. Surprised, Nadala wrapped her arms around her and squeezed. She let go and pushed away a lock of wayward hair from the girl's forehead.

"Bye."

"Bye," Tindel said with a flutter of tiny fingers.

Nadala opened the rear door and buckled up. "Let's go."

"What was all that about?" the driver demanded gruffly.

"Mistaken identity," she snapped. "Take me to the Southbank forensics lab."

"You're the man, Sergeant."

As the car pulled away, she saw Woods standing in the doorway, Tindel clutching his hip. Something warm flowed through her and she felt a rush of enormous satisfaction. She may have crossed an invisible line of duty, but some things cannot be reduced to blind obedience to orders. Possible repercussions? Probably none. She'd update Lenny's file, close the case on

Woods, and give him his life. As for Frederick Goldsmith, she wanted to see his brain peeled.

A short trip to Southbank beside the Yarra River, the driver stopped at the Institute's glittering glass entrance, and Nadala climbed out. She announced herself at the large curved reception desk, and the small brunette sitting there beamed.

"I finally get to meet the voice behind the phone. I'm Marg. Goldsmith isn't here yet, and Professor Zimmer is able to see you. Wait, I'll page his office." She spoke quickly into the phone and looked up. "He'll be out in a minute. Isn't it awful what happened with Hacker? And people are already protesting."

"I hope it remains only protests," Nadala remarked, taken in by the woman's bubbling character.

A middle-aged man in a dark pinstripe suit strode into the cavernous foyer, saw her, and lifted a hand. Black hair, temples touched with frost, he carried his medium height with authority borne of heavy responsibility. A small goatee covered a square chin. Not classically handsome, but attractive enough, she observed. Not her type, though.

"You must be Detective Robinson. I'm Professor Zimmer, head of Taskforce Crimson's forensics team."

His clasp firm and dry, she nodded. "Thank you for seeing me, sir."

"Just Victor. We don't get many of your people here, except for Prada Vishnu. She comes in for an occasional chat. Come with me."

Prada visited? Nadala found this tidbit of information interesting without attaching any significance to it.

She hurried after Zimmer as he marched down a brightly lit corridor, paused at a veneered wooden door, and strode in. Inside, he dragged a black cloth ergonomic chair closer to his desk and waved a hand.

"Make yourself comfortable. Coffee or tea?" he offered and sat behind a large executive desk cluttered with open files and loose papers. Behind him, a ceiling-high plate window showed the city's jagged skyline. Thrown together in apparent disarray, magazines, books, and folders filled a tall bookshelf on her right.

She shifted in her seat and shook her head. "Thank you, but I'm fine."

Zimmer leaned back and steepled the tips of his fingers. "You're new to the Taskforce." He made it a statement, his small black eyes giving her total attention.

"It shows?"

He grinned. "Every new recruit comes to look us over and check out what we do here. After a couple of visits, the novelty wears off and we don't see them anymore."

"Except for Detective Vishnu."

"She's gifted with an inquiring and perceptive mind." He tilted his head. "I sense you might be cast from the same mold."

Nadala allowed herself a small smile. "Should I be flattered or worried?"

He laughed. "Simply making a clinical observation. Now, what can I do for you? A tour of our facility?"

"I'd like that, but first—"

"After decades of research, you want to know why we're still groping in the dark."

"Something like that. With the Hacker Anonymous disclosure—"

"My lab, and eight other centers around the world, will be under increased pressure to produce a magic bullet to reverse sudden aging. Perhaps a good thing, as some of my fellow researchers are too preoccupied with the science rather than focusing on the cure. However, there *is* a cure of sorts. Several in fact."

She raised an eyebrow. "Against sudden old age death?"

"Project Purple is currently running a number of clinical trials with normal and feeder subjects. Normal somewhat relative, because in a very real sense, we're all feeders."

"Yes, I got that from my briefs."

"In most of us, our libido operates within a socially accepted behavioral spectrum. In rogues, the hypothalamus and pituitary gland, helped along by an unknown number of intermediary genes, become overactive. For most feeders, sexual expression is a controlled need. In rogues, they deliberately use their stimulated libido to induce death. Before you ask why feeders must draw energy from someone's bioelectromagnetic field, nobody knows, as there is no apparent evolutionary survival value. Something for social scientists and paleoanthropologists to gnaw on. We also don't understand the mechanism feeders employ to link with a person's field, manipulate it, and control how much energy they draw without triggering onset of sudden aging. There are teams looking into these things, but we're a long way from discovering biological drivers behind them."

"If there's a cure—"

Zimmer shook his head. "Far from marketable, there are nevertheless several promising lines of research. To answer your initial question, it's only within the last eight years or so that technology gave us the hardware tools to manipulate genes, turn them on and off and watch what happens, and build tailored DNA strands. Various MRI and CT scanners enable us to watch in real-time what goes on in a human body, something researchers could only dream of twenty years ago. It's a far cry from observing gene functions in situ, but we're getting there. We finally have sophisticated software to analyze test results and build models in a virtual environment without having to work with live cells. Eventually, of course, we need actual subjects to validate theoretical hypotheses, something I hope your taskforce and taskforces elsewhere will provide. It's one thing to manipulate genes in a petri dish and run scans, we must see what works and what doesn't in an interconnected human physiological package."

"This must have used up a lot of test subjects along the way," she observed candidly, her stomach rebelling at the conjured images, and he nodded.

"And we'll be using up lots more. Naturally, we don't do everything here. The task is simply too complex for any one facility. Our focus, and the focus of our sister facility in Sydney, is pathology, genetics, hematology, and microbiology, but we sometimes send subjects to the Monash Health Translation Precinct for endocrinology testing. Johns Hopkins' Center on Aging and Health concentrate on geriatric effects, while the University of Cambridge in England are looking at epigenetics and immunology. The Bayer Group in Germany are developing drugs. There is a degree of overlap among the nine research centers, the entire program coordinated by the CDC in Atlanta."

"I wondered how everybody avoided stepping on each other's feet," Nadala mused, and Zimmer smiled.

"It gets complicated sometimes, and CDC had to knock heads when some of my colleagues got too possessive about their work." He took a deep breath and sat back. "You're now thinking, what is our authority that allows us to conduct experiments on someone that often prove fatal?"

"A quandary I struggled with since joining the Taskforce, Professor."

"No doubt. We use volunteers—"

She gaped at him in disbelief. "You mean people actually volunteer to be experimented on?"

"It's not a perfect world out there, Detective. Many struggle to make do, and we pay them well."

"To die!" Nadala snapped, and immediately winced in contrition. "I'm sorry, Professor—"

Zimmer lifted a hand. "No need to apologize. I would be judgmental as well."

"Where else do you get your subjects?"

"Terminal patients with the usual signed waivers, inmates on death row where capital punishment is practiced, and genuine rogues, of course, with normal feeders and ordinary subjects as controls. Some authoritarian regimes who aren't fussy about legality experiment on brains obtained from traffic accident victims, deceased hospital patients, and…" Zimmer gave her a probing look, "children of all ages, including babies. We obtained valuable data from them. I'm not a hypocrite, Detective. The world faces a grave threat from rogue feeders. Largely psychological than actual, as worldwide incidents of sudden old age deaths is a fraction of daily car fatalities. A threat likely to become exaggerated by the Hacker disclosure and far-right groups."

She did not want to engage in a prolonged discussion in morality and ethics, understanding the problem all too clearly. Still, the notion that Project Purple, with tacit government approval, used a segment of human beings for what amounted to uncontrolled experimentation did not sit well. The image of someone dissecting a baby's brain made her want to puke.

"Do any Western research centers experiment on children?"

"What we do sounds abhorrent, but it's a price society is paying willingly to cure sudden old age death. Let me add this. Western judicial systems don't recognize feeders. With the secrecy lid lifted, that will undoubtedly change when legislation is enacted to tell courts and law enforcement organs how to deal with them, especially rogues. In my opinion, they forfeited their life by intentionally taking someone else's. I have no moral qualms using up such a person, and I hope whatever legislation the Australian government passes will not go soft on those killers."

Nadala sighed and shook her head. "I'm sorry I came. Tell me something. How far have you progressed to categorize genes in the pituitary gland and the hypothalamus specific to feeders?"

"There are a number of candidates, but we don't understand how they operate, not entirely. If the pituitary and the hypothalamus were the only responsible organs, we'd already have our cure. Our genetic blueprint consists of 3.42 billion nucleotides packaged in twenty-three pairs of chromosomes. Only about two percent of our DNA codes for proteins to catalyze chemical reactions within cells necessary for their function.

"Early in the genome project, Dr. Susumo Ohno coined the term 'junk DNA' to describe the 98% of our DNA under the assumption they were leftovers from our evolutionary past. We came to learn that those nucleotides form a giant switchboard that regulates all gene functions. We hardly understand the two percent we know about. You can then appreciate the daunting challenge coming to terms with the remaining percentage.

"For a long time, research everywhere centered on causal factors why feeders have an exaggerated libido, and rogue feeders especially. The DRD4 gene, commonly known as the 'thrill-seeking' gene, looked promising, but libido is controlled by a multitude of genes that produce a variety of hormones, their function still poorly understood. Research became a grind of elimination to identify specific mechanisms. With advances in genesplicing technology and software, we now have tools to pursue a number of promising treatments to block excessive sexual expression responsible for onset of sudden old age.

"We once thought to simply suppress libido in feeders by blocking production of testosterone and estrogen, and we'd have our cure. Unfortunately, those hormones play an important role in maintaining many bodily functions, and blocking them quickly leads to serious side effects. Moreover, suppression had only a marginal effect on a feeder's need to draw bioelectromagnetic energy. The feeding drive interacts with male and female libido, but is not controlled by it." Zimmer smiled and gave a small shrug. "We learn by doing.

"The other avenue is treatment of victims. This is extremely complicated, as cell aging is influenced by several systems, commonly referred to collectively as the epigenetic clock. If we could point to a set of specific genes that suddenly sends the epigenetic clock into fast forward and switch them off, we'd have your magic pill. Unfortunately, we can't, not yet anyway. Do you know anything about telomeres?"

Nadala nodded. "They came up in my research."

"They also play a vital role in cell aging. How it all works as a coordinated system within the human body is still a subject of much heated discussion and experimentation. You see, Detective, when we switch a particular gene on or off, it sets off a cascade of activation and deactivation in other genes, the process not at all clear. Right now, we're using the sledgehammer approach in the hope to stop a rogue feeder killing his victim, or stop the victim dying suddenly. The overwhelming problem we face, by the time a victim notices onset of aging, usually a day or two after a sexual episode, the process is usually irreversible. To make things even more complicated, if infected themselves, some feeders are able to reverse it, apparently voluntarily, which caused many of us to tear out our hair trying to understand how they do it."

"What we need is that morning after pill," Nadala observed wryly.

"Or the before doing it one!"

She grinned. "Any successes?"

"Some. Mostly preventing rogue feeders triggering onset of sudden aging. With victims, there is still a way to go. In normal clinical trials, we'd use thousands of volunteers to prove efficacy and eliminate undesirable side effects, done after years of laboratory testing on mice, rats, and primates. Unfortunately, mice and rats don't exhibit rogue feeder tendencies."

"A problem peculiar to homo sapiens?" she queried softly.

"It appears so."

"I thought you'd have stacks of test subjects. Research centers around the world must surely hold hundreds of feeders."

"They do, but it's difficult to conduct rigid double-blind clinical trials over necessary time periods to make the results meaningful. We also cannot use these subjects for anything else without compromising the data. In many ways, Hacker Anonymous did us a favor. We can now expect an influx of additional feeders."

"At what cost to the cohesiveness of our social fabric, Professor?"

"There is always a social price we pay for eradicating any malady, and I suspect we'll be paying a heavy one to cure sudden old age deaths. I don't allow myself to dwell on such things for too long or I'd be forced to pack a bag and live in a cave somewhere, and probably end up devoured by a wolf," he added with a chuckle. "Anything else on your mind?"

"There's something I don't understand. How do you determine if someone is a feeder?"

"Ah, I thought you'd never ask. Simple, really. We let them starve," Zimmer said, then smiled at her goggling reaction. "Not conventionally, of course—"

"You don't allow them to link with a donor."

"That's right. A feeder must normally draw energy roughly every twenty-two days. It's only an approximation, as an individual's physiology and psychological condition influences the drive to feed. They can draw bioelectromagnetic energy in a crowded environment, linking repeatedly to extract an incremental charge, but the process takes time. Eventually, they must feed through coitus. In absence of a genetic test to ascertain if someone is a feeder, we sit back and wait until the subject shows signs of physical and emotional distress."

"Then you let them feed?"

"Not always."

Nadala stared at him, appalled at an image of a human being locked in a cell screaming to feed, and not allowed to do so.

"This facility has never done that, but Mumbai regularly conducts deprivation trials. We're not intentionally cruel, Detective. Until we develop an identity test, that's all we have."

"What happens when you do allow them to feed?"

"The encounter is often terminal for the donor."

She slowly nodded. "The compulsion to draw energy overrides the self-control mechanism as the feeder sinks into a frenzy to satisfy his need."

"Exactly. For those we don't allow to feed, the subject goes into a catatonic state. Within three weeks or so, they begin to exhibit symptoms of old age. They don't die, but the debilitating effects drastically curtails the person's lifespan. In presence of a donor, the subject subconsciously links to feed and recovers, but the subject is never a hundred percent again."

Nadala frowned. "This doesn't make sense. Somebody must have observed symptoms in isolated prison inmates and conditions where someone spent a prolonged time alone."

"You're right. In such cases, clinics like mine took possession of the subject for examination, and the authorities were told to keep silent."

Her shoulders drooped. "This is horrible."

"Our work can be grisly at times, Detective, but necessary."

"What about Russia and China? What do they do?"

Zimmer shrugged. "I'd say pretty much whatever they want. Project Purple has no control over their activities, and they rarely share data, even though they get everything from us."

"It seems we cannot get away from politics."

"That's how it is, my dear. Now, how about that tour?"

Half an hour later, knowing far more than she bargained for, feeling a degree of disgust, Nadala promised Zimmer she'd call on Monday to see what they did to Frederick Goldsmith and anybody else the Taskforce brought in. Uber took her back to the Police Center.

She walked in to a deserted floor, strode to her desk, and logged on. She opened Lenny's file, made a notation against Homer Woods, and closed it. Not certain she should do this,

Nadala opened case file KZ-9362-B11, then appended a brief notation against Frank's details. Lower lip between her teeth, she retrieved the special black ops number and lifted the phone.

"Code word," the harsh voice demanded after two rings.

"Crimson."

"State your request."

"If installed, retrieve monitoring devices from Frank Hram's office and apartment, and discontinue surveillance."

"Understood."

She replaced the receiver into its cradle and gazed out the window, deep in thought. No turning back now.

If Porter asked why she closed the Hram case, she had a perfect response: lack of admissible evidence. If Prada could do it with Mercer, a much stronger case, she could do it with Frank. *A judgment call*, she told herself, uncertain of her judgment right then.

Damn you, Frank!

Chapter Five

Nadala twitched the yellow pearl necklace to center the single black onyx just right. Onyx earrings and a black Rado completed the ensemble. A low cut white silk blouse over a stylish pleated black skirt with matching pumps showed off her long legs to best effect. She wiggled her butt and smiled, remembering fondly the few men lucky enough who caressed it.

Frank did not say to dress formal, but her last experience told her not to take any chances. In T-shirt and jeans, she'd simply sink into the ground from embarrassment if he took her to some classy restaurant. A touch of lipstick finished with a little gloss, she felt ready, determined to enjoy herself. The face in the bedroom vanity mirror nodded with satisfaction. It would do.

She walked into the lounge, the Christmas tree lit with flickering colored lights reflected off glass baubles, glittering tinsel, everything festooned with cotton wool streamers. A little over the top, she did not have the heart to stop Valerie going all-out. The little troublemaker cooed with delight when it came to put wrapped presents at the base, eyes glowing with anticipation to see what Santa brought her. As usual, the festive lunch to be held at Mom's place. Somewhat of a tradition that went back to her childhood. Before lunch, Angela would come over and let Valerie go berserk tearing wrapping off presents.

To be so carefree again, Nadala reflected wistfully.

The door clacker went off, which jerked her into reality and made her heart flutter. She switched off the decorative lights, deciding to leave the wall air-conditioner on—she did not fancy returning to a hot house—snatched the black leather purse off the coffee table, activated the small Sony voice recorder, and shoved it into the purse. As a detective, she *had* to know if he…The thought did not want to crystalize. Pursued by a nagging conscience, she hurried down a narrow corridor to the front door. One day, she planned to tear down the wall and create one open space. Another item to tick on her lengthy to-do list.

She opened the door and smiled warmly at her visitor. Frank bowed and held out a bouquet of four white roses. "For you." Decked out in a somber blue suit, black shirt, a thin maroon neck scarf, he cut quite a figure. A package she wanted to unwrap now. *Later,* she promised herself.

Without saying anything, she wrapped slim arms around his neck and kissed him. When a wave of heat coursed clear down to her toes, she broke off before deciding dinner did not really matter, and stroked his cheek.

"Thank you," she murmured huskily, took the roses and sniffed them. The clean, delicate fragrance made her breathe in deeply. "Come in while I put these in a vase."

Conscious of his presence, she strode through the lounge into the kitchen. Roses set in a tall purple ceramic vase, she placed it on the coffee table.

"Nice and cozy," he remarked as he looked around.

"A little rustic and old-fashioned, but I like it," she told him.

"Ready? Let's do this."

A polished charcoal gray Audi A8 waited at the curb, the driver standing beside the open back door. Nadala raised an eyebrow.

"Also the only thing you could get?"

He winced in apparent contrition. "I'm afraid so. Saturdays always so busy and all."

She seated herself and he slid in beside her. The car immediately pulled away and purred down the narrow street through sharp shadows cast by a bright sun. Cabled lights hung from gutters and windows on a number of houses. When night fell, the street sparkled with color. Nadala did not have any, resisting her dad's offer to put them up. She preferred things simple, not into religious things anyway. Her Christmas tree? A concession to Valerie more than anything else.

"Busy day?" Frank queried. His penetrating eyes made her feel he could read her thoughts.

"I don't have any more secrets, do I?"

"You'll always have those, doll."

"You know what I do for Taskforce Crimson." She made it a statement.

"I've seen some of the Hacker documents, Detective Robinson."

"And…"

"And what? Because you're chasing rogue feeders, I'll walk away? You can't get rid of me that easily."

"It's more than that and you know it."

His lazy smile melted her heart.

"You want to get inside the Covenant? Good luck." He shook his head. "I could hardly believe the stuff I read about them and Project Purple. To keep a lid on everything for seventy-six years…but I suppose that's not news to you."

"Let's not talk shop, okay? I want to forget the world for a few hours."

"Suits me. We'll concentrate on having fun instead."

"By the way, where are we going?"

"Heston Blumenthal at Crown Casino."

"Sounds posh."

"It is. You can't get in without a tux and a ballroom gown."

She glanced at his outfit. "Then we're both in trouble."

"If they kick us out, there's always Hungry Jack's."

Nadala laughed at the absurd image and fisted him lightly on the shoulder. He took her hand and gently stroked it, which made her tense a little despite the pleasure his touch gave her.

"I like the way sunlight shines through your hair," he told her softly.

"If you don't stop, Mr. Hram, I'll be forced to tell the driver to take me home."

He leaned toward her and brushed his lips against hers. "A delightful idea."

They crossed Queen's Bridge over the Yarra and parked under the enormous Crown complex portico behind two other cars. People moved slowly along the Southbank riverside promenade on her right. A tour bus pulled away in front of the Audi, belching diesel smoke. The driver hopped out and held open the door for her. She climbed out and nodded to him. Frank slipped him something and the driver beamed.

"Thank you, sir! Ping when you're ready to depart."

Nadala walked into the spacious foyer and slowly looked around, mouth agape. The triple-story high entrance, walls and ceiling cycling through exotic colors, opened to a grand staircase that led to the luxury hotel. A premier gambling establishment, the owners had not stinted on comforts.

Frank took her arm and guided her toward the main public casino area. She stopped and stared. Rows and rows of glittering slot machines clanging and whirring drowned out the background chatter of patrons hoping to strike it rich. The profusion of bright overhead lights made her feel she had stepped into a magical Arabian cave.

"O my gosh. I've never seen anything like it," she gushed in enthralled wonder. "I lived here all my life and it's my first visit."

"Fancy a fling at something?" Frank remarked with a smile.

"No thanks! I can throw away my money on more useful things."

"In that case…"

On the third floor, a tall, reserved woman in a maroon blouse and trousers escorted them to a window table. They were not the only guests. Nadala observed the black walls and floor with interest, square and round tables among crescent couches, marveling that such a place existed. Waiters stood behind a long bar mixing drinks. Chefs were preparing meals in a spacious, glass-walled kitchen. Split panel windows showed the Yarra and the city skyline.

"This is unreal."

"Wait until you taste the cuisine," Frank told her. "You'll never want to leave."

She tilted her head. "Are you a gambler?"

"I'm an investment consultant, which makes me a gambler by definition, but I don't frequent casinos, if that's what you mean. When I gamble, it's with my client's money. They don't like to lose, and neither do I. It can get intense sometimes when the market does something unexpected, which makes my job interesting." He peered at her. "What about you?"

"I gambled with my life every time I went out on the street. You can never tell what might come up, and incidences of violent crimes are increasing. Doesn't say much for our society."

Frank shrugged. "Melbourne is growing. More people means more crime. Were you ever shot at?"

She gave him a hard look. "I killed a man, a kid really, during a failed 7-Eleven robbery. They found $260 on him."

"Hardly worth it," he murmured.

"It wasn't. He missed, I didn't."

The attendant showed up, which broke a tense moment.

"A cocktail or something to start?" Frank prompted.

"You pick," she told him, keen to shake off an unpleasant memory.

They gave her counseling afterward, and she had largely gotten over the bad dreams, but the memory of the kid lying in a pool of blood would be with her always. For a lousy two hundred and sixty dollars, not worth it at all.

"The lady will have an Aperol Aperitivo, and I'll settle for a Mortell XO," Frank told the attendant.

"Very good." She placed black leather menu folders in front of them and departed.

Nadala opened it and her heart skipped a beat at the prices. "My goodness! This is insane."

Frank laughed. "Pick whatever appeals to you and indulge yourself. We're supposed to have fun, remember?"

"Is this how you draw women into your expensive trap?"

His face lost all expression, and she feared she opened a door meant to be closed.

"I don't bring anyone here. I used to, but not in quite a while."

"Who was she, if you don't mind me asking?"

"Rainey. Four years ago, we were engaged to be married. A week before the wedding, a truck driver ran a red light and killed her."

Contrite, she placed her hand on his. "I'm sorry, Frank."

"Memories best left in a drawer. Anyone special in your life?"

"I married one of my professors a year after I graduated from Swinburne. Deliriously happy, I thought my life complete. Then I learned he played around, and that ended it. There hasn't been anyone else since."

The attendant brought the drinks and waited quietly for their order.

Nadala opened the menu again and bit her lip. "A grilled lobster to start, please. For the main, Hereford ribeye, done medium."

"Scallops frumentry for me, and charcoaled barramundi," Frank told her. "A mixed salad for two with Italian dressing."

"Anything to drink?"

Nadala frowned over the selection. "A glass of Grgich Hills Chardonnay."

"A Sutton Grange Syrah," Frank added. "And a Gold Emotion Rose for the entrées."

"Excellent choice," the attendant declared with a flashing smile and withdrew.

Nadala gave Frank a sheepish grin. "I know you're supposed to drink red wine with red meat, but I prefer whites."

"I don't subscribe to that snobbish idea either, and I'm having a red with my fish. The people here are sophisticated and won't sneer at you for breaking a silly convention." He lifted his cognac balloon in a salute and took a sip. "To fun."

She nodded and tried the Aperol. A cascade of tastes galloped across her tongue, the slightly bitter orange and rhubarb flavors prominent.

"This is so wicked!"

"I'm glad you like it. It's available at any Dan Murphy's bottle shop."

"I must get some," she announced firmly and took another sip. "Last time Amaretto, and now this."

"One never stops exploring."

She regarded him over the rim of her glass. "You're a very easy man to be with, Frank Hram."

"I wish all my clients said that," he quipped, and she laughed, beginning to relax and genuinely enjoy herself.

"Nobody has come after you with a shotgun when you lost their money?"

"Not yet, but someone will get around to it sooner or later. Financial markets are driven by perception, not facts. The Chinese fast rail network goes bust and everybody rings their stockbroker to unload. It doesn't make any sense, but most people are sheep. Some high brainpower went into deriving a predictive formula to describe stock market movements, but the problem doesn't have a solution because you cannot quantify emotional responses or pigeonhole irrational human nature."

"What do you do?"

"Rely on historical trends and personal intuition, not always reliable. In any complex, multi-component system, failure isn't caused by a single element. There is a cascade of small break-downs that eventually leads to a major collapse. It's the same with economic and financial structures. My job is to spot minor down-turns and tremors, and take preemptive action before everything falls apart."

She nodded a couple of times, impressed with his holistic out-look, realizing that financial consulting involved more than simply telling someone what stocks to buy or sell.

"Very heavy, Professor."

He lifted a finger in warning. "There'll be a test before the class breaks."

She slapped his arm. "Blockhead!"

"Your work must involve understanding human nature," he countered.

"It does, and I delved deeply into Freud, Skinner, Piaget, and several other highbrows. To tell you the truth, a lot of it sent me to sleep, but if I wanted that degree, I needed to bone up."

"And I wanted to be an astronomer."

Nadala thought she understood him. "You didn't want to be an astronomer, but an astronaut roaming the stars."

His eyes seemed to expand and she felt warm all over. The sensation faded, as did the momentary connection. Did he at-tempt to link with her bioelectromagnetic field just then?

For goodness sake, girl! Stop it!

"You're perceptive," he murmured at length. "I did want to be an astronaut. To get there, though, you need a PhD, be a pilot, an engineer, all rolled into one shrink-wrapped package. Even if you make it into the program, your chances of going into space are infinitesimal. At least with NASA, more interested in sending up probes these days than people. The manned program is a withered rump of a lost vision. I hope SpaceX will be a game changer." He tilted his head. "Do you ever regret not becoming a lawyer?"

"I like being a police officer. Actually, what I really like is enforcing the law and going after criminals. Not all of us are sugar and spice."

He guffawed. "I know what you mean, having tasted some bitter fruit."

Before she could compose a suitable rejoinder, their attendant appeared with the entrées. She filled tall flutes with sparkling rose-tinted wine and left the bottle in an ice bucket. Frank lifted his glass and Nadala followed suit. The crisp bouquet filled her nose and she took a cautious sip. Mildly dry, the light, delicate flavor permeated her mouth and left a hint of cherry aftertaste.

"Heavenly," she said and eyed the lobster.

"*Bon appétit*," Frank offered, took a sip, and studied his scallops.

The dining room slowly filled and background chatter stole into all the empty spaces. Most guests were middle-aged or elderly, able to afford such a restaurant, but she also observed several young couples. Probably courting, she figured. Like Frank courted her? The realization made her smile as she turned her full attention to the dish.

She tasted lobster perhaps twice in her life, more familiar with local freshwater crayfish, which had a similar look and taste. Nadala crunched one of the claws with stainless steel pliers and gently pried loose the delicate white flesh with a small two-pronged fork. She glanced at Frank tucking into his fried scallops and pointed at the surviving claw.

"Care to try one?"

Without saying anything, he spooned several scallops onto her plate and helped himself to the lobster. She figured his gesture probably done out of politeness. A sophisticated worldly man, he undoubtedly dined on most fine things. The realization made her feel awkward and self-conscious, uncomfortable in a setting alien to her, more used to something like Hungry Jack's.

She lifted her head and saw him looking at her, eyes soft and warm, not beneath his consideration. He managed to accumulate a measure of wealth and enjoyed the fruits of his labors without adopting an air of snobbishness from his successes. That's what his eyes told her. What really went on behind their gray façade, she could not say, hoping it might be something nice.

"Thank you," she said softly.

"For what?"

"For bringing me here…taking me out…for everything."

He reached across the table and took her hand. Something more than warmth flowed from him and she savored the sensation.

"This fancy restaurant means nothing. A place to eat like any other."

Her eyebrows arched. "I wouldn't say like any other."

His serious expression did not change. "People matter. You and I matter. What's inside us matters. You're a wondrous woman I'd like to spend my days with. A future we can have together if you're willing to share it with me."

Men propositioned her who did a very good job, but they all had one objective in mind—get her to bed—and most of the time, she played the game willingly. After Leo, she did not shy away from satisfying her needs. As a man, Frank also wanted her in bed, she could tell, but his approach had a qualitative difference that stirred her soul. He laid his feelings bare, which left him open and vulnerable. Men were supposed to be tough, ready to defend a mate in any situation, but they were not. Their veneer of toughness protected a soft, sentimental core easily bruised by rejection. With Frank, she saw a rare combination of genuine toughness, sensitivity, complexity, and something else she struggled to understand. Struggled ever since she first saw him in Blink's security footage. He projected masculine magnetism and an aura of power that drew her inexorably to him. An attraction she did not want to resist.

"I can see the words forming in your head." His deep voice created a resonance within her she found unaccountably pleasant. "He's been out with so many women before. Am I simply another one for his collection?"

Her mouth twitched. "Actually, I planned to add you to *my* collection."

"Ah, an interesting reversal of roles I hadn't considered."

She took a sip of bubbly. "Let's not rush it, okay? I'm in a complicated situation—"

"Investigating me?"

Her eyes hardened. "Since you brought it up, yes. You're involved, perhaps innocently, with Kaneel Mercer's death. I cannot dismiss you until I establish who killed her."

"You can say it. I won't be offended. Go ahead."

Her throat tightened. "I can't, because I don't believe it."

"You think I'm a feeder?"

"Given the circumstances under which you took Kaneel, I had my suspicions. Even if you're a feeder, I can't prove anything, and I don't want to. Do you understand what I'm saying and why I'm saying it? You captivated me somehow and I cannot break free. There, I've said it." She could not believe her words, the whole situation so bizarre. She only met him on Thursday, for goodness sake! He must have manipulated her. She wanted to sink into his misty gaze and lose herself forever, not wanting this moment to end.

"No shop talk, okay? We're having fun." He looked down and forked a piece of lobster. "Perfect. You must be careful not to overcook seafood, or it becomes rubber."

She sensed his desire to steer them from a path that led to emotional quicksand and nodded.

"That's me when I fry calamari. You can use them as elastic bands."

He chuckled. "In that case, our next culinary experience is at my place and I'll show you how to do calamari. Where do you buy it?"

"The supermarket."

"That's probably why they come out like rubber. Get them at the Victoria Market fish section."

Nadala peered at him. "You cook?"

"Living by myself, I cook or starve."

"This isn't a spider, fly gambit, is it?"

"I'll be a perfect gentleman."

"I must be slipping, but okay. You don't mind if I bring along my Glock semiautomatic?"

"Be my guest."

The entrée finished, she refused a refill of bubbly. Their attendant quietly removed everything and left them to enjoy the cozy ambiance. A few minutes later, she returned with the Chardonnay and Syrah, and filled fresh glasses.

Nadala touched hers to Frank's and the crystal sang to her. She took a sip of the smooth, fresh wine, and nodded.

"I could get used to this."

He grinned. "You could if you went out with me again."

"You keep a wine bar in your apartment?"

"Guilty. I can't afford to drink in restaurants all the time."

"Blockhead!"

The main course arrived and Nadala sniffed the lightly charred ribeye smothered in mushroom sauce, cooked vegetables on the side, and small slices of what she presumed was truffle. She cut a piece and chewed. Delicate tastes coursed through her mouth as the meat seemed to dissolve. She could not remember what this dish cost when she looked at the menu, some scandalous figure against it. Determined not to worry about it, she dug in with gusto, helping herself to the side salad.

"I love to see a woman who enjoys eating," Frank declared with a smile.

"Your barramundi isn't swimming away either," she retorted sharply. "Want some steak?"

"It's all yours." He pointed at his plate. "Fish?"

"Keep it."

During the meal, Nadala stole surreptitious glances at him, traced the outline of his strong jaw, the eyebrow ridge that overshadowed captivating eyes, soft lips she wanted to feel again, powerful arms holding her, never letting go. At one point, she caught him staring at her and their eyes locked.

All the romance novels she read prolonged the moment of first meeting and eventual surrender, injecting minor dramas and arguments along the way to keep readers wanting to find out how everything ends, knowing all along how it would. She imagined that's how all romantic encounters developed, but to fall for someone she barely knew broke all the rules. She knew her encounter with Frank had developed into something she did not want to shy away from. Was he a feeder? She did not care, eagerly anticipating his embrace, belonging there for all time.

"…should be exterminated on sight!" a harsh voice declared from a nearby table. For a fleeting moment, all conversation died as heads turned toward the source. The atmosphere eased as everybody resumed whatever they were doing.

Nadala put down her knife and fork, dabbed her lips, and took a sip of wine.

"It started. I thought people were better than that."

Frank shrugged. "What did you expect? There are ardent pacifists and radical haters in every social group. The vast majority sit back and wonder why this has to be and do nothing. There aren't any answers. It simply is. The one thing we all must fear is popular apathy. Extremism thrives in such environments to disrupt order and turn social structures into autocracies. Politicians of all persuasions know this well and use it to enact laws to limit our rights and freedoms under the guise of protecting us from those elements, the danger often vastly exaggerated. Once the perceived danger passes, the laws remain, and governments are happy to operate within the artificial rule of law bubble they created."

Nadala stared at him, surprised at his cynical view of the world. "You really believe Australia is heading toward an autocracy?"

"All Western-style governments are already partway there. Some are prompted into that state by external factors such as imported terrorism. Others feed the population extremist views to divide the country, allowing authoritarian grab for more power. Look at divisions in the United States, created by polarization of political and religious views. In many respects, Australia is in a similar position, not because we became polarized, but because we live in a fictional democracy. The system supposedly allows anyone to stand for election as a representative of a constituency. In reality, unless you're part of a major party machine able to back a candidate, an independent has little chance getting elected. We don't choose our candidates. We're given a list prepared by the parties, which creates an illusion of democratic choice. In turn, parties are influenced by commercial interests who don't care who sits in parliament, as long as laws aren't passed to limit corporate power and freedom to do what they want. It's the same for all religious organizations."

"You make it sound hopeless."

Frank tilted his head in the general direction of the table where the comment came. "He isn't really an extremist. He's simply uneducated or doesn't want to accept facts, preferring to believe his prejudiced position, and becomes belligerent when challenged. Did you see this afternoon's Channel 10 news?"

Nadala shook her head. "I had things to do."

"I skipped most of it, but I got enough to see sensationalism at work at the expense of informative journalism. The other two commercial channels weren't any better. Unless Prime Minister Griffin does something quickly to inject rationality, our daily news will become rallying cries for open witch hunts against feeders."

"I hope you're wrong, because the alternative will give rise to chaos everywhere."

"I'd like to be proven wrong, but history is on my side. Don't misunderstand me. Rogue feeders should suffer the full penalty of legal retribution, but an ordinary feeder trying to survive and look after his or her family doesn't deserve to be swept up in the same net."

His words resonated within her, mindful of what she did for Woods. "You paint a grim picture."

She could not argue with him, not with conviction, lacking his breadth of experience and knowledge, which prompted a disturbing thought. Once the sexual frenzy of their union ended—her skin prickled at the pleasurable prospect—would a man like him be satisfied with someone not able to match his intellectual capacity?

He gave a sheepish smile. "Sorry, I didn't mean to be serious. I forgot you don't want to talk shop."

She spent the next few minutes concentrating on food, his words echoing in her mind. Gradually, her mood lifted and she started to enjoy herself again. The restaurant's gay atmosphere helped, as did Frank's amorous glances. Finally satiated, she sighed and pushed back the plate.

"I don't think I'll eat for a week, and it's all your fault."

He blanched in mock surprise. "Mine?"

"You tempted me with wicked food, knowing I couldn't resist. So it's your fault."

He lifted both hands in surrender. "Guilty. Cuff me, officer."

"I'll let you off with a warning. Seriously, that was so good."

"The point of the exercise. Dessert?"

She patted her stomach. "Are you kidding? Nothing else will fit into this dress."

"Not to worry. Things aren't that desperate. Coffee or a liqueur? You can have both."

"Perhaps an espresso."

"Done." He lifted a finger to catch the attendant's attention. When she walked over, Nadala nodded to her.

"Thank you. A super meal."

"I'll tell the chef."

"Two espressos," Frank added as she cleared away the plates.

"Anything else?"

"A Johnny Walker Blue."

Nadala peered at him. "Do you do this often? Dine out, I mean."

"A couple of times a week. Depends on how I feel and what I'm doing. After work, I like going to a bar or club. Blink's is one of my favorites and I can chat with Walt. He's a character who's seen almost everything there. People are funny, tragic, stupid, and I like to watch their antics. I can't explain why, as I'm not usually gregarious."

"Except when you want to pick up—" Chagrined, she felt a blush suffuse her face. "I'm sorry. That slipped out."

"I don't pick up women every day, Detective."

"I said I was sorry!"

"Just pulling your leg."

"Blockhead!"

Soft orange hues melted into deep red streaks above a bloated sun as it gradually sank toward a night's embrace. Stirred into new life, buildings began to glow with inner light in response to people infecting the streets. A fairyland magic gripped the city and Nadala spent a captivating moment gazing at it.

"It's so peaceful," Frank murmured. "Almost otherworldly."

A hush fell over the dining room as others allowed their imagination to drift into sunset. The magic faded, as did the sun, and reality returned.

Their coffee arrived and she nibbled on a chocolate-covered peppermint wafer, satisfied and at peace, all doubts banished. She knew what to do, prepared to face the consequences, professional and personal.

The hard world crashed into her with harsh sounds of rushing traffic when they stepped out of the casino. The glare of headlights along the boulevard almost painful, she averted her eyes. Along Southbank, trees sparkled and twinkled with decorative Christmas lights, the riverside promenade packed with strolling masses enjoying a pleasant evening despite an occasional hot gust.

Their Uber car pulled in under the portico. The driver jumped out to open the rear door for them, and peaceful silence returned as she buckled up. Frank reached for her hand and held it, not saying anything, his gesture saying it for him. She did not look at him, sensing his eyes on her, content to bask in his closeness. A different world existed inside the car. A world that went on and on, one she did not want to end.

They stopped in front of her house, the street lit with bright festive streamers. She stepped out and Frank escorted her to the front door. Something flashed between them and he gathered her into his arms. His lips found hers and she melted against him, comforted by his strength. He pulled back and brushed lingering fingers through her hair.

"Care to come in for a nightcap?" she offered, not wanting him to leave with one stolen kiss.

He turned to the driver and nodded.

Nadala opened the door, welcoming the cool interior, flipped on the overhead light, and turned, aware of the electricity running between them. Without saying anything, she led him up the stairs to the bedroom. In the doorway, he pulled her against him. She leaned back and felt his hot breath as he nuzzled her neck and kissed the tip of her ear. The rush of sensations sent a surge of wanton desire through her, and the purse made a soft thud as it landed on the carpet. His fingers worked the buttons of her blouse, then lingered on the swell of her bra. She reached behind her, unclipped the thing and pulled it off. Warm hands cupped her tight breasts and she arched her back. Restless and eager, she turned and wrapped her arms around his neck, her mouth eagerly seeking his.

She removed her necklace and earrings, placed them on the bedside cabinet, and waited. He lifted her and laid her gently on the large bed. His body hard, clearly honed by regular exercise, he positioned himself, the foreplay ritual forgotten. He entered her gently and her arms grasped his torso.

The coupling urgent and demanding, both climaxed quickly. Then he entered her again and loved slowly in a cloud of passion without end, his mouth lingering on her face, throat, nipples, gradually moving down her belly. She squirmed and moaned when his tongue found her sensitive spot.

At a point of climax, he pulled back, then sent her peaking again until she finally screamed with unbounded pleasure when the release came. She never believed lovemaking could feel so intense. He finally rolled off her and lay back. She rested her head in the crook of his arm and her fingernails traced patterns on his broad chest.

"I'm glad you're not hairy," she reflected with a smile. "I went out with somebody once, a total rug." Her finger lingered on the bridge of his nose, lips, chin, before returning to explore his chest. She pushed herself up on one elbow and stared into his glinting eyes from the dim light coming through the curtains.

"There is something about you, Frank Hram, I cannot figure. You radiate consuming power I'm helpless to resist, not that I want to." In semi-darkness, she could say those words because he could not see the uncertainty and puzzlement on her face.

"You have that power yourself," he said at length, his strong voice vibrating through her. "I felt it when we became one."

"Are we one, Frank? Can we be one? Goodness! I've only seen you a couple of times. I don't usually—"

"I don't either."

"But—"

"I regularly go out with women? It's something I must do."

Nadala tried to make out his face, her heart hammering. "Because you're a feeder?"

"Yes."

Knowing who and what she was, he willingly laid himself open to her, and her mind reeled. She did not feel revulsion, only relief that he chose to be honest. That seemed important right then. His words damned him, though. If she wanted, he could suffer unspeakable horrors at the Southbank Forensic Institute. Instead, she felt protective, determined to shield him from whatever came.

"What's it like?"

"Nothing much to tell. A hunger I must satisfy. If I don't, I grow weak. Over time, I would start to develop symptoms of old age."

"Do you feel anything while you feed?"

"It's akin to getting a slight buzz after having a glass of wine. It's easy to connect in a crowd. I simply draw a little from everybody. Once I'm satisfied, the need recedes and I'm fine."

"What about when you're with a woman?" she asked, and felt his hand run gently down her bare back.

"Like you?"

She fisted him in the ribs. "You know what I mean."

"I experience exhilaration and profound satisfaction as energy seeps into my body. My senses become keener and my mind works faster. I feel powerful, able to do anything."

"Mmm. Did you feed when we…you know…"

"I didn't. Actually, whether you know it or not, you fed off me."

"What?"

"All women do it when the experience is especially intense. It happens when we open ourselves and touch souls. It's a corny way of putting it—"

"No, it's not," Nadala told him firmly. "I did feel a connection with you. Are we connected now?"

"We are, but I didn't force it. We both wanted it to happen."

"Can you force it?"

"I can, and I did it to attract a woman when the compulsion to feed demanded I satisfy it."

"You did it to Kaneel, didn't you?" she finally said it, hoping he understood why she needed to know.

"You must understand something, Nadala. She wantonly killed Dan. The Covenant warned her, tried to rehabilitate her, but she rejected us. As far as I know, she killed four times before. We should have terminated her then, or at least given Inspector Porter a heads-up. If we had, Dan Poole might still be alive. When I saw him last Friday, his life destroyed, I couldn't let her keep doing it."

"If you reported her, we never would have met," she told him softly and snuggled closer to him. "Why do you do it? Feed, I mean."

"I don't know. Nobody does. The Covenant researched this for a long time and hasn't come up with any answer that makes scientific sense. Lots of hypotheses around, but it's not clear what biological function feeding satisfies, or its evolutionary purpose."

"It must have some survival value or the tendency would have been bred out of us."

"One day we'll find out." He smiled and stroked her cheek. "What now?"

"What do you mean?"

"You drag out the cuffs?"

"Blockhead! I love you." She gave a long exhale, vastly relieved she said it. "This is so silly. I hardly know you." Her eyes tried to cut through the darkness to see his face. "You didn't manipulate me, did you?"

"When I first saw you on the street, I almost turned to go after you. Then you were at the office pretending concern for my welfare."

She glared at him. "You played me?"

"You subconsciously reached out and our fields touched. I knew then you liked me. That's why I asked you out, seemingly on impulse, even though you represented a serious danger for me. Danger or not, I couldn't let you go without seeing you again. Its madness, I know, but there it is."

"Are you a Keeper?" she asked on impulse.

"Not anymore. With the Hacker disclosure, we're out of a job."

"I don't want to pry, not now, did you—"

"Kill? That's been my job, Nadala. Despite our training, using a conventional weapon has become too dangerous. One mistake and we'd get caught, and it's easy to make a mistake. That's why we increasingly switched to alerting taskforces of suspect rogues rather than sanction them ourselves. Sometimes, taskforce bureaucracy takes its time to move and rogues continue to kill. To prevent loss of life, we're forced to step in."

Her head full of new revelations, she gave up trying to analyze it, not wanting to spoil the moment with him. A wave of tenderness swept through her and she hugged him hard. "Don't worry. I won't let anything happen to you."

Frank stroked her back. "A futile gesture, my dear detective. Inspector Porter will get orders to round up every suspect feeder. On Monday, Prime Minister Griffin will table legislation to give state and federal police sweeping powers of arrest and detention."

She jerked back in surprise. "How do you know all this?"

"I don't, but it's likely. Take it from me. You'll see a major curtailing of basic human rights for everybody, not only feeders."

"I can't believe Griffin intends to go that far."

"She's a politician, Nadala, her mind on the next election. She'll do whatever it takes to keep herself and her party in power, even if that means allowing open experimentation on people to cure sudden old age death."

"You conjure a grim scenario."

"We'll know on Monday."

"The Covenant has Porter's taskforce penetrated?"

"What do you think?"

Her thoughts a jumble of confusion, she did not want to ruin the night with images of mobs rampaging through streets looking for feeders or anyone else they could vent their rage on.

"Tell me something. How long can you last before you must feed?"

He looked at her in surprise. "Why do you want to know?"

"Just curious."

"It varies. After prolonged physical or psychological stress, I must feed more often. Usually, I can last about thirty-five days."

She sighed and snuggled against him. "Make love to me," she whispered with deep longing.

* * *

Frank Hram lay propped against the pillow, hands crossed on his chest. A predawn gray hue stole through the curtains. Colored lights flickered on the house guttering across the street. Fast asleep, Nadala had one arm and leg draped across him. When he tried to move, she subconsciously tightened her grip as if afraid he might disappear.

He looked down at her relaxed, peaceful face and slowly exhaled. How could he have been so stupid? He'd seen the girl twice and blabbed everything. To a federal cop, no less. *Idiot!* Nobody knew him for what he was, not his parents nor friends, and he revealed himself to a woman he hardly knew.

Around fourteen, puberty hormones raging through him, he felt the first tugs of strange hunger food could not satisfy. He did not think much about it at the time, shrugging it off as one of those things. At sixteen, Brenda, an older girl at his high school, introduced him to the wonders of sex. Already tall, muscles starting to bulge, clear features without the curse of acne, he had little trouble getting a Saturday night date. Sometimes a girl let him fondle her, but both understood it went no further. Brenda wanted more than simply fool around. With her parents away for the afternoon, they had the house to themselves.

His first sexual experience, and with a feeder!

Clumsy, nervous, eager, he hurried until his need threatened to overwhelm him as she held him in her arms, murmuring soft encouragement. He felt a stirring of something strange emanate from her as she stared deeply into his eyes. He did not understand what linking meant or how to do it. He simply felt an inexplicable bonding with her. Before his desire to draw from her peaked, she pushed him away, surprise on her face. Gently, lovingly, she steered him past the point where he could harm her, although he wanted more. Later, her cheek against his, she told him about feeders, a secret he must never reveal to anyone. Before he left, she slipped him a note with a phone number for the Ardor Helpline, saying they would help him. They saw each other at school in passing and remained friends, but she refused to sleep with him again.

Frank never forgot her, or what she did for him. Without her guidance and kindness, he could have done something dangerous.

He kept his secret, until last night. In a fog of juvenile passion, he spilled everything. He could understand if he were an inexperienced twenty-something, but to blurt it out at his age, he could not excuse no matter what.

He told Rainey, of course. She did not find him strange or repulsive, and neither did Nadala. From that first chance encounter on Spencer Street, his surprise total when she showed up at the office, he instinctively linked with her, and she linked with him. It did not make any sense, but in her, he saw a woman he wanted to make his. Could he have a meaningful relationship if he kept his secret from her, regardless of what it might cost? She wanted him, and not only for a romp in bed. Last night, she gave herself to him without reservation, prepared to be hurt if he turned out to be another predatory wolf.

Did he have to tell her, though?

He saw a touch of blue sky and the shadows fled.

Frank gently brushed back a strand of silken hair from her cheek and Nadala stirred. Her eyes fluttered open and he gazed into their green depths. She rolled onto her back and stretched like a contented cat.

"Morning," she murmured and a smile tugged the corner of her mouth.

"Morning. Sleep well?"

"Mmm. I remember dreaming about you. Naughty dreams."

"Why dream when you can have the real thing?"

She gave a tinkling laugh. "You're a wicked man. One day you'll get me into trouble."

"No need to wait, you know."

She fisted his shoulder. "Randy old goat." After a satisfied sigh, her eyes remained fixed on him. "The dessert last night? The best."

He knew exactly what she meant. "Want to go out tonight? Somewhere quiet this time. My place?"

"How about here? I'll have my Glock handy."

"It didn't save you last night."

Her smile tender, she touched his cheek. "I didn't want to be saved."

She sat up and the beige satin sheet fell away, revealing pointed breasts. Her arms went around his neck and dragged him against her. After a lingering hug, she pulled back.

He slid down and held her, not saying anything. She linked with him and he felt a bond time and distance could never break. How this wondrous woman did it to him, he could not say. Could she be another type of feeder who did not rely on sex, but used some strange sympathetic magnetism to draw men to her? Once snared, would she suck him dry like a spider, then discard his withered shell and look for another victim? He snorted at the ridiculous idea.

Her eyebrows arched. "What? Did I say something funny?"

"Nothing. A passing thought. I should be going."

"Breakfast? I make a mean bacon and egg omelet."

"I *should* replenish the energy I lost last night, but I must go."

"Why? Business?"

"I just do."

"Six-thirty tonight. You won't forget?"

"I won't forget."

Frank slid off the bed and started to pull on clothing discarded on the floor.

Wrapped in a silk nightgown, Nadala followed him downstairs to the front door. He gave her a tight hug and kissed her. Jacket over his shoulder, he made his way down the empty street. Despite the hot northerly promising a scorcher later, he wanted to walk, stretch his legs, and do some hard thinking.

What did he have now? An empty apartment, an occasional drive somewhere, thinking the trips filled a void he felt inside. When compelled to feed, a casual one-night stand satisfied his hunger, but the experience never left anything behind. He did not even remember their faces. Did they remember his? He always walked away from everybody and did not allow himself to feel or get emotionally involved. Then the fates screwed him and took Rainey away, the only thing that mattered in his life, leaving him torn and battered inside. When he stood over her open grave, he promised to never again allow another person get close and hurt him. Up to now, he kept that promise, but perhaps the price he paid for personal insulation a tad excessive.

Then Nadala walked into his life…

Loneliness gave him a shield against life's barbs, but it also deprived him of the joys and companionship having someone close to him.

His footfalls sounded loud on the lonely sidewalk. A car whispered by and left a stink of exhaust in the air, which kind of reflected his feelings. He reached the intersection, watched a tram clatter by, and dragged out his cell to call Uber. Still early, he did not wait long.

The driver threaded her way downtown through mostly empty streets, empty city, silence, the people yet to stir. Like protective arms, tall cranes leaned across new towers clawing ever higher to pierce the sky. Did anybody hear its cry of agony? Did anyone care?

Energized after repeated lovemaking, his senses sharp and alert, he should feel calm and rested, not moody and despondent. He finally found a woman he could love, and she clearly loved him. Why did he slink away instead of sharing the morning with her and simply talk? He knew so little about her, and he felt she wanted to know the raw side of what it meant to be a feeder. Yet, he left her after one fleeting kiss. What went through her head as she stood in the doorway watching him walk away?

Tempted to tell the driver to turn around, he said nothing, letting the car whisper to him.

When he dug deeper and laid everything bare, he knew why he left, not wanting to admit it to himself, preferring to bury the reason under a flimsy blanket of chores. *Damn!* He still hadn't ironed his shirts.

Shadows made the wide streets dark as the car entered downtown canyons. A lone pedestrian hurried past closed store fronts.

Farther up, a huddled figure in a dirty sleeping bag lay on the sidewalk. Something sad seemed to hang over the city yet to wake.

Unfamiliar emotions coursed through him in rambling confusion, emptiness prominent among them. For a long time now, that emptiness sheltered him in a protective cocoon and kept the world out. Kept at arm's length, it could not hurt him, and he considered himself safe—most of the time. Subconsciously, he knew it for a lie and sought bars, clubs, restaurants, and theaters to connect with others. Even then, he kept it from touching him, considering himself sophisticated, above the mundane needs of scurrying masses around him. Gradually, he allowed the emptiness and silence of his apartment to fill his world. Then he meets a woman who wants to be with him and he slinks away. He forgot how to be close to someone, satisfied with random encounters that filled his physical needs, but left his soul barren. He forgot how to let someone else be part of him, thinking himself complete in his shell.

He dug out his cell, powered up, and the red encryption dot immediately blinked, which meant he had a text message from Manuel. Not in the mood for Covenant business, he pressed a preset icon in the Contacts list.

"Nadala Robinson."

Her lyrical voice sent comforting warmth through him.

"It's me, Frank."

"Frank! Is anything the matter?"

"Nothing's wrong...and everything. I want to say I'm sorry for running out on you. I wanted—"

"Don't say anything."

"I wanted that breakfast and spend more time with you. I wanted to keep hearing your voice, but I couldn't make myself stay. It's complicated—"

"What are you afraid of, Frank?"

"I'm afraid of what I've become. You shattered my protective shell and I'm not sure I can reach out to anyone anymore."

She did not say anything for several interminable seconds that felt as though time stood still.

"Come back and we'll talk. Once you get to know me better, you may let me into your shell and it will protect both of us."

He sighed. "How about this? I'll come around at three o'clock and we can go places. Botanical Gardens perhaps, the Art Gallery or something."

She giggled. "Or something."

"If you don't feel like going anywhere, we can veg out in your lounge. Later, I'll help with dinner. How does that sound?"

"I like it better. It's supposed to be thirty-six today with a gusting northerly. Not exactly strolling weather."

"I can feel it already. It's settled, then."

"Let's veg out now," she murmured in a sultry voice, which sent his hormones bubbling.

"Keep that thought," he told her softly and cut contact.

The driver stopped in front of the Oaks building and Frank climbed out.

He set the percolator going and showered, which made him feel better. Thinking of Nadala's offer of a bacon and egg omelet, he made one, adding chopped tomatoes. The chore done, he washed up and refilled his mug in time to watch the Channel 7 8:30 news.

The intro music finished and the two presenters fixed on starched smiles.

"I'm Forbes McLean…"

"And I'm Edith Wright. Welcome to 7 Weekend Sunrise on December 17, 2023. The main points…Last night, Prime Minister Elena Griffin responded to the revelation of Project Purple and the Keepers of the Covenant."

"Chinese fighters violate Taiwan's airspace," McLean continued. *"The US 7th Fleet confronts PLAN carrier group. Quad warships stand firm exercising their right of free passage in the South China Sea."*

"The Victorian government to fast-track the rail link to Melbourne Airport," Wright added. *"Australia wins the second Ashes test by an innings and 174 runs following the collapse of the English top order batsmen. Today's weather, a blistering thirty-six Centigrade and possible late evening showers."* She shifted in her seat, face grim, and stared hard at the camera. *"The details. Yesterday morning, Australia and the world were shocked by the Hacker Anonymous revelation that an organization calling itself the Keepers of the Covenant is operating assassins to kill rogue feeders, sometimes known as energy vampires, who can induce sudden old age death in a victim. What is more disturbing, the revelation claims we're all feeders."*

McClean cleared his throat. *"We also learned that Project Purple, created in 1947 by President Truman, and its worldwide network of task-forces, worked to apprehend rogue feeders and Covenant assassins, known as Keepers. Absence of appropriate legislation left a large hole in our legal system, which allowed research institutions to secretly experiment on feeders in an effort to develop a cure for sudden old age death, which led to gross violation of citizens' rights. The government faced severe criticism for allowing Taskforce Crimson to operate virtually unrestricted since its formation in 1982 by Prime Minister Malcolm Fraser."*

"Last night, Prime Minister Griffin announced an immediate review of Taskforce Crimson's operating charter," Wright continued. *"Tomorrow, the Attorney-General will table legislation that clarifies Federal and State police force powers to arrest and detain suspected rogue feeders. With Coalition support, the government expects the Feeder Bill to pass through the House and Senate without debate. In substance, unless proven a rogue, feeders are considered citizens with all the rights, privileges, and obligations. A rogue feeder convicted of willful murder will face a maximum term of life imprisonment. Forensic laboratories will also have the right to hold a convicted rogue for testing. A special ninety-minute program will air tonight at 7:30 PM that will fully explore this startling development."*

Frank did not feel reassured at all with the proposed legislation. He recalled what he told Nadala about violation of individuals' rights.

"At 3:43 PM local Taiwan time, nine Chinese PLAAF J-20 fifth-generation stealth fighters encroached into Taiwan's Air Defense Identification Zone," McLean went on. *"A squadron of Taiwan's F-16Vs, supported by US Air Force F-35A Lightnings, intercepted the Chinese fighters and forced them to withdraw. The US Secretary of State—"*

He grabbed the remote and switched off the TV, not particularly interested in the Taiwan incursion, or how the Aussies creamed the Poms in the Test match. He had the information he wanted.

Coffee mug topped up, he leaned into the comfortable recliner. Faint traffic sounds came from outside as the city wakened to a most unusual Sunday. Yesterday, the relatively placid world people knew turned into bewilderment and uncertainty, nobody knowing what tomorrow might bring. When they woke this morning, did anything actually change? For feeders, the Prime Minister's announcement probably generated a surge of relief, knowing they can finally shed the daily veil of maintaining their existence a secret. Not right away, perhaps, but in time. Enacting a law did not erase community prejudice and irrational fear. For rogues, public exposure meant going further underground to hide their carnal excesses, which as a side benefit should drastically reduce the incidences of sudden old age deaths, at least in Western-style countries. For normals, things went on more or less unchanged.

Would public exposure prompt further protest marches by the ultra far-right agitators, demanding eradication of all feeders? Not if state governments clamped down on them. Unchecked, such social expression only served to embolden the agitators. Life cannot return to yesterday, but tomorrow need not be so dire either. Still, he expected everybody would have a nervous time for a while.

Nadala…

A federal cop and Taskforce Crimson investigator, she said she would protect him, but could she even if she closed his file? He told her why he killed Kaneel, but she had no evidence for prosecution. The conventional jobs he did like Lenny the Finger? Again, no evidence for a case. That might not stop Inspector Porter from hauling him in and have the Southbank facility work on him. Not a rogue, they could not detain him. One call to Marrick, Ward, and Thatcher and he'd be out in ten minutes. Or would he? Until the Attorney-General presented his bill, he must think in worst-case terms.

He sighed to shake the gloom and doom out of his head, looking forward to spending the afternoon, and possibly a night, with Nadala. A smile tugged the corner of his mouth at the expectation of holding her squirming body in his arms.

The phone's ringing jerked him out of his reverie, and his eyebrows climbed when he saw the flashing red encryption mode dot. He input the PIN and pressed the connect icon.

"Frank Hram. Identify."

"It's Manuel, amigo. Got you at last. I hate sharing bad news, but the feds took Sierra."

Frank felt his stomach tense as all sorts of bad images raced through his mind. "You're shitting me."

"Shitting you not. It happened yesterday evening. I called you, but your phone—"

"I had a date."

"You're supposed to be available 24/7!"

"I have a life outside the Covenant, you know."

"While you were out romancing, you could have been arrested."

"I wasn't, so let's drop it."

"Anyway, our contact said two Taskforce Crimson investigators brought Sierra to the Police Center around six o'clock. Two hours later, three men from Canberra showed up and took her away."

"How could this happen? I thought security around her made her safe."

"Normally, it should have. That's not all. They also have Charlie and Victor."

"Shit! Who stiffed us?"

"Echo."

"Echo? Bastard! I never liked the greasy weasel."

The slime made a deal with Inspector Porter for immunity from prosecution to save his bloated carcass, knowing it would destroy the Covenant's Melbourne branch and cost lives.

"He apparently came to the Center at three-thirty and spoke to Inspector Porter at length. Our contact said Porter called in a police artist who produced several identity sketches."

"Damn! They ran them through their databases and identified Sierra," Frank added in disgust.

"Not only Sierra, amigo. Me, trainers Echo met, and all you guys. No way to tell if the sketches were sufficiently detailed for a face recognition match—"

"But we're vulnerable. You sent somebody after him?"

"A full team. So far, nada. Porter probably has him stashed somewhere. Our contact only realized what went on after Porter ordered Sierra arrested. When I got the tipoff, I immediately sent out a general alert. Echo doesn't know Sierra or any of the Keepers by name, but as a former Navy counterintelligence operative, he probably has a good memory for faces. You saw the Prime Minister's TV speech last night?"

"I got a summary this morning."

"Ah, your date. Porter could charge Sierra as an accessory before and after the fact for every Keeper operation since the dawn of man, but they lack evidence for the charges to stick, and we have legal resources. Anyway, that's not what they're after."

"They want what's in her head."

"This is a major organizational fubar, but not necessarily a total disaster. As the Melbourne Master, she set operational policy, planned ops, exercised due diligence, and supervised the Victorian intelligence network. She doesn't know anybody by name, except for several close aides like me. If Porter tries to pump her, he won't get what he's hoping for."

"He'll get enough to come after you, shut down her office, and our safe houses."

"Count on it, but they won't find me."

"Sierra has access to Covenant databases. With her passwords, Porter could—"

"Won't happen. As soon as we learned he had her, we revoked all her access privileges."

"Something here doesn't smell right, Manuel. Why didn't your tipoff call Sierra and warn her?"

"I don't know, amigo."

"This isn't only about Sierra, is it? You're going to ruin my day even more."

"Until whatever legislation the Prime Minister intends to table tomorrow is enacted, Taskforce Crimson won't stop its efforts to penetrate the Covenant. If you know of a convenient hole somewhere, crawl into it for a day or so."

"I'm not running," Frank told him firmly. "If Porter wants me, he'll get me eventually. I'll take my chances with Griffin's legislation and Covenant lawyers. I can still call them, can I?"

"Of course, but why stick your neck out to be sawed off?"

"Even if Porter gets me, he can't hold me. I'm not a rogue. He'll know I killed in my role as Keeper, but without proof, he cannot charge me with anything, and I'll tell him to blow."

"It's not about prosecution, amigo! Project Purple needs experimental subjects."

"I know what they want." The wheels in Frank's head went into overdrive. "Why are you telling me all this? I don't have a genuine need-to-know."

"Ah, my dense friend, the answer should be obvious. Sierra and the Master Keeper want you to be the next Melbourne Master. She watched you for some time. With her apprehended, we urgently need a replacement."

Frank gaped in shock. "Me, a Master? After what happened yesterday, my Covenant days are over."

"There's more to the Covenant than hunting rogues. A whole hidden world."

"You're talking like you've written her off."

"She considered retirement for a while."

"Even if I entertained such a preposterous idea, I've got something more pressing on my mind than be a Master. I want Echo."

"You'll have to stand in line. Tango also wants him, and you don't tell that woman no when she's set on something."

"She can have Echo's heart, but I'll stomp on the rest of him. Text me her number and I'll talk to her."

"You'll be chasing your tail. Echo is gone."

"It's my tail. I want everything you have on him, and I mean everything since the day he hatched."

"Tango already has it."

"If your people find him first, she and I get the first shot, comprende?"

"Take care, amigo. Consider using that hole."

Contact broken, Frank stared at the cell for several long seconds before he slid it onto the coffee table. They wanted him to take Sierra's place? He burst into uncontrolled laughter. A few moments later the phone gave a ping. He opened the text message, memorized the number, wiped the text, and dialed.

"Zenola. Is that you, Manuel?"

"It's Frank. How about you and I get together and talk about Echo?"

* * *

Cup of strong black coffee in hand, Inspector Kurt Porter stared at the computer screen and the monthly summary report he should be working on. The longer he stared the less it made sense. Bureaucratic manure nobody would actually read. Like a mouse on a circular treadmill, he could not rid himself of the meaningless chore. A heavy sigh did not relieve his frustration, but wallowing in morbid introspection did not get the job done either. No use putting it off, he glanced at the phone, touched a preset number icon, and waited for Nadala Robinson to pick up. He expected so much from her and she let him down. Another disappointment.

"Morning, Kurt. What's up?"

"My office, now!" he grated and hung up. He swiveled the chair to face the ceiling-high window. A clear sky heralded what promised to be a hot one.

He did not intend to come in. Especially not this morning. About to enjoy breakfast, ready for some beach fun with Estella and the boys, a call from his surveillance ops team totally wrecked the day and upset his wife. Rather than start an argument, she left him to pick over his sausages and eggs and retired to the bedroom in a huff. The drive into the city along the mostly deserted Calder Freeway did nothing to perk up his mood. Some days were simply shitty.

He stared at the Westgate Bridge, easily describing himself as thoroughly pissed. It took very little to get him there, and he readily identified the source of his profound misery—Detective Sergeant Nadala Robinson.

The woman could have shacked up with a million men in Melbourne, but no! She did it with a damn feeder! Not just any feeder, but a Covenant Keeper she investigated! Did she know who crawled into her pants? It did not make any difference really. She broke protocol and deserved a dressing down exemplary in its severity. He never wanted women on his taskforce, but understood why they were useful. Male rogues went after females…usually.

Last night, Estella beside him, chattering away in eager anticipation, like most Australians, they watched the solemn PM give her speech. Whatever his personal feelings, he gave the woman her due. A polished presentation to reassure people the world tomorrow would not see marches, hooligans breaking store windows, police in riot gear holding back rock-throwing protesters demanding action against feeders. Everybody would wake to a Sunday little different from Sundays before. On Monday, life went on, and work went on for those not on annual leave. The Keepers of the Covenant were not the bad guys, she claimed, although they took the law into their hands to pursue rogue feeders. Instead of some secretive Big Brother, she regarded Project Purple as humanity's protectors who sought to produce a cure for sudden old age death. The bad guys were rogues who preyed on the helpless and the innocent to satisfy their sexual appetites. Face serious, body language sympathetic, Griffin promised to stamp out this dark menace lurking in their midst. No wild finger pointing at a spouse, relative, neighbor, or boss as a feeder. Leave law enforcement to duly appointed police forces.

A whole lot of PR bullshit Porter figured most people swallowed whole. Had she left it at that, he'd have gone to bed, Estella warm beside him, and slept soundly. But no, the PM waded in to announce a bill to recognize feeders under law. Given the circumstances, a predictable and necessary measure. Feeders might be different, Griffin declared, suffering under a compulsion to draw energy from their fellows science did not understand, but they were still human beings. Rogues were criminals and deserved to be punished accordingly. Until a cure for sudden old age death becomes available, she urged patience and restraint. Then came the kickers.

When her speech ended, he stomped into his study and immediately called Commissioner Trusk.

"We can only hold a suspect for three days before charging them as a rogue? That sucks."

"It's what the legislation will say, Inspector," Trusk confirmed quietly.

"How in hell does the PM and the Attorney-General expect us to prove someone induced sudden old age death? Make every person in Australia wear a bodycam and we watch them as they couple?"

Trusk actually laughed at the absurd idea, which added to Porter's annoyance.

"Sorry, Kurt. There's nothing funny about this, and I know it'll place our forensics facilities under intense pressure, but those are our new operational guidelines. The legislation aims to recognize feeders as normal citizens under law."

"I get that part, but we'll be working with both hands tied behind our back."

"Rogues will be with us in some shape or form forever, Inspector. I'm not trivializing the problem these restrictions place on us, but Project Purple and its taskforces have a broader responsibility than just finding a pill to cure onset of sudden old age, something you forgot in your cloud of indignation."

"I haven't forgotten anything. I'm simply annoyed that Griffin expects us to get results under an impossible mandate."

"Not so impossible."

"What do you mean?"

"Since Truman created Project Purple, we had seventy-six years to penetrate the Covenant. They're aware of our activities, of course, and placed roadblocks to sabotage our efforts. By going public, they've successfully diverted attention from feeders and made governments everywhere look like conspirators experimenting on innocent citizens."

"What's that got to do with the PM's legislation?"

Porter heard empty silence at the other end.

"Can I trust you, Kurt?"

"That's a fine thing to ask, Commissioner!"

"Sorry, but I could get my ass in a sling if this got out. On Monday, the PM will confirm the Covenant's worst fears. With everything out in the open, we can step up our activities, and believe me they won't like it. People out there don't give a shit about feeder rights. They want a pill for sudden old age death, and my Taskforce will do whatever it takes to help them get it. You will do whatever it takes. The Covenant wants feeders recognized under law, and they will be, but not in the way they think."

"What do you mean?"

"I'll try and get you a copy of the proposed legislation, but if you leak, I'll personally shoot you in the head. Understood?"

"Got it." Porter grinned, glad to find his faith in the Taskforce still held.

He eventually crawled into bed and Estella's embrace. They talked long into the night, both looking forward to a day at the beach.

Dawn broke, followed by a call from his ops team. No beach, Estella upset at him, and he in turn upset at everybody and everything. It did not make for an enthralling Sunday morning.

His job ruined the day for him, but nothing could upset the planned trip to Cairns in February, relishing the prospect to forget feeders, rogues, Keepers, and the rest of that crap. If only for a while. He wished he were going now, but nobody on the Taskforce could take leave until mid-January, the festive season tending to generate a spike in rogue feeder activity. Too much celebrating, too much temptation, and people suddenly died old.

In the tropical setting, he would take time to reconnect with Estella and rebuild the intimacy that somehow slipped away, and he knew why. Her job as an RMIT lecturer, him tracking down nutty rogues, often left little time for closeness and warmth. They had alone time in bed, but an occasional romp did not fill the soul like it used to. He should take her out to an opera, a symphony, expensive restaurant, or simply walk together hand in hand along one of the trails Sunbury provided. It should replenish a little of what they lost.

Accepted into the PhD program, unless he started to inject intimacy into their lives, their house might turn into something cold, a place to sleep and nothing else. The grotty part, he did it to himself. If he did not show in myriad little ways he loved and cherished her, she would find meaning in life pursuing a doctorate. He wanted to be the primary meaning in her life, but he needed to get off his butt and show her. How easily love and passion faded, turning into dull cohabitation. Porter promised himself to turn his life around, even if it cost him promotion. Nothing mattered with Estella gone.

As his eyes drifted across the Docklands landscape, he figured yesterday hadn't turned into total disaster. The gods did relent, if only a little. He had Sierra, aka Gianna Arben, the elusive Melbourne Master, and Hogan Lovell—codename Echo—the man who betrayed her to save his traitorous hide. Worth two red stars in his report book from Trusk. Porter pumped him dry, then ordered Neil Ferris take him to the Southbank facility for a full course of treatment, ignoring the man's voluble protests of indignation.

The identity sketches not entirely accurate, Clearview produced eighteen possible photo IDs. Far more people than Lovell had contact with. An inconvenience, but not a problem. He told Prada to send all relevant details to everybody with an order to bring them to the Southbank facility where Lovell would proof their identity.

Apart from Lovell, the effort snagged two Keepers. He expected others to be apprehended in due time. As for Foxtrot, aka Frank Hram, he had something special in mind. Lovell also provided a lead to Arben's right hand man, Manuel de la Kass. A valuable catch, if he could find him. According to Prada, the man disappeared.

Instead of dragging his frustration all over the place, he should be pleased he cracked the Covenant's Melbourne operation. Instead, he kept wondering how de la Kass knew that Lovell betrayed them? Only Ferris, Young, and Vishnu were on the floor when Lovell showed up. Did one of them tip off de la Kass? If so, why not Arben? Yet they had her, not that he complained. Something did not add up here. Time to look more closely at his three investigators. Too bad he could not check their encrypted cellphones for recent activity. He reminded himself to call his special ops team and have them sift through Ferris, Young, and Vishnu's records—after he dealt with Nadala.

Porter logged on again—the computer shut him out after ten minutes of inactivity—opened his monthly summary report and began to update salient details at hand, his heart not on work. If he didn't do it, Trusk and his busybodies would be all over him. The team's weekly reports not due until tomorrow, the report had gaps. Anyway, he didn't need to send in the cursed thing until Friday. If it were not for the never-ending administrative chores, he could actually like his job, mostly.

The cursor blinked behind the last word he'd written, waiting for more. He started at the screen, then exited Word with a growl of disgust.

He heaved himself out of the chair and went to the kitchenette for a refill. On the way back, he paused and glanced around the empty floor, the silent workstations, and hanging Christmas decorations that produced no cheer. He should not have come in. Robinson's problem could wait until tomorrow, but he wanted to chew out her ass for being stupid.

Flowers and dinner somewhere with Estella tonight? A small thing, but it might mean a lot to her. It might mean a lot to him as well.

A couple of thirsty slurps, he placed the cup on the desk and glared at the computer screen. About to open the expenses spreadsheet—the twitchy little bean counters always gave him a hard time over what he and his people spent—a knock interrupted his train of bad wishes on all accountants. No Christmas present for them!

"Come!"

Robinson walked in, handbag slung from her left shoulder. Short ash-blonde hair framed a puzzled expression. His plans for the day in the dumpster, he thought it only appropriate that he ruin hers.

"Morning, Kurt. Am I the only one in?"

"Sit down, Detective. This isn't a team meeting."

A look of concern crossed her face as she sat in the visitor chair and crossed her legs.

"I went over your case files yesterday. You've done well in the short time on the team, but that's what I expected from you."

"Thank you."

"I gather you're still floundering with the Lenny the Finger hit." He made it a statement.

"I'll close it as unsolved."

"I see."

"I did bring in one possible rogue Lenny identified."

"One Frederick Goldsmith, but you left off Homer Woods."

Robinson shrugged. "A man cheating on his wife. Lenny probably reported him as a feeder to ingratiate himself to you."

"It's been done before." Porter crossed his arms on the desk and leaned forward to pin her with his eyes. "I'm told you canceled surveillance on Frank Hram. Why, Detective?"

"Nothing there, Kurt. When I sifted through the events, I realized I had no case. Everything that links him to Kaneel Mercer is circumstantial."

"Indeed?" He lifted his cellphone and showed her a picture. "Florentino Grill, very nice." A cold frown on his face, he displayed another picture. "Last night, Crown Casino, followed by an interesting time at your place. Your Mr. Hram knows what he wants and goes for it."

Robinson lost all color. After a second, her cheeks turned bright red, not in consternation, but anger. Regardless of her sins account, he liked his investigators spunky. It would not stop him from chewing her out, though.

"You had me followed?"

"Of course I had you followed! It's not the first time a young and impressionable investigator fell for a smooth-talking suspect, and Frank Hram appears to be very smooth. He played you, Detective!"

"What if I did go out with him? So what?"

"So what? Did you lose all your objectivity? You trusted your instincts that he might be a feeder, even a Keeper, and placed him under surveillance. Yesterday, you suddenly called off the team. Can't you see what's happening here, Nadala? Hram manipulated your emotions to make you like him and ignited a spark of romance to deflect you from your investigation, and you fell for it."

"I admit a certain attraction existed between us when I met him on Thursday, but he did not manipulate me."

"So, you're an expert, are you? Let's look at some facts, Detective. Hram is thirty-eight years old, a wealthy financial consultant, and very worldly-wise. He's had more women than you have birthdays. Clearview links him to four possible eliminations. On April 15, a rogue got shot with two .22 rounds. Last Saturday, Lenny the Finger meets an untimely death from two .22 rounds in the heart. Ballistics show all four rounds had the same rifling marks, and I'm to believe you failed to connect the dots? You did, didn't you? I can see it in your eyes. Swept up in a romantic haze, you forgot to be a detective and allowed your hormones to take over."

"It's all circumstantial, Kurt," she blurted, clearly unsettled.

"That's why you wanted him under surveillance to get proof! You still refuse to admit he manipulated you?"

"He—"

"Is a Keeper and both of us know it. Do you understand what that means? Every Keeper undergoes extensive training not only how to kill and evade capture, they learn to manipulate a subject by linking their bioelectromagnetic fields. A Keeper can project desire, attraction, and suck energy from a victim to trigger onset of sudden old age death—or not. It's all in your intro brief.

"Hram is ten years older than you, Nadala. Can you appreciate the depth of experience that separates you from someone like him? Ten years more of life to become a master at deflecting those who got in his way, or terminated them. You think he swooned at the sight of your obvious charms? You're the one who swooned! He made you like him to conceal the fact he killed not only Mercer, but possibly others!" he roared and banged a fist against the desk. "And that's only this year! If you did your job properly and bothered to check Clearview, you'd see he's implicated in over a dozen other deaths."

She gaped at him, mouth open in shock as she appeared to weigh up his words. Right then, he hated himself for shattering her dream. Instead of a future with a man she thought loved her, he handed her ashes.

After several tense seconds, color returned to her face and she straightened, mouth set in resolve.

"If you knew everything, why didn't you arrest him? I'll tell you why. There's no evidence to pull him in, and you're taking it out on me."

"What I'm doing, Detective, is demonstrating that you must never get involved with a suspect. I'm sure the subject must have come up in your Academy training. As for evidence, I don't need to see anything more."

"With all due respect, Inspector, you're a bastard," she declared coldly.

"That's right, I am. It's what the job calls for sometimes."

"Your job sucks."

"It has its moments. Chalk it up to experience, Detective. What I want you to do is arrest Frank Hram and transfer him to the Southbank forensics facility for testing. That clear?"

"Yes, sir."

"If you warn him, it'll mean your badge. That's all."

Robinson stood and glared at him. "You said Hram is a Keeper. How do you know?"

"There'll be a team meeting first thing tomorrow and I'll explain everything."

She shot him a look of loathing, opened the door, and paused. "He didn't play me!" she declared and walked out.

Porter nodded, his smile grim. He wounded Robinson's tender sensibilities and earned her disdain, but she had a job to do, a detail forgotten in a moment of romantic tenderness.

After a moment, he touched a preset number button on his phone station.

"Victorian Institute of Forensic Medicine. Marjory speaking. How can I help you?"

"Inspector Porter. Please convey a message to the Taskforce Crimson section. Detective Sergeant Nadala Robinson will deliver a Keeper, Frank Hram, within the next two hours. I want to be informed the minute she comes in."

"Of course, sir. I'll pass it on."

Chapter Six

"Hacker Anonymous didn't leak it. You did!" the President of the United States declared flatly, voice tense with anger.

Aiden Conrad smiled without humor. "An amusing notion, sir."

"Nothing amusing about it at all, Mr. *Smith*. I had the emails and documents checked. At first glance, a damning collection that exposed Project Purple's organization, its network of task-forces, and research centers. When looked at more closely, it's very thin on detail. A lot of history, mostly about past operations, but hardly anything on the Covenant itself."

"We weren't the ones hacked, Mr. President."

"I'm told it's a carefully compiled leak to create public unease, possible civil unrest, and economic disruption. If Hacker did it, they'd have dumped everything on the Internet without sifting it first. Do you realize the damage you caused? By close of trading yesterday, the Dow Jones fell 967 points. In Europe, the FTSE by 297. Euronext, CAC, and DAX all took hits. The only thing that saved everybody from total meltdown, markets closed for the weekend. I dread to see what might happen on Monday."

"Is that all you're worried about, sir? Dollars and cents?" Conrad replied mildly, his electronically altered voice not designed to convey emotion by the encrypted cellphone, courtesy of the NSA not even the Oak Ridge National Laboratory's 'Frontier' super-computer could hack. Given sufficient time, it could. That's why his NSA contact regularly provided upgraded handsets.

"Those dollars and cents represent the world's economic health and the wellbeing of billions. You've jeopardized the life-savings of countless ordinary householders."

"You're right, and I apologize if I appeared to trivialize the knock-on effect of this disclosure."

"Knowing what it would do, you still went ahead."

"The markets will recover if everybody remains calm."

"That's exactly my point! People react irrationally when they see trusted investments bottom out."

"If I may, sir, you need to look at this event in a more rational light."

"You presume to lecture me?"

"Remember our discussion last week?" Conrad asked, dropping all pretense at subterfuge, the Hacker leak having achieved its objective to expose Project Purple. "I approached you in good faith, and you rejected my proposal outright without any discussion. I offered almost everything Project Purple wanted since its creation in 1947. The one thing you demanded, I couldn't do. You didn't really expect us to open our database of known feeders, did you?"

"You voluntarily disbanded your Keepers, promising to provide taskforces with information on potential rogues. Fine, but that's hardly everything. More like a throwaway gesture, since the Covenant already shares such information, albeit sporadically."

"You wanted jurisdiction and I gave it to you."

"To protect your Keepers from prosecution when they killed! Let me tell you something, Mr. Smith. The law doesn't care how you kill or why. It cares that you did kill. Your Keepers committed murder, regardless of the reason behind it. The age of vigilante assassins no longer belong in any civilized society. That's why you disbanded them. You had some traction to use them in centuries past, but no longer. Despite your magnanimous gesture, we'll hunt them down and exact retribution for their crimes."

"What about the lives they saved, Mr. President? Is this about revenge or eliminating rogues?"

"Your city Masters should have reported all suspect rogues to local taskforces. That's why we set them up. They administer law!"

Conrad laughed. "What law? Instead of following established criminal statutes, inadequate as they are, your taskforces conduct a virtual program of kidnapping, then subject innocent citizens to unspeakable medical procedures in search of a pill to prevent onset of sudden old age death. Many died for that noble cause, which left their families devastated and grief-stricken, wondering why someone dragged away a loved one. A loved one they often never saw again. When one of our Keepers killed, it's murder, but when Project Purple kills a rogue or feeder without due process, it's a necessary sacrifice for the good of humanity. I expected better from you, Mr. President, and that's why I exposed your evil. You'll never get those databases. I'd rather destroy them first," Conrad snarled, tempted to end the call, tired of shallow banter with Everett.

After a tense moment of silence, he heard a heavy sigh.

"I'm aware of Project Purple's excesses—"

"Instead of reining them in, your administration and governments everywhere did nothing, hiding behind a contrived fiction that feeders don't exist, tacitly supporting the idea they're blood vampires and a menace to be destroyed. Well, the world now knows feeders exist, and they're not a menace. That title belongs to Project Purple and its taskforces. The truth is out there, and you're faced with a new reality, sir."

"If you intended to force my hand with the leak, it failed. I won't be subject to blackmail, and I'll not disband Project Purple. The infrastructure, communication lines, and networks it established are too valuable. Even if I were predisposed to do so, I cannot order other governments to break up their taskforces."

"You don't need taskforce units to track down rogues. Local police precincts are set up with the necessary communication lines and networks to do the job just as effectively."

"Taskforces do far more than simply apprehend rogues, Mr. Smith."

"So I know. You want to penetrate the Covenant. We're a source of irritation because you don't control us. Continue to be irritated, Mr. President. We will not allow you or any government to shut us down."

"I consider the Covenant a dangerous cabal that undermines the very fabric of democracy everywhere."

Conrad let out a guffaw. "Democracy? What the West has is not democracy, but autocracy whose guidelines are set by the transnationals, stamped into legislation by puppet politicians."

"You mean guidelines set by the Covenant!"

"We're the only ameliorating force that stands between un-feeling global corporate rule and a semblance of genuine freedom people can enjoy. Fast disappearing, by the way."

"Be that as it may. I won't deny that we want to see you un-masked, but Project Purple's primary function is more than play-ing politics."

"I know. It supposedly manages research programs to obtain a cure for onset of sudden old age death. A most worthy en-deavor."

"You mock me?"

"Far from it! I applaud the effort. That's why the Covenant makes healthy financial contributions to those research institu-tions."

"Rogues are mutants, and everybody wants that pill to survive an encounter with one. What you have overlooked, people don't care how we get it."

"They'll care when the Covenant reveals images of children's brains dissected to find your magic pill."

"We don't do that!" Everett retorted indignantly.

"Then you weren't told everything, Mr. President. Instead of acting to amend existing criminal codes to protect our basic human rights, you allowed the situation to fester. Without judicial oversight, Project Purple's activities openly flaunt existing law. Is my demand to put a stop to such practices so unreasonable?"

"Climb off that moral pedestal and recognize a brutal reality, Mr. Smith. People on the street were not ready to hear the truth about feeders."

"Because populist media branded them as vampires, with all the negative connotations that go with it!"

"Our education programs gradually changed public perception, but not enough for full disclosure. Your premature action caused incalculable social and economic damage."

"Face it, sir. They were never going to be ready. It's in the open, and everybody'll have to deal with it."

"With your leak, you have nothing else to bargain with," Everett replied with evident relish. "Project Purple's operating mandate will remain unchanged, and I'll wear the sacrifice paid by the few for the good of the many."

"Is that the beacon of freedom and justice you want the world to follow?"

"Sometimes doing the right thing is unpleasant, but it still must be done."

"Spoken like a polished political pragmatist you are. I shall not bandy words with you, Mr. President. You force me to make my point in a way you will understand. Last year's midterms cost you a Senate majority, which made life more difficult for your administration when you want to pass legislation. Next year, the House and the Senate face elections. A number of states will also hold their gubernatorial elections. I imagine most Republican governors would be keen to keep their cushy jobs. It's also a presidential election year, and I know how badly you want that second term. Your job approval ratings are slipping, while Senator Oswald Garich's star is on the rise. I think he'll make a good Democratic Party president…with some help from us."

"You would interfere with the national election process to serve your ends?"

"Come, sir. Let's not play the naïve innocent. Both parties use gerrymandering, Big Money, and Super PACs to influence elections ever since the 2010 Supreme Court Citizens United versus the Federal Electoral Commission ruling corrupted the process. The Covenant is merely another concerned organization exercising its legal right to protect US national and global interests."

"You mean your interests!"

"Right now, they're one and the same. Of course, the Republican Party *can* regain the Senate and increase its House majority—"

"If I bow to your demands."

"—and you'll enjoy four more years in the White House. The Covenant is not asking for much, Mr. President, and I recognize the pressing need to provide a cure for onset of sudden death. It's one of the reasons why we exist. We'll inject extra resources into research institutions to get that cure. Whether you believe me or not, we're anxious as you to see the end of needless suffering."

"If I don't cooperate—"

"You and your party will face ruin. The Covenant will not stop with the US. Next year, the European Parliament also holds elections in line with the 2007 Treaty of Lisbon, as do some individual EU member countries. If not next year, then the year after. It doesn't matter when. What is salient to our conversation, the influence we can exert on the US electorate can be applied with equal force to Europe if it persists in its policy that allows their taskforces to operate above the rule of law to violate individuals' rights. Sacrificing a minority for the greater good of the many is a bankrupt excuse used by authoritarian regimes everywhere to repress their populations. The world will treat feeders as equal citizens or face ongoing political and economic disruption."

"You're nothing but self-serving criminals!"

"I'm disappointed at your shortsighted view, sir. Let me expand it a little. The US Federal Reserve Board next sits on January 30. The market expects the current borrowing rate to remain steady at 5.25%. Not a good look if the Board raised the rate by seventy-five basis points or more. The economy might slow down, money becomes tight, businesses suffer, people out of work, and you'd wear the blame. Not a good image to project in an election year, and we'd make sure it wasn't favorable. You want to see global power in action, Mr. President? I'll show you its application."

"And I'll show you another side of power, Mr. Smith. So far, our efforts to expose you were an interesting sideline for my administration and governments around the world. That ends right now. I will employ the full weight of my intelligence services and international organs to penetrate the Covenant and dismantle it, and see you personally prosecuted. Nobody is above the law!"

"And neither is Project Purple and its taskforces. I believe we're done, sir."

"I'm not finished!"

"I beg your pardon. You have something else you wish to discuss?"

Everett snarled and cut contact. Conrad shook his head and slid the cellphone across the desk with a flick of his wrist. Dangerous to bait Everett like this, but his administration must be made to realize the seriousness of their predicament. Governments don't stand above the law, although all too often they behave as though they do.

If the President proves to be intransigent, Senator Garich already appeared more malleable to rational persuasion for a chance to occupy the White House and hold Congress. Conrad did not underestimate the power of intelligence services available to Everett in his ongoing campaign to penetrate and destroy the Covenant. However, past Administrations learned the hard way that issuing directives and signing Executive Orders were ineffectual when the Covenant had those services compromised. Over the decades, a number of Covenant operatives were identified and apprehended—always expected—but others remained to warn the Covenant of dangerous developments that threatened its integrity. Steps were then taken to neutralize the threat and its effects. The same procedures were applied in most countries around the world. The Covenant spent 300 years protecting itself from meddling regimes, and along the way learned all the rules. He generally did not apply Machiavelli's principles on the use of underhanded manipulation, but he would not hesitate to employ them when more palatable choices were removed. Besides, everybody used those same rules whether they admitted it or not at diplomatic cocktail parties.

He absently glanced at his wristwatch. Time to call Sybille Konigen and give her an update. First…He stood and strode to the wall cabinet where a steel carafe of percolated coffee always sat to serve his needs. He had a very efficient personal assistant who knew him as President and CEO of Hale & Associates, Importers. He smiled as he imagined her face twisted in horror if she knew how he actually spent his days.

A look out the window showed a patchy blue sky that allowed bright morning sunshine to light Manhattan's dark canyons. Still bitterly cold, the frozen vista only good for a postcard, not actually living in it. Perhaps he should shift the Covenant HQ to somewhere more pleasant. Hawaii maybe?

Once done with his counterpart, he could enjoy a relaxing afternoon. He and Ethel had a reservation to see Verdi's *Nabucco* on Broadway, followed by dinner at the exclusive Le Bernardin on 7th Avenue.

Two quick sips of strong coffee shot a burst of energy through him, and he reached for the cell.

"My day always perks up when I get one of your calls, Aiden," Konigen replied after three rings.

He pictured her smile sitting relaxed in a black leather chair, gazing at Lake Geneva. Not always a comfortable relationship, they nevertheless remained focused on critical issues affecting the Covenant. Most of the time.

"In case you were wondering, we're having some sunshine for a change," Conrad told her.

"It's raining and gloomy here."

"Not too late for that Hawaii trip, you know."

She laughed heartily. "I wish. I think the reaction to our disclosure generated a response within predicted parameters and created some discomfort for Hacker Anonymous who deny doing it. All good things."

"I agree. Australia and Canada already announced tabling legislation to recognize feeders, as has New Zealand. I've read the bills and they look good."

"I'm keen to see what happens. We spent enough time negotiating the clauses. Europe didn't sit on its hands either, my boy. Germany, France, Italy, and England made similar announcements. Others will follow. Amazing what twenty-four hours can do when people are properly motivated. You spoke to President Everett?"

"Just got off the phone with him."

"You sound enthusiastic, Aiden."

"I am, although he didn't find the conversation satisfying. I had to present my argument in germane terms he understood. He'll pass legislation recognizing feeders if he wants to save his political hide. He's a pragmatist. He'll deal."

"In the process, he'll redouble his efforts to penetrate us."

"Of course. What's the general reaction at your end?"

"When the popular press learned how taskforces got their research subjects, it created a wave of protest through most of the

EU. I believe governments took notice, but not everybody in the EU Executive is amenable to the idea of shutting them down."

"Tough chilies."

"That magic pill is the political driver here."

"It's a driver everywhere, Sybille. A driver we support, but not in the way they're doing it now."

"I'll talk to the hardline Executive members. If positive persuasion doesn't work, the threat of disendorsement for the 2024 parliamentary election might be viewed in more sanguine light. We'll bring them on board if they want to keep their seats."

"As will the threat to manipulate the EU's fiscal and monetary policy," Conrad added. "Let's initiate the next phase of our plan and expose Project Purple's research center practices. It should make for interesting evening viewing."

"Talk to me about Everett."

* * *

Acutely unhappy, Nadala closed Porter's door, not quite slamming it. She stomped to her workstation, sat down, and felt the sting of welling tears. Her thoughts in total disarray, unable to think straight, a wave of profound disillusionment washed through her. When she joined Taskforce Crimson, she looked forward to a change of pace, excitement, fresh police work, not heartbreak. Throat tight, she exhaled loudly and snatched a tissue from a box beside the computer screen. A quick dab at her eyes dried the tears, but did nothing to quell the uncomfortable tightness in her chest.

Frank didn't *play her!*

Despondency resolved itself into smoldering anger, and she gave the desk a hearty kick that only bruised her toe and did nothing to the desk. She let out a short, unladylike expletive to vent rage, disappointment, and a feeling of helplessness that threatened to overwhelm her.

Last night, entwined in his comforting arms, his soft words washed away all doubts that he genuinely wanted her. She felt safe, certain she belonged to him as he belonged to her. He gave her everything and placed his life in her hands. What man would do that if he only intended to use her? He allowed her to peer into his soul, which must count for something. She saw a complex person, physically and emotionally powerful, knowing how to live in a world intolerant of his kind, and manipulated it to his advantage not only to survive, but gain professional and material success. So what if he had lots of women and bent their will to serve his need? They merely satisfied a biological urge without any emotive attachment. Held tight in his embrace, she connected with him at a level that transcended physical intimacy. Their spirits touched and they were one, something she knew with utter certainty. Or did she?

Could Porter be right? Did Frank play with her feelings after all to divert her Mercer investigation and his involvement? Ten years older, she expected Frank to be adept at influencing people, channeling their behavior that deflected attention and suspicion he might be a feeder. Not only a feeder, but as Porter said, a specially trained Keeper able to use his bioelectromagnetic field in ways ordinary feeders were not aware of, or did not know how to use. Such a man saw life in so many different ways she could hardly imagine and could not hope to match.

To keep his identity secret, something his training reinforced, did he lure her into his embrace only to one day silence her to remove a life-threatening risk? Nadala refused to believe it. *He loved her!*

Love…A bitter brew, as she found out with Leo. The man took advantage of her youth and innocence and played on her needs, one eye on other women. After the divorce, it took a long time to get over her hatred of all men, driven partially by her body's desires. Understanding the biological basis for those desires did not blind her to the dangers of allowing herself to fall for another male predator. Yet, it seemed she had done exactly that with Frank. He told her he never manipulated her, and jokingly said she manipulated him. A play on her ego to reinforce her want for him and further cloud her professional judgment?

She sniffed and dabbed at her nose. Something else occurred to her. Something dark and chilling.

What if Porter did the manipulating?

Ruthless, driven by the demands of his job, willing to do whatever it took to apprehend rogues and feeders in general, she expected the Inspector to be an expert at it. The same gap in age and experience also existed between them. Did he maneuver her to get his hands on Frank? A captured Keeper would look nice on his record. Porter could have taken advantage of her emotional vulnerability to sow suspicion about Frank's feelings for her, casting him into a hardened feeder mold only interested in self-preservation. Not only a feeder, but a murderer who deserved the full wrath of the law, playing on her sense of duty. Porter told her where her duty lay, and he expected her to carry it out, even if it involved arresting a lover.

Duty…

She hated the word, and hated Porter for shattering something she regarded precious—a future she wanted with Frank.

Nadala reached for her bag and dug out the purse she snatched off the bedroom floor when Porter called. After Frank left, instead of showering and getting breakfast, she luxuriated in bed, a contented smile on her face, thinking about last night. Getting up meant facing another day she felt in no mood to do. Too bad if the world minded that she daydreamed for once.

In a hurry to dress and attend what she presumed to be a team meeting, she completely forgot the Sony recorder. She held the slim device, amazed to see a little red dot that said it still faithfully recorded. She powered up the computer, logged on, and rummaged in the drawer for a connector cable. Plugged in, she opened VLC Player and scrolled through the conversation at

Crown Casino, the words coming through fairly clearly. She fast forwarded past their time of delicious intimacy at her place. Their voices soft, hardly audible, she listened intently, waiting for Frank to damn himself, confessing to be a feeder and a Keeper...and Mercer's murderer. Only jumbled mumbling came from the computer's speakers, the recorder not sensitive enough to pick up the pillow conversation inside her closed purse. Frustrated, she replayed the recording, upping the speaker volume to maximum. An occasional word came through, but not what she wanted to hear. Perhaps a forensic lab could make out the muffled sounds, but she suspected it might be a futile gesture.

Why take the thing to a lab anyway? As a federal police officer and member of Taskforce Crimson, she had a responsibility to arrest Frank as Porter demanded. Could she set aside her love-stricken attachment to a Keeper and do her duty? Be a woman and protect Frank, thereby becoming a felon herself, or a professional as her training demanded?

As a Keeper, Frank almost certainly killed more than once and deserved to be punished in a court of law regardless of circumstances, even though no law existed to tell courts how to deal with feeders. Laws did exist to treat ordinary murderers, and sufficient circumstantial evidence existed to arrest Frank for killing a rogue on April 15, and probable execution of Lenny the Finger. Insufficient to prove guilt beyond reasonable doubt, but would his confession to her be adequate to hand him over to the Southbank facility. Porter said he knew Frank to be a Keeper without divulging his source. That alone should be sufficient to execute an arrest.

Did Frank play her? The nagging doubt kept bothering her.

She suspected it from their first meeting in his office, but pushed the realization away, swayed by physical attraction. Despite his reassuring words that he did not, could she believe him? Nadala placed herself in his position, trying to be coldly objective. Would she manipulate someone if it meant saving her life?

With the Hacker announcement yesterday, she intended to call Angela for a serious sisterly talk, able to finally tell her all about her job. A busy day and an even busier evening, the opportunity slipped by. Right now, she badly needed to unburden herself to someone, and Angy would understand. Her sister always seemed more attuned to things of the heart. *Tonight*, she told herself, the planned afternoon and evening with Frank now firmly in the dumpster.

Overwhelmed by raw emotion, she buried her face between her hands, the comfortable world she knew torn asunder. Nothing appeared real, and she felt cold fear at the thought she could not trust her own judgment. Stranded on a major life's crossroad, she could not decide which way to go.

"Why are you still here, Detective?" Porter demanded behind her.

Startled by his quiet appearance, she swiveled the chair and gazed at his hard features devoid of expression. If he had any feelings, he probably left them at home before coming in, she reflected uncharitably.

Did he see her cry? So what if he did? *Damn him anyway*.

"Just checking something, Inspector." Right then, she could not bring herself to call him Kurt.

He glanced at the Sony recorder. "Evidence?"

"I took it with me when Mr. Hram and I went to Crown Casino."

"And…"

"Nothing. Not that I expected him to suddenly reveal everything. As you said, I only met him on Thursday."

"Too bad you didn't think to tape what happened in your bedroom."

"As a matter of fact, I did, not that it's any of your business what I do with my time, or who I see."

He stared at her. "It is my business when the person you're going out with is a Covenant Keeper. You have a job to do, Detective. Do it." Mouth pursed in a tight line, he scurried toward the kitchenette.

Nadala disconnected the recorder and shoved it into her bag, then logged off. Her hand hovered above the phone, then dialed the Criminal Investigation Unit duty desk.

"Sergeant Polsky," a bored voice answered, clearly not wanting to be bothered with things like work on a pleasant Sunday morning.

"Detective Sergeant Robinson, Taskforce Crimson."

"What can I do for you, Detective?"

"I need a car and an armed constable."

"Main entrance, five minutes."

"Thank you." She hung up, stood, and slung her bag on the right shoulder, the decision which road to take made for her with a little push from Porter. Did that make her weak?

Duty or love? She should have stayed at the Collingwood Station and remained blissfully unaware of the Covenant and its associated baggage. She would not have met Frank...and had her heart ripped open.

A hot northerly gust played with her hair as she stepped out of the building, the street almost devoid of traffic. A tram hissed by heading for the Southern Cross railway station. A lone pedestrian strolled slowly along the sidewalk. She slipped on her shades and walked down the steps toward the waiting police sedan. She slid onto the cloth front seat and buckled up.

"The Rialto building," she told the woman senior constable and turned to watch the lonely street.

The car pulled away from the curb and glided down Spencer Street. A right turn at Collins and they were there.

"Come with me," she told the driver and stepped out.

Her eyes traveled up the sheer façade of the Collins Tower across the shaded street the sun yet to penetrate, checked for on-coming cars, and walked briskly across, the woman close behind her.

The ride to the sixth floor of Oaks done in silence, she headed for apartment 62. She stopped, motioned to her companion to stand close to the wall outside the peephole range, took a deep breath, and pressed the doorbell button.

What if Frank went out? It did not matter. She would call him, arrange a meeting, and pounce.

After what seemed an eternity, her thoughts still in a jumble, the door opened and Frank's eyes registered surprise.

Nadala steeled herself and focused on her job. It did not quite quell the feeling of self-loathing.

"Mr. Hram, you're under arrest on suspicion of three counts of murder and being a Covenant Keeper," she grated coldly.

He flinched as though struck, and something heavy pressed down her shoulders. His eyes bored into her and she saw disillu-sionment, regret, and resignation. Her betrayal complete, she turned to the senior constable and nodded. The woman immedi-ately dug into her jacket and produced a set of cuffs.

"I opened my heart to you!" he managed at length. "I can't believe you're doing this."

She could say so many things, but the words did not come. Too late to turn back time, she clamped her mouth and said noth-ing, weeping tears no one could see.

His face lost all expression and his gray eyes turned to stone. He swung his hand and slapped her, the sound like a gunshot. Her left cheek stung with fire and she blinked hard.

"Hey!" The cop quickly drew her Smith and Wesson semiau-tomatic.

"Cuff him," Nadala told her in a voice that came from a tomb. *Oh, Frank!*

* * *

Eyes closed, his mind drifted to Grieg's *Peer Gynt's* haunting melody. The depth and timbre from the surround sound speakers made him feel he sat in the middle of an orchestra. Frank's right index fingers tapped the armrest of his recliner in time with the music. Nothing mattered in this eternal moment except the music and the soothing images it created.

He reached for the mug of coffee, took a sip, and glanced absently at the towering face of the Rialto building across the street. His apartment did not offer much of a view, but he did not buy it for the scenery. He should go out for a run or have a workout in the downstairs gym. A little later perhaps. After he concluded his business with Tango.

Immersed in the music, his thoughts drifted and he closed his eyes, at peace with himself and the world.

Four lonely years, he held himself back from reaching out, keeping Rainey alive in his mind, finally managing to let go with the prospect of a new life with Nadala. A startling state of affairs. It beggared belief he could fall for someone he'd met only a few days ago, certain it was much more than a hormonal reaction.

Rainey had a special place in his heart, but no longer a ghost to haunt his tomorrows. A shitty turn of fates took her from him, but he mourned long enough. With Nadala at his side, he could stop seeking women in bars and clubs to feed. At least nowhere near as much. His Covenant Keeper days over, killing rogues behind him, he felt a release from a burden he carried for nine years ever since the Covenant recruited him. On reflection, Keepers were a necessary cauterization tool in decades and centuries past, but social structures had changed, as did law enforcement capabilities and techniques. They can have the rogues, and welcome to them. Playing the assassin had become too dangerous…and unnecessary, something the Covenant probably recognized, but refused to let go. Organizational inertia can be a bitch, resisting change unless moved by a visionary individual or an external event. Frank could not say which moved the Covenant to disband the Keepers, and did not particularly care.

They would probably maintain the Ardor Helpline network and support feeders how to manage their need, but as Manuel hinted, only as a secondary activity. What exactly did the vast Covenant organization do? Frank shook his head, vastly amused at the notion of becoming a Master. Nevertheless, the possibility did hold a germ of interest. With his commitment to Urbi Investments, did he want to consider such a radical life change?

In a way, he knew what the Covenant did behind closed doors. Echo said they ran an intelligence network to identify rogues. An obvious assumption, but their role must extend beyond such a narrow parameter. According to his indoctrination, to protect itself, Covenant members infiltrated every government, commercial, and social institution, placed there to sabotage attempts to penetrate the organization. Not only stop penetration, but exert influence and control. That represented a lot of power as Charlie hinted. Power and control exercised by an underground world government? Although somewhat farfetched, exercised to what end? From what he knew, in its early days, the Covenant did exist merely to protect feeders, but as its influence expanded, it undoubtedly applied it to commercial ventures to finance its Keepers, intelligence network, and the Ardor Helpline, which meant bending political systems to stop them from interfering. Frank knew what it meant to pursue profits, but the Covenant must be much more than a transnational money-grubbing business. Its decades-long social conditioning program to dispel the public specter of energy vampires roaming the streets proved the Covenant had a humanitarian conscience. There had to be more behind that facade.

His thoughts shifted to a planned afternoon with Nadala. The prospect of spending another night with her sent a tingle of pleasant anticipation through him. Before then, he wanted to finish a more pressing task…Echo.

A glance at his wristwatch showed 9:25 AM. In five minutes, he expected Tango to show up. Yesterday, she told him she could not wait to get her hands on the revolting son of a bitch and suck him dry. His only concern, and a very real one, if Echo betrayed every Keeper to Porter, he and Tango may not be given the luxury of time to track down the creep before the feds came for them.

A soft knock made him turn. He placed the coffee mug on the coffee table and hurried to the door. A squint through the peephole showed Tango gazing down the corridor, long straw-colored hair splayed across the left breast. He grinned with pleasure and unlocked the door.

"Welcome to my humble abode, Zenola."

Wearing white sneakers, white slacks, and a pinkish long-sleeved shirt, she stepped in and flashed him a warm smile. A quick look around the apartment, she nodded.

"Not so humble, Frank. I wish my place looked this neat. You can't believe what twin girls can do to a house."

Over brunch yesterday, they exchanged names and personal details, codenames no longer necessary. He enjoyed chatting with her, finding her easygoing and unpretentious, conversation he missed. When he confided his attraction to Nadala, she gaped at him in horror.

"Did you flip your switches? She's a federal cop, for Chrissake! Not just any cop, but one of Porter's. What the hell were you thinking? The woman will rip out your trusting, love-stricken heart, break it into little pieces, and grind the rest of you into mince."

He wagged a finger at her. "She's not like that at all."

Zenola sighed and shook her head in sorrow. "Poor Frank. You don't know much about women, do you? Not where it matters. Don't say I didn't warn you."

He would not mind having her as a friend. A person who understood what it meant to be a feeder and a former Keeper. He also looked forward to meeting her husband, also a feeder, she told him, keen to find out how the two met and managed their needs.

"Care for some coffee or tea?"

She placed a small black shoulder bag on the coffee table and sat on the sofa. "No thanks. My stomach is still sloshing from breakfast. Anyway, Manuel's call yesterday turned me off everything. I still cannot believe Echo sold us all to Porter. I'm surprised, though, that Manuel gave you my number."

Frank sat beside her and grinned. "You're not going to believe this. He said the Covenant wants me to be the next Master."

Her violet eyes grew round. "He didn't!"

"I kid you not. I guess he figured that piece of confidence rated a small breach in security."

"You'd make a great Master, Frank," she declared soberly. "With Sierra gone, Melbourne needs someone strong. Especially now." She tilted her head. "Are you considering taking it?"

"Right now, all I want is to get my hands on Echo."

"I'm with you. Manuel said there's a team looking for him. If Porter has him in protective custody somewhere, it'll be tough finding the bastard."

The doorbell chimed and he lifted his eyebrows in surprise.

"Expecting female company?" Zenola queried with a grin.

He stood and pointed at the guest bedroom. "In there."

She nodded and got up.

He grabbed her bag and held it out. "Don't forget this."

A quick peek through the peephole showed Nadala tense and uncomfortable, and he immediately became concerned. He opened the door, saw the uniformed cop, and felt color drain from his face. Totally taken aback, he could not believe she betrayed him. Not after last night, not after he shared everything with her. It's the only reason for her to be here.

He'd been an idiot to trust her. His instincts warned him not to get involved. Swayed by her magnetism and physical charms, he allowed her to peer into his soul. To compound his moment of juvenile foolishness, he told her everything, trusting her completely.

"Mr. Hram, you're under arrest on suspicion of three counts of murder and being a Covenant Keeper," she grated, voice cold, and glanced at the senior constable, who pulled a set of cuffs from her pocket.

In shock, he groped for something to say. "I opened my heart to you! I can't believe you're doing this."

He saw a flash of regret in her eyes, then it faded. Something he built around his heart crumbled and turned to ashes. Disillusioned, his hope for happiness broken shards at his feet, he pursed his mouth and slapped her. She winced and her left cheek turned red.

"Hey!" The constable immediately reached for her gun.

"Cuff him!" Nadala told her.

Frank glared at her. "I'm entitled to make a call."

He could overpower them easily and walk away, then what? Instead of having moral justice on his side, he'd be a genuine fugitive. He suspected even the Covenant's lawyers would not be sympathetic to his plight. On the other hand, forsaking moral justice might be better than what the Southbank facility had in mind for him.

"You'll get your chance."

"Can I at least get my wallet?"

Her green eyes contracted, and she glanced at the cop. "Go with him."

He strode into the kitchen, jerked open a drawer, and extracted his wallet, keys, and cellphone. In the corridor, he locked the door and placed his arms behind his back. The woman constable cuffed him and they marched toward the elevator, her hand firm on his shoulder.

Outside, startled pedestrians stopped to watch as the constable secured his right hand to the car's rear safety bar and buckled him up. Nadala got in up front and he stared at the back of her head, hoping the whole thing to be a nightmarish flashback. It proved all too true when the car did a squealing U-turn and headed toward Spencer Street. He knew with absolute certainty where they were taking him—the Southbank forensics facility. Where else would they take a feeder?

At least they did not get Zenola, expecting her to alert Manuel.

First on his list, Frank had to contact the Covenant lawyers. Did Porter have the balls to go after Marrick, Ward, and Thatcher? Every Keeper knew them to be a Covenant front, and he presumed Echo betrayed them to Porter. One of the most respected decades-old law firms in Australia with two former High Court judges and several King's Counsel barristers in their fold, the Taskforce would find the firm formidable opponents. Porter might try to arrest the principals, but he had no evidence that firm members were feeders. Porter arrested him without evidence, Frank reflected. No, he did it on Nadala's say-so. The likely scenario? The Inspector may be waiting to see what legislation the Prime Minister trotted out tomorrow before doing more. He could not act totally outside the law…for now.

If Porter had already moved, Frank knew he'd be in some seriously smelly trouble.

He stared at Nadala's ash-blonde hair and wondered what made her do it. Duty? Orders? It did not matter. She chose a life without him in it, and he now had a life without her. He tried to exorcise her from his heart, but could not. The attempt caused him too much anguish. He would let her wither and die inside him until only a dusty memory remained of what might have been. A poignant lesson reinforced: never get involved with a non-feeder.

When the car crossed Queens Bridge, he knew with absolute certainty where they were going. This early in the morning, traffic still light, pedestrians nonetheless strolled along the Southbank riverside promenade enjoying a warm Sunday. Judging by packed seating everywhere, the restaurants were doing brisk business. Gulls fluttered above the tables hoping for a throwaway morsel. Two girls in skimpy outfits jogged along the waterfront. A four-man scull powered up the Yarra.

He took everything in without focusing on anything in particular, cleared his mind, stilled his troubled feelings, and attempted to merge with the Self. No matter how hard he tried to enfold himself in a bubble of peace and tranquility, release did not come. The emotional wounds inside him still bled and he could not let go. Giving into the Self also meant surrender, and he could not surrender. What he expected to endure shortly, it might be better to keep the flames of anger fanned. It should help keep him alive.

Frank knew what the Southbank facility did to feeders. Their Taskforce contact gave everybody sufficient details. The facility did not conduct prolonged deprivation to see how feeders reacted when denied the need to feed, although several centers around the world did. He could hardly imagine what that felt like. However, their contact may not have known everything. He expected to find out soon enough.

Taskforce Crimson section of the Victorian Institute of Forensic Medicine primarily carried out anatomical and chemical pathology, which meant tissue extraction. Would some green-garbed, masked examiner start slicing strips off him, or drill into his head? They might feed him drugs, then diligently observe his reactions, take blood samples, do MRI scans, or wire him up to do old-fashioned brain response tests to various stimuli. On the other hand, they might give him the whole package, and then some.

He shook the gory images from his mind. None helped his composure, his thoughts on what Nadala did to him. He struggled to wrap his head around it, everything so surreal.

The police car drove past the Institute's glass front, turned into a side alley, and stopped before a wide metal freight entrance. Nadala got out, walked to a small side door, and pressed a black pad. A moment later, the door opened and a bulky individual in a dark gray suit came out and spoke to her. She showed him her badge, and he nodded. She then glanced at the car and the constable undid Frank's cuffs. He slipped out and waited. Nadala signed something on the proffered clipboard, got into the car, and it whispered down the alley. He spent a moment gazing after it.

The gray suit hooked a thumb over his shoulder. "This way."

Frank never considered disobeying. Getting a broken arm or shot not in his survival plan. Despite his intensive martial arts training, he doubted his chances taking the guy. His minder looked too professional. Freedom, however temporary, might be preferable to lying on a cold examination table getting carved up. He always wanted to find out what this facility did, but not necessarily from the subject's point of view.

His minder marched him down two deserted corridors and shoved him into a whitewashed, windowless room with a black table and four black chairs.

"Empty your pockets into the tray," the gray suit said coldly.

Frank hesitated for a second, then complied. His minder took the tray and walked out. The door closed after him with a loud click. With time on his hands, he pulled back a chair and sat down, only mildly wondering what to expect. A CCTV camera mounted above the door stared at him. He stared back, then crossed his legs and waited.

Perhaps two minutes later, the lock clicked and in walked a youngish man wearing a white lab coat. Somewhat on the short side and a little overweight, his deep blue eyes glinted with clinical detachment. Pink scalp showed beneath sparse brown hair. He placed a clipboard on the desk and sat down.

"I'm Dr. Bayer, Mr. Hram, your pathologist. You won't be mistreated during your stay, not in the conventional sense, but don't try to leave. Security here is specifically designed to cope with feeders. I will also block any attempt to link your bioelectromagnetic field with mine. You see, I'm also a feeder," he added with a wry smile.

Frank fought to suppress his astonishment. On reflection, it made sense for research facilities to employ feeder investigators. Who else could understand what feeders felt? A useful datum for the Covenant if he ever got out of here.

"You'll have a room in our dormitory section, but no contact with other feeders. Some time ago, we found that a group of feeders can link and use their combined ability to render unconscious up to four individuals from a distance of nine meters." Another smile from Bayer. "Lesson learned, we don't want you tempted."

Frank's mind raced. Individuals can group to act as a single controlling force? Did this represent the evolutionary survival value everybody looked for? A social unit such as a neighborhood or village, and conceivably even a city, could repel a land attack from ordinary humans. He immediately dismissed the thought as absurd. For one, there simply were not that many feeders to form such groups. Apart from the ability to attract a potential mate and stimulate desire, a feeder could not actively influence someone's actions…as far as he knew. From what Bayer said, one definitely could.

An additional datum for the Covenant? Could they already be aware of these things? If they penetrated every research center, they likely did know. Why didn't this ever come up in his indoctrination? Probably no need-to-know. Even if he did know, the knowledge would not help him be a better assassin.

He finally realized something harsh and it left a bitter taste. Keepers were trained to be killers, nothing more. Tools to eliminate rogues, who in turn threatened Covenant's survival as a body. No need to burden Keepers with extraneous information.

The perception of his importance as a Keeper shrank, and he at last understood his insignificance in the larger arena the Covenant played in. He might be a minor pawn in their game, but he refused to admit he did not matter. If they were prepared to abandon him, it betrayed everything he knew they stood for. The rub, he admitted, he did not know what they stood for, or the price they were prepared to pay to remain anonymous.

Betrayed by Nadala, and now the Covenant itself?

If true, he faced a hostile world alone, and would likely never get out of here.

"I want to call my lawyer," he declared.

Bayer cleared his throat. "I'm afraid that only works in the movies, Mr. Hram. While you're here, you have no rights. When you stepped into this facility, you ceased to exist."

Frank stared at him. "You intend to keep me here indefinitely?"

"That remains to be seen, but it will be a lengthy stay. If you're hoping for some legislative reprieve the Prime Minister intends to table tomorrow, I wouldn't raise my hopes. Our Institute, and others like it, operate under a singular mandate—"

"I know about your mandate."

"I am sure you do." Bayer pulled a pen from his lab pocket and lifted the clipboard. "Before we get started, I want to confirm some medical details."

Frank leaned forward, prepared to dislike the individual on principle. "Let's get something straight, Doctor. You're holding me here without any legal basis, which amounts to kidnapping, and you plan to carry out medical procedures on me without my consent. That must break a raft of laws. Even if I don't exist to you as a person, people will look for me. You can kill me, but it will not erase my existence. There is no reason I should cooperate, and I won't."

Bayer shrugged. "Very well. We'll find out what we need in due course. You see, your willing cooperation is not actually required."

"Fuck you!"

"That's been tried."

"Tell me something, Doc. When did you sell your soul?"

"My soul?" Bayer laughed. "I'm a scientist, and you're a research subject. A lab rat, nothing else. Moreover, you're a killer."

"Not proven!"

"The fact that you're here is enough proof. In any court of law, you'd face death or life imprisonment. Instead of languishing in a cell, you're serving society in atonement. My conscience is clear." He got up and knocked twice on the door. "I shall see you in a little while. We need to run some preliminary tests, and then you'll be shown your room."

A little later, his bulky minder appeared. Frank pushed back his chair and stood. The guard took him to Serology where a nurse impersonally extracted two 10cc vials of blood. In Radiology, he had a full-body MRI and CT scan, both lingering on the head. The examination done, Bayer showed up, accompanied by a man dressed in a dark blue suit. Tall, probably 180cm, black hair and eyes, he carried himself with authority.

"Ah, it looks like I'm just in time," the man declared in a neutral voice. "Mr. Hram, I'm Inspector Kurt Porter, your host."

"It's not a pleasure, Inspector," Frank grated, wondering why he rated such personal attention.

"No, I suppose not." Porter glanced at Bayer. "Is the other subject ready?"

"All set."

"Excellent." Porter grinned at Frank. "Before Dr. Bayer starts his probing and stuff, I thought you'd enjoy meeting a fellow Keeper. His information enabled us to net two of your colleagues yesterday. That doesn't mean I like him. You may enjoy the encounter more than he, but we shall see. All the monitoring equipment set up, Doctor?"

"Cameras, IR, EMR, and magnetometers," Bayer replied.

Porter nodded, and everybody proceeded down another corridor. Bayer stopped before gray ceiling-high double doors above which a sign said 'Examination Room 2'. He pressed a large, green mushroom button, waited for the lock to click, and pushed in one door. Frank stepped into what appeared to be a small operating theater equipped with a portable table, overhead lights, instrument trays, monitors, and stuff he did not understand. He recognized the antiseptic smell, though. He also recognized the heavyset individual, the chiseled features, and crewcut of the man who stood beside the table, a guard at his side.

"Echo!" Something hot surged through him and he lunged, driven by a visceral hate reaction.

Echo stepped back in alarm and lifted a hand. "Wait! It's not what you think, Foxtrot."

Frank lashed out with his right leg and caught Echo on the chin, which sent him spinning to the floor. Frank leaped, straddled Echo's chest, and sent his fist crashing into the man's face with all the fury he could muster. Blood spurted from the mangled nose and Echo went limp. Frank connected with his field and began to suck, revenge the only thing on his mind. A few seconds later, he stopped as his wave of anger subsided. He ought to kill the slime, but doing so would give Porter undisputed evidence to charge him if he survived whatever Bayer had in mind for him. He wouldn't give the asshole the satisfaction.

He grabbed Echo's shirt, lifted the limp body a few centimeters, and shoved him against the linoleum floor. Blood flowed freely from Echo's crushed nose, slowly spread across his chest, and seeped down his neck. Frank stood and rolled the man onto his stomach with a shove of his foot to prevent Echo drowning in his own blood. He wiped his hands against the trousers, turned slowly, and smiled faintly at Porter.

"You were right. I enjoyed it more than he did."

"Will he die?" Porter demanded, seemingly indifferent.

"No. I didn't want to soil my hands with scum like him, or provide you with sport at my expense."

Bayer cleared his throat. "Inspector, Hram's agitated state gives us a perfect opportunity to obtain tissue samples and conduct hormonal tests before his systems settle down."

Porter waved a hand. "He's all yours. An interesting experience meeting you, Mr. Hram."

"I can't say the same," Frank shot back and clenched his fists. If anyone deserved to die here, Porter stood first on his fecal list. The encounter with Echo? Nothing more than a prearranged experiment.

The Inspector smiled faintly, gathered the guard with his eyes, and walked out.

Two individuals in white coats pushed in a gurney and wheeled out the bleeding Echo. Bayer glanced at Frank's muscular minder.

"Take him to Serology, then Radiology. Once he's done, I want him back here."

* * *

Despite her sister's comforting counseling, Nadala felt drained and dejected, her emotions in a mixer. Hands behind her head, she stared at the gloomy ceiling, which perfectly reflected her mood. Faint dawn light came through the window, but did nothing to lift her despondency. She wanted to curl into a ball, hoping to wake into a brighter world.

No matter how hard she pushed back the memories, yesterday kept replaying in her head.

After she dropped Frank off at the Southbank facility, she asked to be driven back to the Center to pick up her car. She definitely did not want to go upstairs and face Porter, the cause of all her misery. Did he really create all her problems, though? The sparse Sunday traffic allowed her to get home quickly.

She threw her bag onto the lounge coffee table, sprawled across the sofa, and cried hot, bitter tears that seemed to scour her insides. Nadala had not wept brokenhearted in years, and moaned in anguish at the dull pain in the pit of her stomach. Eventually the sobs subsided, but she remained prostrate, not wanting to move, her mind churning with memories of her childhood, the fun things she and Angela did, her first crush, kiss, and tender moment of nervous intimacy with a university boy she thought loved her. Then Leo came, followed by two years of delirious joy where nothing could go wrong with life. The discovery of his extracurricular affairs forever shattered her dream world and jaded her view of men…until Frank wiped away the past. She told herself she did the right thing to arrest him, but doubts ate at her insides as she realized she may have made a terrible mistake, duty notwithstanding.

Cried out, she gave a long exhale, gritted her teeth, and got up. She padded into the bathroom, washed her face, and stared at the mirror. Eyes puffed and red, hair in disarray, her reflection showed a stranger. Still her, but also someone different, harder, colder. Did her tears wash away any hope for happiness? If happiness meant moments of passionate madness where nothing mattered except to be in her lover's arms, followed by despair, pain, and loneliness, she did not want it. Better to wall herself in and avoid the anguish of lost love.

In the lounge, she dug out the cellphone and called Angela. She needed to unburden her load of emotions and guilt, and her sister always managed to put a different perspective on issues. That's what she wanted now; a different perspective, and some love and sympathy.

Angela showed up around three bearing a bottle of Chardonnay. After a tender embrace, Angy fetched two glasses and filled them to the brim. Nadala downed the icy wine in four long gulps and held out the glass for a refill.

Her sister only sipped, her mouth set in a small smile. "I see one bottle won't be enough."

Nadala grinned. "There's more in the fridge."

"You want to talk about it or binge?"

"Both."

"Fine. Tell me what ruined your day. By the way, you look terrible."

"Porter ordered me to arrest Frank," Nadala moaned tragically.

"The man you were investigating? And…"

"What's to say? I arrested him and took him to the Forensic Institute." Nadala felt her eyes fill. "I think I ruined everything." The tears came and she did not hold them back. Angela's arms held her as she sobbed, unable to stem the tide of raw despair. "Of all the men in the world, why did I have to fall for a feeder?"

Angela pulled back. "Wait a minute. Frank's a feeder?"

Nadala nodded miserably.

"And you know that how?"

"He spent the night here and told me."

"Wow. I see why you're in the dumps."

"I had no choice! If I didn't, Porter would have my badge."

"Would that have been so bad?"

"I arrested a man I love and destroyed a future I hoped to have with him," Nadala said brokenly and reached for a box of tissues on the coffee table.

Angela shook her head. "You can be so thick sometimes."

Nadala sniffed and dabbed at her eyes. "Thanks. I needed to hear that."

"You are, you know. Don't you see? Instead of warning Frank, doing what's right, you took the easy way out and followed orders, which only compounded your problem."

"It'd cost me my job if I didn't arrest him!" Nadala snapped angrily, her cheeks hot with indignation. "I worked all my life to have a career. I'm a federal police officer, and Frank killed—"

"Please! Save it for the PR. Frank killed in the eyes of the law, but from what I read in the papers and seen on TV, Covenant feeders killed rogues to protect the rest of us. Did that deserve his arrest? You had to know Porter's order was illegal and violated everything your training said you shouldn't do."

"We cannot allow self-appointed vigilantes to—"

"Ah, for Christ's sake! You talk about Covenant vigilantes, when all along, it's your taskforce who are the vigilantes. You joined Porter because you thought you had justice on your side. You were protecting us from Covenant murderers. I'm not excusing what they've done, but you need to reset your moral compass. Don't you get it? Your taskforce wasn't protecting us. They protected their own interests. You're working for the enemy."

Nadala groaned and her shoulders sagged. "I'm so mixed up, Angy. I thought I was doing the right thing, and in the process, I screwed Frank, and I screwed myself."

"Screwed yourself? What crap is that?"

"What do you mean?"

"Be a cop for a minute. Never mind his pillow confession, is there proof to convict Frank of anything?"

Nadala thought of her Sony recorder. "Nothing that can stand up in court."

"In that case, the only reason you arrested him is because Taskforce Crimson needs test subjects in their drive to develop a pill to stop us suddenly dying. A convenient cover to bring in Keepers and penetrate the Covenant. From Hacker Anonymous documents I've seen, Project Purple taskforces virtually kidnap feeders and subject them to unspeakable medical procedures. If anyone needs to be strung up, it's them!"

Nadala remembered what Professor Zimmer told her about experiments on infants and shuddered.

"A small evil for the greater good," Angela added. "Ask yourself something, Detective Sergeant Robinson. When does evil become large enough before people say enough? As a police officer sworn to protect society from criminals, decide who are the real criminals."

Nadala pondered that same question ever since she joined Taskforce Crimson. "It's not that simple."

"Nothing ever is, but if you want to do what's right, you must reduce things to fundamentals."

Nadala smiled faintly and gently brushed her sister's cheek. "You're wise, did you know that?"

Angela smiled. "Older, you always took it for granted that you were the smarter one."

"Mea culpa. Okay, O wise one, what do I do?"

"You still don't know?"

"I must get Frank out of there, but after what I did to him—"

"Poof! He'll forgive you. Men are suckers when it comes to shedding a few tears of contrition on their shoulder."

Nadala bit her lip. "I don't know, Angy. I hurt him badly. He may not want me anymore."

"Don't work yourself into a state. Do what needs to be done and see what happens."

"Easy for you to say. Getting him out of the Southbank facility might be impossible."

"Not my problem. You're the detective. Detect something."

"You're a lot of help."

"It's what sisters are for." Angela glanced at Nadala's empty glass. "A top-up?"

Nadala held it out, waited for the refill, and downed half of it. She tilted her head at Angy. "Have you told Mom about him?"

She loved her mother deeply, but when it came to feeders, Mom had a firm no-tolerance policy. To her, they were all vampires to be exterminated. Her dad had a loose live and let live attitude. As long as feeders didn't bother him, he would not bother them.

Angela scowled. "Dummy! What goes on between us stays between us. Still, you'll have to tell her if your relationship with Frank becomes something important."

"I guess."

"Now, when did you eat last? If you keep filling yourself with wine, you'll be on the floor."

Nadala's insides gnawed at her, and she shook her head. "Not since breakfast."

Angela slapped her thighs and stood. "Right! Let's go somewhere and fix that. Afterward, we'll come back here and talk some more. I want to know everything about this feeder dreamboat of yours. All you told me is that you two had dinner on Thursday, and you apparently romanced him last night. By the way, how's he in bed?"

Nadala laughed and punched her sister on the shoulder, her world no longer dark and forbidding. Some of the crushing load lifted off her shoulders and the day became a little brighter. "I have no complaints, snoopy nose."

"I want all the details, okay?"

On impulse, Nadala pulled Angy against her and held her tight. "Thank you," she whispered, her voice thick with feeling.

That's how yesterday passed.

She slept fitfully, but no longer chased by demons of guilt. Not much anyway.

Hands behind her head, she watched the brightening dawn. She pushed back the jumble of her thoughts, exhaled loudly, and climbed off the bed. A quick shower perked her up a little, and she pulled on her favorite navy blue business suit. Makeup done, she padded downstairs. A tall glass of pineapple juice, followed by a cup of freshly percolated coffee, set her up for an omelet mixed with diced tomato and finely chopped red capsicum. Usually done by 7:30, she did not care if she ran late. At any rate, she planned to make this her last day, and Porter can bitch all he wants. By the time she cleaned up and got into her Suzuki Swift, the dashboard clock read 7:56 AM. An underground parking spot at the Center made the twice-daily commute bearable.

Squeezed between six other eager, or maybe not so eager, Monday morning office types, the elevator took her to the eleventh floor. She slapped the keycard against the sensor, pushed her way in, and headed for the kitchenette. Armed with a mug of Earl Grey, she strode quickly past occupied workstations to her seat. Before she could power up the computer, Prada Vishnu walked up. Without saying anything, she pulled up a visitor chair and sat down.

Nadala noticed the tension on her face and frowned. "Bad morning?"

"You didn't watch the news?"

"No time. What happened?"

"A forty-second clip showed a dissected infant, its chest a gaping raw hole. A few minutes later, another one popped up. This time of a young woman, her brain held in a stainless steel pan. At end of each clip, a stern voice said, *Is this the price you're prepared to pay to cure sudden old age death?'* It's on all the channels. Apparently, it's been showing all night."

Nadala's stomach churned in disgust at the invoked images. "The Covenant is hitting back."

"And so is the National Rally Party, but not against the clips. They're applauding action against feeders. They assembled a group of protesters at the state parliament, and the fringe are flocking in to join them, banners waving. There are similar gatherings in every capital city. They aren't the only ones there. The

Family First Party, pro-lifers, and ordinary people who saw the clips are standing toe to toe with the agitators. They're not alone, though. Anti-NRP and FFP protesters are ready to confront them. We could see widespread riots today."

"Surely the police won't let things get out of hand?"

"I hope not, but that's not why I'm here. I know about you and Frank Hram. Porter told me everything. I also know you took him to Southbank yesterday. Although it's not much consolation, I'm sorry."

"Not the nicest twenty-four hours I ever had," Nadala told her with a brittle smile, images of rioting, looting agitators galloping through her mind.

"There's a team meeting at nine. Afterward, you and I need to talk." Prada stood and walked off, leaving Nadala staring after her.

She checked emails, filled the expenses sheet, and nursed her tea to make time march. At exactly nine, Porter emerged from his office and stood in the relatively empty space between two rows of bullpen dividers. Everybody quickly shuffled toward him.

"We had a most interesting weekend," he began briskly, his gaze lingering momentarily on Nadala. "And Saturday afternoon proved most productive for the Taskforce. What some of you don't know, a Covenant Keeper came in seeking a protection deal and provided valuable information that enabled us to apprehend two Keepers and the Melbourne Master. A big win for us. Yesterday morning, Detective Robinson apprehended another Keeper. Out of a cell of six, two are still at large, as are a number of administrative personnel, but I like to think not for long.

"This morning, the Attorney-General will table the Feeder Bill to codify their status into law. It will also define operating parameters for Taskforce Crimson and how we interact with other taskforces and research centers. The Governor-General is expected to sign it into law later this afternoon. As I told you on Saturday, the government and the Coalition had the bill prepared a while ago. They waited for a trigger to enact it, and Hacker Anonymous gave it to them. I understand countries around the world will pass similar legislation."

"Do we know what the bill will say?" Nadala ventured.

"Prime Minister Griffin's speech on Saturday night gave us some indicators, but we don't have any details. Focus on your jobs, not the Feeder Bill. If anyone needs help, Detective Robinson is there to assist. That's all." He swept everybody with a hard look and retreated to his office.

The group immediately broke into excited chatter, becoming more animated when Neil Ferris mentioned the gathering agitators. Nadala caught Prada's glance and strode to her desk. She grabbed her bag and headed toward the exit. Simone Washnik cut her off before she reached the door.

"Nadala, since you appear to be a spare wheel, I could use a hand with a case."

"I've got a chore, but I'll see you when I get back, okay?" Nadala told her and walked out, not wanting a discussion.

In the corridor, she stilled her rapid breathing and waited. Prada emerged and immediately headed for the elevators. One came with a soft *ting*, and the doors opened. Nadala hurried in and saw Prada touch the level four underground parking button. Still not saying anything, Prada walked quickly to her car, a white VW Golf, and got in. Puzzled by the cloak and dagger stuff, Nadala took the passenger seat.

"The cafeteria is more comfortable," she observed with a grin.

"I think we're safe here," Prada said. "For the moment at least."

"Safe?"

"You know you were followed?"

Nadala's features clouded. "Porter told me. That's how he found out about me and Frank Hram."

"There's probably a tail on me, Ferris, and Young. What Porter didn't say just now, when that Keeper came in on Saturday, we three were the only ones on the floor. Porter suspects one of us tipped off the Covenant."

"And you know who did it?"

"It's me."

Nadala went pale. "You're a Covenant plant?"

"Remember our weighty talk? I could tell right away you weren't happy working for the Taskforce. You're a straight cop with a conscience. Before Porter recruited you, he asked me to go over your record. I told him you did not fit the personality profile he wanted in his people, but he overruled me. He played on your sense of civic duty to make you set aside your moral misgivings how the Taskforce went about its business. I watched you closely, and I thought you'd make it. You might have, but for Frank Hram. The rest followed naturally. If it hadn't been him, sooner or later, something else would have tripped your circuit breaker."

Nadala sighed. "I don't hate Porter, not exactly. I hate what he and Taskforce Crimson represent, operating as though laws don't apply to them."

"They don't, as there are no laws. You didn't want to arrest Hram, did you?"

"No, and it has me all messed up. I know he killed rogues, but he's not a murderer! He doesn't deserve what Professor Zimmer and his people will do to him if they aren't already doing it."

Prada gave her a long look. "What are you going to do about it?"

"What *can* I do?"

"Get him out, of course. Not only him, but the other Keepers as well."

Nadala goggled at her. "Are you serious? Although I thought about it, how do we penetrate Southbank security?"

"There's a way. Are you game?"

"If we're caught, it will mean our badges, and we'll probably face charges."

"Followed by a lengthy, all-expenses-paid holiday at some correctional facility. Just now? Porter lied to all of you. He knows what's in the bill, and so do I."

"How?"

"As his 2IC, I can access most Taskforce server directories. When I came in this morning, I found a file sent to Porter by Commissioner Trusk. What the PM intends to table is our worst nightmare. It will recognize feeders, all right, not to protect, but persecute. Taskforce Crimson will be able to hold a suspected rogue for twenty days before they're charged, and that's where the kicker comes in. The evidence she spoke of…reasonable suspicion."

Nadala stared at her in shock. "It means we can arrest anyone we like."

"And the Institute can hold them almost indefinitely without access to legal counsel."

"The High Court will strike down such legislation."

"More than likely, but it may take months for them to hear the case. While the legal wheels turn, there'll be a lot of suffering by many."

"Civil liberty groups will protest."

"And their protests will be drowned out by agitators wanting every feeder in a cell or strung up. The need for that sudden death pill will give the government a credible excuse to ignore the rule of law, and people on the street will swallow it. Despite public conditioning programs, the specter of energy vampires roaming the streets is a powerful image, and the National Rally Party for one will make the most of it. Are making the most of it."

"Jesus, this isn't what I signed up for." Nadala did not have to think hard. "How do we do this?"

Prada gave a whimsical smile. "You could be Porter's star investigator if you handed me in."

"I'd have to slash my wrists first."

The older woman chuckled. "Okay, let's get it done."

"You mean now?"

"I have a signed order from Porter to transport all Keepers to the Monash Health Translation Precinct in Clayton. They do specialized research—"

"I know what they do. Zimmer told me."

"I've done this thing before, and Marjorie knows me. Professor Zimmer normally arranges such transfers, but—"

"Porter actually gave you a signed order?"

"Not exactly. I write his signature better than he does it himself."

"If we get them—"

"*Once* we get them."

"Okay, once we get them, what then?"

"The Covenant will probably take us to one of their safe houses."

"A raft of things can go wrong with this, you know."

"I know, but the longer we wait, the harder it will be to pull off."

"What if Marg calls Porter or Zimmer to query the order?"

"She might, but she never has before. If she does, we'll be in some trouble," Prada deadpanned.

Nadala laughed, taken in by the woman's pragmatism. "You're crazy. You know that, don't you? What's more, I'm crazy for listening to this crap."

"A perfect reason why we should do it."

"Well, I planned to hand Porter my resignation. Let's go," Nadala said firmly, realizing she just trashed her career.

Prada retrieved a cell from her bag. "Before we rush off, we'll need help. I'll be on speaker so you'll hear both sides of the conversation." She set encryption mode and tapped in a number.

"Manuel de la Kass," a gruff voice answered after three rings. "Identify."

"It's Prada Vishnu, amigo, and I've got Detective Robinson with me. Don't worry. I'm not under duress."

"Morning, Detective."

"Not a good one, sir," Nadala replied awkwardly, never imagining she would be talking to someone from the Covenant.

"Just Manuel. Are you secure, Prada?"

"For now. I have an update for you. I tried to reach you yesterday—"

"I had my phone off. Dodging the feds."

"The Taskforce has Frank Hram."

Nadala heard a heavy exhale.

"I know. One of our surviving Keepers called in yesterday morning and told me."

"My fault, Manuel," she said.

"She wants to break them out," Prada added.

"You plan to walk into the Southbank facility and demand their release? Even we can't do that, and we considered it."

"I can get them out, but I need backup. The excuse I'll use is that I'm taking them to the Monash Precinct. They'll give us a standard van, but our getaway won't last scrutiny and they'll undoubtedly mount an intercept. What I need, Manuel, is a transfer vehicle."

"When do you plan to do this?"

"Right now."

Manuel laughed. "I admire your pluck, chiquita. I'll arrange a black Toyota Granvia to pick you up at the Ink Hotel City Road main entrance, or close to it. It's a stone's throw from the Institute."

"Perfect."

"By the way, thanks for sending us the PM's proposed bill, but the Master Keeper already had a copy."

"What's the Covenant going to do?"

"I'm not in the need-to-know loop, but I'm sure they'll think of something unpleasant. If your plan works out, I'll see you all at our safe house. Sorry, I can't tell you where," he said and cut contact.

Nadala looked at Prada. "The Australian Master Keeper?"

"You must know by now, several state and federal parliamentarians are feeders, as are a considerable number of public servants. Once the PM announced she'll table the Feeder Bill, it didn't take us long to get a copy."

"On Saturday, Porter said that successive governments had the bill ready for some time. It's only now the Covenant managed to get a copy?"

"They must have prepared the altered version in secret, and for once, its existence remained a secret. Given what it says, you can understand why." Prada tapped a new number into her phone. "We better use a constable vehicle to take us to Southbank. If I'm tailed, I don't want to be seen in my car." She made the call and turned to Nadala. "Switch off your cell. We don't want Porter tracking us."

Nadala gaped at her. "You mean the damned thing has a GPS locator?"

"For our own good. It came in handy once or twice when one of us got into trouble, but—"

"Porter can also use it to find out what we're up to."

Prada smiled. "He plans for every eventuality."

"This isn't going to make you very popular with him."

"It had to happen sooner or later."

They took the elevator to the ground floor and waited outside. An ordinary police sedan pulled up and they walked down the steps. Prada jerked open the rear door and the driver looked at her.

"Sergeant Vishnu?"

"That's right."

She and Nadala piled in and the car pulled away from the curb.

It did not take long to reach the Institute. The car stopped at the entrance and Nadala swallowed her nervousness, worst-case scenarios racing through her head. She also felt excited at the prospect of seeing Frank. Could she patch things up between them? Would he want to?

At the reception desk, Marjorie looked up in surprise, then flashed them a warm smile. "Prada...Nadala! Nice to see you guys. What's up?"

"Just another dull Monday morning," Prada told her and fished out the fake order.

Marg's forehead creased in concentration, then she picked up the phone. "Dr. Bayer? There's an order from Inspector Porter to transfer all Keepers to the Clayton facility...Right, I'll tell them." She replaced the phone and beamed. "It'll take a few minutes to load them up. While you're waiting, help yourself to coffee or tea."

"Thanks, Marg, but we're fine," Prada told her. "Main freight bay?"

"Right."

"We'll wait there."

Marg fluttered her fingers. "Have fun, dear."

"All the time," Prada assured her, then glanced at Nadala. Without saying anything, she strode down the left-branching corridor.

Nadala grinned. "That went—"

Prada glared at her, shook her head, and looked up at a CCTV camera mounted in the ceiling.

Chagrined, Nadala felt her cheeks burn, realizing the facility naturally monitored everything inside.

Down another corridor, Prada stopped before wide double doors. She pressed a green mushroom knob and walked into a small freight bay filled with odd boxes. Above a workbench along the back wall hung various tools. A nondescript white VW Kombi appeared at the open entrance and drove in. The driver got out and strode toward them.

"Detective Sergeant Vishnu?"

"Yes."

He nodded, walked back to the van, and pulled back the sliding door.

Nadala turned when she heard the door behind her open. A youngish man in a white lab coat led three handcuffed men and a woman. She tried not to show reaction when Frank pierced her with his eyes. One man, face swollen, white plaster across his nose, glared at Frank.

"I'll get you for this, Foxtrot."

"Quiet!" one of the guards snapped and shoved him toward the van.

Prada nodded to the young man. "Dr. Bayer…"

"Nice to see you again, Detective Vishnu. Please sign the release form."

Prada dashed off her signature and Bayer waved toward the van. "They're all yours. By the way, any special reason for the transfer? We just started work on them."

"I'm just the delivery girl, Doc. Nobody tells me anything, and I don't tell anybody anything."

"I know the feeling," he said with a grin, glanced at Nadala, and went out. The door locked with a click.

The two guards cuffed everybody to side rails and the older one held a key to Prada. She climbed into the front seat and the driver started the engine. Nadala scrambled into the back and slid the door shut with a clang. A moment later, the van backed into the alley.

She forced her heart to slow, not believing they actually made it. When she thought about it, why shouldn't it go smoothly? Prada made such transfers before and everybody knew her. It would never occur to them to query a routine pickup. It did not keep Nadala's hands from sweating.

She slowly turned her head and found Frank staring at her. She wanted to reach out and touch him, hug him, smother his face with kisses, and tell him she loved him. Not yet, but soon, she promised herself.

"Stop at the Ink Hotel," Prada told the driver. "One more package to pick up."

"You're the man, Detective," the driver replied cheerfully.

In what appeared only a minute, the van approached the hotel's wide portico and slowed.

"Stop behind that black Granvia," Prada ordered. When the van braked, she reached into her bag and produced a semiautomatic with a fitted suppressor. "Don't move and don't make a sound."

"Hey! What the hell is this?"

Prada ignored him and glanced at Nadala. "Get everybody out."

Nadala slid back the door as two men in brown coveralls hurried toward her. Prada tapped her shoulder and held out the cuffs key. Without saying anything, Nadala quickly unlocked the prisoners.

"I'm not going anywhere," the man with the plaster nose declared.

Frank frowned and crashed his fist against the man's chin. The other two occupants cheered with obvious pleasure.

"He had it coming," the woman added.

"Hurry up in there!" one of the coveralls men hissed impatiently. "We don't have all day."

Nadala jumped out and watched as her prisoners helped the stunned Keeper into the Granvia. She felt strong arms embrace her and she sagged against Frank's firm chest. She turned and welcomed his hard kiss.

"I'm so sorry," she mumbled against his lips. "I had no choice. I did, but—"

He silenced her with another kiss, pulled back, and cupped her face between his hands. "We'll talk later."

"Come on, you two!" Prada snapped and ran toward the black van.

"What about the driver?" Nadala shouted after her.

"I gave him a sleepy pill!"

Everybody hurriedly buckled up and the van moved smoothly into the traffic. Nadala leaned against Frank and sighed when his arms went around her, vastly relieved that he appeared to forgive her. The thought of his rejection terrified her.

A chubby Keeper grinned broadly. "The cop who investigated you, Foxtrot? She obviously found what she looked for."

"Zip it, Charlie, or you'll end up like Echo," Frank shot back with a broad smile.

"Ah, our comrade against the rogues, except he turned out to be the worst type of rogue," Charlie muttered, shook his head, and glanced at the man in coveralls. "Where are we going?"

"A safe house. It's best if you don't know where."

Charlie lifted his palms. "Peace!"

Nadala sat up and looked at each of them. "Is everybody all right?"

The woman Keeper nodded. "Dr. Bayer didn't have time to start on the gruesome stuff," she said and tilted her head. "I presume you're one of Porter's investigators?"

"Former investigator."

"Welcome to the ranks of justice."

Nadala glared at her. "Whose justice, lady? Your vigilante justice? You didn't have to go after the rogues, but you loved to play your games."

The woman gaped in surprise. "Why the vitriol?"

"Shove it, Victor," Frank told her softly, his voice carrying authority. The woman shot him an angry look, but didn't say anything. "We'll dissect everything later." He nodded at the man in coveralls. "Thanks for delivering us from purgatory."

The man grinned. "Thank Manuel."

"All of you should thank Detective Vishnu," Nadala retorted, still angry at Victor. "She planned it all."

"She's our plant?" Charlie looked nonplussed.

Nadala leaned against Frank and held him tight, content to have his arms around her. Nothing else mattered. Nothing else ever did.

She closed her eyes and listened to the whisper of tires.

Chapter Seven

Inspector Porter stared at the screen in disbelief. Whatever agreement the Prime Minister had with the Covenant, it could not be for the legislation he now read, which meant Trusk lied to him last night. Or perhaps Griffin lied, something Porter readily believed. All politicians lied, he reminded himself, and the Commissioner was more a politician than a cop. It came with the rank. It did not matter either way. With the shackles finally off, the Taskforce could go after feeders in earnest.

He glanced at his watch, almost 9:45. The Attorney-General should have tabled the Feeder Bill in the House by now. Porter allowed himself a grim smile, clearly picturing the consternation of the independent MPs, gallery visitors, and covering reporters when the AG read the controversial bill. He liked what it said, but the government surely did not expect to get away with it. With Coalition support, they obviously did or would not have tabled the thing. He expected civil liberty groups across the country to march up and down the Canberra parliament lawn in alarmed outrage, while behind the scenes, busy preparing to mount a High Court challenge. A useless gesture even if it succeeded, as other countries would have passed similar legislation, and Project Purple would have secured enough test subjects to find that damned pill.

What Porter read, the bill contravened several UN and international agreements to which Australia was a signatory, including violation of existing Commonwealth criminal statutes. When passed, it would face some serious legal criticism. However, with federal elections still more than two years away, Griffin appeared prepared to wear the ensuing heat.

He wondered if people would protest all that vigorously. After all, the legislation only affected feeders, not the ordinary bloke on the street. Everybody wanted a medical solution to overcome onset of sudden old age death and rid the streets of prowling energy vampires. The National Rally Party and other far-right extremist groups would no doubt celebrate, ready to support what they'd see as a bold and overdue government initiative. A few minutes ago, getting coffee, Neil Ferris told him the NRP were already gathering below the steps of the state parliament demanding immediate action against feeders. Well, they got their wish, and then some.

The sweeping reach of the bill staggered him. It gave Taskforce Crimson sole authority to arrest suspect rogues on mere circumstantial evidence. It had twenty days to obtain proof that can stand up in court, with provision for an extension of another twenty days to validate forensic results before formal charges of premeditated murder were laid. During that period, the suspect had no right to direct legal representation. On conviction, the court can release rogues to the Taskforce for whatever additional testing the forensics facilities saw fit. The bill also required the Taskforce to establish a national register of all identified feeders, a retrograde step as it already maintained such a register, although far from complete. The insidious part of that clause demanded sharing information with other federal agencies, which effectively branded known feeders as undesirables and placed them on the suspicion list as potential rogues, with all the negative social connotations such a label generated if the information became public.

In an attempt to stifle inevitable alarm at such sweeping powers, the bill reaffirmed that Article 2 of the UN Universal Declaration of Human Rights adopted in 1948 applied with full force to feeders, which stated, '*Everyone is entitled to all the rights and freedoms set forth in this Declaration, without distinction of any kind, such as race, color, sex, language, religion, political or other opinion, national or social origin, birth or other status.*'

Interestingly, the legislation had no sunset clause, which meant Taskforce Crimson could wage unrestricted warfare against feeders forever, unless some future government amended or repealed the bill. It did provide a complaints avenue to the National Anti-Corruption Commission. A worthless fig leaf for anyone detained, as the bureaucratic process took weeks before anything happened. The complainant could launch civil action against the Taskforce for wrongful arrest—if he or she survived forty days of experimentation and could afford to mount a challenge. While the legal wheels turned and trial proceedings dragged on, feeders would continue to enjoy Zimmer's probing hospitality.

Professor Zimmer always bitched to him for more test subjects. From today, he'd likely get more than he could use. Ship them to the sister facility in Sydney, provided they had somewhere to hold them. Porter shrugged. Not his problem, although a looming issue for Trusk and the government.

They may have another and more serious difficulty, he mused. At breakfast this morning, he and Estella watched the news to catch up with the latest local and international shenanigans. An open window into how the world works. Neither enjoyed the dissection clips. He forgot about breakfast and boarded the train to the city deep in thought.

As a federal police officer, Porter harbored several personal reservations about the bill. As an ordinary citizen, he understood why the government tabled it, pushed into taking action by the Hacker Anonymous revelation. People wanted a pill to stop them dying, simple as that, and he suspected most would turn a blind eye to how the government got it for them, setting a most dangerous precedent. Even if it meant ongoing experimentation on helpless infants? He'll ask Zimmer why researchers needed infants.

If one of the pharmaceutical giants involved with Project Purple managed to produce the pill within the next two years, Prime Minister Griffin and her Labor Party would be hailed as national heroes and likely voted in for another term. If not…but that lay in the future and not worth expending too many brain cells on now.

Despite some moral doubts, he served the Taskforce, which in turn served the social greater need. The rationale did not sit entirely comfortably, but as head of the Melbourne branch, he would see to it his people did not abuse their powers.

He took a sip of the tepid coffee and sat back.

The desk phone rang and he picked up. "Porter!"

"Dr. Bayer, Inspector. Excuse the interruption—"

"What is it, Doctor?"

"Some fifteen minutes ago, Detective Sergeant Vishnu presented an authorization to transfer all Keepers to the Clayton facility. We've done it often enough. Ordinarily, I don't question your orders, but it seemed somewhat unusual to transfer them now before we finished even preliminary examinations."

Prada!

Porter gripped the phone until his knuckles began to protest. He eased his hold and took a calming breath.

His trusted 2IC stabbed him in the back. With the Taskforce from the beginning, she proved an invaluable guide when he took over the branch, familiarizing him with the personnel, operational procedures, and cases. On Saturday, after Hogan Lovell spilled all, Prada must have tipped off the Covenant. It explained why his team only caught two Keepers, not counting Frank Hram. The likely explanation for her betrayal, she might be a feeder.

He felt the hurt more keenly than he anticipated. Although he knew for some time that one of his investigators worked for the Covenant, it never occurred to him it would be Prada.

It reinforced the grim truth that he could not trust anyone. *Even Trusk*, his cynical side reminded him with a smirk. Porter did not want to believe it, but he had to accept the stark possibility. A manipulative Canberra operator, Trusk probably took steps to cover his back if mud started to fly over his Taskforce's activities. He could claim the city branches did it on their own. Porter and his colleagues might get the chop to save the higher-ups. Shit always flowed downhill, he reflected.

Something else occurred to him.

"Doctor, did Detective Vishnu come alone?"

"She had someone with her. I don't know her name—"

"Description?"

"Tall, ash-blonde—"

"Thank you. I know her."

Nadala Robinson, of course. The revelation did not come as total surprise. She never wanted to arrest Hram and cooked up a plan with Prada to break him out, taking the other Keepers with them in the bargain.

"You said Detective Vishnu came fifteen minutes ago. That means they already left?"

"They used one of our white VW Kombis. I don't know the rego—"

Porter ground his teeth in frustration. The fool should have queried the irregular transfer immediately, but he could not actually blame Bayer. He did not know that Prada played him.

"Please email me the full details, including the vehicle used. Under the circumstances, you did the right thing to call. Somebody will be in touch." He hung up, then dug out his cellphone, and opened an app that tracked his team's phones. He pressed Vishnu's icon and a 'Not connected' message flashed back at him. Wearing a wry smile, he tried Nadala's with the same result.

Frustrating, but predictable, he reflected with a tinge of pride. His people were following procedure.

He activated encryption mode and tapped in a number for his special ops team.

"Code word," the electronically altered voice demanded.

"Crimson One. An immediate for you. Apprehend a standard Southbank Institute transfer van containing four Keepers scheduled for the Monash Precinct at Clayton. The vehicle may or may not be under Taskforce control and is likely not heading to Clayton. Detain and return all occupants to the Institute."

"Acknowledged," the voice answered and broke contact.

Every Institute vehicle came with a transponder for exactly such a contingency. His team should find it with minimal difficulty. Of course, once they had it did not guarantee the occupants would be inside. One step at a time.

Porter replaced the receiver and nodded, eminently satisfied at the notion of adding Prada Vishnu to Zimmer's list of subjects. As for the charming Nadala, she could look forward to joining the ranks of the unemployed. With his negative reference, she'd be lucky to get a job at McDonald's. Too bad, as he had high hopes for the woman. He understood perfectly why she did it, but she forgot to be a cop and crossed to the other side. A sin he could not forgive.

Twenty minutes later, his cell demanded attention. The red encryption light blinking, he input his PIN.

"Code word."

"Red One," the electronic voice answered. "Subject vehicle located at the Ink Hotel on City Road. We found the Institute driver unconscious. Probably drugged."

Porter frowned, understanding what happened. Finding Prada and the Keepers had now become a major problem. Instead of a red star of approval from Trusk for breaking up the Melbourne Covenant operation, he could expect an icy blast of acrimony.

Trusk expected results, not interested in explanations why something failed.

Screw yourself, Commissioner!

"I'll forward pictures of all subjects. Coordinate with the local Criminal Investigation Unit and issue an all-points bulletin."

"Acknowledged."

He broke contact and slid the cell across his desk. After a heavy sigh, he logged on, attached the photos to an email, and sent it off, not expecting much to happen. Prada and the Keepers were gone. The Covenant would see to it. Nadala might show up, but apart from facing dismissal, he could not do anything else to her. As a Taskforce investigator, normal federal police disciplinary procedures did not apply, and punitive action lay with him and Trusk. He *could* charge her with violation of the Official Secrets Act 1911, but doing so could generate publicity neither he nor the Taskforce wanted. But why should he charge her at all? For being disloyal? Because she followed through with her convictions and prevented what she saw as injustice?

If she went public?

It did not matter. Once the Feeder Bill became law, nobody would care what happened to her. Most people would regard her as a dumb woman who forgot to do her duty by falling for a Keeper. Serve her right what she got, they'd say. Anybody prepared to run her story would first validate it with him, and he prepared himself to totally discredit her. If somebody did run the story on her say-so only, the Taskforce had mechanisms to quash it.

Not his best morning and the day far from done.

Sometimes it did not pay to get up at all.

Around 11:30, someone banged on his door.

"Come!"

Simone Washnik flung back the door, flushed and breathless. "Have you heard?"

He stared at her and blinked. "Heard what?"

"The Governor-General declined to provide royal assent for the Feeder Bill, citing it violated the Constitution, and sent it back to the House. Prime Minister Griffin is boiling mad and threatens to dismiss him. You do know about the bill and those horrible info clips?"

"Only what Griffin announced on Saturday night," he told her. A barefaced lie, of course. "I saw the info clips this morning."

"Is Project Purple really doing those things? I almost puked when I saw them."

"Our Southbank facility isn't, but other research centers probably are."

Her gaze lingered on him. "Is this what we now do, Kurt?"

"How do you think drugs are developed, Detective?"

"I'll print you a copy of that bill," she murmured and closed the door after her.

He waited a second, swore, then picked up his cell, wanting to wash the damned info clips out of his mind. Did the end justify the means?

"I expected you'd be calling," Commissioner Trusk announced gravely. "You're not the first."

"Is it true about the Governor-General?"

"It's a disaster, Inspector. All our planning and maneuvering undone in one stroke. Griffin never figured the Governor-General would refuse to sign the bill, although in hindsight, given what is at stake, she should have."

"Lots of things become clear in hindsight," Porter added. "What now?"

"The PM said she'll dismiss him, and she can, but it will take time. With the bill now in public domain, the damage is done. My Taskforce has the ground cut from under us, and the government is in for some rocky times. The Liberal Party is already distancing themselves from the bill to salvage something from the debacle."

"But they supported the bill!" Porter protested.

"Rats are the first to abandon a sinking ship, Inspector."

"Where does that leave us?"

"We keep doing our job until told otherwise."

"After seeing those dissection clips, public sympathy may swing to favor feeders, which will leave us walking on legal eggshells."

Trusk chuckled. "Succinctly put and accurate."

"You know what will happen next, Neville. With the bill tossed out, the Covenant will stomp on Griffin, the Labor Party, and the Liberals. They were betrayed and won't hold back. People want a cure for sudden death, but those clips were devastating. We can expect to see more of the same or worse."

"Griffin can limit the damage if she asks the networks not to run them."

"As you said, the damage is already done. Besides, why should the networks stop running them? They'll be raking it in for the privilege."

"Probably. Griffin can mitigate the situation if she tables a watered down bill."

"If she survives, the Covenant will demand that she shuts down the Taskforce and rein in the more extreme medical procedures. All of us could face charges."

"Let's not get carried away, Kurt. A number of political heads will have to get chopped first before somebody comes after us."

"Cold comfort. Those clips, were they Australia-wide?"

"All over the eastern hemisphere. I suspect Europe will wake up and see the same thing."

"After what happened here, other countries will be nuts trying to pass similar legislation. Politicians don't like to stick their neck out to be chopped. Do you have an island hideaway I can go to?"

Trusk laughed. "Keep your activities low key and pursue genuine rogues. Don't attempt to arrest someone without verifiable evidence. It will make life difficult for our Melbourne and Sydney forensics facilities, but it cannot be helped."

"And I thought I had my day made," Porter groused.

"You managed to break up the local Covenant operation, which is good. Well done."

Porter wanted to hold back the bad news, but it wasn't something he could do.

"Not all good, Commissioner. This morning, one of my investigators walked into the Southbank facility and sprung four Keepers."

"A Covenant plant?"

"Everything points to it. My special team is on it. I take full responsibility. Knowing I had four valuable prizes, I should have initiated extra security protocols."

"Forget the Keepers, Kurt. I want you to stop all activity against them, and notify your Covenant contact to that effect. Add this, though. Taskforce Crimson will not pursue them, but should one kill a rogue and we can prove it, they'll face murder one. However, we'll accept any intelligence they care to share. As of now, the Covenant is out of the rogue hunting business...all over the world."

The Commissioner's message left Porter nonplussed. Instead of a dressing down, he had a new operating mandate.

"They were out of it when Hacker made their announcement."

"In case you're wondering, this is going out to all Taskforce Crimson branches," Trusk added.

"What about my Covenant plant?"

"Deal with it as you see fit."

The line went dead and Porter gently replaced the receiver. He reached for his cell and called off the special ops team. Still digesting what Trusk told him, he picked up the desk phone and pressed a glowing button.

"I'm still printing the bill, Kurt," Simone answered.

"Don't bother. I already have a copy. My office, now," he snapped and replaced the receiver.

Shortly, a knock, and she opened the door.

"Take a seat. As of this moment, you're my 2IC," he told her as she pulled up a chair.

Her eyes grew round. "What happened to Prada? She isn't—"

He lifted a hand. "She betrayed us to the Covenant. After our morning meeting, she and Nadala went to the Forensic Institute and released our Keepers."

"She was a Covenant plant? I don't believe it."

"I'll email you what you need to know to be my 2IC. You'll also get access to most Taskforce servers. Apart from doing your job, you'll be responsible for every active case file run by the team. I just came off the phone with Trusk and he filled me in on the Feeder Bill. There'll be a meeting at one PM and I'll explain where we stand. Make sure everybody is there. That clear?"

She grinned and stood. "Does my new job rate a pay increase?"

"Get out."

"Prada a feeder?" She shook her head, unable to accept the idea.

Before she could close the door, Nadala pushed in past her, which earned her a curious look from Simone.

Porter's eyebrows climbed in surprise. "You're the last person I expected to see, Detective."

She pulled an envelope from her jacket and placed it on his desk.

"My resignation."

He met her steadfast gaze and pursed his mouth. It took courage and conviction to come back and face him, but he always knew she had those qualities.

"Close the door and sit," he told her softly.

Expecting him to rage, his mild response appeared to confuse her. Still wary, she slowly sat down, fingers locked on her lap.

"Mmm. Not the same Nadala I saw yesterday," he continued. "You've matured."

"I did some hard thinking," she temporized.

"Not only thinking, but doing. Care to tell me what happened to the Keepers?"

"The Covenant took them to a safe house. I don't know where. They dropped me off at the South Melbourne Market and I took an Uber to the Center to pick up my car."

"I presume Prada went with them?"

"Yes, sir."

"Did you hear what happened to the Feeder Bill?"

She frowned and shook her head.

"The Governor-General refused to sign it into law."

"I see."

"You don't, but it doesn't matter." He tapped her resignation letter with a stiff finger. "There is no justification for what you and Prada did, Detective, although I understand why you did it. With the bill dead, many things will change how the Taskforce does business. I'll need able investigators more than ever, and you proved yourself very able. Tell me. Do you want to continue hunting rogues? They're the society's real enemy, not the Covenant, which is a different dimension altogether."

Porter gazed steadily into her green eyes, surprised at what he said. He should rake her soundly for what she did, exemplary in its drastic quality. Instead, he tossed it all out in a gesture of grand magnanimity. Why? She believed in what the Taskforce did. Otherwise, she would never have accepted the appointment. Prada warned him that Nadala did not have the personality or temperament required for the job, but he disagreed. He wanted his investigators to show spunk, determination, and a degree of moral fiber. Qualities Nadala had in heaps. What steered his brand new investigator down the wrong path wasn't her romantic attachment to Hram, although a factor, but objections to how the Taskforce went about its job.

"I agree that rogues are everybody's enemy," she declared at length, "and deserve to be treated as murderers. What I cannot sanction is open abuse of individuals' rights by apprehending them on mere suspicion they might be a feeder. There is a vast gulf between arresting a genuine rogue, and someone whose only sin is to be a feeder. Your Taskforce, and taskforces everywhere, don't appear to see the difference, or chose to ignore it in their drive to obtain experimental subjects. I'm resigning because I *can* see the difference."

He expected something like that, but not the force of her delivery. "I'm not going to paper over what Project Purple did, or how they did it, Detective. However, Hacker Anonymous changed the calculus for everybody. By refusing to sign the Feeder Bill, the Governor-General demonstrated the error of everybody's approach to feeders. His action created a minor Constitutional crisis, but that's not our concern. Despite personal question marks, I wanted that bill passed, but it's done. What is important for both of us, this Taskforce, if it continues to exist tomorrow, will stick to its original charter, which is to track down and apprehend rogues, and you can be a contributor."

Playing the politician himself now?

Nadala gave a sour chuckle. "Hunt rogues? What Project Purple's charter demands is not apprehending rogues, but penetration of the Covenant for political reasons. Everything else is window-dressing. I don't want any part of that."

"Project Purple *is* attempting to penetrate the Covenant, but not at taskforce level. Not directly anyway. My branch is not involved in penetration activities, although I passed useful intelligence to Trusk. So, Detective Robinson. Do you want to be a player?"

"You're prepared to forget what Prada and I did?"

"Not forget, but I won't hold it against you professionally. If you need time to think it over—"

"I'll stay," she replied without hesitation, and he smiled, liking her decisiveness.

"There's a team meeting at one. Be there. That's all, Detective."

With the Commissioner's new directive, Nadala could resume her relationship with Frank Hram, which should please her no end. As for Prada...

Pondering what to do with her, he came to a startling realization. He shaded the truth when he told Nadala his team did not actively seek intelligence to penetrate the Covenant, and they didn't. His special ops team handled that end.

Poor Nadala. Sharp, thorough, she could not understand why Prada dropped her Mercer investigation. A judgment call, he told her, which did not sit well with her at all, her detective alarms clanging. What he could not tell her, Prada did not drop the investigation. Instead, she used it to entrap and eventually apprehend a Keeper sent to kill Mercer, which opened a small window into the Covenant's Melbourne operation. A very small window, as Keepers had scant knowledge of the organization's administrative arm. Why go after them, then? Porter asked himself the same thing more than once. All Trusk said, it created cracks in the Covenant hierarchy, something Porter dismissed. Who gave a toss anyway how Trusk played it, the whole tangled mess way above his pay grade.

He swiveled his chair and gazed at the Docklands sprawl. His flash of soul-searching? He believed in pursuing rogue feeders. They were murderers of the worst kind and deserved whatever society dished out to them. All too often, with little justification, ordinary feeders were dragged in with the same net simply to provide Project Purple's research institutions with test subjects. He understood the need, but as Nadala said, not how they did it. Instead of being a standard bearer to protect people from energy vampires—he might as well admit what they were—he became an Inquisitor, and Project Purple his religion.

Traffic crawled across the Westgate Bridge. In the background, towering cranes waited to swoop on a container ship. Bright sunshine colored the world with light. But Porter did not enjoy the vista, having lost his faith. In a way, the Governor-General had done him a favor.

He cracked a smile when he reflected on his senior investigator.

If he could overlook what Robinson did, he should not damn Prada either. He hated to lose an experienced investigator and administrator, but after what she did, he could no longer trust her. Best to transfer her back to regular police duties where she could still have a career. Doing two such good things did not come easily to him, and he savored the unusual feeling of satisfaction.

Perhaps he should review his own career objectives. Estella wouldn't mind if he expressed more interest in her.

He picked up his cell, set encryption, and tapped in a number.

"Identify," the electronic voice demanded after four rings.

"Crimson One. We need to talk, Manuel de la Kass."

* * *

Frank Hram stood in front of the Oaks building and watched the black Uber sedan pull away from the curb into heavy traffic. Sunshine slanted through golden elms along the avenue's median strip and made everything livelier. A hot gust stirred his hair and he took a deep breath, not minding the raw smell of car exhausts, the noise, or pedestrians along the sidewalks. He felt at home, in his element, something he did not expect to experience again for some time, if at all. Definitely a morning to remember.

He walked up the steps, paused until the heavy glass panels slid aside, and strode toward the elevators. Inside his apartment, everything looked the same as though he stepped out only a minute ago, which in a sense, he did. No sign of Zenola, of course. He'd call her later with an update, but first...

He dug out his cell and tapped in a number.

"Manuel de la Kass. Identify."

"It's Frank."

"Where are you, amigo?"

"At home. I just got in. My thanks for getting us out of the Institute and the deal you made with Porter."

"Thank India for getting you all sprung."

"India?"

"Our Taskforce plant."

Frank recalled the Indian woman and smiled at her choice of codename.

"As for the deal with Porter, after the Governor-General vetoed the Feeder Bill, the PM and Commissioner Trusk were forced to do some reevaluation."

"I don't doubt it. Those awful clips I'm told the Covenant aired on all channels probably helped speed their deliberations," Frank added.

"The fallout is still falling. By the way, I can't contact Echo. We planned something special for him."

"We left him at the Institute."

Manuel laughed. "Poetic justice, and perhaps a better solution for everybody. I've got another call coming. Glad to hear you're safe, amigo. Talk to you later. We have much to discuss."

Frank scrolled through his Contacts list and pressed her icon.

"Frank! O my God! Where are you? What's going on?"

"Remember that pleasant afternoon we had in mind for yesterday? We can have it today if you can make it."

"You come right over, Frank Hram, and tell me everything!" Nadala commanded.

"How about four o'clock? I must take care of a few things."

"Not a minute later, hear?"

"Deal. Love you."

"Love you too, you lug."

He cut contact, a large grin on his face, looking forward to having her in his arms again.

Almost 1:30 PM, he showered, changed into a fresh suit, and made himself a toasted pastrami and cheese sandwich on brown bread, accompanied by freshly squeezed orange juice. Years back, he bought a juicer that produced colored water, keeping back all the healthy fiber. He switched to a Nutribullet thing, which liquidized everything.

Cathy looked up in surprise when he walked into Urbi Investments.

"Frank! Owen and I tried to reach you all day. Is everything all right?"

He saw their text messages, but hadn't the time to respond.

"Everything is fine. I had to take care of some personal business. I trust you apologized to my clients scheduled for this morning?"

"Owen dealt with them. You have another one at three."

"I know. Ask Owen to take him, or reschedule. I won't be in."

"More personal business? The hot lady detective who came to see you last Thursday?"

"It's possible."

"Go for it." She also tried to get him married off at every opportunity. Her face suddenly turned serious. "Have you followed the news?"

"About the Feeder Bill? I know all about it."

"I'm glad the Governor-General quashed the thing. By the way, the police broke up a serious scuffle at Parliament House and everything is peaceful again. I wonder for how long," she mused. "Those awful clips on TV? They made my skin crawl. I knew feeders and the Covenant existed, but the things Project Purple are doing is unbelievable. I want a pill to stop me suddenly dying, not that I'm promiscuous or anything," she added quickly with a disarming grin, "but I had no idea what they were doing to get it."

"I hope more people feel the same way. I'm going to catch up on some administration. Buzz if you need me," he told her and made for his office.

He barely powered up his computer when he heard a knock and Owen peered in.

"Got a minute, partner?"

"Grab a chair," Frank said with a wave of his hand.

"I tried to reach you—"

"I know. I saw your texts. Sorry for not getting back to you. Something unexpected came up." Like having his phone confiscated at the Institute.

"Important?"

"Could have been. It's all sorted out."

"You're up on current events?"

"I know what's going on, Owen. That's why I came in. I wanted to check the market indicators."

"The All Ordinaries dipped 256 points when the Exchange opened, but it recovered most of it by noon when people realized the PM's bill wasn't law."

Frank shook his head. "Our life would be simpler if markets were driven by logic and facts, not emotions."

"Then we'd be out of a job," Owen replied with a smile.

"There is that. Anything I should know about my two clients? By the way, thanks for seeing them."

"A routine update. One wanted to liquidate some of his holdings, fearing a market plunge, but I persuaded him to sit tight."

"I asked Cathy if you could handle my afternoon appointment—"

"Sorry. My day is full."

"Not a problem. She'll reschedule."

Owen cocked his head. "You're leaving early?"

"I have a date," Frank said with a grin.

"The federal cop?"

"The same."

"I'm glad for you, Frank. I mean it. About time you crawled out of your shell."

"I've had a tough few years after Rainey."

"Remember, you're coming over for Christmas lunch. Bring your lady friend along if you like. Karen would love to meet her and talk girly things."

Frank originally planned to spend a few days with his parents at Airlie Beach, but they were taking a fourteen-day cruise around New Zealand. He didn't fancy spending Christmas alone in his apartment.

"We'll see. Things are a little fluid right now."

"Not a problem." Owen stood and gave him a long look. "Are you okay, Frank?"

"What do you mean?"

"You seem preoccupied, distant."

"I'm fine. Hectic morning."

"Catch you later, then," Owen replied, not entirely convinced.

Frank hated to keep a major personal secret from his friend, and perhaps one day, puffing a cigar, a snifter of cognac in hand, he would reveal all, but not right now. When he said things were fluid, he did not mean with Nadala. Life needed to settle down for everybody, and feeders a normal part of it, before he could talk openly about himself, mindful of what happened when he blabbed, although a very special case.

Nadala's betrayal still a little raw, he wanted to hear her side before he buried the episode into a memory drawer. She came back for him, he reminded himself. In his book, that squared away all sins…mostly.

At 3:00 PM, he logged off and waved a cheery goodbye to Cathy. An apartment in the building where he worked proved its worth. His lifestyle may lack some things, but not having to endure a numbing twice-daily crush made up for it.

He did not mind the idea of driving to Nadala's place, but finding a parking spot in that narrow street would be next to impossible. Let the Uber driver do all the worrying how to get there.

With a jerk, the dark blue SUV stopped in front of her terrace house. He stepped out eager to see her, a little tense, recent events fresh in his mind. She opened the door, also a little tense. Probably for the same reason, he reflected. A touch of gloss made her lips shine. Lips he wanted desperately to feel against his. Wearing a black T-shirt over white slacks, she looked poised and dignified. He heard the Uber drive off and gathered her into his arms.

"You make my heart sing, Detective Robinson," he murmured and brushed her lips with a finger. Yesterday, though, he wondered if it ever would again.

She trembled against him, eyes glistening, ready to spill tears. "Oh, Frank. After what I've—"

His mouth clamped on her tender lips and her arms wound around his neck. The need for oxygen forced them to break up. Her eyes went dark green and her happy smile vanished. Without saying anything, she took his hand and led him upstairs.

Eyes locked on each other, pieces of clothing quickly littered the floor. She pressed her yielding breasts against him and waited as he slowly pulled down her black panties. On one knee, he kissed the tuft of pale hair between her legs. Nadala moaned and pressed his head against her belly, wanting more. He ran his hands up her thighs, sides, cupped her breasts, and stepped back to admire every subtle curve of her superb body.

"My God, you're a miracle."

She flashed a sparkling smile and tugged his hand toward the bed. The cover flew back and she threw herself across the mattress. His need urgent, he thrust into her hard. She yelped and her fingernails left trails of fire across his back as she smothered his face with kisses. About to peak, she let out a stifled scream, then shuddered as waves of pleasure rippled through her, which prompted his own release. She let out a low growl, pushed him onto his back, and rode him with wild abandon until both climaxed again. After a huge exhale, she sagged against him, cheek to cheek.

"I needed that," she murmured and bit his ear.

"Ow! Eating me isn't part of the package."

"That's where you're wrong, buster," she purred, eyes intense. "You're mine, and I'll devour every part of you."

He raised his eyebrows. "Every part?"

She giggled and slapped his chest. "His turn will come."

"As will yours," he growled, leaned across her, and began to lick her neck, chest, lingered on each nipple before moving down to her navel. She grasped his head, pulled him up, and wrapped her arms around him.

"You're a wondrous man, Frank Hram, and I can't imagine life without you. Promise you'll never leave me?"

"Not even the end of time will make me leave you."

He gazed deeply into her magical orbs, kissed the tip of her nose, then brought his mouth gently over her inviting lips, supremely satisfied and at peace. Tomorrow remained to be written, and all the days after, but right now there were no tomorrows. Only the eternal now.

On his back, hands behind his head, Nadala smiled as her finger slid down the bridge of his nose, traced the outline of his lips, chin, and moved to roam randomly over his chest.

"I like hard, craggy men. Do you work out?"

"I make use of a gym and pool in the building. You?"

"I take long walks, runs, and do calisthenics."

"I can tell."

She glared. "Are you saying I'm lumpy?"

"You're gorgeous and you know it," he assured her with a smile. "How come you never married again?" he asked on impulse. "Men must have chased you."

"They did, but they were the wrong men. Then a mysterious feeder showed up. I'm still half certain you manipulated me to draw me into your snare."

"My sweetie, you're the one who cast the snare, and I hope never to escape."

"You can't. It's unbreakable." She bit her lip and pulled back. "I almost did break it, though."

"No need to explain," he told her, finding to his surprise that he meant it.

"I must get this off my chest—"

"And what a perfect chest it is."

She laughed gaily and playfully punched his shoulder. "Blockhead. What is it with men and breasts? Seriously, you have to understand why I did it. The cop part of me demanded I bring you in, even though the part that loved you said I shouldn't. Porter called me in after you left yesterday, and I told him I'm shutting down the Dan/Mercer case. Lack of evidence. He got stuck into me then for being a silly woman who allowed a Keeper, an expert at playing women, to sweep me off my feet. He may have been right. I swore an oath to uphold the law, and you were a confessed killer, although I didn't tell him that. It meant my career if I didn't arrest you. You know what happened then." Miserable, ready to cry, she stared at him.

He reached for her and held her tight. "You came back for me," he said gently. "That means everything."

She sniffed and pulled back. "I almost didn't. Angy, my sister, straightened me out." Nadala smiled at the memory. "And I always thought I had the smarts in the family."

"What did she say?"

"That I worked for the enemy. I always knew it in a way, but I believed in what Porter and the Taskforce did. Or I thought I did, and buried my moral reservations. As a federal law officer, I could not reconcile the need to apprehend rogue feeders and the methods we used to get them. Not only rogues, but anyone we suspected to be one."

"It takes a lot of courage to stop obeying an illegal order," he told her softly.

"On Saturday, I went after a man Lenny the Finger identified as a rogue. He had a wife and an adorable little girl who reminded me of Angy's kid. He admitted to being a feeder, but he never killed, and I believed him. An ordinary man who suffered from an impossible affliction trying to live a normal life like the rest of us. That's when I crossed the line between duty and compassion. What sealed it for me was seeing Professor Zimmer—"

"In charge of the Taskforce Crimson section at the Institute?"

"That's him. He opened my eyes to what he and other research centers do to find that magic anti-death pill. When he told me they experimented on babies, my insides rebelled. I asked myself, how can governments pursue their own people to satisfy the perceived need of the majority? When Angy said I worked for the enemy, I realized I've been deluding myself from the day I joined Porter's taskforce." She let out a long exhale. "There, I've said it."

"It's a mixed-up world out there, Nadala. I didn't enjoy killing rogues, although I believe some Keepers did. Maybe I did a little. The Covenant screened us thoroughly before we started our training. They didn't want zealots among them. I enjoyed killing Kaneel, though. She represented the worst in a rogue. She didn't need to kill Dan, but she did it anyway. There were undoubtedly reasons for her behavior. Reason's we'll never know. The Covenant tried to rehabilitate her, but she didn't want any part of us. In hindsight, I should have let another Keeper handle her. Never get emotionally involved with your target, they told us repeatedly. I threw training and discipline out the door and went after her. I never knew Dan, but I believe we were friends."

"And you couldn't forgive Kaneel for taking him from you," she added.

"That too, but most of all, she represented a cancerous cell I had to cut out. We could have told Porter about her and let him deal with her, but all too often, your Taskforce moves at glacial speed and does nothing. While it sits on its hands crossing the T's, rogues continue to kill."

"Are you glad you're no longer a Keeper?"

"I am," he told her truthfully. "I began to tire of the game we played some time back, and in many ways it was a game. When Hacker Anonymous broke the story, I felt relieved. The Covenant has hunted rogues for centuries, and I like to believe whoever runs it was glad to leave that side of its operation to Project Purple. They could have done it much earlier, but there it is."

"Who runs the Covenant, Frank, and what do they actually do?"

"You know already. It's all in your indoctrination brief."

"You know about that?"

"The Covenant has Project Purple and its taskforces totally penetrated."

"Prada," Nadala murmured.

"Who?"

She smiled. "A colleague."

"Ah, India."

"Is that what you call her?"

"I'm told she picked the codename herself. It tickled me when I found out."

Nadala laid her head on his chest. "At the Institute, they didn't mistreat you, did they?"

"Dr. Bayer had me prodded, scanned, weighed, and took about a liter of blood, but nothing painful. If I stayed longer, I fancy my days would have been less pleasant. The way India got us out? A slick, professional operation. Do you know what happened to her?"

"No idea. Porter might charge her if she shows up. She broke every rule in his book, but after what happened to the Feeder Bill and those horrid TV clips, he may have thrown the rulebook away. He did it with me."

He gaped at her. "What? After everything that happened, you're still working for him?"

"Rogues haven't left the building, Frank," she declared primly. "That part of the job, I can handle. As for everything else, I believe there'll be changes to how Taskforce Crimson operates. Besides, Manuel will need an insider."

"You?"

"Why not?"

"You've changed, Detective Robinson," he said after a thoughtful moment.

"Taskforce Crimson changed me. You changed me. How do you like the makeover?"

"I like it a lot."

"You know, I had a nagging fear I wouldn't be able to keep up with you."

"Keep up with me?"

"Older, more knowledgeable, experienced, I wasn't in your league. When the intimacy ended, you'd get tired of me and seek new prey."

He stroked her cheek. "I can understand your feelings, but that's the cynic inside you talking. Love cannot be measured with any yardstick, Nadala. You possess qualities that drew me to you from the first moment I saw you. What you never considered, Detective, I feared you would not find me worthy and discard me for someone younger."

"You got me used to vintage wine, Frank Hram. Now, I can't go back to cheap knockoffs."

"Glad to hear it."

"Say! Whatever happened to that man with the broken nose?"

"Echo? A fellow Keeper. He's the one who betrayed us to Porter."

"Wow. Who gave him the broken nose?"

"Yesterday, Porter arranged for the two of us to meet. He expected I'd kill Echo by linking with him and sucking him dry. Believe me, I wanted to, but I'd be handing Porter evidence that I willfully killed. Instead, I smashed in his nose."

She laughed. "Where is he now? The Covenant safe house?"

Frank chuckled. "I hoped the Covenant would deal with him in some drastic manner, but after Porter arranged to let us go, I had a better idea. I suggested we leave Echo with Dr. Bayer to play with."

Nadala grinned, liking the idea. "Serves the bastard right."

"That's what we all thought."

"What now? You'll revert to a dull investment consultant?"

"Not exactly." He wanted to tell her about Manuel's crazy idea of him being a Master, but decided to bide his time, not prepared to be completely open with her right now. When the moment comes, he hoped she would understand. Instead, he nibbled her nose. "I need to feed and I want to ravish you. Later, I'll help make dinner. I plan to get mighty hungry."

"Blockhead!"

He rubbed his chin against her cheeks and she squealed, small fists pounding his back.

* * *

"What are you going to do?" Sybille Konigen's voice came clearly from the phone's speaker.

Snow drifted down in large flakes from a dark sky and blurred the Manhattan skyline. Aiden Conrad wondered if it snowed in Zurich, not giving a damn. Warm air whispered from the central heating system that made his office nice and cozy. He should not be working at all. Most of the TD Bank Building had shut down for the Christmas/New Year break, and he should do the same; shut down and enjoy personal time with Ethel. If it weren't for the Aussie business, he would, but his job owned him.

The job…A relentless taskmaster that allowed no peace, only unfailing duty. It did not allow for weekends, holidays, or personal needs. It wanted him 24/7, simple as that. A high price for running half the world, and he often speculated whether the privilege compensated for making him old before his time. No wonder Grand Masters did not last long—he hated the title, a 300-year-old throwback to an archaic time. He did not actually run the world, his Council did, but it often felt like it. Once the current situation resolved itself, he would take Ethel somewhere warm, perhaps Down Under. Given what they did yesterday, the irony of that choice did not escape him. Still, he never visited Australia and the experience might prove enlightening.

"Strike back hard to contain the situation," he replied promptly. "Her head will roll as a warning to others. I already spoke to our Australian Master Keeper. He has compromising evidence that should force Prime Minister Griffin to resign, which will effectively derail her government's efforts to pass what is horrendously repressive legislation."

"Her government already passed it. If it weren't for their Governor-General—"

"I know. A tactical miscalculation on Griffin's part. One we must exploit fully, but I don't intend to stop with her."

"You want to disrupt her cabinet? Is that wise? With Griffin out of the way, her party would have gotten the message. Your action will needlessly destabilize the Australian government."

"That's the general idea, but I want more than Griffin's cabinet. I want the leader of the Liberal Party served on a plate. We made a deal, Sybille, and they shafted us. Nobody does that without consequences."

"New Zealand and Canada delayed submitting what I understand were virtual copies of the Australian Feeder Bill. The Aussies didn't do this alone. They were obviously part of a coordinated plan."

"One that almost worked."

"I'd like to know who put it together. It didn't happen yesterday."

"Agreed. The Hacker Anonymous announcement merely served as a trigger to set it into motion."

"Which sets me to thinking," the western hemisphere Grand Master reflected. "Why didn't we see it coming?"

"European governments had similar bills ready to table?"

"That's what I'm getting from my Master Keepers."

"In that case, the answer to your question is simple. We were the subject of a very clever misdirection plot. We entered into negotiations figuratively hugging and shaking hands that feeders the world over would be recognized and protected under law, and Project Purple's taskforces reined in. We obtained copies of the proposed legislation and didn't bother to look beyond the obvious. A major strategic blunder on our part," Conrad added ruefully. "While all along, they prepared an entirely different bill. I shudder to think what might have happened if the Aussies succeeded."

"There'd be a cascade of legislation coming down on us from all over the world, which would have taken years to repeal, if at all," Konigen added. "I still find it incredible that our people never got an inkling."

"A salutary lesson for us, and I blame myself." By extension, he also blamed her. Their intelligence apparatus let them down badly, something to pick over diligently. "With our hands on most political and economic levers, comfortable exercising our power, we grew complacent. We cannot afford to let that happen again. That's why I want to destroy Prime Minister Griffin and the Liberal Party leader. If he hasn't already, the New Zealand Prime Minister will get an enlightening email from their Master Keeper that should make him pause and reconsider if he wants to save his political hide, but I'm not stopping there. All government heads in my hemisphere will receive a similar email, and I suggest you do the same thing."

"Aren't you overreacting a little, Aiden? Rake the Aussies until they bleed is fine, but going after others could trigger a damaging backlash."

"They declared open war on us, which makes it our move, and I don't intend to fire back with a popgun. The objective of every government is to remain in power. Everything else is secondary, which includes serving the electorate who supposedly put them there. The Covenant must give everybody a sharp rap across the knuckles as a reminder that *we* got them elected, or at best allowed them to stay in power. You and I know that exercise of so-called democracy where people are free to elect their representatives as an expression of popular will is an illusion. They may cast the ballot, but money and the media directs them to vote for candidates who are obedient to our policies. Prime Minister Griffin ignored that reality and will pay the ultimate political price. You must reinforce that reality in Europe and Africa."

"It's a little more complicated here. I must deal with individual governments and the EU Executive, and they're in recess for the holidays."

"You have a phone. Call them."

"If we initiate a destabilization response, it could create an undesirable economic ripple effect."

"Some market correction is inevitable, but I anticipate a short-term effect only. We don't want to actually topple any government, provided they do the expected thing."

"And holding a Damocles sword over them will make them tractable," Konigen replied, clearly amused.

"Precisely. After all, in our own fashion, we also serve the people."

"As long as they also do what we tell them."

"Of course. That's man's history, and those in power write the history. The vast populace out there are sheep, or at best children to be guided and kept happy. The way we do that is by sat-isfying their basic needs and giving talented individuals opportu-nities to grow—"

"And join our ranks," Konigen added softly. "Why did I ever think you were not fit to be a Grand Master?"

"Because of your disdain for a New World upstart who thought he knew more than you, backed by centuries of Euro-pean glories and past empires," Conrad replied promptly, and Konigen laughed with genuine mirth.

"True."

"That's why one of your predecessors tried to assassinate the American Master Keeper when he declared independence from Europe."

"Let's not rake over old corpses, okay?" she admonished sternly.

"I apologize. I shouldn't have said that. You and I had our differences, but we managed to put them aside in pursuit of Cov-enant objectives. Although I don't say it often enough, I always valued your input even if I did not follow it."

They had their power rivalry spats, and Konigen would love to rip out his heart to unify the Covenant under her rule, but realized the impossibility of that ambition. Because she did real-ize it, they focused their energies on business. So far, their coop-erative endeavors had worked—until the attempted Aussie coup. That is why he wanted his response to be so drastic in its quality.

"You're a scheming bastard, Aiden, but that's okay. I'm one too. I'll set things into motion at my end. What about President Everett? Regardless of our threats, the EU will follow if he ig-nores what happened in Australia and introduces a draconian bill in Congress. A challenge in the Supreme Court may or may not succeed. He could cause a lot of misery for feeders everywhere and trigger major social discord. I wasn't kidding when I said our tactic could set off a global backlash. Governments and politicians are jealous of their power and abhor the notion they're beholden to somebody. If Everett is prepared to absorb some political casualties, countries around the world might be prepared to do the same to curb our influence. Especially if they mount a negative media campaign against the Covenant, blaming us for everything."

"We'll counter with our own campaign. When you send out those emails, point out the value of genuine open cooperation and understate the threat corollary. We can all get what we want if we work together instead of trying to stab each other in the back. A confrontation might be emotionally satisfying for me, but it would be a Pyrrhic victory."

"Despite my warning, you don't believe a unified global response will ever happen, do you?"

"Everett may pound the drum to rally the world against us, but governments are too parochial to unite. There's no immediate percentage in it for them."

"You're not underestimating possible damage if Everett is even partially successful?"

"That's why we must talk softly, our cannon barely visible, but still visible. I haven't spoken to him since Saturday, but I did sound off Senator Oswald Garich. He's very receptive to what I had to say."

Konigen chuckled. "I'd also be receptive if someone offered me the White House."

"We push hard against Australia, but hold a candy stick to others. I think they'll take the candy stick. If not…"

Conrad felt confident his response would work, provided Konigen did her part, and he could not see why she should not.

"Even if Everett is prepared to deal seriously, and he hasn't demonstrated that he wants to, he won't disband Project Purple and its taskforces," she added. "It has too many tentacles in too many governments, and it *does* serve to coordinate research into sudden old age deaths."

"I don't want to disrupt research programs," Conrad shot back. "I want him to curb its excesses. As I told him before, the Covenant will expand its support. A solution is in everybody's interest. If he wants to fight me, I'll make sure he never gets that second term, and I'll decimate the Republican Party and the Christian nationalists behind it."

"Even if we get partial cooperation, he and the EU will never stop their attempts to penetrate and eventually dismantle us."

"It gives them a hobby," Conrad quipped.

"I'm serious, Aiden. What if we shifted our focus to purely economic ventures? Just saying."

"Our predecessors toyed with the concept, Sybille, but they all came up against the same wall. To exercise corporate influence means control of fiscal and monetary policy, which in turn requires meddling in politics. Whether we like it or not, the Covenant is a worldwide net. To extricate ourselves would create more damage than any realized gains."

"Like I said, just a thought. I wonder sometimes whether the Covenant has the monopoly on wisdom to decide what's best for the world."

"A rhetorical question, and one I wrestled with myself. There are internal checks and balances against abuse of power, but they can be subverted by a ruthless Master Keeper—"

"Or Grand Master," Konigen pointed out with a chuckle.

Conrad let out a soft sigh, not bothering to affirm the obvious. "Something to add for your next Council meeting. If we can get common worldwide legislation, or enough countries where it matters, that recognizes feeders and curbs taskforce power, we can gradually loosen our control."

"Sounds attractive, Aiden, but hollow, for reasons you already stated. The bottom line? You and I are power addicts, and so is every Master Keeper. We must be to run the world."

"In that case, let's run it. By the way, still thinking about a Hawaii getaway?"

"I want to jump on a plane right now, but with this business in the works…"

"I know. Take care, Sybille," Conrad said briskly and broke contact.

A hell of a way to celebrate Christmas!

He turned and gazed out the window. Snow still fell, soft and silent.

* * *

A humongous speck and egg sandwich in hand—Frank felt hungry after a night out with Nadala and more relationship repairs—he paused when the ABC *Breakfast* presenter interrupted a clip about an avalanche in Austria and announced Prime Minister Griffin walking out from the executive annex. He picked up the remote and upped the volume a bit. Somber, dignified in a gray business suit, she stood behind the lectern and swept her eyes over the gathered reporters.

"Effective immediately, I am resigning my position as Prime Minister and leader of the parliamentary Labor Party. Our country faces serious challenges, and I did not make the decision to leave lightly. However, for personal and family reasons, I must step aside to enable the party to have a fresh start how to resolve those challenges. It has been an honor and a privilege to represent my constituents and lead our great country. Thank you all." She turned and strode quickly into the executive annex, followed by a flurry of questions from the stunned gathering.

The camera switched to the show presenter in the studio, looking equally stunned. *"We're told the Labor Party will hold a caucus meeting at 10 AM to elect a new leader who will automatically become Prime Minister. I now turn to our political correspondent who witnessed this astonishing—"*

Frank's cellphone went off and he muted the TV. He read the caller ID and grinned.

"Nadala! A pleasant surprise. Want to join me for breakfast?"

"I'd love to, Foxtrot," a harsh masculine voice replied, "but I'm already dining on your young lady."

A chill ran down Frank's spine. He gripped the phone, teeth clenched in anger.

"Echo!"

"Your former fellow Keeper, against them, the bad guys, until you proved to be one of them. If you want to see your lady friend again, come to her house and you can have breakfast together. I have coffee and toast all ready for you."

"If you harm her—"

"Come, come. I'm not a sadist. She's safe, for now. Getting out of the Forensic Institute left me somewhat famished and Detective Robinson kindly volunteered to feed me. Not with cereal, though, if you know what I mean. Now, the longer it takes you to get here, the hungrier I'll get. Comprende, as our friend Manuel is fond of saying. By the way, I'll be paying him and all the other fellow Keepers a visit as soon as you and I settle some unfinished business, like thanking you for leaving me in Dr. Bayer's care. You might be interested to know he's beyond care now. Such a delightful chap too. In case you're concerned about your darling, here she is."

"Frank! Don't come! He plans to—"

"Such poor manners from someone so lovely," Echo declared in an amused voice, clearly enjoying the pain he inflicted.

"Twenty minutes," Frank grated flatly.

"You don't know how keen I am to see you, Foxtrot. Or should I say, Frank. One more thing. If you call the cops, she'll be the first to go." Echo cut contact and Frank glared at the cell.

He had no idea how Echo managed to escape the Southbank facility, but with his training, he obviously did. His guts churned at the thought of Nadala hurt, or worse. The image of Echo forcing himself on her, sucking her life, made him determined to kill the traitorous scum…if Echo gave him a chance to strike.

Ignoring the warning, he activated encryption mode and quickly typed in a number.

"Manuel de la Kass," the electronic voice declared. "Identify."

"It's Frank. Echo has Detective Nadala Robinson. He's at her house and I'm going there now."

"I'll send in a team."

"No! I presume you know how to contact Inspector Porter?"

"I'll talk to him."

"No wailing sirens, okay?" Frank warned, horrified at the terrible images the thought created.

He broke contact, switched off the TV, the Prime Minister forgotten, and quickly pocketed his cell, wallet, and car keys. He yanked back the second drawer set into the breakfast bench, pulled out a short steak knife, and slid it behind his back. He expected Echo to search him, and pushed another knife behind the sock of his right foot. If Echo had a gun and shot him as soon as he showed up, he expected to have a bad day. He did not think Echo would shoot immediately. His type liked to gloat and savor the moment of victory.

The elevator opened to the second level underground parking lot and Frank hurried to his Subaru Impreza. With a surge of power, tires squealing, he raced toward the exit. As he drove, weaving fast through the traffic, but not recklessly—no value at getting a ticket or cracking up the car—he played through possible meeting scenarios with Echo. Mouth clamped tight, he turned into Nadala's street and parked a few houses before hers. Most residents gone to work, there were a few empty spaces. He would have double-parked if necessary.

He slammed the car door shut and hurried toward the entrance. Before he could grab the round clacker, the door opened and Nadala rushed into his arms.

"Get out of here, Frank! He'll kill you!"

"How touching," Echo remarked, standing feet apart in the lit corridor, gun in hand. "Get in and close the door after you."

Frank walked in and lifted Nadala's chin. "Are you all right?" He saw she knew what he meant and nodded. "He—"

Without warning, he pushed her hard toward Echo and she gave a startled yelp. Echo stepped back in reflex as she stumbled and landed at his feet. In that second of distraction, Frank pulled out the steak knife, threw it at Echo, and immediately dived for the floor. The entire eleven centimeters went cleanly into Echo's chest with a soft thump. He grunted in surprise, staggered, and squeezed off a shot at the ceiling. His nerveless fingers opened and the gun thudded to the floor. He tried to say something, but the words failed him, and slowly toppled back heavily.

The stink of burnt powder sharp in the air, Frank crawled to Nadala and gathered her into his arms. Instead of falling apart and descending into hysterics, she hugged him and planted a long kiss on his mouth. She smiled when he pulled back and stroked his cheek.

"Thank you."

"He'd have offed both of us if I hadn't got him," he murmured gently, trying to slow his racing heart.

"I know. I never expected you'd shove me at him. Covenant training?"

He grinned. "One of my homemade specials." He pulled out the short knife from his sock and flicked it to the floor.

Her eyes arched. "I see you came prepared."

"How did he get in?"

"I heard the clacker," she said. "When I opened the door, he pushed the gun into my face. I waited for an opportunity to get him, but he never gave me a chance."

He winced. "Training. We were taught how to take down rogues in different scenarios and live to do it all again another day."

Her arms went around him and she began to tremble. He held her tight and stroked her back.

"You're going into shock. It'll pass soon."

She sniffed twice, then leaned back, eyes glistening with tears ready to spill. She brushed them away with an abrupt gesture and gave him a tight smile.

"Look at me. Behaving like a frightened teenager."

He kissed the tip of her nose. "Nothing to be ashamed about. You held your nerve where it mattered."

She searched his face. "You don't seem to feel anything," she told him, making it sound almost like an accusation.

"Reaction will set in later. Right now, I'm simply glad that you're safe. I wouldn't want to live without you. Killing him, I felt nothing because he did not deserve anything. I didn't want to give him the satisfaction of seeing me upset." He looked into her eyes. "When he called and said he fed…"

"I felt his connection, nothing else. If he fed off me, I couldn't feel it."

"You wouldn't. You must touch to feel it."

"He planned to do much more after he killed you," she added.

"I know."

She squirmed and he helped her up. He gave Echo a glance as she led him into the kitchen.

"Coffee?"

"I could use some."

She put down the carafe and reached for her cell. "I better call Porter."

"Talk to me, Nadala," the Inspector demanded abruptly.

"Echo is in my house. He's dead."

"I see. I'm on my way with backup. And Mr. Hram? I presume he's with you."

"He killed Echo."

"Ten minutes," Porter said harshly and broke contact.

Frank smiled at her puzzled expression. "After Echo called, I rang Manuel and he contacted Porter. That reminds me…" He pulled out his cell, set encryption mode, and dialed. "I'll have this on speaker," he added.

"Manuel de la Kass. Identify."

"Frank."

"You're still walking, amigo?"

"Your concern is overwhelming, Manuel, but unwarranted," Frank replied dryly, and his friend laughed.

"I *am* concerned. What happened?"

"Echo won't bother us anymore. Porter is coming over and the place will be swarming with federal cops shortly. Keep our people away."

"Got it. By the way, you heard about the Prime Minister?"

"Watching the news when you called. If I had a suspicious nature, I'd say her sudden departure had a helping hand."

"She's not the only one who had a sudden yearning to retire. Ransome is also gone."

"The Liberal Party leader? Wow."

"Yeah, that's what I said."

"I smell the Covenant's hand in this, Manuel."

"Nobody's talking, but if we did it, it'll filter down. I've got some more cheery news. Sierra is back."

"No shit! When did that happen?"

"I'm on my way now to pick her up at the airport. I'll call you later with an update. We still need that long talk. Glad you're okay, Frank."

He pocketed the cell and grinned at Nadala. "Sierra is our Melbourne Master. Taskforce Crimson picked her up on Saturday after Echo identified her."

"What's this about the Prime Minster? I haven't had a chance to watch the news."

"Ah, with Echo here, you couldn't have. She resigned. I think it's payback by the Covenant for the Feeder Bill. Now, how about that coffee?"

She picked up the carafe and filled a mug for him.

"Does this mean you won't be the Master?"

"Looks that way," he said as he added one sugar and took a sip. "It's up to Sierra. She's pretty old, and after what happened to her, she may have had enough. Anyway, I'm not sure I want to be a Master."

"Oh?"

"There's my business and us."

Her mouth twitched in a smile. "Us?"

"You and me, together. Isn't that how it's supposed to work?"

"Blockhead!"

He reached for her hand and squeezed. "How about we elope and go somewhere tropical?"

Her eyes became dreamy and she sighed. "Sounds heavenly."

He heard the door clacker go off and tilted his head. "I think your boss is here."

About the Author

Stefan Vučak has written twenty-one novels, which include eight SF books in the Shadow Gods Saga. His *Cry of Eagles* won the coveted Readers' Favorite silver medal award, and his *All the Evils* was the prestigious Eric Hoffer contest finalist and Readers' Favorite silver medal winner. *Strike for Honor* won the gold medal.

Stefan leveraged a successful career in the Information Technology industry, which took him to the Middle East working on cellphone systems. Writing has been a road of discovery, helping him broaden his horizons. He also spends time as an editor and book reviewer. Stefan lives in Melbourne, Australia.

To learn more about Stefan, visit his:
Website: www.stefanvucak.com
Facebook: www.facebook.com/StefanVucakAuthor
Twitter: @stefanvucak

More Books by Stefan Vučak

https://www.stefanvucak.com/Books/

  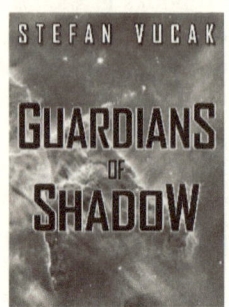

 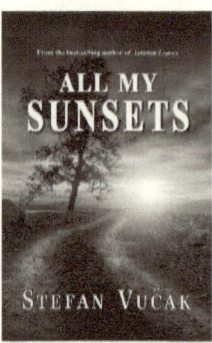